remy

EDEN SUMMERS

*To all the readers who see the red flags
but pretend they're colorblind,
this book is for you.*

OLIVIA

"You look beautiful, Skylar." I lean closer, adding a faint layer of blush to her cheeks. "As requested, your makeup is understated but elegant. It's some of my best work."

Her mouth sits gently pressed, her eyelids closed as I work my magic.

I grab one of my custom lipsticks—a dark ruby shade that almost perfectly matches the hue Skylar wore to her wedding—then my favorite lip brush. I get busy painting the luscious color on her mouth as the soft hum of my mellow pop playlist carries from my cell on the stainless-steel counter on the other side of the room.

"Have I told you how much I love your hair?" I finish her lips and readjust the lock of strawberry blonde resting against her forehead, guiding it to frame her jaw. "It's breathtaking. So uniquely pretty."

I could've done something more with the thick strands. Maybe a braid like mine, or gentle curls, but subtle class was the goal and I won't stray from the style brief.

"Almost done." I reach for the foundation to add a final layer over her chin, making sure the bruising from her car accident is fully concealed. "The fluorescents aren't doing us any favors." Every blemish and shadow is painfully highlighted. "Thankfully, the event room is more forgiving."

The warm down lights will help her glow once it's her time to shine.

"There. Stunning." I sit back, admiring my handiwork as a knock sounds at the door, the hinges squeaking softly as it opens.

Ivy's stunning face greets me, her long dark hair curtaining her shoulders as her attention turns to Skylar. "She looks fabulous."

"I know, right?" I raise my protective face shield, then lower the mask from over my mouth. "I think the family will be happy."

She approaches, her voluptuous body gliding forward in her stylish pantsuit with my family business name—*Pelosi Funeral Home*—emblazoned over the left breast of her jacket.

She grabs the picture of Skylar from beside my makeup kit and glances from the image to the dead woman laid out on the metal gurney. "She looks peaceful. It's all the family can ask for. Well done."

"Thanks." A tingle of pride unfurls in my chest.

Praise is hard to come by in my profession. Typically, those paying for the service have other things on their mind than complimenting their loved one's mortician. But when those welcomed words do occasionally brush my ears, it sinks deep.

"Do you need any help?" Ivy places the photo back beside my makeup kit.

"I'm good, thanks."

"You sure? Aren't you meant to be going out for your dad's annual birthday dinner?"

Shit.

I rush to my feet, my stool rolling along the tiled floor behind me. "I forgot." Well, not entirely. I remembered when I was at home getting ready for work. Then the birthday cake we had in the break room was another reminder… Until Skylar's family decided to bump up the private viewing to tomorrow—Saturday—even though my dad usually finds a gentle approach to guide mourners away from weekend services for the sake of our sanity.

"Go." Ivy jerks her head toward the hall. "I can return Skylar to the cool room. If I need help I'll ask the new guy."

"You really need to stop calling him that." I hustle to the stainless-steel counter where I place my face shield before tugging off my blue surgical clothes shield to dump in the trash with my face mask. "Hugo has been here two months. I think that warrants you learning his name."

She shrugs. "Two months too long if I'm being honest. He's not the most empathetic of men. He wasn't built for this job."

I should ask why, what has he said or done this time to warrant her wrath, but that's going to have to be a conversation for next week. "We'll discuss this on Monday. And putting Skylar away will only take a minute." I rush back to the gurney and shove my foot down hard on the wheel brakes. "Has Dad said anything about dinner tonight? Does he think I forgot?"

"He hasn't said a word to me." Ivy sidles up beside me, helping direct the heavy weight inside the room-sized cooler. "Where are you two going?"

"I don't know." I slide Skylar between Jamar Starr, an elderly man who passed from a stroke, and Richard Noack, who suffered a traumatic construction injury. "We haven't discussed dinner at all."

Fuck. I left his present at home.

I follow Ivy out of the refrigeration unit and close the door behind us. "I haven't even mentally prepped for socializing."

She chuckles. "You know most people don't have to prep before stepping into society. You seriously need to get out more. Why don't you meet up with me and Allison for a drink after you finish with your dad?"

I shoot her a playfully scathing scowl.

Her laughter increases, ending in a dramatic sigh. "Why God gave you such beauty paired with a phobia of people is beyond me."

"It's not a phobia." I pull off my surgical gloves and place them in the trash as I pass. "I just don't like people."

"Nobody does. At least the rest of us can stand interaction enough to have a life outside of work, though. You live for the isolation of the mortuary and resent leaving it."

"You know me so well. But I now also have to be back at work first thing tomorrow to prep for Skylar's viewing. So I have a legitimate excuse for an early night."

"Fine. I'll try again next week." She flicks off the light as she follows me into the hall, then the reception area where Allison sits behind her desk, peering up at me from her computer.

"Fri-yay." She beams.

"*Yay.*" I sarcastically wave imaginary pom-poms, not feeling the vibe.

She snorts. So does Ivy.

"I've never met anyone besides you who doesn't live to get away from work." Allison taps at her keyboard. "It's unnatural."

I shrug. "I enjoy my job."

"So do I," Ivy drawls. "But I also like to get tipsy, flirt with outrageously attractive men, and get laid."

I cringe, not wanting to give her a warning about appropriate workplace conversations in a house of mourning.

"Don't worry." Alison gives me a knowing look. "Nobody else is in the building apart from your dad. Hugo left two minutes ago."

"Well, wasn't it lovely of him to say goodbye," Ivy mutters.

"Be nice." I continue to my father's office across the far side of the reception area to rap softly on his closed door before letting myself in.

"Are you ready for your birthday dinner?" I smile sweetly, pretending I didn't forget the special occasion. "What restaurant did you decide on?"

He stands behind his large oak desk, pausing in the middle of pulling on his suit jacket as his eyes snap to mine. "Damn it, Liv. I'm sorry. Dinner completely skipped my mind. I already made plans."

Made plans? Is he joking?

I bite back the accumulating guilt. "But we go out for dinner on your birthday every year."

We've done it for as long as I can remember. Since I was a toddler. Even when we were in the deep trenches of grief over Mom's death. It's a tradition. The only one we have.

"I guess I've been distracted." He winces. "I didn't even realize it was my birthday until Ivy brought out the cake this morning."

He's definitely not joking.

We've both thrown ourselves so deep into the trenches of work life that his birthday became nonexistent.

"It's okay." I fake a smile. "We can reschedule for tomorrow night. What do you have planned?"

"It's nothing." He adjusts the collar of his business shirt to sit perfectly atop his jacket. "Just a casual business meeting."

After hours? On his birthday?

Is this a date? Like a *date-date?* The first non-business-related interaction with a female since Mom passed?

It's about damn time. Seven years to be exact. Yet, the secrecy stings.

"I'm really sorry, *fragolina*. Can I get a rain check?" His use of the Italian childhood endearment only makes this situation worse. "I'm running late."

He crosses the room and squeezes my arm, not waiting for a response before he glides past me and enters the reception area where Ivy remains chatting to Allison. "I'll see you all tomorrow." He waves us farewell and continues to the front door.

"Bye." Ivy looks at me in confusion.

"Have a great night." Allison's gaze finds mine as soon as he's gone. "Aren't you and Carlo—"

"No." I slump against his office doorframe, crossing my arms over my chest. "Apparently this year he has a better offer."

Allison grins. "Does old man Pelosi have a date?"

"He's not old," Ivy scoffs as she glides behind the reception desk to close the door to the admin storage room. "That man is in his prime. If I were ten years older…"

"Ew." I shudder. "If you were ten years older you still wouldn't have been born when he graduated college."

She rolls her eyes. "Exaggerate much?"

"Grave rob much?" I shoot back.

"Wasn't that in the job description?" She grins. "Besides, I like 'em mature."

Allison snorts. "Babe, you need to like 'em when they still have full function of their anatomy."

"*Whoa.*" I raise my voice. "Please remember that's my father we're talking about."

"Your *hot* father," Ivy mumbles under her breath.

I ignore her and retrieve my cell from my pants pocket, navigating to an app that's sat dormant on the device for years.

My dad made me download a tracker when I got my license, stating it was a great safety tool—not that I ever went anywhere other than school or home. But it gave me the same access to his location, too. And from the look of the moving icon on the local street map before me, it still does.

"What's got you so invested in your cell all of a sudden?" Ivy approaches and peers down at my screen. "Are you spying?"

"Maybe a little." I keep an eye on the tiny dot indicating his whereabouts as it moves, taking a left out of our parking lot, then slowly inching down to the end of the road.

"I don't know what's more depressing." Allison stands and plucks a wilted rose from the large arrangement of office flowers beside her computer. "Ivy having a boner for your dad or you stalking his first date in ninety-five years."

"Please never mention my dad and boner in the same sentence again," I mutter. "Can you believe he ditched me?"

"I know, right? Does he not realize his birthday dinner is the only time you dare to leave your isolation bubble?" She launches the rose into the trash bin under her desk.

"Very funny." I roll my eyes. "Also very accurate. But this is out of character."

Ivy shrugs. "He has been acting a little off lately."

"Off how?" I ask.

"I dunno. Distracted. Tired."

"Maybe Mr. P has been dishing out the monster D to a lucky lady." Allison hauls her handbag onto her shoulder and scrounges inside until she pulls out a jangling set of keys. "I'm sure sex has to be quite the ordeal for someone his age."

Ivy scoffs. "You'd be surprised. I once slept with a—"

"Please don't finish that sentence." I pinch the bridge of my nose. "And my dad isn't *that* old. He isn't even fifty yet." Although, now that I think about it, he seemed a hell of a lot younger last year.

Maybe it's a mid-life crisis.

"He's probably just catching up with friends." Allison continues her end of day routine, perfectly aligning the four mauve waiting room chairs that match the feature wall behind, before tidying the grief pamphlets on the glass coffee table in the middle of the room.

"Yeah." Ivy nods and saunters to the hall to switch off the lights. "Friends with vaginas."

I hang my head. "I give the universe permission to swallow me whole."

"Do you know who else is probably going to swallow—"

"*Ivy*," Allison and I snap at the same time.

Well, *I* snap. Allison's reprimand is mostly smothered by an encouraging chuckle.

"Jesus, woman. You need to get laid." I wave a hand in Ivy's direction. "Whatever this is, isn't healthy."

She laughs as she walks for the front door. "Are you going to stalk him?"

I shrug, following after her.

"And if so, can I come with?" She waggles her brows.

"Do you really think I'm going to encourage your unhinged fascination with my father?"

"It was worth a try."

All three of us file out of the two-story building and I lock the door behind us.

We say our goodbyes, my only friends driving from the parking lot while I remain in my idling car, the map on my cell screen haunting me.

Dad stops a few blocks away at a bar I can barely recall noticing, let alone frequenting. I stare at his little dot, my stomach churning.

I don't care if he's dating. I'd actually prefer him having someone to ease his loneliness instead of his out-of-business hours being spent alone.

What I don't appreciate is how he might be hiding it from me out of fear of my reaction.

It doesn't take a lot of mental debate to justify following him.

I only want to confirm my suspicions. Take a quick peek at the woman in question. That way I can ruminate on the situation over the weekend and come up with a plan to broach the subject.

He needs to know he doesn't have to keep a relationship from me. That I'll support him no matter what.

So I trek the same path, drenched in social awkwardness but not feeling an ounce of guilt as I slowly push through the front door of a darkened dive bar, the sound of lively chatter and clinking glasses flooding my ears.

I pause a few feet inside to scan my surroundings, the dim lighting casting a shadow over the room as an eclectic mix of patrons occupy mismatched chairs and booths. It's not crowded by any means, but to this queen of introversion it's a slippery slope into a building nightmare.

"Excuse me. Can I get past?" a female murmurs behind me.

"Sorry." I sidestep, moving out of her way.

"It's no problem." The blonde smiles and sashays ahead in a short skirt and long-sleeved blouse that has the bar's logo emblazoned on the back.

I dawdle after her, my anxiety meter sliding into unwelcome territory as I dart my gaze around.

Two women cackle loudly from a booth to my left. A bunch of barely legal guys crowd a table near the front window. A glass smashes somewhere behind me. A loud curse follows.

I shouldn't be here. And I can't see my father anywhere. I do, however, make eye contact with a burly bearded guy with tattooed arms twice the size of my thighs and a lascivious smirk that irks me enough to snap my gaze back down to my phone.

I check the location app again as I walk for the bar. My father's dot and mine are directly on top of each other. He's here. Somewhere. I just—

I smack into a solid surface. A *man*, judging by the grunt of impact.

"I'm sorry." I fumble to catch my phone, the stranger's warm hands quickly cupping mine to grasp the device before it falls.

"Looking for someone?" he asks, his voice deeply delicious.

I keep my head bowed, not wanting to engage, and instead focus on his polished leather shoes. "Forgive me. I should've been watching where I was going."

"No forgiveness necessary as long as I can get your name."

I cringe, cursing the idiocy of my spying plan and how deep it's taken me into the trenches of society. I really don't like people. But I was raised to have impeccable manners, so I give an awkward smile and raise my gaze, taking in the expensive tailored suit. Black on black. No tie. The top two buttons of his collared shirt undone.

My attention climbs past a chiseled jaw with the faintest hint of dark-blond stubble to become ensnared on the darkest brown eyes peering back at me.

I blink. Twice.

Goddamn. His face matches the deliciousness of his voice—tousled dirty blond hair, warm tan skin, and a mouth that could inspire a wealth of wet dreams. Mine salivates for some ludicrous reason, and I suddenly become religious. There's no way those plush lips weren't sculpted by a god.

I clear my throat. "Ollie," I blurt. "My name, it's… Ollie."

Ollie? Really?

I've never been Ollie in my life.

Olivia, yes. Liv, definitely.

Olivia Cassandra Pelosi whenever I'm in trouble? Absolutely.

But never, ever Ollie unless, apparently, I slip into an alternate universe where my grown ass can't handle basic brain function around a handsome man.

"Nice to meet you, Ollie." He flashes a subtle smirk, heavenly enough to create a slight dimple in his right cheek. "Let me buy you a drink."

2

OLIVIA

The way he says my name—all confidence and charisma—has my pulse surging.

He oozes sinfully dangerous vibes with the profoundly teasing glint in his eyes sending a million red flags ascending to full mast in my mind. Flags my ovaries seem to mistake for green if the way they flutter is any indication.

"No, thanks." I drag my gaze from all the gorgeousness to do another scan of the room. "I'm not staying."

"I'm sorry, sweetheart, but I insist. You can't bump into me like some fairy tale princess, then disappear from my life. That would be cruel." His gaze lowers to take in my work clothes—white blouse, navy pencil skirt, and matching mini heels. "You don't seem like the cruel type."

My cheeks heat under his appraisal. My entire body follows. I should walk away. Skedaddle. The warm sensation weighing down my belly keeps me rooted in place.

I'm not used to being seen. By *anyone*. Let alone an attractive god who screams trouble.

I've never even met a man who fell into the bad boy category—not one that was breathing anyway. The closest I've come is when I've prepped tattooed gang members for cremation and the few men who had been incarcerated at the Baltimore Correction Center at their time of death.

Ivy was right; I need to get out more. The way my body has instigated a meltdown over this guy is ridiculous.

He strides around me, taking the few steps to the bar before gaining the female bartender's attention with the jut of his chin. "Macallan, thanks." His gaze returns to mine. "What do you drink?"

I open my mouth. Close it again.

I will not fold for this man. This *deity*.

I ignore him and continue the visual search for my father, not wanting to be out in public when whatever spell I'm under breaks.

From the corner of my eye I see the guy's smirk increase, still understated yet impeccably striking. "Do you always play hard to get?"

"I don't usually play much of anything." Where the hell is my father?

"One drink, Ollie. That's all I'm asking."

God, why does he have to say my name like that? All sinfully rich and smooth as if the syllables dance around his tongue.

"You've piqued my curiosity," he admits. "Indulge me a little."

My heart pitter-patters.

Pitter. Goddamn. Patters.

It's ridiculous. Top-tier insane.

And the rest of my body? It tingles like I've been hooked up to a low-voltage live wire.

"What would you like to drink?" He keeps staring. Keeps casting his magical trance with those dark eyes.

Like an idiot, I clear my throat again, unsure if I should run or ask him to impregnate me.

I hear myself say, "Champagne," the word spoken by whatever man-hungry demonic force has possessed my body.

I rarely drink. The last time I indulged was four years ago at my twenty-first birthday, and the only reason for the indulgence was to ease my way through the forced social activity when Ivy and Allison dragged me to a club.

"Champagne for the lady." He instructs the bartender.

The woman nods and gets to work on our order.

"So who are you looking for?" My new deity friend grabs a coaster from the bar, drawing my attention to the rings on his fingers. Thumb, pointer, and pinky.

A confirmation of the bad boy trait, no?

He has strong hands. I bet they're talented, too. Rough. Warm. A pretty necklace.

"Ollie?" He grins. "Tell me who you're looking for."

I shake my head, trying to think of a less embarrassing response than the truth when my gaze catches sight of my father seated at a table in the far back corner of the building.

Shit. I lunge toward the stranger, crowding into his larger frame, using his personal space as a hiding spot.

"You okay?" He stiffens, standing taller, broader, creating more of a shield. "Are you in trouble?"

"No. Nothing like that. I just don't want to be seen."

He inches closer, wrapping a protective arm around my waist, the delicious scent of his woodsy aftershave sinking into my lungs. "Need me to get you out of here?"

"No." I chance a peek over his shoulder. "Just, um… don't move. Please."

My father's back is to me, his younger dark-haired companion facing the room. I don't recognize the guy, but like the man beside me, he's wearing a suit, the strong stance of his shoulders and posture speaking of power and prestige.

"How 'bout I do you one better?" The deity protects me from view as he pays the bartender and hands me my flute of champagne. "I'll walk behind you to keep you hidden while you lead the way to the free booth at the front of the building."

"You wouldn't mind?" I stare up at him. At such close proximity, he towers at least a good six inches above my five-three height.

"Trust me, I have no intention of letting you out of my sight until I learn your secrets." He taps the bar, murmurs to the waitress to keep our drinks coming, then indicates the booth with a nod. "I'll follow close behind."

I should decline the offer.

Should've declined the drink and those to come, too.

I'm not sure what has me acting outside my normal hibernation regime—maybe the guilt over Dad's birthday or Ivy's taunts that I don't have a life—but I lead the way, downing half my flute of champagne in the few yards it takes to reach the booth.

"He's going to recognize me." I absently touch my braid. "I always wear my hair like this."

Now that it's confirmed there's no date, I don't want my father knowing I was crazy enough to follow him.

The walking wet dream takes in my hair with open reverence. "The room's dark. I'm sure he won't see."

I'm not as optimistic. I feel like I'm a bright beacon waiting to draw my dad's attention.

"Here, let me help." He pauses a few feet in front of the booth and hands me his tumbler.

I stiffen, juggling both drinks and my cell. "What are you doing?"

"Nothing untoward." He reaches for my hair, then pauses. "Am I likely to get my hands broken for touching you?"

I balk. "No, why?"

"Because if you were mine I'd do far worse to any man who dared to do far less."

All my nerves dance as he undoes the elastic holding my braid, our gazes entranced as his fingers gently loosen my hair.

My sanity blows me a kiss of farewell and flees the building, leaving attraction to grasp the controls of this high-speed train derailment.

I hold my breath, my tingles turning into tremors when his touch reaches my nape, gently massaging my scalp. I'm forced to smother a groan, but it's still audible, the needy sound meek in my throat.

He doesn't smirk. There's no longer cocky confidence in his expression. What stares back at me is curiosity. Intrigue.

He continues to undo my braid until the shoulder-length strands of my brown hair are tangled waves around my cheeks, my heart a rampant vulture beneath my ribs.

"God, you're beautiful," he murmurs.

The words steal my thoughts. My composure.

I swallow to alleviate the ache in my throat. "How long have you had sight problems?"

"How long have you had self-esteem issues?" he counters.

"I don't. I'm just smart enough to know something isn't right here."

He continues to massage his hand through my hair, his fingertips causing mini orgasms along my scalp. "You don't like my attention, Ollie?"

"I don't *understand* it," I correct. "You're an incredibly attractive gu—

"You think I'm attractive?" His smile returns.

I roll my eyes and pull back until his hand falls to his side. "I'm sure you're well aware of your appeal."

He shrugs. "Maybe. But it's always nice to receive praise from a gorgeous woman."

"Oh, my god." I chuckle and slide into the booth, discreetly gazing around the wall of my wavy hair as I glance behind me.

My father remains at the back of the building, his companion leaning closer as he talks.

"Who are you spying on?" Mr. Deity startles me by sliding in beside me. I would've assumed he'd take the opposite side of the booth, not nestle into my personal space close enough to awaken goose bumps along my thighs. "A boyfriend? Your husband?"

"Who says it's a guy?"

"You," he states simply. "When you said *he's* going to recognize me."

Shit. This man is paying attention.

So much dreamy, gratifying attention.

I place his Macallan on the table, still too embarrassed to admit the truth, and chug the remainder of my champagne.

"Would you prefer if I didn't sit so close?" His eyes narrow, reading me, increasing the scrutiny. "I thought you could use me as cover instead of making it obvious when you glance over your shoulder… but if you'd prefer—"

"No, it's fine." I shake my head. "I appreciate it."

"Then tell me who you're hiding from. Is the situation scandalous, Ollie?" His voice dips to a deep purr. "Are you dating a married man?"

I want to swoon at his tone. Instead, I lick my drying lips, my pulse thudding when I return my gaze to his and find his attention on my mouth. "It's far from scandalous."

My cell vibrates in my hand, thankfully giving me an excuse to look away in case I break into a fit of idiotic giggles. I check the latest message in my long-standing group chat with Ivy and Allison.

ALLISON

Update please.

I type back—

ME

I found Dad in a darkened corner of a dive bar with a younger man.

IVY

Has Daddy found himself a twink?

I choke on air.

ME

What the hell, Ive? No. Why does your mind always default to sex?

IVY

Why doesn't yours?

"I admire how you don't hide your emotions," the stranger murmurs as if to himself. "Usually women are cagey in an attempt to be mysterious. Yet your feelings dance across your features untamed."

"They do?" I slide my cell onto the table and raise my gaze, becoming dumbstruck by his heated scrutiny all over again.

Nobody has the right to have eyes so dark and hypnotizing.

"Yeah, Ollie, they do. I'm going to need all the details on this man of yours. The jealousy is eating me alive."

I scoff, not buying his player game, but enjoying it all the same.

With any other person, in any other place, I'd be attempting to frantically escape the social interaction. In fact with any other stranger, I'd be in a full-scale meltdown over being caged in this booth. Instead, I find myself wanting to scoot closer. To sink deeper into the woodsy scent invigorating my lungs.

"Well, you can inform your jealousy that the reality of my current situation is extremely dull."

He raises a brow. "I find it hard to believe that there's a single thing about you that isn't entirely fascinating."

There are more tingles. Flutters. Pitter-patters.

"Nice line." I chuckle.

"Not a line." He takes a mouthful of scotch, the bob of his Adam's apple making me salivate. "If I thought I was worthy of a woman like you, this conversation would've breeched X-rated territory the moment our eyes met."

My cheeks flame. Parts down south do, too.

He smirks. "You're too fucking cute."

I force myself to maintain our stare even though my blush spreads, the heat traveling down my neck. "What do you mean by *a woman like me*?"

"Timid. Respectable. Innocent." He casually places his tumbler on the table. "I would ruin you, and hate myself as I enjoyed every minute of it."

"Ruin me?" The question whispers between my lips. "I think you've got the wrong impression."

"Really? I'd place a solid bet that you've slept with no more than five men."

Ha. That's five too many, bucko.

His eyes narrow further. "Make that less than three."

Perceptive bastard.

I school my expression. "I don't like this game."

He gives another sinful snicker, but it's short-lived. "You're wholesome, Ollie. Far too virtuous for a guy like me." He reaches out, gliding my hair behind my ear with an electric touch. "That's not a bad thing."

It kinda feels like it is when my so-called wholesomeness is the reason why being *ruined* isn't on the table.

"Do I get a turn at making unsubstantiated assumptions?" My gaze is drawn to the female bartender who arrives to deliver another round of drinks, then grabs my empty flute before leaving.

"You think you can read me?" He hands me my fresh glass. "Let me have your worst."

I take a strengthening sip and sit taller, taking my detective role seriously despite the ache between my thighs.

I leisurely scan my gaze over him, from the tousled hair that seems freshly cut, along the slightest trace of stubble peppering his chiseled jaw, to the perfectly fitted suit clinging to his broad shoulders.

"You come from money," I say with confidence. "Your suit is tailor made, and from memory, your shoes were Italian leather."

Enough of my clients have been laid to rest in designer brands for me to tell the difference between a luxury and a knock-off. This guy oozes wealth.

He inclines his head. "Does money excite you?"

No, it doesn't. I don't bother telling him, though. "Please don't interrupt my assessment. The customer is to remain quiet so I can focus."

He grins. "My apologies."

God, the tingles.

"Whatever your job, it's a position of power. You hold yourself to a high regard." It's his posture. The almost arrogant tilt of his chin. "But I wonder if that confidence hides something."

His humor retreats as he raises a brow, silently questioning.

"Your eyes, they're soulful." I stare into the rich depths, swimming in the earthy brown peering back at me. Without the smirk he's almost someone else entirely. "Your eyes hold pain. Or maybe sorrow."

Something flickers in his expression.

It's slight. Maybe I imagine it.

Then leisurely, his grin returns, from subtle to blinding in the space of a few heartbeats.

"Have you been spying on me, too, Ollie?"

I snort. "I don't even know your name."

"I'm starting to think that's for the best," he drawls. "You already know too much."

He's mocking me. *Damn it.* And here I was thinking I'd been somewhat flawless in my assessment.

"You've never been in love," I say, desperate to make an accurate claim—to find something to knock this deity off his pedestal and send him toppling to mere mortal status.

"True." He inclines his head. "But I'm creeping closer by the second."

I bark a laugh and quickly clap a hand over my mouth to obliterate the sound. "*Shit*. That was loud."

"It was." He leans closer, shielding me further from prying eyes as he discreetly glances over his shoulder to the bar. "Nobody is paying us attention. Your cover remains intact."

Dear Lord, he smells incredible. If flawless confidence had a scent the intoxicating elixir sinking into my lungs would be it.

I want to nuzzle my face against him. To lick the deliciousness right off his skin.

God, I'm turning into Ivy.

"Don't think I haven't noticed you never told me who you're hiding from," he murmurs.

"And don't think I haven't noticed you never told me your name," I counter.

Dark eyes return to mine. "Has this become a negotiation?"

"Does it need to be?"

His smile softens, another glimpse of sorrow making my chest ache. "You don't want to know me, Ollie."

"And why is that?"

"I'm not a man that women like you want to get acquainted with."

Aww. What a cute yet ridiculously ill-advised assumption.

"You're wrong, kind sir." All thought of my dad vanishes. *Poof*. Gone. "I want to know everything. Most of all how you would ruin me."

I attempt to play it cool, marking the end of my declaration with a casual sip of champagne.

I don't know who this woman is, the one who volleys outrageously flirtatious lines with a straight face. But I like her. She's far more fun than the hermit with flunking social skills.

He slides one arm along the top of the booth behind my shoulders, his other hand coming to rest on my knee.

I tense at the sizzling contact, my skin erupting in blissful goose bumps.

He leans close, his scotch-sweetened breath warm against my lips. "Tell me what man has claimed so much of your attention and maybe I'll give you a taste of what it's like to be ruined."

I swallow. Lick my lips. Perish.

It takes what little grip I have on my composure to speak without groaning. "It's my dad."

"All this time I've envied your old man?"

All this time?

I swear I only just met this guy, but it feels like I know him. That I could trust him. Maybe even hand over my beating heart neatly wrapped in a nice little bow.

It's weird, but after living and breathing death for years, I feel alive.

The switch is euphoric.

His heated palms slides up my inner thigh, scorching my skin. "Tell me, Ollie, why is a gorgeous woman spending her Friday night spying on her father?"

"We had plans." My breathing turns ragged, his touch driving me wild, his gaze holding me captive. "At least I thought we did. Then he told me he had a business meeting. He wasn't himself and I thought…" I place my flute back on the table.

This guy doesn't want the inane intricacies of why I'm here. I don't want to give them to him either. Not when the conversation would inevitably lead to the family business, then devolve into the usual morbid questions that inspire my lack of faith in humanity.

"You thought?" he prods, his lips a slight tilt from mine.

I could kiss him. Could incline my chin and claim his mouth.

Would the contact scorch me as much as his hand?

Would it ruin me like he promised?

"Ollie?" he whispers. "Tell me your secrets."

"They're not worth knowing."

"I'm not so sure about that." He moves in and nuzzles the sensitive skin below my ear. "At least tell me if I was right earlier." His hand creeps higher. So slowly. So teasingly painful. "How many men have had the pleasure of touching you? Tasting you?"

Oh. Dear. Lord.

I shake my head, denying him an answer.

"How many?" he murmurs.

I clamp my eyes closed, hiding from humiliation as I dig my nails into the leather of the booth seat. "None."

His hand pauses its ascent, his body turning rigid.

Silence rings in my ears.

There's nobody else. Only him and me. Only my mortification and his unease.

He pulls back, his gaze like a beaming spotlight behind my closed lids, his attention illuminating my inexperience.

Goddamnit.

I force my eyes open and face the regret staring down at me.

A battle wages war in those deep brown irises—one I don't understand.

"Forgive me, Ollie." His voice is barely audible. "But I don't mess with virgins."

Rejection leaves me chilled. "I may be a virgin, but I'm not virginal."

His nostrils flare. "It's not because I don't want you."

"Please." I glide my hand over the wrist between my thighs like a lust-drunk fool. "I haven't come close to tasting ruin yet."

I don't know what the hell I'm doing. What the hell I'm begging for.

I just met this guy and he's touching me in public, for heaven's sake. But I can't help craving more. He's got me hooked. Drugged.

His jaw ticks.

I hold my breath.

Heartbeats pass. Wild and crazed.

Then his fingers move again, the slightest brush of fingertips teasing over the elastic bordering my crotch. I suck in a shuddering breath, the exhilaration from the simplest of movements almost blinding.

His other arm slides around my shoulder, his hand returning to my hair, my scalp. "Are you wet for me, Ollie?"

My throat restricts. Every part of me is alive for this man—nerves jangling, heart thrumming, soul dancing.

I nod.

He leans back in, his stubble grazing my cheek as his mouth moves near my ear. "Such a good girl."

I shudder and clench my legs to stem the needy ache in my core, trapping his hand between my thighs.

A deep grumble emanates from his chest in delicious approval. "I bet you taste so sweet." His voice is low, dripping with lust. "My perfect, pure princess." His fingers shift, the slightest brush of contact over my panty-covered clit nudging me close to the precipice.

I dig my nails into his wrist. Gasp for air. "I'm…" I swallow. *Gasp.*

I'm lost for words. Drowning in greed.

I've never craved anything like this before. Never yearned with a ferocity so fierce it made me mindless.

I want to touch him. To be so daring as to slide my hand over his crotch. To feel his length. I'm summoning up the courage to reach for him when a masculine throat clears close by.

I startle. Panic.

I grasp the handsome stranger's shoulder and push back an inch, mortified to find another suit-clad man standing at our booth, his expression emotionless as he looks down his nose at us.

"Boss," the intruder drawls.

My deity doesn't move. Doesn't seem to care as he remains focused on me, his fingers continuing to gently slide back and forth along my underwear-covered slit. "Russo," he growls.

"We're ready to leave. I've already fixed up your bill."

"I'll be there in a minute."

I keep clinging to his shoulder, praying the dim lighting and the tilt of his body hides where his hand is hidden.

"I'll meet you at the car." The interloper walks away, unfazed.

I slump into the booth, my breathing ragged while the touch withdraws from beneath my skirt, the fingers in my hair retreating.

"It was a pleasure, Ollie." The slightest shadow of guilt creeps across his face as the mysterious stranger slides along the bench seat.

"Wait. I don't even know your name." I reach for him, but he's already moving to his feet. "Will I see you again?"

His lips kick at one side, the most solemn grin hitting me in the chest as he smoothes his ring-covered hand down the front of his suit. "Not if you're lucky."

3

OLIVIA

SIX MONTHS LATER

"Liv… sweetie… my darling, precious baby girl… I know you don't like to be rushed but we're getting a little stretched for time before the viewing, and Alexandra's mother isn't someone we should keep waiting." Ivy gives me an apologetic smile from the mortuary doorway.

I sigh, still fiddling with the bobby pins failing to hold the decedent's hair. "I know. I just can't get her part to sit right, and before that I wasn't happy with the reconstruction of the stab wound to her cheek."

Some clients are more difficult than others.

I'm not sure if today's issues are due to it being the end of another long week, or if it's because Alexandra's mother is a high-profile news anchor—one with an extremely unfavorable demeanor.

If anything goes wrong during the services leading up to her daughter's funeral, the world will hear about it.

"Give me a few more minutes." I run my glove-covered hands gently over the back of Alexandra's head, paranoid the screws holding her skull together weren't placed as perfectly as they could've been. "If you can get Hugo to wheel in the casket, I'll start placing her right away."

She nods slowly, her attention remaining on Alexandra.

"Was there something else?" I ask.

"Other than how ridiculously cold it is in here?" She wraps her arms around her waist and shivers. "I don't know how you handle it in winter."

"Layers." She already knows that, though. "What's really on your mind, Ive?"

She winces, the expression scrunching her beautiful face. "Well… speaking of Hugo…" Her gaze finally meets mine. "You know I'm not one to snitch and all that…"

"But?" I straighten, as if better posture will make whatever mess my least-favorite employee has created become somewhat easier to digest.

Her hands fall to her sides, her eyes blinking back at me with sympathy. "The cremator was warm when I came in this morning."

What the fuck?

Again?

"He did a pickup last night, didn't he?" I remember the additional body bag in the cooler when I dragged my half-asleep ass into work earlier but haven't had time to learn about our latest client.

"Yeah. At around ten. An eighty-year-old woman from Settler's Nursing Home."

"*Goddamnit.*" I yank the face shield off my head.

Her wince deepens. "I'm sorry for telling you. It's just that—"

"Don't be. There's no way you could've kept this to yourself." I cross the room, dumping the face and mouth shields to the bin. "What did my father say?"

She gives me a funny look. "Carlo has the day off, remember?"

I turn my back to her and grab the counter with both hands, briefly closing my eyes. *Shit.* I hate how frequent my dad's casual days have become. I hate even more how I'm now going to have to deal with Hugo when he should've been fired the first time he messed with the retort.

"I'll speak to him." I paste on a half-hearted smile and turn back to my friend, my braid seeming overwhelmingly tight despite some of the loosened hair tickling my cheeks. "Don't worry about it."

"I am worried." She approaches, her sympathetic expression sinking under my skin. "I know how much you hate this sort of stuff, and if your dad were here I would've taken it straight to him. But…"

"But he's not." And I'm yet to learn how to explode into a million bats and disappear whenever an unwanted human interaction arises, so… "I need to start learning how to handle management issues. This'll be good for me."

She raises a slow brow. "Are you trying to convince me or yourself?"

Me, obviously.

I shake it off. "I'll be fine."

"You'd be fine if you didn't hate socializing… or people in general."

"I don't *hate* those things." Well, not *all* the time. Not since one dreamy night six months ago.

Ninety percent of interactions and ninety-nine percent of people—for sure.

Her other brow hikes to meet the raised one. "Really? Tell me the last time you conversed with the living in a pleasurable way, my sweet, hermitted Olivia."

"I talk to you—"

"Other than me, your dad, and Allison."

Okay. Fine. That makes things more difficult. Yet she's well aware of my one exceptional experience.

I beam a sultry smile. My heart does a little pitty-pat. "That night—"

"Do *not* relay the story about you and the guy from the bar. That happened a freaking lifetime ago, Liv."

My face falls. The game is lost.

It was a good night though.

The only instance I can recall where I didn't imagine placing a plastic bag over my head and tying it tight around my throat when a random man dared to speak to me.

He'd been smooth, suave, and sinful. And those hands… Not that I have much of a base for comparison, but it was a five-star experience in my book.

Two thumbs up.

Highly recommended.

"Seriously, stop thinking about him." Ivy claps my shoulder with a chuckle, jolting me from the memories. "You need to get out more."

"No, thank you. Dealing with Hugo will be enough association with the living to last until the new year."

"It's February," she drawls.

"Exactly." I tug off my clothes shield, volley it into the trash, then backtrack toward the door. "Do you mind bringing Alexandra's casket in while I talk to him? And get the cooling pads, too? Pretty please."

"Sure. I'll have everything ready for your return from battle."

"You're so kind." I cringe, trying not to imagine how Hugo and I are about to butt heads.

Even though I don't see him all that much these days due to my workload and the favorable need to lock myself in the mortuary, when our paths do cross it's never short of discomforting.

How could it not be when I was the one who discovered the warm retort last time? Then proceeded to rat on him to my father.

I was also the one who adamantly argued he should be fired, right in front of his face, when my dad decided to let him off with a warning.

"If I'm not back in ten can you wheel Alexandra back into the cooler?" I pause at the threshold, anticipation wreaking havoc on my stomach.

"Of course."

"You're the most awesome person I know."

She rolls her eyes. "That's not the compliment you think it is when you only know four people."

"It's the thought that counts, right?" I close the door behind me and attempt to ignore the dread filling my gut.

It wasn't easy growing up the only daughter of two proud funeral directors.

The soundtrack to my teenage years was a constant stream of tears and guttural sobs—none of them mine. I'd come home from class to our living space upstairs, and more often than not I'd have to skirt a crowd of mourning families.

Kids at school teased me. Boys didn't want to date me. And in the few instances when they did, it was due to morbid curiosity not romantic interest.

It was only natural that I tapped the brakes on socializing at an early age. I cut and run from the whole stitch.

The only exceptions to my antisocial rules are my dad, Ivy, Allison, and my sweet elderly neighbor, Lesley.

I don't even talk to grieving families anymore. That's my father's domain, and Ivy steps in like a dutiful protege when he's not around.

I drag my feet along the hall, the heating from the main part of the two-story funeral home blistering in comparison to my usual space of solitary confinement.

I pass the staff break room and poke my head inside. It's empty. No sign of the accused.

I continue past the cremation room, then further to the reception area where Allison sits behind her desk, typing into her keyboard, her face partially blocked from view by the large crystal vase beside her filled with white roses and carnations.

"Good morning, Ally." I force a smile as she glances up from her computer.

"Morning," she beams, her enthusiastic expression quickly fading. "Are you looking for Hugo?"

"Yeah. I—"

"Did someone say my name?" The man of the moment walks out from the admin storeroom behind Allison's desk holding a stack of Alexandra's service booklets. "Look who crawled out of her dungeon to grace us with her presence."

Funny joke from someone about to take pole position on the unemployment line, you horse's ass.

"Morning, Hugo." I divert my path toward my father's closed office door. "Can you please follow me?"

He frowns. "Why?"

"There's something we need to discuss." I keep walking, not stopping until my fingers grip the door handle. "It shouldn't take long."

"No thanks. The last time I was requested in your father's office I got accused of shit I didn't do."

I fight not to react to his unprofessionalism. He shouldn't curse so loud in case grieving families are on the premises. Not only that, but the so-called *shit* was true. He confessed. Maybe not to me, but it all came out in the end.

"It's a private matter." I force calm and swing my father's door open.

"I don't care if it's private." Hugo dumps Alexandra's booklets on Allison's desk. "You can speak to me out here."

My cheeks flame hot. "That would be unprofession—"

"Just spit it out, Olivia. Whatever you want to accuse me of, you can do it in front of an audience."

Wow. He really is holding a grudge. Two-fisted grip and all.

"Did you get up on the wrong side of the bed?" Allison mutters.

"No," he snaps. "I just hear her judgment loud and clear when I've done absolutely nothing wrong. I won't take that bullshit again."

I drag in a deep breath, wishing I could crawl back into my death sanctuary where conversations are one-sided and the only people I have to deal with lack a pulse.

"Fine." I stand my ground, square my shoulders, and hold his gaze. "And I'm glad you brought up last time because what I need to discuss seems to be an extension of the issues that arose back then."

He chokes on a cough. "I didn't *do* anything back then."

"Come on, man, you admitted it two weeks later at that nightclub." Allison rolls her eyes. "You told me you used the retort on your Labrador after she passed."

"It was a *joke*," he says. "A drunk one at that. How was I to know you were still holding me accountable for something I *didn't even do?*"

He did it.

I know he did.

The retort had been used. And although he'd done a decent job sweeping out the tiny bone fragments after the cremation of his goddamn canine, his standard of cleaning wasn't as high as mine or my father's, and we're the only two allowed to use the equipment.

"You then went on to slur about how you should start a pet cremation side-hustle," Allison drawls.

"It was a fucking *joke*," he repeats.

"I'm not here to rehash the past." I clasp my hands in front of me, my palms sweating. "What I do want to speak about is why the cremator was warm again this morning."

"Warm?" He glares. "You're accusing me of the exact same shit? Really?"

"You did a pickup last night. You were the only one that came into the building after we closed."

"Well, I sure as hell didn't touch your precious cremator."

"Hugo, please. I hate this as much as you do—"

"Hate what? Accusing me of things I haven't done? I just told you I didn't go anywhere near the stinking cremation room. I put some old crone from Settler's on ice, then went the fuck home."

And that right there is another reason why his disrespectful ass should get the boot.

Ivy told me months ago that he had no empathy for the deceased. It just took me a little longer to notice.

"I wish I could believe you." I shrug. "But when moments ago you were still denying the whole cremated dog story after you previously admitted to it, there's no trust here. You—"

"No trust?" He raises his voice. "Are you firing me?" He shoots a glance to Allison. "This is bullshit. She has no proof." His furious gaze returns to mine. "Does your dad know you're doing this?"

God, how I wish my father knew. There's no way he'd let me suffer through this on my own if he were privy to another Hugo stint. And even though my dad is probably right upstairs watching television or reading the biography of some random sports athlete, I refuse to break the sacred oath not to contact staff on their day off. He deals with enough hours on call and deserves his downtime to be uninterrupted.

"You're well aware I don't need Carlo's permission to handle something like this. Every time you misuse the retort you put our livelihood at risk. We could lose our license. Not to mention how unethical it is."

If news broke that a local funeral home was cremating pets in the same sacred space as loved ones, we'd be blacklisted.

Closed.

End of story.

"But I didn't fucking do it." He thunders toward me, his height seeming so much taller than mine now that he's enraged. "You can't fire me on an assumption."

My pulse increases, my hatred of social interaction skyrocketing to nauseating heights.

"Your past is damning enough at this point." I sidestep, cautiously walking around him to make my way to the entry. I pull the door wide, the freezing winter air swooping in to swallow me whole. "I suggest you leave quietly so this doesn't become a legal matter. I'll pack your things and—"

"*Legal matter*?" His face is red now. "It's currently a *fictional* matter. I didn't touch the damn retort when I came in last night. You probably left it on after you fried that junkie with the rich parents."

"What did you say?" Ivy's voice carries down the hall, her heels furiously clapping as she approaches along the tile.

Shit.

"Hugo, leave." I cling to the door handle, wishing I would've thought this through before taking action.

"Aaron Jefferson was *not* a junkie." Ivy marches into the room, scowl fully engaged. "He was a returned serviceman who was injured fighting for *our* country. The health system let him down—"

"Ivy." I give her a pleading look. "It's okay. Let me handle this."

"Yeah, Ivy," Hugo mocks as he trudges toward me. "Mind your own goddamn business."

My heart pumps harder. Faster.

He stops before me. My pride has me standing taller when I should probably shrink back.

"You can't do this." He gets in my face. "You fucking can't. I need this job."

"I'm sorry," I lie because I don't have a death wish. "Please, just leave."

"Or what?" He stares at me. "What are you going to do, Liv?"

I'm more concerned about what *he's* going to do. If my cremation-obsessed friend over here will turn violent.

There are no weapons on the premises apart from my surgical supplies in the mortuary.

No monitored alarms to trigger.

Why the hell hasn't Dad let me bring this building into the twenty-first century?

"I'm not sure what she'll do." Ivy snarls. "But if you don't move out of her personal space I'll—"

"*Ivy*," I warn.

"I'm calling the cops." Allison grabs the office phone. "Good luck getting another job after news of this breaks."

Shit. Shit. Shit.

News of this *can't* break.

"Everyone needs to calm down." I raise my palms in placation, glancing from Ivy to Allison then finally, the man of the moment—who seems slightly subdued after the cop threat. "Why don't we take a step back from all this? Go home, Hugo. Use the weekend to think about what's happened. If you're still adamant you did nothing wrong, then come back on Monday and speak to Carlo."

"After you've already cemented my guilt?" he snips.

"I'll tell him the facts. That's all. He can come to his own conclusions. Don't forget he fought for you last time."

He shakes his head. "You're ruining my life."

You're not filling mine with sunshine and daisies either, asshole.

"Take the weekend," I repeat. "Nothing good can come from continuing this conversation today."

He glowers but complies, stalking outside and into the parking lot.

It isn't until he's out of view that I close the door and slump back against the cold glass with a relieved sigh.

"You should've asked for his keys." Ivy crosses her arms over her chest. "I wouldn't be surprised if he comes back tonight and torches the place."

I slump farther. "I seriously didn't think that through."

Dad is going to kill me.

I want to kill me.

I push off the door. "On a positive note, at least I'll be here if he does return, because the additional workload I've just given myself will keep me on the premises until midnight."

REMY

I saw into my sirloin, one brow raised as I listen to my brother, Salvatore, talk business with our Uncle Lorenzo at the old man's extravagant Baltimore penthouse.

"I told you we needed to handle them both," Salvo says around a mouthful of meat. "Didn't I predict this would happen? We tap the son and the father retaliates. I lost three men today because we should've snuffed Javier the same night we dealt with his kid."

Steak, salad, and slaughter has become the theme for these delightful family luncheons. You'd think the combo would spoil an appetite, but after unending months of the same ol', same ol', this shit no longer fazes me.

"What do you think, Rem?" Salvo looks at me, deliberately pinning me under the microscope before Lorenzo can voice a protest.

I swallow my bite, taking my time to digest the question. "I think I need another scotch."

My brother glares.

My uncle sighs.

"What?" I dump my cutlery on my plate. "I'm thirsty." And bored. It's not like Salvo gives a shit about my opinion anyway. All he cares about is if I'll support his request to snuff more threats.

As far as I'm concerned he can stew on his newfound psychotic tendencies for a minute.

It's closing in on a year since we moved from Denver to become part of our uncle's family business on the East Coast. The biggest and most loyal family business of all—the Italian fucking mafia.

At the time, we'd had little choice. We didn't have a penny to our names much less any prospects for the future after our parents royally screwed us. And in hindsight, it may have been better to become destitute. But the authority and god-like complex that comes with the threatening role is addictive.

At lease Salvatore seems to think so.

"Grow a set," my brother mutters. "We need to move fast on this."

I stare at him with tired disinterest, not giving him the enthusiasm he craves.

Was I not the one who pulled the trigger on the son last night? The one who watched Miguel Rodriguez's brains explode over the dark alley wall? The very same extremely talented motherfucker who got the job done without witnesses or bullets flying in my direction?

Yes, yes I was.

Fucker.

"You should feel flattered." Lorenzo's Italian accent is thick as he rests back in his chair, relaxed and distinguished as always. "The cartel wouldn't have attempted to make a move on our territory unless they felt threatened. Obviously, they heard about your upcoming promotion into my role and wanted to get on the front foot."

My brother's promotion is definitely an issue.

And not just for the cartel.

The world is on notice now that Salvo has had a sniff of power. The guy has turned into a fucking junkie, wanting to do lines with that shit.

"I don't feel flattered in the least." Salvatore's tone borders on a snarl. "And I disagree with your assessment. These cartel pricks don't feel threatened and you know it. Instead, they assumed your retirement means the organization has been weakened enough that they can diversify into our line of work. They don't see me as a threat and I need them to realize their mistake."

"Well, you proved your point by ordering the hit on their boss's son." I reclaim my cutlery and continue sawing into my steak. "Taking the head of the snake is overkill."

"I agree." Lorenzo reaches for his tumbler and takes a sip. "They've been punished for their recklessness. Now we let them scurry away to lick their wounds."

For months we've worked like this, with Salvatore acting as our tyrannical leader behind the scenes while our uncle steps down into more of a consigliere—advisor—role.

It's like an apprenticeship of sorts.

The thing is, Salvo never appreciated training wheels.

The egotistical bastard has rarely walked into a situation where he didn't think he knew best, and that whole god-like confidence boost he's gained by being part of one of the most notorious fractions of the underworld has only heightened that delightfully psychotic attribute.

"Trust that your men on the streets will handle any retaliation," I add. "That's their job."

"I don't give a shit about trust." Salvo snatches his cloth napkin from our uncle's ostentatious dining table and dabs his mouth. "This is about me showing everyone I'm not to be fucked with." He slaps the material back down to the polished wood. "I want to send a message. To let every single piece of shit on the East Coast know I'm more than just some pencil-pusher from a fashion label."

"This is about ego," Lorenzo corrects.

Exactly. One hundred percent. Give the man a prize.

"No." Salvo screws up his face. "It's about strength. About safety for the organization. Word on the street is that you're handing over the reins to your *'nephew in fashion.'*" He uses a derisive tone while making air quotes. "They think I'm weak, defenseless, and fucking gay."

"Well," I drawl, "it's been a minute since you had a woman in your—"

"Shut the fuck up, Remy." His glare skewers me before he returns his attention to our uncle. "What do you think will happen to everything you've built if I take over while our enemies think I'm a joke?"

I roll my eyes.

Lorenzo seems to ponder the question, regal authority ebbing off him. "I understand, and I can agree to a point. But this move is substantially larger than those you've previously made. There will be ramifications. Instability. Unrest."

"I can handle it," Salvo vows.

"We will lose men."

"We're already losing them. Why not do it while making a statement that everyone on this side of the country will hear?"

Lorenzo massages his chin. Pondering. Scrutinizing. Until finally he drags in a deep breath. "Okay. I'll allow it." He takes another drink from his tumbler. "But let me be clear, *you* will be the one who handles any backlash."

Salvatore squares his shoulders. "I'm ready."

I dump my cutlery again with another eye roll and shove my plate away.

My brother is *not* ready.

He'll *never* be ready.

We come from a background in the fashion business—a barely legitimate business at that. And now we're meant to learn how to juggle the overseeing of nightclubs, hotels, and a mass of small—mainly cash—businesses which all launder money for our main focus—drug distribution.

For the love of commonsense, even someone who was born into this takeover role would be nervous filling Lorenzo's unfathomably large shoes.

Yet it's been obvious for a while now that my brother has something to prove. God only knows what it is, although I'm confident it has everything to do with our messed up childhood and our deranged parents.

If our father wasn't already dead, I'd pigeonhole this as Salvo's way of giving dear ol' Dad the metaphorical bird. And it's not like our mother will get the memo when she remains in a cell in the basement of our uncle's Virginia Beach mansion.

Why the hell can't Salvo pick a trauma response with a little less bloodshed or potential years in prison?

"Are you going to protest, brother?" Salvatore sneers.

I scoff a laugh. "Me? Protest?"

As insidiously ruthless as my brother is, I can't claim to be any better.

He may be the one laying plans for our generation to take over Lorenzo's mantle, however, I've been the one to instigate his threats. The severed fingers. The executions.

I chose this life just like he did. I made the decision to be his right-hand man through it all. His underboss. His loyal disciple.

Well, as loyal as a younger sibling can be to an older, more annoying, less attractive brother.

"No, Salvatore." I throw back the last of my scotch and thump the tumbler down on the table. "I do not protest."

"Good." He stares at me, a silent message of thanks passing between us. "Now go kill Javier Rodriguez."

5

OLIVIA

I stand behind the closed door leading into Alexandra's viewing, listening to the soft cries and muffled words as her family grieves their loss.

"She looks beautiful," a female says. "Angelic."

There's a murmur of agreement. An underlying thread of appreciation.

My pulse hums.

"They approve?" Ivy whispers as she tiptoes toward me from the hall.

I nod.

"I don't know why you're always surprised. You do the best work in Maryland. Probably this side of the country, to be honest. I don't hear of anyone putting in as much effort or care as you do."

I may be the best, but the attention to detail comes at a cost.

The family business isn't as profitable as our competitors' because we can't take on as many funerals when our only mortician is an idealist who wants everything to be perfect. I bet my father kicks himself on a daily basis for guiding me into the role.

"It's not that I'm surprised," I whisper. "It's just that grief can trigger unpredictable responses, and I don't want anyone to be upset with my work." Like I was with my mother's presentation.

Her lips had been glued into a thin line. Her makeup, tacky.

I'd wanted to prepare her myself. To bathe her. To massage the stiffness from her limbs and lay her to rest in her casket.

But I'd been too young. Still in high school. With no formal training. And then there was the overwhelming grief.

So instead I live with the unwanted flashbacks of the final moments I saw her, and I don't want any of our grieving families to endure similar trauma because of me.

"Be careful, Liv." Ivy links her arm with mine and leads me back to the hall. "You seem like you're skating toward an unwanted path." Otherwise known as *taking on the grief of our clients.*

"I'm not." I pat her hand. "I promise."

"If that's true, then prove it. Come out with me tonight. Let your hair down. Live a little."

"Hard pass." I unlink our arms as we walk by the reception area where Allison is fully entranced by whatever she's tapping away at on her computer. "Not only do I have a crapload of work to do because of Hugo's absence, but I'm on call due to Dad having the day off."

"Let me handle any call-outs." She follows me into the break room. "I can be the designated driver."

I grab three mugs from the cupboard and fill them with coffee from the drip machine. "*You* as designated driver? Girlfriend, you wouldn't know how to go to a club without getting white-girl wasted if your life depended on it."

"I could so." Her face falls. "I'm professional when it comes to my work responsibilities."

I hand over her filled mug, her expression of genuine forlorn shaking away my exhaustion.

Although tongue in cheek, I insulted her. It's a low blow given how hard she strives to impress my father.

"I know you are, Ive." I wince in apology. "I was only messing around."

"So you'll let me take the van and be on-call tonight while you come out drinking?"

"Nope." I make my way back into the hall. Ivy follows. "I need to start on next week's work."

"You realize you're going to leave this Earth with cobwebs in places there shouldn't be, right?" she asks quietly.

I smother a smile as we return to the reception area. "I dealt with the cobwebs a few months ago." *Kind of.*

I place a coffee in front of Allison who lunges for the mug.

"You're the best," she gushes.

"She is *not* the best," Ivy argues, keeping her voice low. "She thinks her dating card is full because of one random guy last summer."

I scoff. "I didn't say that."

"So you don't still think about him incessantly?" Ivy taunts.

She's got me there, but that doesn't prove her point. "Of course I still think about him. He was the only seemingly normal, mentally stable, extremely attractive guy I've spoken to in my entire life. No exaggeration."

Allison pulls a face. "Hon, that only proves you don't get out enough."

"Don't you start." I shoot her a playfully stern look. "Dating is a minefield in our profession, and I don't have the social bandwidth to handle the crazies. I already lie about my job to anyone who asks."

"You mean your grocery delivery guy and the little old lady who lives next door?" Ivy hits me with a smug stare over the rim of her mug, then takes a sip. "They're the only people you talk to besides us."

I shrug. "I still stand by my statement."

"The morbid topics of conversation do get a bit much." Allison sighs. "I've lost count of the amount of immoral questions I've been asked by men since working here."

"Why are they so disgusting?" Ivy cocks her hip against Allison's desk.

"Because most are probably aspiring serial killers?" I hedge.

She nods. "Probably."

We all fall quiet, sobering with matching sighs that seem to state how pathetic we consider our love lives.

It's the varying scale of misery that makes my position so pitiful.

Ivy considers a dry spell anything over two weeks. Allison would be around five to ten.

If either of them knew my sex card is yet to have one hole punched they would throw a fit.

But it's not like I'm clinging to my virginity.

I would've happily given it to the unholy deity from the dive bar. No holds barred. I was enthusiastically willing to be ruined.

If only I'd had the sense to ask for his number before he fled.

"Stop thinking about him," Ivy mutters. "Those googly eyes of yours are pathetic."

Allison chuckles. "She definitely gets a look about her when she thinks of him."

"I was *not* thinking about him." I turn my back and start across the room, attempting to hide the blatant lie.

But seriously, those dark eyes. The tailored suit. The playfully arrogant smirk…

I'm still exquisitely scorched from his attention.

"He couldn't have been *that* good," Allison grumbles.

"I agree." Ivy raises her chin. "What could he have possibly done to get near that imprisoned heart of yours?"

I choke on thin air. "Who says I let him near my heart?" My dusty ovaries, on the other hand…

"Don't go," Ivy calls after me. "We need to talk about tonight."

I pause before the entry to the hall. "So you've finished making fun of me?"

"Never." She grins. "Do you need any help before we close up? Alexandra's family shouldn't be too much longer, then I'm done for the day."

"No, I'm fine. But thanks." I turn my focus to Allison. "If you can switch the after-hours number to my cell before you leave that would be great."

She nods. "Sure thing."

"Liv…" Ivy sighs. "Please let me be on-call tonight. You're already swamped."

"I can handle it." More importantly, I want to show my father I'm not a monumental fuck-up after the Hugo fiasco. The least I can do is put in the extra effort to make this place run smoothly while we're a man down. "But I really appreciate the offer."

I return to my prep room.

Turn on my playlist.

Dive into work.

The next decedent on my list is Amisha, a young woman who had been heavily pregnant when she passed.

I wheel her from the cool room and unzip the body bag, my throat tightening when I see the tiny child nestled in her arms.

We don't cry.

We have to be strong.

Always.

My mother's words ring in my head, the rule of our family business having been drilled into me since childhood.

If I cried every time something sad happened around here I would've lost my mind long ago.

And it's not like the forensic examiner hadn't warned me about Amisha's circumstances. But there's rarely a more heart-wrenching sight than that of a baby who's never taken its first breath, resting in the arms of a mother who only got to hold her child in death.

I set up my equipment in silence, turn the air-conditioning down a smidge lower, and let the gentle hum of my music console me as I take my time preparing their bodies.

I barely notice when Ivy wheels Alexandra's casket back into the cool room. I'm too busy washing Amisha, describing out loud how beautiful her precious daughter is in case she can hear me in the afterlife.

It's a tough end to an exhausting day—one I don't realize has passed quicker than normal until I glance at my watch and see it's close to ten p.m.

"Shit." I raise my face shield and rub my tired eyes with the back of my gloved hand.

It's been a long week.

An even longer six months with my father's newfound love for taking days off. If this is his subtle way of preparing me to take over the business, I don't like it. I much prefer when he's the workhorse, putting in the long hours beside me.

I stretch my back, my muscles aching as I massage my thumbs in a circular motion over Amisha's wrist, kneading away the stiffness to make her limbs more pliable. "I'm going to have to call it a night."

I continue the gentle manipulation farther along her arm up to her elbow. A yawn hits me, forcing my eyes closed and the mask over my mouth to stretch. "Yep. I definitely need a nap."

I place Amisha's arms over her middle, holding them together with a material bandage, before nestling her daughter back against her chest. "I promise I'll finish up once I get a few hours' sleep."

I cover them both in a clean white sheet, yawning the entire time, then wheel them back into the cool room.

I remove my protective gear. Switch off the air conditioner and light. Then drag my heavy feet into the hall. I'd been in an enthusiastic mood for exercise this morning and rode my e-bike to work. There's no way I'm going to risk returning home the same way at this time of night.

I make my way to the break room, every step like the final yards of a twenty-mile mountain climb, and dramatically collapse onto the two-seater sofa.

I lose consciousness as soon as my head hits the stiff polyester cushion.

The next thing I know I'm jolted awake, my body snapping alert before my brain can catch up.

It takes a few seconds to get my bearings. For the lumbering weight of grogginess to leave my head, and the kink down the right side of my neck to announce itself with a twinge of pain.

Why do I do this to myself?

I should've knocked on my dad's door and asked to sleep in my childhood room. Better yet, given that I'm on-call, I could've driven the damn van home instead of thinking I was stuck here because of my bike. "Idiot."

I shove to my feet. Eye the coffee pot. Check my watch—*two a.m.*

I could go home to my fabulously comfortable bed… or I could finish preparing Amisha and her daughter so I don't have to return over the weekend.

I sigh, trudging my feet toward the coffee pot when a loud rumble followed by a weighty *smack* rumbles through the building.

I freeze. My pulse kicks.

Was that the delivery van door?

I leave the break room and make my way down the hall.

Did I miss a pickup? Or did Ivy take on-call duty even though I told her not to?

She hasn't been on-call before—at least not on her own. Dad has been with her a few times, but that was before Hugo's employ—

Oh, shit.

I stop dead in my tracks before the closed double doors to the delivery room.

Was Ivy right about Hugo coming back to cause trouble?

Shuffling carries from inside the room. I pat my pockets for my cell. Pull out the device just in case I need to call the cops. Then I open one side of the doors and my stomach plummets to my feet with an agonizing whoosh.

A gasp escapes.

Two men dressed in black snap their attention in my direction, the limp body they're carrying dropped to the cement floor with a sickening thwack.

They draw weapons. Life-threatening, panic-inducing guns.

I turn to stone, my cell a dead weight in my frozen hand.

"What the fuck?" one of them mutters, his narrowed eyes murderous.

The other jabs his firearm in my direction and retreats toward the overhead external door, the now open space partially filled by a white van exactly like the one we use for decedent transportation except for the different license plate. "Don't move."

If only I could.

"Who are you?" I pant, my breaths coming thick and fast.

"Grim," the retreater calls out, focusing past the van into the dark of night. He seems familiar somehow.

I don't know what to do. Scream? Run? Chance dialing 911 and hope my quick fingers outpace a bullet?

"*Grim,*" the guy shouts louder.

"Look…" I swallow over my achingly dry throat. "I don't want any trouble."

"Then shut your fucking mouth," the remaining man snaps.

I clamp my lips closed. Send out a silent prayer.

Both men turn their attention outside, and I chance a tiny step backward, my entire body trembling.

Footsteps approach from the dark of night. Slow, calm steps that seem like the advance of the devil himself.

My pulse is an erratic mess in comparison. Hard. Fast. Chaotic.

Then the *Grim* they're calling to walks beneath the delivery room door, bypassing the doppelgänger van, the man's familiar midnight gaze meeting mine.

Relief overwhelms me. My heart pitter-patters.

Then the stupidity vanishes and I'm dropped back into the hellish pit of reality.

Everything inside me shuts down.

Head… heart… soul…

I know this man. The one who strolls around the limp body on the floor with threatening grace and menacing confidence. The same guy who had those ring-covered fingers up my skirt six months ago. Who made my ovaries flutter. Who made my knees weak for reasons other than terror.

"Hey, Ollie." He continues toward me, giving a sympathetic smile. "I'm afraid I'm going to have to kindly ask you not to scream."

6

———

OLIVIA

"Continue with the plan." The man from my past speaks to the gun-wielding sidekicks. "I'll deal with her."

Deal with her?

My frantic heart rate reaches a whole new level, the beats manic as I attempt to discreetly slide my cell into my trouser pocket.

"Are you going to kill me?" I whisper.

"Now why would I do that?"

His voice is the same as it was the night we met—all smooth seduction and subdued power. But there are added layers now. He's different. Calculated and utterly confounding.

The men behind him holster their weapons and reposition themselves to pick up the motionless male, one grabbing the ankles, the other the shoulders.

"What are you going to do then?" I ask in a rush, my body trembling.

"I just want to talk." He stalks closer, a predator approaching prey.

"Then talk. From there. Don't take another step." I retreat into the hall and thankfully, he complies. "Where are they taking him?"

My newfound nightmare glances over his shoulder to his companions. "It's okay. Just ignore them."

"Are you kidding?" My eyes widen, my breaths sawing in and out of strained lungs. "Is that man dead?"

"Ollie…" He slides his hands into his pockets. Dauntless. "Baby, calm down."

Baby? Calm Down?

I don't know what part of his statement is more grotesque—the horrifically familiar endearment or the outrageously sickening request.

I open my mouth to speak but out of nowhere he whistles, high-pitched and shrill.

"Take a walk, guys." He keeps his gaze on mine while the men snap to attention like obedient dogs. "Leave and update my brother on our success, but don't mention my current audience. I can handle the rest from here."

"The rest of what?" I blurt.

He gives me a sympathetic look.

No, it's patronizing. Like I lack the brain capacity to formulate simple math—*two plus two equals you're about to be murdered by the man you've religiously fantasized about for half a year.*

He starts toward me again and I stumble back into the hall wall, the other men not paying me attention as they follow his command, dumping the body on the floor for a second time, then walking beneath the raised delivery door and disappearing into the night.

I glance to my left, down the dimly lit hall. Should I run?

"Don't do it," my nightmare murmurs. "We just need to talk."

"Then stay where you are." I divert my retreat toward the reception area when he doesn't listen. "Whatever you're doing here I promise I'll forget it. I'll pretend it never happened. I don't even know what *is* happening. I'm clueless." I backtrack toward the front of the building, him matching me step for step. "Please just stop. You're scaring me."

"I'm not trying to scare you. But you're a smart woman. You already know this is a serious situation. I can't let you out of my sight in case you call the cops."

He's definitely going to kill me.

I can already read the headlines—*Murdered in her own funeral home. No need to transport the body.*

A car door slams in the distance, the sound echoing through the building where it seems I'm destined to take my final breath.

An engine hums. Asphalt crunches.

I've been left alone with him, and at this point I'm unsure if that's my preference.

"My father lives upstairs." I say on instinct. "If I scream—"

"You're not going to scream," he says with confidence. "And even if you did, I'm certain Carlo isn't nearby to provide assistance."

My stomach hollows.

How does he know my father's name?

"His Audi isn't parked under the awning," he continues. "Neither is the pick-up van or your little blue Volkswagen. Thus the basis of this unfortunate interlude. We thought the place was empty."

I shake my head, confused.

How does he know so much? The cars we drive? That my father isn't home? And where the hell is my dad at this ungodly hour if not in bed upstairs?

"Did you do something to him?" I whisper.

"Ollie, come on. You've got the wrong impression." He pulls his hands from his pockets to hold up his palms in placation. "I'm no threat to you or your dad."

Yet he keeps stalking toward me. Prowling.

I reach the reception area and glance over my shoulder, searching for an escape.

I could sprint, but even if I reached the front door I wouldn't get the deadbolt unlocked before he caught me.

I can't hide. Not when I'm already in plain sight.

I could potentially call for help. Yet somehow I don't think this man will pause his wolfish approach to allow me the time to retrieve my cell and dial a number.

"I can see your mind running a mile a minute." He enters the brighter light of the entry, the gentle glow beaming down on his too handsome face, highlighting the tousled curls of his hair. "But everything is going to be okay. Is there somewhere we can sit and talk? Maybe the staff break room."

Of course he knows about the staff break room.

Does he know what color underwear I'm wearing and my email password, too?

"Can't we talk right here?" I take another retreating step, my ass colliding with Allison's desk, her crystal flower vase teetering on impact.

I gasp.

He slows his advance, but doesn't stop. He continues until he's right in front of me. Foot to foot. Savagely close.

Those dark eyes stare down at me with a wickedly sinister brutality I never noticed all those months ago.

And somehow he's no less beautiful—all carved lines and perfect symmetry.

"Why are you here, Ollie? It's two in the morning. You should be home in bed." His tone is a delicious purr, perhaps attempting to remind me of our past. Of the heat. The lust.

"Why are *you* here?" I murmur back.

He scrutinizes me for long seconds—*reads* me—as if trying to determine if I'm capable of withstanding the truth. "I require the use of your facilities."

My stomach drops.

Bottoms.

I swallow. Lick my excessively drying lips. "Our office hours are from nine to five. If you'd like to come back when we're open, I'm sure—"

He snickers. Goddamn laughs.

And I'll be damned but my insides tingle at the carefree sound.

"This is more of an after-hours type of situation." He smirks. "But I adore your wit. Just like I did the first night we met."

My stomach picks itself up off the floor, climbs back into its rightful cavity, then proceeds to give birth to a mass of butterflies, their rapidly beating wings conducting a symphony of gastrointestinal stupidity.

You are not *still attracted to him, you dumb bitch.*

"Which facilities do you require the use of?" I swallow.

He's previously admitted he comes from money, which makes it clear he's not in need of a cheap deal on a funeral. That doesn't leave a lot of desirable alternatives, but a girl can always hope.

"Is the man in the back room still alive? Does he require medical assistance?" It's such an idiotic question. I'm grasping at straws. "If a sterile workspace is what you're after I can take him to my preparation room. I have stitching supplies and surgical—"

"He doesn't require medical assistance." Grim encroaches, his legs pressing into mine, his hands falling to the desk on either side of my hips.

I'm caged.

Trapped.

The pity returns to his features, making his eyes gentle and lips plush.

His handsomeness attempts to manipulate me into a false sense of security. I'm sure Ted Bundy relied on the same aesthetics to lure his victims to slaughter.

"I think you know what's going on." He reaches out, his arm raising in slow motion and gently swiping at a lock of loose hair that's fallen from my braid.

My pulse thunders, the heavy thuds pounding in my ears.

I want to shove him away. To scream. To escape.

But I'm caught here, trapped between him and the desk. Between a life-threatening situation and the misplaced optimism that he can somehow explain everything into a neat little package that doesn't end in my blood being splattered all over the floor.

"I h-have a wild imagination," I stammer. "The possibilities I've come up with aren't favorable."

"Think the worst of me, Ollie, and you'll be on the right track."

I hold my breath, not wanting to think those things. Refusing to believe this is real.

"This isn't the first time I've been here after hours," he admits.

Bile scalds my throat.

He inclines his head as if sensing my revulsion. "It's not the most ideal situation."

My breathing kicks back in, full speed ahead. I fight not to hyperventilate. To remain conscious despite the terror threatening to undo me.

I spread my fingers out behind me, trying to find the heavy crystal vase. "You're a criminal."

"Yes," he admits without pause.

"You want to use the retort." To cremate a victim. To dispose of evidence. To manipulate someone's life into nothing but tiny grains of bone where DNA is all but impossible to find.

"That was the plan."

I swallow and lick my lips again, my parched throat in agony.

His eyes catch the movement, his focus lowering to my mouth.

What the hell is he thinking?

He looks like he wants to kiss me. As if we're back at that bar with his hand teasing my thighs instead of in a funeral home with a criminal conviction hovering between us.

"I assumed you were a businessman." My fingers brush the side of the vase, spiking my adrenaline.

"I am… of sorts." His attention raises to my eyes. "But the stakes in my line of business are life and death. It's what I signed up for."

"I didn't sign up for it." I lean back, edging closer to the vase.

"I know and for that, I apologize. Nobody wanted you to get involved."

Memories of this morning return to punish me. How the retort was still warm. How I fired Hugo despite him vowing he hadn't touched the cremator.

"You were here last night." I wrap a hand around the neck of the vase, my palm slippery from sweat.

He inclines his head. "I was."

Two murders in two nights?

My limbs shake. "How long has this been going on?"

"That doesn't matter right now."

He's right. It doesn't. One murder is more than enough.

So with all my strength, I swing the vase and aim for his temple.

7

———

REMY

I WAKE, MY BRAIN SLOWLY COMING ONLINE WHILE MY EYES REMAIN SHUT.

I've got a headache, my skull already throbbing—no doubt from another night with one too many drinks—but at least I'm warm.

Goddamn fucking toasty actually.

I shift, trying to settle farther into the comfortable heat, but the solid surface beneath me becomes evident, the rigidity grinding into my hip.

I snap upright. My head collides with another solid surface. The pain in my brain skyrockets as I flop back down.

"What the—" My words vanish as I take in my surroundings, slowly rising onto my elbows.

I'm in a compact brick enclosure. The glow of tiny flames poke out from the bottom of the walls of my hellish cave. The only opening is a square of space near my feet.

Reality sinks in. The snapshots of Javier's murder. The funeral home. The alluring Olivia Pelosi.

Fuck.

I'm in her motherfucking cremator.

"Ollie." I attempt to keep my voice neutral and fail, her name coming out as a lethal warning. "Although I appreciate the ambiance, I'd like to check out of this unscheduled Airbnb."

She comes into view, hunched over at the opening near my feet, her pale face peering back at me. "I don't think I can let you do that."

She doesn't *think?*

At least the hesitation works in my favor.

"Well, turning me to ash isn't a good plan either. What would that achieve apart from a murder charge?"

She gnaws on her bottom lip, the glow of flames dancing in those innocent hazel eyes. "I'm thinking on my feet here. Excuse me for using the only tools at my disposal."

"You've made your point. Now move so I can get out." I skootch toward her.

"No." Her arm lunges to the right, out of sight, the flames licking higher a split second later.

Heat engulfs me. "*Jesus fucking Christ*. Are you insane?"

Her beautiful eyes widen with terror. "I don't know what else to do. You're going to kill me."

I hold her gaze, hating how her vulnerability affects me even while my face melts from the hellfire temperature. "I already told you I have no plans to hurt you. But your self-preservation techniques are making me rethink the lenience."

"You gave me no choice. What else was I going to do?"

"Maybe let me explain without the threat of a concussion and third-degree burns."

"There's nothing more to explain. You kill people, then break in to my family's funeral home and illegally cremate them."

"I don't break in." I yank at the top of my button-down, the heat and confinement triggering my first introduction to claustrophobia. "I was given a key."

She balks, those magnetic rosy lips parting.

"*See?*" I scowl. "You don't know as much as you think. So move out of the way and we can talk. It's fucking hard to breathe in here, and this can't be sanitary. What would Grandma Betty think if she knew I was rolling around in her remains?"

"That's not funny."

No shit. It's going to take a hell of a lot of dry-cleaning to get the minute remnants of dead people out of my favorite suit.

"You're right." I reposition myself on my protesting elbows, my head almost colliding with the brick ceiling again. "This is serious, especially if the news of this threat against my life becomes known to my family. They're not people you want to get on the wrong side of."

Her face loses more color. Or maybe that's just the effect from the brighter flames that are slowly dehydrating me to death.

"I don't know what to do," she rambles, exquisitely vulnerable and meek. "I don't want to hurt you, but I wasn't sure if I could call the police. And my dad isn't answering his phone. If word gets out about illegal cremations…"

"So you didn't call the cops?" I ask slowly, keeping my temper in check.

"Not yet. But you know I have to."

"If you do that I won't be the only one going to prison, my pretty little pyro. This family business of yours isn't an innocent party."

"What does that mean?"

"Let me out and I'll tell you."

She shakes her head.

"At least turn the heat down before I fucking roast."

Her breathing increases, her chest rising and falling beneath her black blazer before she finally reaches for something that makes the threatening flames recede. "Who are you?"

"Remy Costa," I offer without pause, wanting the fuck out of this scorching hot pocket asap. "But you might be more familiar with my uncle's reputation—Lorenzo Cappelletti."

I'm not sure what reaction I expect but the breathy laugh that escapes her isn't it. She gasps a chuckle. Then another. The manic humor is delirious before it transforms into ragged gasps of hyperventilation.

I guess leaning into my family's notoriety wasn't the best strategy.

"It's okay." I skootch forward again, gaining an extra inch toward freedom.

"*No.*" Her grabby hands snatch at my Gucci loafers. "*Stop.*"

I've imagined those pretty little fingers doing a lot of scandalous things these past six months, but none that surge my anger like this. I grind my teeth. Suppress a snarl.

I could kick her. Could force my way out of this… *Wait a minute.* I pat my waist, searching for the hardness of a familiar bulge and come up empty.

"I already took your gun." Her voice shakes.

Am I surprised? Yes.

This woman was such an awkward slip of a thing in that dive bar. Sarcastic and self-deprecating, yet timid and so fucking tempting. And somehow she managed to knock me out, get me into this death vault, and successfully steal my weapon.

Kudos, princess.

"I guess it's only fair you took your turn to scrounge around in my pants after what happened the last time we met," I drawl.

Her eyes narrow, her lips tightening in the cutest show of subdued aggression. "Yeah, and I bet you were left just as satisfied as I was."

I take the insult with a smirk. "Move, Ollie."

"*Talk,* Remy."

Fuck this.

I skootch again, snapping my feet around her hips.

She squeals. Wiggles. Fights. She retreats in an attempt to escape my hold and I keep scoot, scoot, scooting my ass along with her, not releasing the deadlock around her body until my waist is free from the oversized pizza oven.

She stumbles backward, bumping into the corner of a metal gurney with a wince and a whimper.

Shit. First fear, now pain.

"How the fuck did you get me into that thing, anyway?" I prowl toward her.

"Half my life's work is moving lifeless bodies." She sidesteps along the side of the gurney, turning toward it, her attention straying to my gun that lies on the far end of the steel surface.

Fuck.

She lunges.

I sprint, my longer legs catching up to her as she reaches for my Walther.

"Don't do it." I skitter into her, grabbing her arm as she grips the barrel. "I don't want to hurt you."

"Please stop," she begs. "*Please*."

The plea fucking kills me, but I'm well aware that the gun could do a better job.

I slide my palm to her hand. Squeeze her fingers. Not too hard. Just enough to let her know I'll strengthen my hold into painful territory if she doesn't concede.

"*Please*." A sob escapes her. "I don't want to die."

Her terror sinks into me, tightening my lungs.

I briefly close my eyes, hating the guilt that thunders through me. Despising how it's so effortless to remember the ease of our last time together. How she still smells of the same sweet strawberry scent. The way her dark hair tickled my face while my dick begged to plunge inside her… at least until she said she was a virgin.

"You're not going to die," I vow, "as long as you follow instructions."

She *should* die.

If she were anyone else under these circumstances, the air would've been stripped from her lungs the moment my men were caught entering the premises.

But she's not anyone else.

She's Olivia Pelosi. A valuable asset. And the woman I've failed at trying to forget for half a goddamn year.

I lean close, daring to rest my forehead to her temple, hating the tremor that vibrates through her. "We have some heavy shit to discuss."

She shudders with a shaky breath.

"Let go of the gun, pyro."

She winces. Concedes.

"Good girl." I remain close, returning the weapon to the gurney in a gesture of good faith, although my palm rests on top of it because I'm not a fucking idiot. "Now before we talk, I'm going to need you to help me dispose of evidence."

8

OLIVIA

I turn to him, taking in the seriousness of his expression.

"You're going to follow me down the hall with this gurney of yours," he states simply. "That's how you got me in the cremator, right?"

I shake my head, the slow movement denying his request, not his question.

Because he's right. After he crumpled into a pile of muscled limbs on the floor, I rushed through the building to retrieve the gurney so I could transport his heavy weight. I'd flipped him onto it like a sack of potatoes, the adrenaline in my veins potent enough to give me superpowers. But now all that energy is gone.

I'm exhausted. Defeated. On the brink of collapse.

"I'm not going to help you." I hold my chin high through the fear.

He gives a sympathetic smile. "Yeah, you are." He pivots the gun on the gurney, the barrel pointing in my direction.

My pulse stutters. "You said you were no threat to me."

"I said you wouldn't die as long as you followed instructions, my pretty little pyro."

Stop calling me that.

Please *stop calling me that.*

I shake my head. "I won't do it."

"You sure?" He raises the gun, the barrel creeping toward my face until the cold metal brushes my cheek, gently directing my loose hair behind my ear.

I stand frozen. "You can't make me."

Am I willing to die for my morals? No. Will I put up a heroic fight until I'm forced to concede? God, I hope so.

He drags the gun along my jaw. Under my chin. He adds pressure until I raise my face flush with his. "We both know you'll do exactly as I ask."

Anger builds inside me. Disgust, rage, and ferocity, too. "I trusted you."

We both know what I'm talking about.

The trust I gave him with my body. With my vulnerability.

"I know." His dark eyes hold my gaze. "But we all make mistakes. Don't make another one by defying me." He juts his chin toward the hall. "Lead the way."

"No." I step back. Square my shoulders. "How did you get a key? Did you bribe Hugo? Do you know I fired him today because the retort was warm when staff arrived this morning?"

"That's a tough break for the poor guy. But no, he has nothing to do with this. You need to think a little closer to home."

Allison?

Ivy?

I shake my head. They wouldn't give away a key. Not for legitimate reasons, let alone criminal ones... would they?

Remy sighs, returning the gun to the gurney, the barrel still aimed in my direction. "It started the night we met, Ollie. It wasn't fate that brought us together. It was the meeting your father had scheduled with my brother, Salvatore."

Icy dread enters my veins.

I keep shaking my head, denying the connection, refuting the implication.

"They formed a partnership of sorts," he continues. "One that's been smooth sailing until now."

My head works on a swivel. Back and forth. Back and forth. "You're a liar. My father would never—"

"Your father needs the money, and we pay him generously."

No. Times were tough after my mother died. Not that Dad admitted to anything out loud, but I'd seen the medical bills scattered across his desk. I'd noticed how he cut back on expenses. How he scrimped and saved for years while he put me through my degree in mortuary science until the dust seemed to settle. Or, more accurately, until a pandemic made our family business a far more prosperous career choice.

We don't need the money.

We might not be filthy rich like the murderer before me, but we're comfortable. We've had the means to invest back into the business. Dad purchased the brand new hundred-thousand-dollar retort last year, for heaven's sake.

"If my father is involved it's because you blackmailed him." I stand tall. "You're threatening him."

"Did he look threatened that night?" Remy raises a brow. "When you were at the bar, batting your lashes at me, were you concerned for his safety? Or were you comfortable enough to leave him to his conversation while you fucked around with a stranger?"

My throat burns. My cheeks, too. "He doesn't need the money."

"Parents have secrets, Ollie. Believe me, I learned that lesson the hard way."

"*He doesn't need the money,*" I repeat, almost shouting my denial. "He wouldn't do this."

"He has for six months." He taps the gurney with the hilt of his weapon. "Now tell me how to get this thing moving. My men usually dump the bodies straight into the retort."

He attempts to push the heavy weight, the brakes making it impossible.

He glances beneath the metal tray, scrutinizing the wheels while I stand numb and hollow.

"Like I told you—" He shoves the gun into the waistband of his suit pants and stomps the closest wheel brake. "—it's going to be okay. You're in shock, but it'll wear off." He strides around the gurney, tapping off each brake. "All you need to do is keep your head down and toe the line."

Toe the line? *Impossible.* I can't be involved in this. And I refuse to believe my father is. At least not willingly.

"Olivia," he grates. "I don't have time to fuck around. Lead the way before I lose my patience."

My arms fall to my sides, my feet heavy as I numbly comply.

I don't understand.

The panic is too loud to think through.

I enter the hall, the soft squeak of the gurney following behind me to the delivery room.

How could the guy at my back be the same man who inspired the last six months' worth of sinful daydreams? How could I have missed who he truly was—a criminal? A murderer?

I hold open the double doors of the delivery room, allowing Remy to pass me and continue to the lifeless body sprawled on the floor.

The van is gone. The overhead door, closed.

"Come over here," he demands.

I shake my head and look away, the scent of urine and vomit permeating my lungs. "No."

"Ollie, do you really want to do this the hard way? Where I force you to comply?" He grabs the guy's shoulders, hauling his lifeless upper half off the ground. "Given how much I enjoyed your body against mine all those months ago, I don't think that's the way you want to play this."

I scowl at the wall, hatred consuming me.

"Or maybe it is a preference." He drags the guy closer to the gurney. "Do you want a repeat of that night at the bar?"

Bastard.

I cross the room, nauseous, murderous.

"Grab his feet," he instructs but I barely hear the words. I'm stuck staring at the face of a man slightly older than my father, his skin a warm brown, his black hair curtaining his forehead. His head hangs limp to the side, his jaw slack, his eyes wide.

"Come on, Ollie. I want him gone before sunrise."

I do the math, assessing the deceased, guesstimating his weight. It will take roughly two hours to cremate him. At least it would if he were in a casket.

I'm not familiar with a man-only incineration equation.

"*Olivia,*" Remy barks. "Snap out of it."

"You don't need me for this." I meet his eyes, all that earthy darkness staring back at me. "If you lower the gurney you can roll him on yourself."

"Yes. But if you participate, you'll be far less inclined to run to the cops."

Fucking bastard.

"Feet. Now." He keeps dragging the man across the floor.

I follow slowly, waiting for him to pause before I grab the dead man's ankles and help carry him to the raised platform, my actions feeling out-of-body.

"See? That wasn't so hard, was it?" Remy smirks at me, and I hate knowing that I would've swooned over the expression had it been given under different circumstances. He guides the gurney across the room, pushing against the doors, then briefly pauses to make sure I follow.

Once we reach the cremation room, he aligns the gurney beside the retort conveyor, shoves the body onto the movable metal slab, then presses the button to send it into the cremation cavity.

When the metal slab is fully extended, Remy leans in to hold the man's feet, then retracts the conveyor, leaving the body to flop unceremoniously to the retort floor.

It's wrong. So incredibly wrong, and disrespectful, and morally corrupt... but he does all the right things. Knows how to work the equipment. Has evidently been taught the drill.

He just skipped the casket and consensual disposal part.

"Come here." He pushes the gurney aside and beckons me forward with a jerk of his chin.

My legs work without my permission.

I stare at the man inside the retort, bent and crumpled, the gentle flames flickering from the walls inside.

"I want you to do the honors," Remy murmurs.

My gaze snaps to his. "*No.*" I lunge back.

He grabs my wrist, holding me tight. "I apologize if I made that sound like you had a choice."

His eyes are stunning. *Why* are they so stunning?

How can he be incredibly beautiful and soul-shatteringly horrific at the same time?

"You're going to do it, Ollie. This won't end until you do."

My body goes into meltdown, panic and helplessness turning me into a trembling wreck.

"It's okay," he says with such gentle conviction that a stupid part of me still wants to believe him. "This is almost over."

My heart threatens to explode beneath my tightening ribs as I force myself to comply.

If he wants me implicated, that means he plans to keep me alive... right?

He won't kill me if I participate?

"Let go." I twist my wrist from his grip and then pull down the rectangular door to close the retort, locking it in place with shaking hands.

He remains close, forever tainting my personal space, his mouth closing in near my ear. "Now dispose of him."

My pulse thuds everywhere. My temples. My throat. No place more adamant than my chest.

I sidestep to the control panel, my limbs heavy as I slowly turn the dial to increase the flames. I take my time, the build of heat incremental while I pray for something or someone to save me. To save this victim's body.

I itch to grab Remy's gun. To change this unfair power dynamic. To shove it against his beautiful face and—

"Stop fucking around, Ollie." He closes in at my back. "Finish him."

A sob lodges in my throat. "I hate you."

There's a pause of silence, then: "I'd expect nothing less given the circumstances." He places a gentle hand on my waist, the touch painfully familiar as he shadows me. The lingering effects of that night in the bar come back to haunt me. "But your fragile feelings are the least of my concerns."

"You won't get away with this."

"I suggest ditching the pessimism." He speaks against my neck. "*We need to get away with this, pyro. The alternative isn't favorable for anyone involved. Including you *and* your father.*"

I clench my teeth. Scrunch my nose.

"You can do it." He squeezes my hip. "This is the final step."

I suck in a deep breath. Swallow.

Just do it, Liv. Save yourself and figure out the rest later.

It takes all my strength to twist my hand, jerking the knob to maximum capacity in one fell swoop.

My arm falls to my side as the whoosh of familiar flames fills my ears and residual heat envelopes me.

Then a guttural groan carries from inside the retort.

A. Goddamn. Fucking. Groan.

9

———

OLIVIA

Bile rockets up my throat as I rush to reclaim the knob and kill the flame, but Remy wraps his arms around me from behind, hugging me tight, trapping my hands at my sides.

I fight against his hold. Battle for breath. War with hysteria.

"He's dead," he vows. "You know as well as I do that a groan is normal given the circumstances."

I shake my head. Wiggle. Buck.

"Calm down." His voice is terrifyingly composed.

I keep fighting. Keep bucking. Keep gasping against the tightness taking over my throat.

I don't know how long he holds me in his unwavering grip—seconds, minutes, hours… It feels like a lifetime passes before every ounce of energy is wrung from my limbs and I'm left frozen, staring at the closed door of the cremator.

Eventually I'm released, Remy stepping out from behind me in an agonizingly slow withdrawal.

I'm sure he says something. Asks something. But I can't hear him. I can't hear anything other than the deafening flames from inside the retort and the thunderous pulse in my ears.

The man wasn't dead.

I can't bring myself to believe otherwise.

Remy might know the textbook details of how common it is for the deceased to moan and groan if air is trapped in their lungs. But those noises tend to occur when the body is moved. Not while being incinerated.

You never know. Maybe this is the norm when unlawfully disposing of a body.

I've never cremated someone so soon after death. Have never cremated anyone without family or government approval either.

But the sixth sense churning in my belly tells me that Remy has turned me into an unwilling killer.

I pivot to the room. Slump to the floor against the bottom of the retort. Hug my legs to my chest.

Remy moves about as I stare at the tiled floor.

He cleans the gurney, spraying it with chemicals that tickle my nose in scents of lemon and pine.

He says something else, the words not registering before he disappears into the hall.

Is he fleeing? Calling for reinforcements? Maybe he's decided to leave and indulge in more slaughter so he can capitalize on the cremator while it's in full swing.

Either way I remain comatose on the floor.

I relive the last hour over and over. How calm and methodical Remy had been. How familiar he is with my sacred space.

He's nothing like the man who charmed me months ago, yet exactly the same in equal measure.

How could I have been so oblivious?

He told you he was trouble.

"Jesus Christ." I bury my head in my hands.

I'd wanted him.

Pined for him.

Our time together at that dive bar had felt so heaven-sent that every second of it still clings to my memories.

My cell trills in my pants pocket, blinking me out of my catatonic state and yanking me back to the nightmare of reality with the retort continuing to fire behind me.

I'd been such an idiot.

Such a goddamn fucking fool.

I pull out my phone as thunderous footsteps echo along the hall. Remy comes into view at the threshold, his piercing eyes scrutinizing me.

"Did you call the cops?" he asks.

I shake my head, still trying to rid myself of the painful memories.

"It's okay." He adopts the demeanor of a hostage negotiator, all feigned patience and concern. "You can tell me the truth. Did you speak to the cops or not? Have you called anyone?"

I want to laugh. To scream. To disembowel.

Instead, I mutter, "The truth would've been nice six months ago."

He flinches. It's only slight, or maybe I imagine it, wishing it into existence as he stops in front of me to lower to his haunches. "Who's calling you in the middle of the night, Ollie?"

I glance at the cell screen, alight with a number I don't recognize, the device still vibrating.

"Answer it," he says. "Put it on speaker."

I want to comply. Connecting with someone outside of this hellscape is exactly what I need. A lifeline. A way out. But my brain is too sluggish and my hands to heavy.

Remy reaches for me. I flinch.

"Jesus fucking Christ." He glares as he swipes at my cell screen, connecting the call.

Silence follows.

"Hello?" an unfamiliar woman finally says. "Is anyone there?"

Remy nudges my leg, prompting me to talk.

"Hi," I croak. "Yes. Hello."

"Is this Olivia Pelosi?" she asks.

I nod, still so incredibly numb, the flames continuing to billow behind me. "Yes. Who's calling?"

The woman clears her throat. "I'm so sorry to wake you, but my name is Pearl Scott. I'm calling from The Johns Hopkins Hospital. Your father has just been admitted after arriving in the ER roughly twelve hours ago. He's got you listed as his emergency contact."

My shocked gaze turns to Remy, my feelings quickly vaulting from devastation to anger.

Did *he* do this?

"What happened?" I ask.

"I'm sorry; I don't have the full details. I'm only admin staff. All I can tell you is that he's currently in a stable condition, but due to the circumstances, you've been cleared to visit now if you'd like."

I push to shaky feet, using the cremator as leverage. "Umm… okay… Thank you…"

"You're welcome. And again, I'm sorry to have woken you at this hour with unfavorable news. I wish your father all the best."

The line disconnects, leaving me with a million questions.

I stare at Remy, trying to interpret his expression. To find any hidden guilt. "Did you have my dad—"

"No." He snatches the cell from my hand. "Your father is an asset. My people aren't responsible for this."

My people?

He sounds like the leader of a guerilla warfare group. But he also doesn't seem surprised about the hospitalization.

I square my shoulders, attempting to portray tenacity. "If you're lying…"

"You'll what?" He cranes a brow. "You had the chance to kill me and you couldn't do it."

"That was before you turned me into a criminal." My voice hitches, the pathetic weakness ricocheting around my throat. "Before you made me murder someone."

"None of this would've happened if you weren't here."

"None of it? You mean that man wouldn't be dead? And you wouldn't have used my family business for illegal means?"

He sighs, long and weary.

Fuck him. Fuck all of this.

I need to get out of here. To somehow make my way to the hospital. But even if I could get away from my prison guard, I have no car. And then there's the whole issue of the incinerating body.

The cremation won't be finished for at least an hour. Then I'll have to clean up and ensure the remaining bone fragments are placed in the cremulator. Will I also have to dispose of the cremains?

Oh, God. What if Dad's health declines while all this is going on?

"Take my car." Remy shoves a hand into his pocket and pulls out a key fob.

I blink at him, confused. "You're letting me go?"

"I'm allowing you to drive to the hospital, and *only* the hospital." He grabs my arm and places the fob in my palm. "If you divert from your path, you're as good as dead. Carlo, too. Understood?"

Adrenaline floods my system for the millionth time. "I can't leave when there's a body in the retort. If—"

"I'll handle it."

I shake my head.

He can't. I shouldn't. But my dad…

"I know what I'm doing. What's important is that you fully grasp the weight of this situation." He strengthens his hold on my arm. "If you find another phone or go to the cops—if you so much as breathe a whisper of distress to hospital staff—"

"I won't." I attempt to pull my arm away, but he digs his fingers deeper.

"I don't want to have to—"

"I understand," I snap.

I don't need to hear how he'll kill me. I've never been a slouch in the imagination department. I can picture my blood on his hands just as well as I can remember his palm scorching my inner thigh.

"Good." He loosens his hold. "I'll meet you at the hospital later."

I turn rigid. "No. I don't want you there."

I don't want Remy anywhere near my father, especially if this criminal is responsible for my only remaining parent being hospitalized.

"It's not up for debate," he states simply. "There's still a lot to discuss. You will take my car. Drive to the hospital. Then wait for my arrival."

Does he expect a *yes, sir*?

Or maybe a *heil, Hitler*.

I give neither, instead glancing away in indignation.

"Good." He tugs on my arm, making me stumble closer, his face an inch from mine.

I shudder at the proximity, the hint of his heavenly cologne poisoning my lungs, the subtle warmth of his breath brushing my cheek.

"I promise to keep you safe from the repercussions of this." His thumb rubs in lazy strokes along my wrist. So gentle. So sickeningly vindictive. "But that generous coupon expires as soon as you open your pretty little mouth to anyone other than me. Am I clear?"

I glare at him. "Yes."

He doesn't release me, doesn't even loosen his hold as the weight of his scrutiny intensifies. Those dark eyes read me, imprison me, seeming to judge if he's making the right choice in granting my temporary freedom.

But I'll keep tonight's secrets safe.

At least until I can figure out what I'm up against.

"I didn't want this for you, Ollie." His grip becomes tender, the tight lines leaving his expression as something softer takes their place. Exhaustion? Guilt?

For a split second I see him again—the Remy I first met. The temptation. The dreamy god.

His attention strays to my mouth for the briefest moment, a deep breath escaping him. "I hope your dad is okay."

10

OLIVIA

I snatch my arm away and all but run for the door.

I make it outside without breaking down and unlock his seemingly brand-new black Bentley with a scream still bottled in my lungs.

My fingers clench the steering wheel, the threat of a nervous breakdown hot on my heels as I drive across town in the dark of early morning. The smell of new leather clogs my every breath—but worse is his aftershave.

The delicious scent of the man I despise is embedded throughout the car's interior, poisoning my lungs with each inhale.

I'm tempted to sideswipe every vehicle I pass just to spite him, yet all that will do is attract the authorities, and I meant what I said about the cops. I won't run to them. Not yet. Not until I know the risks of what I'm up against.

I dump his luxury penis extension in the parking lot across the street from the hospital, then shuffle jog to the main entrance, my breath fogging in the freezing air.

The information desk isn't hard to find. The middle-aged woman who sits behind a computer greets me with kind eyes.

"I'm looking for my father, Carlo Pelosi." My stomach twists with the unknown. "I received a phone call a little while ago to say he'd been admitted."

"Let me take a look." She taps at her keyboard. "Here he is. The oncology ward. You're going to want to take the elevator to the second floor for room two hundred and three."

"Oncology?" All the blood seeps from my face. "But he doesn't have cancer."

She winces. "I'm sorry. I can only advise the patient's location. He may have been relocated due to bed shortages on other wards."

I stand dumbfounded, blinking, barely breathing. "Okay… um…"

"His doctor will be able to explain the situation." The woman stands and indicates the elevators with a gentle hand. "Go see him. It'll be all right."

I hear the placation for what it is but nod my thanks and hustle to the elevator. I escape on the second floor, then rush to the dimly lit nurses' station only to find it empty.

I don't pause to wait for someone to show. I continue down the darkened hall, my heart stopping when I reach the open door of room 203.

My father rests on a hospital bed a few yards inside the room, his face shadowed, the left side of his forehead covered in a square bandage.

"Ma'am?" a gentle voice prompts nearby.

I glance over my shoulder to the female nurse approaching. She takes me in with tired eyes, silently questioning.

"My father," is all I can muster.

She nods, stopping close beside me. "He just got back to sleep after the request to relocate him to a private room, so please try not to wake him. But he's doing fine. The doctor only wanted to keep him in overnight for observation."

"Observation of what?" I ask. "I haven't been told why he's here."

"He didn't call you while in the ER?"

"No." I wrap my arms around my middle. "I don't even understand why he's on the oncology ward."

Her expression fills with pained sympathy. "I see. He's a closed-door kind of dad. I have one of those, too."

A chime dings and *207* alights from an illuminated sign a little farther down the hall, alerting the nurse to a patient's call.

She shifts to take in the digits. "I'm sorry. I have to get back to Mrs. Slocum before she wakes the entire ward. But don't worry, Carlo is doing great." She backtracks. "Apparently, he had a dizzy spell and fell quite hard onto the corner of a cabinet. And when he lives alone, it's better to be safe than—"

"*Nurse,*" a frail female voice calls from down the hall.

The woman winces. "Mrs. Slocum really does need me." She continues backtracking. "The doctor will do his rounds in a few hours and can fill you in on all the finer details. Until then, sit with your father and try to get some rest."

"But—"

"I'm so sorry." She raises her hands in apology, frantically retreating. "I really need to get to my patient. Maybe one of the other nurses…"

I sigh and nod. "It's all right. I'll wait for the doctor."

She gives another pained smile and turns on her heel, quickly disappearing into room 207.

I turn back to my dad, the snippets of information I've received haunting me as I watch him sleep.

Due to the circumstances… A closed-door kind of dad… All the finer details.

What finer details? What circumstances?

I drag myself inside the room and stop at the foot of his bed.

He rests soundly, his lips gaping. A dreaded mouth-breather, my mom would always say. But he seems healthy enough.

Tired, yes. Run down, definitely.

Yet surely not suffering from cancer, right?

I scan the room, finding a chair in the corner, and drag it to his bedside. I sit next to him, my weariness bone-deep as I attempt to piece together the puzzle, not only about his health but his connection to the man who made me a murderer.

"What the hell is going on, Dad?" I whisper.

I brush my fingers over his, the contact pulling at my heartstrings.

I don't want to wake him, but I need to feel his warmth. His presence. To have a connection to the living instead of the cold isolation of death.

"What are you hiding from me?" I ask.

He whimpers. Stirs.

"It's okay. Sleep. I'm not going anywhere." I stare at him until my eyes ache. My back, too. I try to see all the things I might have missed over the past months. The secrets he's hidden.

Did he willingly step into an illegal arrangement with Remy's family?

I huff a tortured laugh. *No.* That's impossible.

My father's not a bad man.

He sponsors Little League teams. Donates to charity. Refuses to charge for services on infant funerals.

He's a role model. *My* role model.

I don't know how long I sit, failing to understand how my life has brought me here while I fall victim to the weary effects of adrenaline detox. I lay my cheek on the mattress beside his arm, dozing a little, my lids growing heavy. I close them for a moment. It feels like barely a blink. But when I open them again it's to tender fingers stroking my hair, gently coaxing me awake.

I straighten, the room now brighter than before, the orange glow of sunrise seeping in through the window.

Dad gives me a strained smile, a wealth of unmasked sorrow staring back at me.

That's all there is. No words. No admission. Only a pained curve of lips and a regret-filled gaze, and I become acutely aware that this is more than a bump to the head.

I swallow over the questions waging war inside me. Once I have definitive answers there's no going back to the bliss of ignorance.

"How long have you been here?" he rasps.

I check my watch. *7:05.* "A few hours, I guess."

"The hospital called you?"

I nod. "Around three in the morning. They said that given the circumstances I could come see you straight away."

His blank features give nothing away.

My heart twists. "The oncology ward, Dad?"

A flicker of pain dances in his eyes, making the twisting, wrenching organ beneath my ribs morph into an instrument of torture.

"I'm sorry, Liv."

I press my lips tight. Clasp my hands together to stop them trembling.

His palm slides over my tangled fingers. "After what we endured with your mom, I thought it best to keep you as far away from this for as long as possible."

I shake my head. I didn't *endure*. I rallied. I'd wanted to be by her side while she fought breast cancer.

"So it's been going on for a while?" I ask.

He nods, strong and sure. A valiant warrior in the face of his demons. Or maybe just a deceitful parent, giving it his all to lessen my concern.

"I guess that explains all the days off you've been having." I huff a pained laugh. "And here I was thinking you might have found a woman to occupy your time."

He crushes me with a sad smile. "Your mom was all I ever needed."

We don't cry.

I sit straighter, denying the memory of my mother's voice leverage over my wayward emotions. "I want to know everything."

"I understand." He drags his hand away and repositions himself against the pillows until he's seated upright. "But I've decided that won't be happening."

"What does that mean? Surely, you can't think to continue keeping me in the dark now that I'm at your bedside."

"No, *fragolina*. At least not entirely. I just..." He drags in a tired breath. "I don't want this for you again. Not the hospital visits. Not the worry and the heartache."

"Worry is a privilege, Dad. Heartache doesn't exist unless you have people to love. Don't keep me from this. I already blame myself for not noticing—"

"Don't," he begs.

"How can't I? How did you hit your head? How did you get to the hospital? Why didn't you call me? Why couldn't you trust that—"

"This has nothing to do with trust, Liv, and everything to do with protection." He reaches for a glass of water on his bedside table and takes a sip. "Neither one of us have recovered from watching your mother suffer. I promised myself I wouldn't do that to you. At least as much as possible. And besides, I didn't need to call you about the fall when I was already here." He grabs the neck of his hospital gown and drags it down past his collarbone, exposing the small, implanted port in his chest. "Chemo."

I school my expression, refusing to let him see the effects of the punch to my gut.

"The treatments are why I've been taking the time off," he continues. "I schedule them for a Friday, which gives me time to recover over the weekend. For the most part, I can bounce back well enough for nobody to notice by Monday." He shrugs. "Or Tuesday at the latest."

Guilt clogs my veins. "I *should've* noticed."

"I did everything in my power to make sure you didn't. I've given Ivy extra responsibilities. I hide away in my office more than usual. I take power naps at lunch. And with you always squirreled away in your prep room there's no way you could've known."

I shake my head, hating how self-absorbed I've become. "I thought you were working too hard. But it all makes sense now—the lethargy, the thinning hair."

"My vanity doesn't appreciate the side-effects of the treatment, that's for sure." He rakes a hand through his short black strands. "Then again, I've been lucky. The chemo drugs I'm on don't always cause hair loss."

Is that because he's taking a less effective treatment so I wouldn't get suspicious?

"I did buy a wig in preparation though." He chuckles.

"I would've noticed a wig, Dad. At least I hope I would've. But it seems I'm more narcissistic than I realized because I had no clue you were sick."

His laughter vanishes. "You're not narcissistic. You didn't notice because I didn't want you to." He stares at me with the same unconditional love he's given freely for as long as I can remember. Then something at the door steals his attention, his brow furrowing.

I glance over my shoulder, following his gaze.

Remy watches us from the hall, the sight of him flooding me with panic.

I snap my focus back to Dad, the color drained from his face.

He studies my clothes, his eyes widening. "You're still in your work uniform. Why?"

My stomach plummets. "I…"

I don't know what to say. What I *can* say without putting us both in more danger.

"What happened, Liv?" His gaze ping-pongs between me and the hall.

"I, um, stayed late at work. I wanted to prepare Amisha and the baby so I didn't have to go back in over the weekend."

"And?"

"And—" I chance another glance over my shoulder, caught up in the subtle threat of a narrowed gaze that pins me in place. "I fell asleep."

"*Jesus*, Liv."

I want to tell him that cursing Satan would be more appropriate because I'm sure that's who spawned the monster in the hall, but it's too soon for jokes.

I give an awkward smile instead. "It's definitely been a night of revelations."

Footsteps carry behind me. Hinges softly squeak before the door clicks shut. Then Remy's broad frame enters my periphery.

"Carlo," he murmurs.

"Rem." My father offers him an agonized smile. "What happened?"

He calls the monster *Rem?* He looks at him in *apology?*

I keep my attention on my dad, scrutinizing his reaction to the murderer in the room… Well, the *second* murderer now that criminal activity has been forced upon me.

"We had an issue we needed to dispose of. You weren't answering your burner, and there were no cars in the parking lot. The assumption was made that our presence wouldn't be known."

Dad winces.

I fight to remain composed.

"She knows," Remy states calmly.

My father gives a solemn nod, a sheen of unshed tears swimming around his deep brown irises.

"I don't blame you." I grasp his hand. "There's nothing you could've done if they threatened—"

"There was no threat, Liv." He squeezes my fingers. "The decisions I've made were done without duress."

He's lying.

He has to be... If only I could deny the truth staring back at me.

There's no fear in my father's expression. Not even a hint of trepidation. There's only sickening regret.

"Why?" I ask.

He scrunches his nose. "Cancer treatment is expensive."

"We have health insurance."

"We have *basic* insurance," he corrects. "I still have to pay half of all the bills. And with the specialists and treatments... I did what I thought was best for your future. In the event of my death, any remaining debt would be taken from my estate, which means both the house and the business are at risk. You'd lose everything."

"Don't talk like that. I'm not losing anything."

"Liv, it's a mountain of debt. I'm still paying off the new reto—"

"Stop it," I warn. "You can't go through this with a negative attitude."

He concedes with a wince, holding my gaze for long heartbeats before turning his focus to Remy. "I'm sorry this happened the way it did."

Now he's *apologizing*? To the menace who interrupted a monumentally private family moment while standing there without any hint of surprise or concern at my father's cancer admission... just like he wasn't surprised or concerned when I received the phone call from the hospital?

Wait a damn minute.

"Did he already know?" I ask my father.

The wince lingers.

I turn to Remy, hating how his expression doesn't falter from the elite level of composure. "You knew about the cancer?"

My father's betrayal cuts deep. My insides wage war.

Remy must sense my growing unrest because his eyes harden. "Remain calm." There's no comfort in the request. It's a subtle warning.

If I wasn't fearful for my life I'd contemplate clawing his eyes out.

"It's okay, Liv," my dad tries to soothe. "Everything is going to be—"

"Why the private room then?" I blurt, returning my attention to my father. "If money is such an issue—"

"I made that request." Remy strolls closer. "Given the circumstances —and your temperamental state—privacy is a priority. I'll cover the cost."

He's keeping us contained.

Isolated.

Their arrangement may not have been made under duress, but it sure reeks of manipulation.

"Liv, please trust me." Dad holds my gaze, compassionate and sympathetic. "This is a lot to take on. But you'll understand in time. All I need you to know is that your future is my main priority. I don't want you to have to worry about money if I leave you."

I shove from my chair. "You're *not* going *anywhere*."

He stiffens at my outburst.

"You're not," I repeat, softer, clinging to my last slither of self-control. "I don't care about money, or debt, or whatever else has made you keep this from me. All I want is for you to concentrate on getting the best care so you can recover."

"I am," he vows. "And my arrangement with Remy's family has allowed for that. I'm not sure how I would've approached this without their financial backing."

A cold sweat seeps over me. "Please tell me you weren't going to deny treatment due to finances."

I've already lost a mother. I will *not* lose him, too.

"No." He beckons me forward with a curl of his fingers. "I admit I did think about it a time or two. But I promise I'm not in a hurry to be reunited with your mom. I'll do everything in my power to stay with you as long as possible."

The promise hits like a physical blow.

We have to be strong.

"I—" The ache in my throat renders me speechless.

So many questions remain unanswered. What type of cancer is he battling? What's his prognosis? How do we dissolve the arrangement with Remy and his family?

A *tap, tap, tap* at the door claims my attention, followed by a squeak of hinges.

"Morning, all," a jovial male voice announces.

My father breaks our pained stare, giving the intruder his full attention. "Morning, Doc."

I take a few seconds to breathe. To battle against the weakness dragging me under before I turn to see a grey-haired man offering his hand to Remy.

"I'm Doctor Julian Parker. Nice to meet you."

"Remy. Family friend."

My eyes flare at the lie.

"And you must be Olivia." The doctor approaches me with a kind smile. "Your father talks non-stop about you."

"I wish I could say the same." I clear the fear from my throat and release Dad's hold to take the doctor's outstretched palm, pretending there's no threatening murderer in the room. "Unfortunately, your patient hasn't mentioned you at all. Or cancer. Or chemo. This morning is the first I've heard of it."

The doctor softly clasps my hand, the touch exuding comfort. "I can assure you it wasn't something he wanted to hide, but us humans make a lot of hard choices for the ones we love." He gives my fingers a quick squeeze, then releases his hold. "If it makes you feel any better, I promise he's been getting the best treatment available." He turns his attention to my father. "How's the head this morning?

"Good. I'm ready to go home."

The doctor chuckles. "Not so fast. Seeing as though you're already here, I thought we might run my next round of tests slightly earlier than planned."

"Now?" My father frowns. "Is that really necessary?"

"I'm afraid so." Doctor Parker looks to me, then Remy. "I'll have him discharged later this afternoon."

Dad sighs. "I could think of a million other things I'd prefer—"

"Dad," I beg, hating his negativity in light of the life-threatening situation. "*Please.*"

"Don't worry, I'm not giving him a choice." Parker smiles. "He likes to pretend he doesn't enjoy being fawned over by all the pretty nurses, but I see right through him."

Dad barks a laugh. "Yeah, okay. Can you give me a minute to say goodbye to my daughter?"

"Of cour—"

"No," I interrupt. "I'm staying."

"Liv, that's not what I want." Dad's expression turns somber. "Please let me do this my way."

No. Not alone.

"*Please,*" he repeats.

The pressure of everyone's attention weighs on my shoulders.

It's not right. Nobody should suffer in isolation. To walk through darkness alone.

"We'll take good care of him," the doctor promises. "There's no need to worry."

Remy steps closer. "I'll make sure she gets home safely."

I stiffen and shake my head, wanting to protest, *needing* to stay not only *with* my dad but *away* from the psychopath.

"Thanks, Rem." Dad gives a solemn nod. "I'd appreciate that."

He would?

Does he not understand what this man has put me through? What I've seen? What I've been forced to do?

I ache to tell him. To blurt the atrocities for all to know. But Remy encroaches farther on my personal space as if he can sense my teetering sanity.

"We'll talk more once you return home," he says to my father.

Dad nods again, holding my gaze as he throws back the bedsheet, his sun-starved legs on display while he drags them to hang over the side of the mattress. "Until then, try to get some rest, Liv. You look worse than I do."

"Please," I whisper. "I really don't want to leave you."

"I know. But I need you to. Those nurses aren't going to offer me a sponge bath with my daughter hanging around." He winks, yet the stare he gives after is pointed. Pleading.

None of this makes sense.

Why is he pushing me to leave with a criminal? Is it because he thinks I'll be safe? Or that all of us will die if I don't?

The doctor laughs, startling me.

"Come on." Remy grabs the crook of my arm, his grip increasing my panic. "Let's go."

It takes all my strength to remain quiet as the doctor leads my father from the room. Every single ounce of my composure not to run for the nurses' station and scream bloody murder.

"I suggest you quit thinking thoughts that will only get you in trouble." Remy inches closer, the warmth of his mouth nestling close to my ear. "You've been so well behaved, my pretty little pyro. Don't ruin it now."

11

REMY

It takes a couple seconds but Ollie starts for the hall, her posture rigid.

She's scared of me, which I loathe, yet the alternative isn't an option.

I reach the elevator by her side. Remain quiet on our descent. Leave her to her thoughts as we cross the lobby and step into the frigid morning air.

"Where's my car?" I scope our surroundings for the Bentley, having been dropped off at the front door by Russo.

She doesn't have a coat, and I need to get her someplace warm before hypothermia can be added to the goodie bag of treats she's received during the past six hours.

"In the parking lot." She waves an arm to the left, not taking her eyes off the cab rank up ahead. "Here." She retrieves my key fob from her trouser pocket and hands it over. "I can't remember exactly where I parked."

She turns on her heel and hustles for the street as if fleeing a crime scene.

"Where do you think you're going?" I stalk to catch up and grab her wrist. "We leave together."

She gasps. Flinches.

We've done this dance before—me being heavy-handed, her despising my touch. But in the bright light of day it's risky.

"I'll find my own way home." She attempts to yank her arm free.

"Like hell." I step closer, releasing her wrist to wrap an arm around her back, making our volatile standoff seem more like an intimate embrace to the cab driver who watches us from his rested position against the side of his car. "I'm not letting you out of my sight to make a costly mistake."

Her eyes narrow. "I'm not stupid. I know I need to keep my mouth shut."

"You're exhausted and emotional. It's a hazardous concoction." I use my free hand to gently swipe the loose strands of her frazzled braid behind her ear and ignore her cringe. She has such stunning hair—always tied back with ethereal beauty. "One that might unintentionally steer you in the direction of a police station."

"I'm not going to run to the cops." She leans back, trying to inch as far away as my hold will allow. I'm sure she'd stop if she realized the tilt of her waist against my crotch is taunting my dick.

"Don't make a scene." There's a lethal edge to my warning. "There are witnesses. Security surveillance. Do you really think the cops finding out about this is the only problem?"

She's stiff in my hold—a complete contrast to the night we met.

I bet she's relieved I didn't pop her cherry all those months ago when she couldn't stop staring at me with those wanton hazel eyes.

It wouldn't have taken much. I could've seated her on my lap, hitched her skirt, and discreetly fucked her in full view of the bar's patrons.

She'd been hungry enough—a greedy little kitten. One who would've despised those memories for the rest of her life.

You're welcome, Ollie.

"If you want to keep that gorgeous head on your exquisitely delicate shoulders, I suggest you stop seeing my lenience as weakness. I don't want to have to hurt you."

She whimpers. Wiggles. "I'm *not* leaving with you."

"Forgive me if I haven't made this abundantly clear, but for the unforeseeable future you and I are going to remain intimately close at all times." I slide my hand farther up her back, adding pressure to force her toward me. "I gave you leeway to come see your father because I knew making you wait would be detrimental to your emotional state. But from now on, you don't leave my sight. Understood?"

She swallows. Shudders.

She wants out of this nightmare, and I get it. If I was immune to the sight of her, I'd be praying to wake up from this shit show, too. But I'm the fucking asshole who's actually enjoying being close to her again.

"If you want to go home, we go together." I rub taunting circles along her spine with my thumb. "If you take a nap, I'll be right there to coax you to sleep. And if you decide you need a shower…" I let my voice trail, my cock already too unruly.

Dial it down, motherfucker.

Her breathing quickens. "I hate you."

Her statement packs the same brutal punch it did the first time she threw it at me.

Don't ask me how. Or why. It's a mediocre retort. A flimsy backhand at best.

Yet here I stand, the serrated teeth of guilt gnawing into my gut like a rabid dog. "Hate me all you like, just do it discreetly. You don't want anyone noticing your newfound friendship with Italian mafia royalty."

"No, you don't want evidence that shows I'm an unwilling participant," she murmurs.

"Either way, you'd be screwed if this ever got to trial. Do you think a tantrum out the front of a hospital would negate the fact you willingly accepted the offer of a criminal's car to drive into the city in the middle of the night? Does that scream *hostile situation* to you?"

I wouldn't have thought it possible but she stiffens further—a stunning marble statue that radiates terror.

I eat up the space between us until my mouth is poised near her ear. "And the doctor?" I drawl. "Do you think he'll corroborate your story? Or would he maintain that you seemed undaunted by my presence as you sat quietly at your father's bedside? That you freely accepted my ride home and left with me without duress?"

"You bastard." She places a hand to my chest, pushing, digging her nails through my shirt and penetrating my skin. *God*, it feels good.

"I'm merely giving you clarity." She still smells divine. Ripe strawberries and vanilla. I bet between her thighs tastes just as sweet. "If tonight's events are discovered, you're screwed. Not only by the authorities, but my family. I'm trying to keep you alive. Remember that the next time you think about defying me."

Her rigidity loosens, her shoulders slumping in defeat. The pointy teeth of guilt sink deeper.

"The good news is you can rail on me all you like in private." I loosen my hold. "In fact, I encourage it."

I crave her hatred as much as hemorrhoids, but reverse psychology and all that.

She takes the bait, slamming her mouth shut. She wiggles from my hold, daring to give me the slightest glare before turning and starting for the parking lot.

She was never meant to learn about the arrangement. It was Carlo's one stipulation. He even crafted specific guidelines after the first time we almost got caught so that the disposal of *whatever we saw fit* was only to be done early at night, leaving enough time for the retort to cool, and only while he was on-call.

But I fucked up.

Miguel's kill had been done in the heat of the moment. I'd had brain matter and skull fragments to dispose of. And with the growing rivalry between us and the Mexican cartel, keeping a mutilated body on hand wasn't ideal.

So I took liberties.

There wasn't much Carlo could do when I showed up at his doorstep with blood on my hands and a fresh kill in the replica funeral van.

He'd switched the after-hours number to his phone instead of Hugo's to make sure we weren't disturbed. I guess he'd prayed the retort would cool in time.

I'd assumed it had.

Then Salvatore gave the order to get rid of Javier and the game started all over again, except this time Carlo hadn't answered my knock on his door.

My men located the actual Pelosi funeral home pick-up van via the GPS tracker I planted months ago for circumstances just like this. They kept watch on the female employee's townhouse and were told to cause a diversion if she got a call-out.

I'd thought I'd been in a prime position to use the retort.

The staff parking lot had been empty.

The place was quiet.

Then my men had shouted my moniker, Ollie's terrified eyes had met mine, and I'd known my choices had just ruined the life of someone entirely undeserving of the threat her knowledge would bring.

We make it to my car in silence. She climbs into the passenger seat without protest.

I drive onto the Baltimore streets faster than necessary.

There's no music. No playlist. Only the grate of asphalt and honk of horns from the bustling Saturday morning traffic which is going to make the journey across the city ten times longer than it needs to be.

I check my cell at a red light.

Two missed calls. Five texts. All from Salvatore.

Shit.

I'm not surprised he didn't appreciate the message I sent earlier about needing a night to blow off steam. It wasn't the best diversion from the mistakes I've made. But I'd just thrown a man in an oversized kiln and ordered the most stunning and frighteningly scared woman to dispose of his body.

I only get another five miles down the road when *Salvatore* alights on the car's display screen with the option to connect the incoming call.

Fuck.

I can't ignore him forever. The longer I do, the more suspicious he'll get.

I shoot a glance at Ollie. "If you value your life, I suggest you remain quiet."

She crosses her arms over her chest, her chin hitching as her mouth remains clamped shut.

Good girl.

I connect the call. "Broth—"

"Where the fuck are you?" Salvo snaps.

"Good morning to you, too." I snicker, forcing the slightest drunken slur into my tone. "Didn't you get my message about taking the night off?"

"Did you not get mine that demanded to know where the fuck you are?"

"Of course. I just didn't want big brother crashing my party. After everything I've done for you I deserve a night to myself."

"You can have all the nights you want," he growls. "But we've made a lot of enemies in a short space of time, and they're out for blood."

Ollie's gaze shoots in my direction.

Yes, pyro, the list of threats to your existence is extensive.

"Aww, look at you trying to take care of me." I tap the turn signal and change lanes. "Aren't you just the bestest big broth—"

"Don't fuck with me, Rem. I've got enough on my plate without worrying about you."

"There's nothing to worry about."

"So last night ran smoothly?"

"Without a hitch." I take the next corner, turning toward Ollie's suburb.

"There were no loose ends?"

I pause, paranoia skittering down my back at the pointed question. If my men said something about Ollie despite my instruction I'll—
"Everything is as it should be. Like always."

"I fucking hope so. Make sure you keep your head low and your ass out of trouble. And answer next time I fucking call."

"Aww. You're such a sweetie. I'd do anything for—"

The line disconnects.

I discreetly ease out a long breath. I'll have to text him later and pretend I'm leaving town while I keep an eye on my unwilling business partner.

I'm also going to have to speak to my men—Russo and Valenti—and point out exactly what will happen to them if they open their mouths about Ollie seeing them with Javier's dead body.

Having to kill her because she attempts to rat on my family is one thing, but losing her because Salvo is a paranoid, blood-thirsty asshole isn't something my battered conscience could handle.

"You lied for me," she whispers, her attention burning up my periphery. "Why?"

I flash her a taunting smirk. "Because you and I are besties now, right?"

She cringes. "What will happen if he finds out about me?"

Dread thickens the blood in my veins. I switch my attention back to city traffic.

I've already made it clear my family are a threat. But telling her just how quickly and easily my uncle and brother would order the execution of someone capable of putting us all in prison isn't something she should be aware of.

"My brother is unpredictable. And at the moment, so are you. Which means it's best to keep last night's events as contained as possible."

"Will he kill me?"

"Only if he finds out about you."

She falls quiet, her attention trained on me from the corner of my eye.

I drive miles without a peep from her. There's only the deafening sound of her thoughts and the building weight of my concern for her future as I detour down less populated streets.

I'd grown too fucking cocky.

"Why Grim?" she finally asks. "Why did those men call you that last night?"

I roll my eyes through my disdain for the moniker. "I suppose you could say it's a family tradition."

"You all have sickening handles?"

"For the most part. We're quite the eclectic bunch. Anyone on the wrong side of the law could tell you my oldest brother, Matthew, was once known as the Butcher of Baltimore. My sister has also been called the Temptress of High Society." I shrug. "I earned the Grim Reaper title."

In less than a year. Talk about an overachiever.

The shits I have to give for the human race have all but disappeared since my father ambushed me and my brothers with our murder on his mind. In fact, I haven't cared much for anyone outside of my siblings and uncle until I spawned a demented obsession with a woman who has balls big enough to attempt to burn me alive.

"What about your other brother?" she asks. "The one that was on the phone. Does he have a handle?"

I narrow my eyes at her, then glance back to the red Chrysler in front of us. Is she scheming to gain some sort of intel? "Salvo's yet to earn a moniker."

"And your uncle? Does he go by another name?"

I slow the car, easing a few extra yards from the vehicle ahead. "What's with all the questions, pyro?"

She scrunches her nose in disgust. "Please don't call me that."

"Why not? You're one of us now."

"No, I'm not." She stares outside. "I'm nothing more than an unwilling participant."

That's a shame.

I could picture her in the lifestyle. A mafia princess. My treasured queen. I'd kill our enemies. She'd dispose of the evidence.

But she's too honorable for all that.

She'd never be able to make a home amongst my family. In my penthouse. Between my sheets.

I snap my attention back to the road, well aware that building an infatuation with someone on death row is a bad idea.

"There's a danger in knowing too much, Ollie." I snatch my sunglasses from the center console and shove them on as if a thin layer of glass could protect me from her appeal. "Keep that in mind if your intent is to snoop."

"It's dangerous to learn more. Dangerous to defy you. Dangerous to breathe in your presence." Her voice climbs with each sentence. "You've ruined my life."

"I've definitely sprinkled it with a little spice, that's for sure."

Animosity filters from her side of the car, the tension growing the closer I get to her suburb.

"I don't want to go home," she states once we're a few blocks away. "Please drive me to work."

"Not going to happen." I continue on my predetermined path. "You've barely slept. Or eaten. You need—"

"Drive me back to work, or as soon as I get home I'll drive there myself."

My dick taps in to the conversation, her audacity having the opposite effect of what I assume she intends.

Fear me, pyro. Don't fuck with me. Otherwise this shit is going to get messy.

"Why work?" I grate.

"I need to keep myself busy. My thoughts will be the death of me if I'm not occupied. I also don't want you at my house, invading my personal space. It's bad enough you seem to know where I live."

"The invasion is inevitable. You might as well get it over with."

"No. I'm not ready." She hugs her arms around her middle, her heartache doing strange things to me. "And besides, I need to make sure everything is as it should be with the retort."

I itch to concede. To give her what she wants merely for the sake of pleasing her. But I dived headfirst toward that piranha tank six months ago and still haven't been liberated from the aftereffects of my fingers against her damp panties.

I should've known I'd sealed her fate when I slid into that booth.

I could've played last night differently if she hadn't recognized me.

I would've had my men subdue her, ply her with a roofie or two to make what she witnessed seem like a messed up dream. She'd wake up with a headache and a serious case of confusion that Carlo could've blamed on a gas leak. Men in hi-vis gear with clipboards could have corroborated the story.

I should've gone down that path regardless, yet the thought of hurting her, *drugging* her…

I clench the steering wheel.

This woman is fucking everything up.

"Please, Remy. Wasn't biting my tongue at the hospital a sign of good faith? Can't you give me one in return?"

Good faith means jack shit when the sound of her begging has me craving to hear those words in a more sordid setting.

What would she look like on her knees? Wrists bound? Lips parted?

"I may be a virgin, but I'm not virginal."

Fuck.

She's right. Taking her home is a mistake. I can't be trusted in close proximity to the temptation of her bed.

"Fine." I grind my teeth through the carnal thoughts and slap the turn signal to navigate toward the funeral home. "But let me make this clear—the invasion of your personal space is going to happen eventually."

We just both need to be in a better headspace when it happens.

12

———

OLIVIA

His agreement brings the slightest relief.

I need to keep busy, otherwise the murmurs of panic in my mind will become deafening shouts.

I can't fixate on what's happened. Or what the future will bring. Not until I can speak to Dad and get solid answers—ones I can trust.

Remy makes a small detour through a fast-food drive-thru to order breakfast and coffee, his manners sickeningly impeccable as he speaks to staff. A short time later he parks the Bentley at the funeral home and cuts the engine.

After more than thirty minutes stuck in a car, I would've thought the haunting grasp of his hands would've left my body. But the feel of him against me continues to linger.

I hate it. Hate *him*.

Yet apparently that doesn't stop me from being attuned to his energy.

"Me being here during the day is a risk," he mutters. "If I'm seen—"

I unclasp my belt and shove from the car before he can change his mind.

I stride for the delivery room door and the little locked box screwed into the wall, seeing as though my hasty escape earlier meant I left my keys inside. I'm pretty sure I left my innocence and happiness in there, too, but I'm not sure I'll get those back.

I enter the PIN code, press the remote inside, and wait impatiently as the overhead door slowly rises.

A car door slams behind me, Remy's approaching footsteps bringing anxiety. I don't wait for him to catch up. I duck under the half-opened door and enter the delivery room to do a quick scan for signs of illegal activity.

There's nothing. Not even the stench of urine and bile from earlier.

I hustle into the hall and do the same frantic visual sweep. Then move to the cremation room where I flick on the lights and pause in the doorway.

The air is warm, the heat still emanating from the dormant retort.

Everything is as it should be. There's no sign of the struggle I endured or the trauma inflicted.

For some reason, I thought those horrific moments would've changed the space somehow. That my ordeal would've tainted the room, stained the walls, or shifted the foundation in some way.

Yet nothing is out of the ordinary.

I inch toward the retort, my heart in my throat as I wheel aside the gurney placed in front of it and check the primary chamber for remnants of the deceased.

Again, nothing.

No fissures of bone, titanium rods, or ball joints.

"I'm open to critiques if the cleanup isn't to your standards."

I tense, not only at Remy's presence but my inability to critique even if I wanted to.

It's as if the trauma never happened—his victim a figment of my imagination.

I turn to face him standing in the doorway, carrying the take-out food bag and coffee tray.

"How many?" I whisper.

I promised myself I wouldn't ask. Not *him*, at least. I want a reliable answer I can trust, which means it can only come from my father. But intrusive thoughts have me in a chokehold.

He raises a brow. "How many?"

"You know exactly what I'm asking. How many crimes? How many bodies?"

"Enough."

One word. No emotion. Just handsome, detached indifference.

"Enough for what?" I dare to demand. "My disgust? My hatred? The utter decimation of my faith in humanity?"

"All of the above." He leans his shoulder against the doorframe. "Trust me, you don't want to know my stats, pyro."

I flinch at the nickname—how he always throws it in my face like a taunt.

I press a hand against my turbulent stomach. "How can you be so callous?"

"Compassion is something that's taught. I never had a teacher. But you can rest assured that all those who've died at my hands are just as unworthy of life as I am."

"Those people would've had families… Loved ones."

He inclines his head. "True. The guy from last night had both. A wife. A son. But that kid was Thursday night's barbecue."

All the air escapes my lungs.

I stare at him, searching for guilt that has to be hidden somewhere. But no matter how hard I focus on those handsome features, my efforts are in vain.

He's emotionless. Devoid of remorse.

"I need to get to work." I swallow over my building nausea, refusing to let it weaken me. "Can I have my phone back?"

He shrugs. "Depends what you want it for?"

"To message my father. To listen to music." To research the mastermind currently holding me hostage.

He gives me a pointed look as if hearing the thoughts I've left unspoken. "I'll think about it."

Asshole.

He raises a sardonic brow, as if hearing that, too.

I suck in a deep breath to stem the frustration. "Can you at least leave me alone to do my job? My decedents deserve privacy."

He's quiet a moment, his scrutiny giving me goose bumps. "You need to eat."

A scoff escapes before I can clamp it down. "Given my duties, I've learned to stomach food through many emotions, *Grim*, but disgust isn't one of them."

His jaw ticks, my loathing seeming to affect him when the vilest of his atrocities doesn't.

He pushes from the doorframe, towering to his full height. He walks toward me, his predatory steps decimating the space between us.

My pulse quickens and I fight against the need to backtrack as his callous gaze clutches me in its poisoned grip.

"Eat, Ollie." He smacks the food bag on the metal gurney at my side, then does the same with the coffee tray. "God forbid you pass out in my presence. You wouldn't want to learn what someone as vile as me is capable of when left to my own devices around an incapacitated woman."

I remain frozen. Sickened.

He reaches inside his jacket.

I suck in a breath, waiting for a gun to be drawn. But it's my cell he retrieves, clapping the device down beside the food.

Then he turns on his heel and strides from the room.

I don't breathe again until he's in the hall, my gasp for air hissing in my ears.

I ignore the food and grab my cell, unsure why he'd risk giving it back until I realize I don't have to enter my security details to unlock the screen.

He's bypassed my pin somehow. Probably added some form of spyware or blocked me from calling the authorities.

I don't care.

My Google stalking can wait. For now, I settle for contact with my father, the lifeline enough to leave me feeling slightly appeased and naively protected.

I spend the passing hours working in the mortuary, messaging dad whenever my anxiety piques. I ask for updates and try to determine when he'll need a ride home, completely ignoring the mafia noose around our necks.

His answers are vague.

DAD

No need to worry about me.

I'm convinced hospital coffee is just dirt and hot water.

Only a few more tests to run.

There's no elaboration on what the tests are or how he's feeling. He's in full-blown avoidance mode. I'll wear him down, though. I just need to talk to him alone.

God, we have so much to figure out.

It isn't until after lunch that the mortuary door opens and Remy invites himself in to dump a filled coffee mug and a granola bar on the stainless-steel tool tray beside me.

I ignore the peace offering, at least until he leaves the room and my grumbling stomach convinces me that succumbing to his bribe is far better than being violently hangry after I refused to eat the breakfast he bought this morning.

More hours pass. The anxiety roller coaster continues.

I'm sterilizing my preparation bench after finishing Amisha and her daughter's embalming when I hear something over the music humming from my cell playlist.

I pause. Cock my head.

It's faint. Barely a murmur of Remy's voice. But I've heard that all day. I even eavesdropped on a call he made earlier to Russo—the interloper from the bar—until I grew exhausted trying to decipher his deceptive lingo.

I continue busying myself with a deep clean of my instruments in the sink and zone out, watching the water cascading over the stainless steel, my heart heavy, my limbs tired.

I need sleep. Food. Maybe a lobotomy. Not necessarily in that order.

Ten minutes later, the prep room door opens again and Remy strides in to grab my cell from the counter, silencing Billie Eilish mid chorus.

"Obviously you didn't hear me earlier." He returns the device to the counter. "Your dad is here. I just finished settling him upstairs."

I dump my tools in the sink, quickly wrench the faucet, then yank off my protective gear and rush for the hall.

"Choose your words wisely when speaking to him," Remy warns, following me to the outside stairs leading to my father's home on the second floor. "It's best not to give him details on what happened last night."

I pause on the third step. "Why?"

"Because this situation can't handle any more complications."

I slowly turn, needing to see what he means. What he's hiding.

He peers up at me from the cement path, his expression giving nothing away. "Like your father mentioned at the hospital, he requires my family's money for his treatment." He grabs the handrail and takes a predatory step. "You wouldn't want to risk messing that up, would you?"

I hear the threat for what it is.

But it hasn't even been twenty-four hours and I'm already becoming burned out from intimidation.

"Your game plan can't be to keep threatening me forever, Remy. It's unsustainable."

He encroaches another step, suffocating my personal space for a moment of intense eye contact that has my mouth drying. "Have more faith in me."

God, I want to gouge his gorgeous face.

"How this proceeds is entirely up to you." He continues upward, nudging around me. "If you're sick of threats then come to terms with the arrangement and keep your pretty mouth shut."

Fire consumes my chest, the fury heating my eyes.

I may have withheld my tears of sorrow for years, but holding back those of violent rage might break me.

His footfalls continue up the staircase, each thud a hearty punch through my insides.

I have no bargaining power. No collateral. Or do I?

I turn to him, finding him halfway up the stairs. "We could find the money elsewhere. He doesn't need you."

"Well, I need his equipment, so unless you're willing to forfeit your life, I suggest you keep things civil." He pauses at the landing. "If you didn't already notice at the hospital, your father trusts me. I suggest you learn to do the same. Now move your ass. Let's make this short and sweet. Your father has to concentrate on recovery."

His fake concern for my dad only enrages me further.

I stalk up the stairs and maneuver in front of him, cautious not to make contact with the devil as I open the door to my childhood home.

It's been weeks since I've been in here and years since my mother died, but this place is always teeming with her scent of cedarwood and patchouli. I don't want Remy anywhere near it. Near *her*. His presence spits in the face of all the good she brought into this world.

I pass the small entry and continue into the open living area, all the air escaping my lungs in relief at the sight of my dad seated on his plush grey sofa, a bandage still covering his forehead.

I rush for him, taking in the fatigue in his eyes as I lunge onto the cushioned seat beside him to wrap him in a hug. "What were you thinking, driving home on your own? You should've called. Why didn't you?"

He returns the gesture, his arms heavy around me. "I wasn't alone. Remy arranged a driver to bring me and my car back from the city."

Fucking Remy. Always one step ahead.

"You should've asked *me*." I withdraw to meet my father's gaze. "I would've got an Uber into the city and brought your car back myself."

"It wasn't necessary." The asshole speaks from somewhere behind me. "One of my men was already close by."

I don't acknowledge him. Don't even look in his direction.

"Tell me what the doctor said." I grasp my father's hands, silently begging for full transparency.

"There's nothing to worry about, Liv. Everything is as it should be."

"But what *is* everything exactly? I want to know the type of cancer. The prognosis. How many chemo treatments you've had…"

His smile turns apologetic. "I've already told you all you need to know."

My stomach hollows. "Dad, you haven't—"

"Why did you come back here after the hospital anyway?" he cuts me off with a blatant segue. "You should've gone home to rest."

I slide my hand away from his to stem the ache of dismissal. "I needed to keep busy. My mind isn't a comforting place right now."

He winces. "I promise I'm fine."

"Your health is only one of many things that worry me, Dad."

"I know." He looks down at his hands in his lap. "My worst fear was that you would find out about the situation with Remy's family from someone other than me. I'm sorry, *fragolina*."

I settle back into my seat. "Then why didn't you tell me?"

"Because I was hoping you wouldn't have to find out at all." Dad takes great interest in the aging skin on the back of his hand, rubbing his thumb repeatedly over his knuckles. "It's not something I thought you'd understand."

"You're right," I whisper. "I don't."

What hurts most is that I'd assumed we had the same values. That we were cut from the same cloth. Has he somehow changed from the man who tag-teamed Mom in teaching me right from wrong?

"I need you to explain it to me." I tilt my head, attempting to meet his gaze. "Because I don't believe you willingly walked into something this morally corrupt."

The hairs on my nape tingle in foreboding, my senses on high alert for a reprimand to my disobedience from Remy.

"I promise I did." Finally Dad meets my gaze. Tired. Solemn. Yet resolute. "I've hidden a lot of pain from you over the years. A wealth of anger, too." He quits rubbing his knuckles, instead tangling his fingers in his lap. "Your mother's cancer battle was a lot more complicated than we made out. And it wasn't only grief that brought me to my knees when she passed but an overwhelming sense of injustice at how the health system let us down."

My heart skips a pained beat. "Let us down how?"

"They denied assistance for costly experimental treatments she hoped to try. And when she went to seek a second opinion from a more experienced doctor, they warned her that doing so would be considered out-of-network care. Even without moving forward on those options we were left majorly out of pocket due to our level of coverage."

My eyes mist. "If I'd known she went without, I could've..." *Could've what? You were a teenager. What could you have achieved that your grown-ass parents couldn't facilitate?*

"There was nothing that could've been done. I tried everything. I even begged. But the corporate greed cycle didn't care. The healthcare system in this country is corrupt and the knowledge has eaten away at me ever since." He straightens his shoulders. "So when I got sick, I knew something had to change. The definition of insanity is doing something over and over again and expecting different results."

I swallow over the lump in my throat. "Dad…"

"I'm not insane, Liv. I entered into this agreement willingly. I chose this path."

I shake my head. I don't believe him. I can't. "But they're killing people. They're illegally disposing of bodies in *our* retort."

"What they're disposing of is none of my business. Any actions taken would still be carried out whether I was financially compensated for the hire of the equipment or not."

Actions?

"They're not *actions*, Dad. They're crimes. *Murders*. Ones that will put us behind bars."

"We won't get caught." He grabs my hand in both of his. "Not if you keep quiet."

I drag my arm away in shock.

They've brainwashed him. Indoctrinated my father into some sort of sick cult.

"Liv, *please*. I know this situation seems appalling, but I've learned that this world isn't as black and white as I once taught you."

I'm definitely seeing more of a spectrum of color at the moment. However, morally grey isn't something I want in my wheelhouse.

"This isn't you." I push to my feet. "They've messed with your head somehow."

"No. I'm more sure than I've ever been. I trust Remy. He's the one who's helped me." He peers up at me, his eyes beseeching. "Our health insurance didn't care about my diagnosis. They didn't offer additional support or assistance. Even the wait to see an oncologist was detrimentally excessive until Rem made some calls."

My gaze turns to the so-called trustworthy son of a bitch who leans with quiet indifference against the side of my father's favorite recliner, emotionless yet still somehow exuding arrogance.

"How did you meet?" I demand. "Tell me how all this started. I want to know everything."

"I crossed paths with his uncle a long time ago," my father offers. "He came here for a friend's funeral, his reputation proceeding him. What I was unaware of, though, was his charisma. He sought me out at the wake for what began as a casual conversation. But the longer we talked, the more I enjoyed his company."

"Of course you enjoyed his company," I press. "You were his mark."

"Maybe." He gives a fond smile. A *fond* fucking smile. "He praised me on his friend's service and then went on to compliment our facilities. He didn't hide who he was. He admitted that his line of work was probably exactly what I imagined—neither moral nor honorable. Then he made a joke about how we should work together. That the use of my equipment would be a great asset to his organization that would be handsomely rewarded."

"He played to your ego."

"He did." My father inclines his head. "And I laughed him off, soon bidding him farewell without a backward glance. He didn't contact me. Didn't bribe, pressure, or threaten me. I didn't even think much of our conversation again until your mom's hospital bills began to accumulate and make life more difficult. But I never sought him out." Dad returns to his knuckle examination. "Not even after we lost Melissa and I became jaded. I did everything I was supposed to—I focused on reducing the debt from her treatments, and we bounced with the helping hand of a pandemic. I tried to be a good father. I kept my anger to myself. I gave back to my community. I helped others with their grief while I remained overwhelmed by my own. Then cancer came for me, too."

My eyes burn, not only with sadness and rage, but resentment at the world. My damn tear ducts are running the gamut today.

"I promised myself I'd never let the animosity that changed me during your mother's battle get anywhere near you. I refused to let the banks touch a dime of your inheritance. And I sure as hell wasn't going to let them take the business and family home that's been a part of the Pelosi name for generations. So years after that one random conversation, *I* reached out to Lorenzo. It was me, Liv. *I* did this."

I don't know what to say. What to feel.

I want to be angry at him. For making choices that can—and have—affected the very foundation of my life. But all that rattles around inside me is anguished heartache and hollowing shock.

He's suffered for so long without me taking notice. Far longer than the months of my ignorance since the cancer diagnosis.

"Dad—"

"No, listen," he begs. "I know the decision I made was unethical, but that's all it was or ever will be—a decision. I'm not a participant in any illegal activity. I don't know what goes on downstairs while Remy's there. I hire out the cremator. That's all. What happens while it's used isn't my business. The agreement is that I don't get involved. I'm not given incriminating information, and I don't bear witness to any unlawful activity."

I drag my attention to Remy. A silent *lucky Dad* sits on the tip of my tongue.

I yearn to destroy the trust my father has in this man. To decimate the relationship that's violently contrary to the one I have with the murderer.

"How much is the hire fee?" I continue to hold Remy's gaze, pretending not to be intimidated. If he's cheating my father, all bets are off. I'll blab. Rat. Whatever the hell he wants to call it. Because putting our freedom on the line for a few hundred dollars isn't going to cut it.

"Twenty thousand." Remy slides his hands into his pockets, a laid-back checkmate gesture if there ever was one.

I snap my lips shut to stop a gasp.

"Does that meet your expectations?" He raises a demeaning brow.

I open my mouth. Close it again.

Twenty thousand? Is that a one-time fee? Per year? Per month?

"Every use," he clarifies, yet again reading my mind.

"It's a lot of money." The sofa creaks as my dad ambles to his feet. "It's allowed me to get the best treatment, Liv. I'm doing far better than where I would've been without his help."

I bite my tongue, refusing to be thankful, loathing that maybe I should be.

"Will you tell me how you found out?" Dad wanders toward me. "I've felt so guilty for not being here. Remy messaged me vague details, but there's only so much that can be shared on the phone without it becoming incriminating."

Hearing him speak freely about messaging a criminal sits like a lead balloon in my gut.

"You said you fell asleep downstairs," Dad encourages.

I nod and side-eye Remy, trying to get a gauge on how he feels about this line of questioning, but yet again, his expression is unreadable. "I started preparing Amisha and the baby. It got late without me noticing so I thought I'd sleep in the break room. Then a noise outside woke me."

Remy's jaw tightens.

Good. Fear my volatility, you son of a bitch.

All it would take is a few words to blow this agreement to pieces —*he pulled a gun on me. He made me dispose of a body.*

"It's okay, *fragolina*." Dad grasps my upper arms, rubbing gently. "You can tell me."

God, how I wish I could. But evil is destined to win this round.

"Remy was standing in the hall—" I swallow over the horrid taste of the lie. "—just as shocked to see me as I was to see him."

The subtlest of smirks tweaks one side of the asshole's lips. Another faint triumphant gesture.

Fucking prick.

"I bet you were so scared." My father squeezes my arms.

Petrified, Dad. Traumatized.

"I still am." I meet my father's gaze, drowning in the waves of apology that stare back at me. "I don't know how I'll ever not be."

His brows soften. "You'll learn to trust him. I know you will."

Before or after hell freezes over? Because right now, I can't think of anything less likely than me gaining faith in a man who sees death as sport. I've got more chance of receiving presidential recognition for my socializing skills.

"We should go." Remy pushes off the recliner to stand to his full height. "Carlo needs to rest."

"*No.*" My eyes widen. "I want to know how long this agreement will last. How many victims there'll be. And what happens if the authorities get involved?"

"The authorities *won't* get involved." Remy starts for the entry. "Not unless someone opens their mouth."

"She won't talk," my father vows. "Will you, Liv?"

I *would.*

I'd sing like a canary, tweet-tweeting my way through every step of what I was forced to do if only my dad hadn't tangled himself up in this horribly criminal web.

"How long will it last?" I repeat, ignoring my father's misplaced faith.

Remy pauses.

My dad falls quiet.

I glance between them as a sense of foreboding enters the chat. "How long?"

"It's a fluid situation." Dad focuses on Remy's back. "There isn't an exact end date."

"Are you saying this could go on forever?" I can't keep the horror from my tone. "How could you—"

"It won't last forever." Remy swings around to shoot what seems to be an apologetic look at my father before spearing me with animosity. "Six months. Maybe twelve. Once the situation with the Mexican cartel is resolved—"

"By resolved do you mean once they're eradicated?" My pulse quickens. "Do you plan on disposing of an entire cartel in our retort?"

How many people would that be? Twenty? Fifty? Two hundred?

"If necessary," he growls. "Their organization has been significantly dismantled this week. I anticipate some retaliation for the sake of their pride, but after that things will die down."

"Dismantled how?" I ask.

"Liv." My dad speaks softly. "It's best not to know."

Maybe. But ignorance isn't a type of bliss I can achieve now that I know I'm straddling a prison sentence while caught in the middle of a war between the mafia and a cartel.

"This is madness." I shake my head. "Dead bodies. Mexican cartels. Fired employees."

"Fired employees?" My father frowns. "Who are you talking about?"

"Hugo." I fling my arms out at my sides in exasperation. "Ivy found the retort warm when she came into work yesterday morning. And after he was suspected of disposing of his dog months ago, I just assumed…"

Dad cringes.

"That's why this is such a mess." My voice hitches. "Carelessness is going to get us caught, if not by the police, then by our staff."

"It's okay." He inches toward me. "I can coach you over the weekend at what to say and—"

"No." Remy grates, his cocky calm eviscerated. "I'll do it. You need to focus on recovery. I'm taking Ollie home."

My stomach flips, fear and anger performing rhythmic gymnastics inside me.

"Say goodbye to your father." There's a warning in Remy's tone. One that couldn't have only been heard by me.

I turn pained eyes to my dad, waiting for him to step in. To admonish my tormentor.

All he does is give a sad smile, spreading his arms wide to wrap me in a hug. "I promise it's going to be okay."

Dread fills my lungs, making it hard to breathe. "How?" I whisper. "He doesn't trust me to be alone. He's going to shadow me."

Dad squeezes tighter. "But you can understand that, can't you? There's a lot at stake, and having someone close by to answer your panicked questions is necessary until you wrap your head around the situation."

"Then let me stay here," I beg.

He winces. "I wish I could. But I already know you can handle this. Remy's the one you need to convince."

I blink through the static taking over my head.

He isn't surprised Remy is going to tail me. Have they already discussed it?

Oh, God, I'm on my own.

"I'm so sorry." He pulls back to meet my eyes. "It's my fault this is messier than it needs to be." He cups my cheeks, his expression distraught. "But I beg you to give this a chance."

My stomach revolts. Twisting. Clenching.

"He's a good man, *fragolina*." Dad's thumbs stroke my jaw, the gentle back and forth a contrast to my riotous emotions. "You may not see it yet. But I promise you will."

"He's a murderer." My voice is barely audible.

"Because he needs to be. Please just have an open mind."

13

—

REMY

Fractured murmurs of their conversation reach me at the door. A heartfelt apology. A whispered plea.

The part that hits me the hardest? *He's a good man.*

Carlo is the only person who believes that. Not even my mother would agree, and she knew me before the Grim Reaper was born.

But despite the situation we're in, the last six months have made me reciprocate that admiration.

Carlo is a good guy. Full of heart, yet oddly pragmatic.

He only wants what's best for his daughter, and given the respect he's stolen from me since this arrangement was made, I'm inclined to help him achieve his goals.

Ollie glances over her shoulder at me, her face pale.

Clearly she disagrees with her old man's assessment of me. With reason. Too bad she's going to have to get over it, and quick. My patience is wearing thin.

"Are you done?" I ask, harsher than necessary.

Anger flares in those pretty eyes.

"Yes." Carlo nods with an appeasing smile. "Take care of my girl for me."

"I'll do my best." I jerk my chin toward the door, wordlessly telling Ollie to get her ass moving.

Carlo doesn't approve of me tailing her. He made that blatantly known when we texted earlier. But his daughter's desire to run to the cops can't be ignored. And someone exhausted and suffering from cancer isn't the right person to sprint after her if she finally makes that move.

So I'm stuck in the ring for now.

Ollie starts for the door.

"Liv, wait." Her dad stops her a few feet from me. "I'd like to keep my health issues between us. Please don't tell Ivy or Allison."

The request furrows her brow, her nose wrinkling.

I clench my jaw, beating back unwanted sympathy.

Then she gives an abrupt nod and continues outside, leaving me to incline my head in farewell to Carlo and follow her back down to the lower level.

I don't say a word as she takes her sweet time tidying up her shit. She needs to adjust to her father's deception. To figure out how she's going to handle my presence in her home. So I bite my tongue even though I'm starving and equally fucking fatigued.

More than an hour later we walk out of there, the sun already starting its descent, the cold of late winter clouding the air whenever I breathe.

I drive her home in silence.

It isn't until I turn into her street that she breaks the quiet with a hearty "I'll never trust you."

It's not the usual way to thank someone for not killing them, but I'll take it as a win that she's initiated conversation.

"As devastating as that is, I'm going to work hard to get over it." I park across the road from her quaint cape cod home, not wanting to risk her safety if my Bentley is recognized in her drive. "Your father trusts me. That should be good enough for you for now."

"My father is obviously suffering mentally as well as physically." She yanks off her seatbelt. "You're taking advantage of a sick man."

She shoves her door open with a huff and climbs out to stalk for her drive.

I sigh.

Where the fuck is she finding the energy for this animosity?

I cut the ignition, and yet again, follow after her, catching up as she strides along her garden path to the three stairs leading to her small porch.

I'm an asshole, so when she stops to unlock her door I stand closer than necessary, breathing in that intoxicating strawberry scent.

As soon as the door is swung wide, she turns on me.

"Wait here." She glowers, then escapes inside.

My dumb ass complies.

How this woman gained power over me is astounding. But I really need to get a handle on that shit. And still, I stand out in the cold for seconds that tick into minutes.

Finally she returns, her arms filled with electrical devices—two tablets, an Echo speaker, and a laptop.

"There." She shoves them against my chest. "That's every form of contact I have with the outside world." She digs into her pants pocket as I juggle the unwanted gifts, then adds her cell to the top of the precarious pile. "You can check if you like, but you're not staying inside. If you're worried I'll do something stupid, the risk will only increase if I don't have space to come to terms with what's happened. I've had enough people-ing for one day. I need time to think."

She's adamant. Her posture carved from the toughest stone. Yet her hands quaver at her sides. Her eyes plead instead of demand.

She's beautifully daring in spite of her fear.

What I wouldn't give to drop the weight in my arms and yank her against me. To eviscerate her hostility by slamming my mouth on hers.

I clear the tightness from my throat. "That's some set of balls you've—"

"My father trusts me. That should be good enough for you for now." She throws my words back at me, then slams the door in my face.

Perfect.

Just fucking perfect.

I'm the murderous motherfucker in this equation, and still, despite the odds, she's the one who's calling the shots.

A humorless laugh escapes me, the pile of devices growing heavy in my hands.

This goddamn fucking woman.

I swear to hell she does unnatural things to me. And it's not just the unruly reaction from my dick.

"I'm not going anywhere, Ollie," I yell through the door. "I'll grant you some space. For now. But my lenience won't last."

There's no reply. Not even another slammed door or hissed rebuttal. The house falls deathly quiet.

It's too fucking cold for this shit.

I swing around to face the yard with a growl.

This never should've fucking happened. Who the hell stays at work overnight? Especially when their place of business houses dead goddamn bodies?

My cell vibrates in my pocket, inspiring another growl.

I drag my feet from Ollie's porch like the unintentionally whipped psycho I am and dump her shit in my trunk before sinking into the driver's seat.

It's no surprise the message is from my brother.

Where are you?

I'm taking the weekend off. Stop riding my ass.

The three little dots of his impending reply pop up, then disappear.

I should call him. Should tell him I'm not a little bitch who needs to check in, but I'm starting to itch for a fight, and having it out with the unhinged dictator won't help this situation when lack of sleep has my wits at an all-time low.

Instead, I stare at Ollie's house, cursing that night at the godforsaken dive bar.

Three of us had watched her walk inside—me, Russo, and Valenti— all of us spaced throughout the building to keep watch on my brother's meeting in the back booth.

I'd recognized her instantly thanks to the background check Salvo had arranged on the Pelosi family. Had known a complication was about to potentially fuck with the diabolical partnership my brother had been exceptionally proud of nurturing to fruition.

I'd wondered if Carlo had been stupid enough to tell his daughter about the meeting. If she'd arrived in a vain attempt to stop the illegal negotiation.

The only thing I'd known for sure was that the photos in the background file hadn't done her justice.

She was beautiful, her dark hair braided in some sort of whimsical artistry that only increased the appeal of her wide, innocent eyes and plush, glossy lips.

Both my men had stood to take action. All it took was a glared warning to seat them back in place.

I wanted to be the one to approach her. To shut down whatever plan she had to derail our success. So I placed myself in her path, waited for her to slam into me, then lost all commonsense when those hazel eyes met mine.

All I'd needed to do was figure out her motive and distract her.

I'd done both.

But touching her? That had been a mistake. I can't forget the softness of her skin. The goddamn moisture between her thighs.

Ollie Pelosi is a clueless temptation—one that's pure as snow, with her fucking hymen still intact.

I glare at her house, waiting for her to turn on a light and give me insight into her activities.

She needs to eat. To shower. To keep occupied.

Yet there's no movement. No glow from behind the curtains.

"Fuck this." I grab my coat from the backseat and climb from the car, convincing myself I'm performing a perimeter check when what I'm really doing is trying to get eyes on her again.

I scan the front windows as I stalk the drive, my head hung low in case she's got nosy neighbors. I listen for movement as I pass the left side of the house and continue into the backyard.

The garden is bathed in twilight, the few trees and shrubs casting dark shadows over the lawn.

I slow my stride along the back of the house and yank on my coat, the chill seeping into my bones. Still, I hear nothing. See nothing. No cries or hiccupped sobs. No flicker of illumination or twitch of drapes.

I turn down the far side of the building, stalking between the vinyl siding and the chin-high pale fence to her neighbor's yard. When I reach the glass sliding door to her laundry, I pause.

Again, there's no movement from inside.

Salvo will fucking kill me if he finds out I've been playing Russian roulette with our lives all because of a pretty face.

I return to the Bentley, pull out my cell, and distract myself from my building temper by making phone calls.

I lay down the law with Russo and Valenti.

I chat with my sister and niece.

I even dial Salvatore's number and pretend my drunken ass is out trolling to get laid instead of being the sober fuck who's freezing his balls off while staking out a woman who makes me dispense more wood than a lumber mill.

Still, no movement.

Did she go to bed? Is she curled up on the sofa crying? Is she the type to self-harm?

Fuck.

I scrub a hand over the back of my neck and stare at those front windows for another ten minutes, my pulse thrumming in my ears.

I clench my way through ten more, my stomach growling in both hunger and frustration.

This damn fucking woman.

If she hurts herself I'll…

I shove from the car yet a-fucking-gain.

I follow the path I made earlier—through the carport and into the backyard. I listen at every window, attempting to spy through curtains. To listen at doorjambs.

When I reach the laundry, I test the handle to the glass sliding door only to find it locked.

"I should've killed you and saved myself the trouble," I snarl under my breath.

I turn, determined to pound on the front door until she answers when a bright light blinds me from over the pale fence.

Shit. I squint, shielding my eyes with one arm as I reach behind my back for my gun with the other.

"Don't move," an elderly female voice calls.

You've gotta be fucking kidding me.

"I have a weapon," the crone croaks. "And I've already called the police."

Fuck my fucking life.

"I'm not an intruder." I continue gliding my right hand beneath my coat, then my suit jacket, splaying my other palm in placation. "I'm doing a welfare check on Ollie."

"Ollie?" She scoffs. "That girl hasn't been called Ollie in the three years I've known her. Now move away from her door before an arthritic spasm has me mistakenly pulling the trigger."

Of all the fucking ways to die, I will not be taken out by a senior citizen.

"Lady, I'm no threat." I chance a glance around my raised hand, blinding myself with the flashlight the old crow has lasered on my eyeballs. "*Olivia* had a hard day. I wanted to check on her."

"By snooping around her house? You don't think I've been watching? That I haven't seen you spying on her from your car for over an hour?"

A light flicks on from Ollie's laundry, a familiar silhouette approaching the sheer curtains covering the glass door. She pulls the material aside, a fucking goddess in light pink winter pajamas with her hair loose and wavy around her cheeks. She squints against the glow and lowers her gaze, her attention snagging on the grip I have on my gun.

Horror bleeds into her features.

"*Lesley,*" she yells through the door, quickly unlocking it and pulling it wide. "It's okay. I know him."

The old bat averts the flashlight's beam to my chest. "Did you also know he's been prowling around your yard like a peeping tom?"

"I wasn't prowling," I snarl.

"It's okay," Ollie repeats, stepping close to discreetly glide her hand beneath my coat, her warm touch attempting to ply my grip from the gun. "I know him. We, ahh…" She winces. "We're friends."

"Friends?" the fossil asks, dubious as fuck.

"Yes." Ollie's fingers dig under my palm. "This is, ahh… the guy I told you about. The one from the bar."

I raise a brow, my homicidal mood interrupted.

She told her neighbor about me?

All I get in return is a pointed glance, the stare pleading.

"The handsome one?" Lesley trains the light back on my face. "Who curled your toes but never gave you his number?"

Ollie winces.

She *did* tell the old witch about me.

The knowledge has an unhealthy amount of blood rushing to my dick.

I grin through my squint, releasing my gun to grasp her wrist and drag her into me. I use the proximity as a silent threat but also to keep her warm. Those pajamas can't be giving her much protection from the cold, and her thin socks are an invitation for frostbite.

"I never said he curled my toes." Ollie places her palms against my chest, attempting to maintain distance. "Could you please turn off the flashlight before we're permanently blinded?"

The crone harrumphs, the illumination vanishing with a soft click. "So why didn't you give her your number?"

"*Lesley*," Ollie chastises.

"For good reason." I stare down at her, my fingers itching to guide the unruly locks of her hair behind her ears. I'm not sure if she's showered, but she's removed the remnants of her makeup, her skin now flawlessly dewy. "I didn't give her my number because my life is problematic."

I hold her gaze, hating how her eyes harden.

"Yet now you're here?" Lesley questions.

"Yes." I keep the bitterness from my tone. "Now I'm here."

"…snooping around her house," she adds.

For fuck's sake. This living history lesson isn't going to let up.

"I told you I wasn't snooping." I turn my attention over the fence, the squinted eyes of the old relic meeting mine.

She can't be a day under three hundred and seventy-five, her skin like crinkled wrapping paper, her grey hair pulled back into a thin pony.

"Well, tell your story to the police, because they're on their way."

"*No*." Ollie pushes harder against my chest. "You need to call them back. Tell them they don't need to come. It's a waste of resourc—"

"It's too late." The old woman shrugs. "Look, they're already here."

The faint glow of red and blue blinks across her face from the front yard, the colors growing more adamant with the sound of an approaching car.

Lesley treks a few steps toward the imminent threat, the crunch of grass carrying from the other side of the fence.

Fury prickles my veins.

I drag Ollie closer into me, her body stiffening as I lean in to nuzzle her cheek.

"Be on your best behavior," I whisper. "Naughty girls get punished."

Her spine straightens. "And what if everyone realizes I'd have better taste than to spend time with someone like you?" she murmurs under her breath.

There she goes with that animosity again. It's such an inopportune time to be turned on.

"Then people will die, my pretty little pyro, and you'll be responsible."

"Over here," Lesley calls out. "Come this way."

I grasp Ollie's hips and turn her toward the path leading to the front of the house, my chest settled against her back. Then I grab my gun and point it against her ass.

Her breathing hitches.

"Just an FYI, your body is fucking flawless." I slide my free hand around her waist to splay across her belly. "But that's not my cock digging into your ass."

She doesn't respond. Doesn't even move as Lesley continues to call for the cops.

"Such a good girl." I nuzzle her hair, dragging her scent deep into my lungs. "Stay quiet and this will all go away."

Another flashlight approaches, the bright illumination slicing around the building and slashing my eyeballs.

Ollie flinches.

I tighten my hold on her.

"We had a report of a suspected intruder," a man states in a heavy Boston accent.

I keep my gaze averted, my jaw tight. "It was a false alarm."

"Apparently," Lesley mumbles.

The flashlight is dimmed and lowered, the silhouette of two officers coming into view near the front of Ollie's house.

"It's my fault." I paste on a charming smile. "I wanted to check on Olivia but also didn't want to disturb—"

"He was snooping around her yard," Lesley talks over me. "Peering in her windows and watching the house from his car parked across the street."

"The Bentley is your vehicle, sir?" a young, male voice asks.

"It is. Is that a problem?" If only they'd lower the spotlight farther I'd be able to see their faces.

Ollie makes to step away, but I increase the pressure of my hold, a subtle growl vibrating from my throat.

She sucks in a breath. "Please, officers, I… I can't take much more of this."

What the fuck is she doing?

I press the gun harder into her back, my pulse thunderous.

"I've had the worst day." Her voice fills with emotion.

"Did he hurt you?" the crone asks. "Tell us what he did."

I dig the gun harder. Press my hand tighter. "*Careful,*" I whisper into her hair.

She slides her palm over my knuckles and digs her nails into my skin. "He—"

The flashlight reclaims my vision, cutting Ollie off with a flinch.

"Is that you, Mr. Costa?" the younger voice asks. "It took me a minute to recognize you."

"And you are?" I blink through squinted eyes.

"Sorry, sir. I'm Officer Hawkins. We've met before."

"You hear that, Ollie?" I murmur against her ear. "He's on the payroll."

"Let her finish," Lesley demands. "Can't you see she's under duress? I've known her for three years, and not once have I seen her act like this. I'm telling you, that man is responsible."

"That's not the case." I keep my tone level. "Olivia has already explained that we're friends."

Ollie remains quiet, her breaths increasing. She wants to sing. Does she have the balls?

"Miss?" the Boston accent asks. "Can you tell us what you were going to say?"

She shakes her head.

"He's crowding her," Lesley demands. "Tell him to step away."

"She's cold," I snarl.

Fuck. If I'm forced to move, Ollie will run, and this shit show will turn into a slaughter scene.

"*Fix this,*" I murmur under my breath. "*Now.*"

She clings to her silence, letting me drown in a disaster of my own making.

"*I swear to God, Ollie—*

"Lesley, please just stop," she finally pleads. "This isn't about Remy. It's my dad. He had a fall last night and was taken to hospital."

Something warm and expansive takes over my chest. Relief? Victory?

"*Good girl*," I breathe.

She shudders, and my dick twitches as if her response was made in pleasure and not disgust.

"It's been a heartbreaking twenty-four hours." She shifts her hips away from mine. "I didn't realize until I arrived at Johns Hopkins that he's been battling cancer. He's even had chemo without telling me. It's a whole big mess that I'm struggling to get my head around."

"Oh, Liv." Lesley awkwardly peers over the fence. "I'm so sorry, dear."

Ollie's hand slides from mine, her arms wrapping around her middle. "Remy was checking on me because I didn't take the news well. I swear, there's nothing inappropriate happening. You can even call the hospital to confirm. My father—Carlo Pelosi—spent the night in the oncology ward."

"I'm sorry to hear that, miss." Boston turns off his flashlight, his short, pudgy silhouette exposed in the moonlight beside his taller, leaner partner a foot to his left. "But I appreciate the clarification. I'm happy to write this off as a misunderstanding and let you get out of the cold if you're certain you're okay."

"I'm sure I will be." Her tone is flat. Unconvincing.

"Don't worry, officers." I glide my weapon into the front of my waistband and discreetly reposition my suit jacket. "I'll make sure she's all right."

She straightens her shoulders, the light from the laundry casting her rebellious shadow across the fence in simplistic beauty.

She despises me. Loathes me.

Why is that such a fucking turn-on?

"Come on, Ollie." I direct her toward the glass door. "It's time for me to take care of you."

She pivots, her panicked eyes meet mine, and it's clear this mesmerizing pain-in-my-ass understands the double entendre.

14

REMY

"YOU WERE GOING TO RAT ON ME." I storm down the darkened hall after her, the sweet scent of strawberries claiming my lungs. "What don't you understand about this situation?"

She ignores me, entering a pitch-black doorway and slapping her hand against a light switch.

Bright light illuminates an open living area where a mass of plants adorn every horizontal space, their vines and leaves creating a forest of green across a television stand and free-floating shelves along the walls. There's painted art in simplistic frames. Tidy furniture. A modest TV.

I grab her wrist to stop her from walking farther into the room. "I said—what part of this situation don't you understand?"

She turns on me, yanking her arm from my grip before shoving at my chest with a burst of aggression I don't see coming. I stumble back a step, my blood rushing south.

"The things I *do* understand is a much shorter list," she snaps. "But contrary to popular belief, I wasn't about to tell anyone anything."

God, how her anger does things to me. Scorching, reprehensible things.

"Bullshit." I snarl. "If it hadn't been for that officer making it clear he knew me, you would've eagerly spilled your guts."

She squares her shoulders and steps up to me.

Steps. Up. To. *Me.*

"It's called acting." She glares. "You know, like the thing you did the night we met?"

I clench my teeth, fucking pissed that she'd dare to turn this around on me.

"I can't believe how you played me in that dive bar," she scoffs. "Why go to all that effort to charm me?"

"What effort? You were all over me like a rash."

Her jaw unhinges, that delectable mouth gaping.

"Is that what you've been fixated on while I was locked outside?" I huff a laugh. "Now you're pissed over me buying you a few drinks?"

"It was more than just drinks." Her hazel eyes turn pleading. "You didn't have to use me like that."

Use. What a remarkably shitty word to describe me succumbing to infatuation.

I'd been the fucking victim.

The one trapped under her spell.

"I needed to keep you occupied." I shrug. "Salvatore and your father were finalizing negotiations, and they didn't need interference."

"You could've done it another way. You didn't have to seduce me. *Humiliate* me."

"I think you're rewriting history, Ollie. As I recall, I warned you that I wasn't someone to get involved with. Yet you fucking *begged* me to ruin you."

She draws back as if I've slapped her, her cheeks darkening.

It's not that I want to fight. Reducing volatility would be a far smarter strategy. But she almost sung to the fucking cops.

"Do you have any other questions before we return to the situation at hand?" I raise a taunting brow.

"There is no situation." She retreats a step. "I followed orders. I did as instructed. Now leave me alone."

"You dangled a fucking carrot in front of that nosy neighbor of yours. You were about to tell them everything."

She crosses her arms over her chest, plumping those beautiful breasts beneath her pajamas. "No, I wasn't."

Irritation burns my veins, the toxicity thrumming through my blood. *God,* she drives me wild.

"Sorry, I forgot—you were acting." I raise my palms in mock apology. "Please enlighten me on what that acting role was trying to achieve other than placing our freedom in jeopardy."

She stares at me for long moments, eyes pained, brows furrowed. "I don't understand you."

"What can't you get through that pretty little head, pyro?"

"Everything. How can you be the same guy as the one at the bar? You had me completely fooled."

That guy had been real enough.

I may have deceived her, but I hadn't lied. My moral compass had been pointing toward fucking saint territory for the most part. "I guess this is a great life lesson on why you shouldn't throw yourself at strangers."

She scowls, all that mouthwatering vulnerability disappearing in an instant. Her lips part, a treasure trove of delicious retorts waiting to be shared, but she snaps her mouth shut and starts for the hall behind me.

Smart.

Restrained.

So fucking beautiful.

"We're not done here," I growl.

"Yes, we are." She makes to walk around me.

"Know your place, Ollie." I block her path. "Because right now you're grating on my last nerve, and I've been nothing but hospitable up to this point."

"Hospitable? Are you kidding me?" She nudges past me, continuing into the hall.

I see red. So much mesmerizing, tempting red.

"Like you wouldn't fucking believe." I prowl after her, returning the nudge to regain my place in front of her, the hall shadowed around us, the air thick with tension. "I let you leave a hazardous crime scene so you could visit your dad in hospital. I relented to your pleas to return to work, then gave you privacy to fulfill your duties. And when we came here, and you squared those feeble little shoulders and raised your dainty chin in a fucking laughable show of dominance, I gave you your goddamn fucking space."

"You think allowing me to see my sick father was generous?" Her tone hitches. "In the whole scheme of things—"

"In the whole scheme of things you should've been dead the second you witnessed my men carrying a lifeless fucking body." I take a threatening step toward her and grin when she retreats in equal measure. "I was being goddamn charitable in letting you live." I take another step, this time angled, backing her against the wall. "And you best believe that's exactly what I was doing the night we met."

She plasters herself against the drywall, chin high, shoulders tense.

"I did you a favor and walked away." I lean in, getting in her face. "Do you hear me? I did your cock-hungry ass a *fucking favor.*"

Her jaw ticks. "And now you expect a thank you?"

"I walked away, Ollie. Even though I wanted you. To feel more than just the material of those slick fucking panties. To kiss you. Consume you."

Surprise flares in her eyes. Or maybe it's increased disgust.

"The ways in which I wanted to ruin you grew like a rampant

fucking virus while we sat in that booth." The admission spews from me. "I'd ached to fuck you. To drag you onto my lap and slide my cock so deep inside your virginal pussy that your dad would've heard you scream from the pleasured pain of it."

Her breathing labors, her chest rising and falling in quick succession.

She's scared.

Good.

"And we both know I could've had you," I snarl.

Her delicate throat works over a heavy swallow. "Too bad you don't mess with virgins."

Anger slams into my temples. Why doesn't she know when to shut the fuck up? "Careful or I might just change my mind."

She gasps.

Great. Just fucking great.

As if our temperamental relationship wasn't bad enough, I had to threaten sexual assault.

"Are you done?" she rasps.

No.

I want to grab her. Shake her. Fucking kiss the goddamn sass out of her until she learns to keep that pretty mouth shut.

God-fucking-damnit.

I step back and shove a hand through my hair. "Get out of my sight."

She doesn't need to be told twice. She slides along the wall until she's out of reach then storms down the hall and enters what I assume is her bedroom.

"And keep your fucking door open," I seethe.

She complies even though her animosity consumes the house.

It takes a good thirty seconds to get my feet moving and return to the living room before I do something else I'll regret... like fucking apologize.

I force myself to crash on the relatively comfortable, oversized sofa, the hours passing with slowly waning bitterness. I spend the night trying to figure out how the hell to fix this mess while also keeping Ollie's freedom and heartbeat intact.

Problem is, every achievable outcome hinges on my trust and her respect—neither of which seem attainable.

Morning arrives with little rest for the wicked. It's barely light out when I message Flynn to bring me a change of clothes, along with a folder of information I requested during the midnight hours from a source within the Baltimore PD, then help myself to a mug of instant coffee while I wait for the kid to arrive.

I'm on Ollie's porch, making more calls, when the testosterone-filled teen pulls up in the Chevy Impala I bought him a few months ago.

"Howdy, boss." He walks along the garden path toward me, a garment bag draped over one arm with a take-out food bag balanced on top, while his other hand is clamped around a manila folder.

"Hey." I jerk my chin at his haul. "Did you get everything?"

"You know I did." He hands over the folder. "What happened to you? You look like shit."

"Watch it." I snatch the offering with a fake glower and flick through the pages to make sure the contents are what I asked for.

He snickers. "Are you angry because of the party I threw last night?"

I raise my gaze to his and wait for him to elaborate. The kid has been living with me since I found him sleeping in a dirty corner of the underground parking lot of my apartment building. Four easy months where I can't recall him attending a party let alone showing interest in throwing one. I'm not sure he even has friends.

"You should've been there," he taunts. "It was huge. The music was pumping. People were dancing. I even figured out how to unlock your liquor cabinet. You might just want to be patient while I clean up. It's going to take days, if not weeks."

I smirk. "Nice try, kid, but I've got eyes on that penthouse at all times."

Disappointment takes over his features. "Really? Well, shit. I thought for sure a party would crack your annoying composure." He sighs. "Why are you always so chill? My dad could never keep his temper. Even over the smallest things."

"I'm not your dad." I rest the folder on top of the metal porch railing and hold out a hand, indicating for the garment bag. *Chill* is far from what I've been these past twenty-four hours, but the last thing I want is him knowing what riles me. Or, more accurately, who. "Are you sure you got everything?"

He hands the clothes over. "Of course. Suit. Shirt. Socks. It didn't skip my attention that you didn't ask for underwear, which is gross, but you do you, man."

I roll my eyes and unzip the garment bag.

"You got a woman in there?" He tips his head toward Ollie's house, drags a vape from his pocket, and takes a puff.

"That's none of your business. And didn't I tell you to quit that smoking shit?"

"Probably." He takes another inhale then releases the mint-scented toxic air. "I can't remember."

"I'm not kidding, Flynn. It'll fuck up your lungs."

He shrugs. "Maybe. But I'm not gonna lie, I feel kinda invincible since you started looking out for me."

Dread worms its way into my gut. "My protection makes you far from invincible." If anything my presence in his life is a threat, but it's better than him dumpster diving for food.

"Don't worry, boss. I can look after myself."

I snatch the folder from the railing and the food bag from his arm. "Quit the vapes or we'll be revisiting the boarding school discussion."

His face falls, and he shoves the device back into his pocket.

I already tried to get him into a nearby school, but that shit didn't stick. Apparently the kid is dyslexic and has a lifetime of judgement hanging off his shoulders. Not even the offer of expensive tutors was enough to get him to stick it out for longer than a day.

So I gave him a job instead. A glorified go-fer role.

He's been on cloud-nine ever since. At least when he's not trying to test my limits to see if I'll kick him to the curb.

"You should get going." I start for the house. "Keep your phone on in case I need anything else."

"Sure thing. Will you be home tonight?"

I pause at the door, the thought of leaving Ollie unsupervised bringing unease. "I doubt it."

I walk back into the house and find the woman in question standing in the kitchen still dressed in those cute pajamas, her hair pulled back in a messy pony as she eyes me over the steaming mug cradled in her hands.

"Morning." I kick the door shut behind me.

"Morning," she mutters into her drink.

Two syllables and eye contact. I guess it's better than a glare and a verbal spray.

"I ordered breakfast." I dump my haul on her dining table beside the cute pea-like plant centerpiece, determined to be civil, and fold the garment bag over the back of a chair. "You must be starving."

"No, thanks."

I ignore the caustic tone and take the response and feigned gratitude as a win.

"Did you sleep well?" I open the food bag and delve inside.

She sighs, long and weary. "It's too early to pretend to play happy families. Can we at least wait until the caffeine kicks in?"

"Of course. I'm nothing if not excessively patient."

She scoffs into her mug and takes a sip, her gaze not leaving mine.

I don't let the animosity get to me. I can't.

We have to figure this shit out or she's dead. Simple as that.

"I'll be the first to admit yesterday was a cluster fuck." I turn my attention to the food bag and shove a hand inside. "I'm hoping we can find a way to see eye to eye."

I was too hard on her.

Too threatening.

She's not merely virginal in the sexual sense but also when it comes to the ways of the world. Her father warned me she's isolated. That she lives in a vacuum. Few friends. Minimal social interaction.

Me storming into her life would've felt like the start of Armageddon.

"I guess that sounds like a good idea," she grumbles.

My gaze snaps to hers.

Is she fucking with me?

Her expression remains impassive. Her stance, emotionless.

"I know I have to comply," she adds. "I've always known. And in my defense, I asked numerous times for space so I could make all this sit right in my head. The sleepless night gave me that. I'll co-operate."

The hair on the back of my neck prickles.

She's definitely fucking with me. Right?

"That's quite a backflip." I pull two breakfast burritos from the bag. "Especially when you came so close to snitching."

She heaves a heavy breath. "I'd like to consider myself a relatively smart woman, Remy. So I can say with complete honesty that snitching was never an option. I wouldn't risk my father's life like that, let alone mine. Obviously I'm not going to win any awards for thinking on my feet in life-threatening situations, but what I was attempting last night was to stall. Lesley knows me too well to have listened to me blurt my private life without hesitation. I didn't want to make her more suspicious."

I remain quiet in the hopes she'll continue trying to persuade me because I'm not convinced. I slide a breakfast burrito across the table in her direction before unwrapping the top of mine.

"She's an extremely perceptive woman. One who's well aware I like to suffer in silence," she says. "If I spewed my father's health secrets without at least a little reluctance, she wouldn't have stopped her interrogation until we'd both passed a polygraph."

Her eyes hold mine. There's none of the venom from yesterday. None of the seething hatred. She's adamant. Possibly telling the truth.

"What I'd been about to say, before you jammed your gun harder against my back, was that I'd had a horrible day but that *you had taken care of me.* That your kindness was the only reason I wasn't a blubbering mess. And that I assumed you were snooping around my yard because I'd pushed you away when I became irrationally emotional." She places her mug on the counter behind her and wraps her arms around her middle. "I was trying to create a believable story. The truth had never been an option. That's why I'd dug my nails into your hand. To get you to hold fire on any knee-jerk reaction."

"I thought you were being vindictive."

"No." Her gaze turns pleading. "I was being strategic."

I'm tempted to believe her. The worst part is that I know exactly why I'm preparing to turn coat so easily.

It's her beauty.

Her innocence.

I'd gobble up her words whether truth, lie, or fiction. Hell, I could listen to her tell me the world was flat and walk away convinced.

"I know what's at stake." Her throat works over a delicate swallow. "And although I don't appreciate the position I'm in, I'd much less prefer to be the next person you throw in my retort."

I take a bite of burrito, praying that outcome doesn't eventuate. "Thanks for the clarification."

"Do you believe me?" She stares at me, her gaze hopeful.

Jesus Christ.

Her viciousness was a drug. Her anger an injection of lust.

But expectant Ollie? Imploring Ollie?

That shit shoves its greedy little hand straight through my chest to grasp my heart in a death grip.

"I'll give you the benefit of the doubt." I take another bite. "For now."

"I suppose that's all I can ask for." She pads toward me, the plush material of her pajamas hugging her curves. "Who was outside?"

"A friend."

"Should I be worried that another dangerous man now knows where I live?"

"No." I shove more food in my mouth. "He's just a kid. He's no threat. He brought me a fresh suit and our breakfast." I tilt my burrito in her direction. "It's good, by the way. You should eat."

She glances at the take-out bag, then the wrapped burrito in front of her.

"You don't like burritos?" I ask.

"I do. It's just…"

"What?" I say around a mouthful. "You think I've done something to the food?"

"No." She scrunches her nose. "I'm still struggling with my appetite. This situation is a gold-star weight-loss program."

I don't want her to lose weight. She's perfect the way she is. Slim and taut in places. Lush and rounded in others.

"But I did spend most of the night trying to justify everything that's happened," she continues. "I didn't get to a point where I can condone what you do, but I'm slowly coming to the understanding that your agreement with my father wouldn't change how you conduct your business. Those people would still die, right?"

"Right." Although the effortless disposal does make the complication of murder a hell of a lot easier.

She continues focusing on the food, her brow furrowing, the etch of dismay digging across her forehead.

"So what part has killed your appetite?" I want to see her eat. To nurture her instead of torture her, no matter how fucking pathetic that makes me.

That cute little scrunch in her nose increases. "I can't stop seeing his body. Can't quit hearing the groan." Her gaze rises to mine. "I feel responsible for that man's death."

Her suffering does shitty things to me. Uncomfortable, fucked up things. It has since the moment I walked into the funeral home's delivery room early yesterday morning.

What a troublesome fucking time to grow a conscience.

I take the last mouthful of burrito and ball up the trash before sliding the manila cardboard toward her. "Open it."

She frowns and takes the chair in front of her, hesitating as her fingers brush the offering. "Do I need to prepare myself for what's inside?"

"Probably."

She sits taller, her eyes curious as she drags the file closer, then finally flips it open.

I expect a gasp. A cry, maybe.

I get neither.

She's a fucking mortician, dickhead.

She stares at the first picture, her lips slightly parted, her shock hidden.

"Is this another warning?" she asks softly, slowly turning over the top photo of a battered and deceased female to display a similar one beneath. "A far more graphic display of what's to come if I don't follow your rules?"

"No. This isn't my handiwork."

Her shoulders relax. A little too much for my liking.

The fact she thinks I'm capable of achieving a crime resulting in those pictures isn't a welcomed news flash.

She turns another page and another. Photo upon photo of raped, bruised, and beaten women. "Tell me what I'm looking at."

"This is the legacy left behind by the man you harbor guilt toward." I snatch the food bag off the table, forcing myself not to become fixated on whatever relief the knowledge might bring, and scrounge inside for another burrito. "This was his favorite pastime."

She doesn't react, only continues to turn to the next photo, then the next.

"He was a murderer like me." I itch to touch her. Soothe her. Instead I keep scrounging around in the bag, my fingers brushing over more burritos I no longer have the stomach to eat. "But one thing we didn't have in common was our treatment of the opposite sex. I never hurt women, Ollie. Except, evidently, the one seated before me."

Her attention raises to mine for brief moments of confusion. Those big, beautiful eyes peer back at me in bewilderment.

"I may scare you," I mutter. "I may sicken and disgust. But you're the only female I've inflicted that upon. I'm a monster to men, pyro. To those who deserve my punishment."

She continues staring for silent moments, anticipation for her reply grasping my balls in a vise grip until she returns her attention to the photos.

I quit the pretense of searching for food and dump the bag, circling the table to stop at her side. "This guy doesn't deserve your guilt." I tap the image of the deceased woman covered in ligature marks, the damage most prominent between her thighs. "He'd done this to more women than you could imagine."

"Is that why you targeted him?"

I wish I could give her the answer she wants. The sweet, virtuous response that would make me seem like a better man.

"No. But it's reason enough for you not to spare him a second thought. You didn't kill him, Ollie. I did. That groan was nothing more than an inopportune coincidence."

Her gaze meets mine. "How did you do it?"

I've risked enough from verbalizing guilt, yet I'm still drawn to give her more. Give her everything. "Lethal overdose—a far quicker death than he deserved."

Thoughts race behind those dreamy eyes, her quiet musing getting to me. I want to know what she's thinking. What she's feeling.

She returns her attention to the photos, her expression pained as she stares at a full-face image of a blonde girl in her early twenties, her pale eyes lifeless, lips parted, skin bruised.

"I know her." She traces a finger over the victim's jaw, her chin. "I think her name was Jasmin Taylor. She was one of my decedents a few years back. What he did to her was…"

"Nothing more than a game to him."

"I can see that." She swallows.

"Do you still feel guilty?"

"Definitely not as much as I did a few minutes ago." She closes the folder and squares her shoulders. "Are all the men you kill like him?"

I'm tempted to lie. To tell her each and every one is a woman-torturing rapist, and I'm performing some sort of worldly Robin Hood-type duty she could excuse.

But that's not me. Not the world I live in.

I can't allow myself to indulge in the fantasy of her approval. To imagine a recreated moment where she grants my hands another trip along her perfect thighs to those heavenly panties.

She's a fucking virgin, for God's sake.

Civility is where this relationship needs to be. And *only* civility.

"No, pyro." I force myself to grab the garment bag from the chair and head toward her bathroom. "I may not kill for sport, but I sure as hell do it for profit and convenience. Never forget that."

15

OLIVIA

My alarm sounds at six-thirty Monday morning but I'm already awake, staring at the ceiling, worrying about my father and promising myself today will be better than the nightmare weekend.

Sunday consisted of absolutely nothing but an epic battle to keep my distance from Remy.

We spoke very little after breakfast when he'd walked away. I'd remained at the dining table, confused over what had happened.

The entire color wheel of emotions I've felt for this man isn't healthy. The heart-crushing rage. The chaotic fear.

The worst is the lust. That unconscious, loathsome feeling had flooded me Saturday night while I'd been smothered against the hall drywall, listening to him paint a verbal masterpiece of what he'd wanted to do to me at the dive bar.

I should've been disgusted. Revulsed.

Yet my pulse had raced with rapture.

Or maybe it was adrenaline.

I'd just escaped another life-threatening situation and my blood was all hot and tingly. Since then, I've promised myself I'll never rile him again.

I don't want him in my face. His cologne drugging me. Those eyes captivating me.

I've accepted my fate for the most part. At least where my father's illegal alignment is concerned.

I'll play nice. I have no choice.

I fling back the covers and haul a fresh set of clothes to the bathroom so I can shower and change into a light grey pantsuit.

When I open the door to step back into the hall, my hair damp around my cheeks and face devoid of makeup, Remy is standing in wait.

I swallow a shocked inhale at his overbearing presence.

He's dressed in yet another dark ensemble. Charcoal suit. Matching shirt.

I want to ask if all the food and clothes deliveries that have made their way to my front door have been fulfilled by the same *"kid"* who was here Sunday morning and not by a long list of criminal psychopaths. But I keep my anxiety at bay for the sake of peace.

"Hi." I avert my gaze and maneuver around him, a renewed scent of woodsy cologne warming my insides as I pass.

I already presumed he'd used the shower. Water droplets had clung to the tile walls when I'd entered. But I should've better prepared myself for the sight of him fresh and cleanshaven, his hair perfectly tousled.

"Morning." He follows me to my room and stops at the door while I continue inside. "How long until you need to be driven to work?"

A resurgence of dread tightens my throat. "I don't need to be driven. I assumed we'd go our separate ways today."

He can't follow me to the funeral home. There's no time for the distracted curiosity he'd attract from Ivy and Allison when Alexandra's funeral is this morning. There's going to be news crews. Local celebrities. A huge crowd. We'll already be down one team member if Hugo accepted his position on the unemployment line. Maybe two, if Dad isn't at his best. Then there's the added catering staff that need to be managed.

"We are going separate ways." Remy cocks his shoulder against the doorframe. "For the most part. But I've arranged for you to be supervised."

The dread squeezes tighter.

Is he talking about video surveillance? Did he bug the funeral home?

Surely that would be counterintuitive.

"What does that me—"

A knock sounds at my front door, the heavy thuds cutting me off.

I raise my brows in expectation. "You and your underworld guests sure like to show up to my house at early hours."

"I'm not expecting anyone." He pushes from the doorframe, concern tightening his menacing features. "Are you sure it isn't for you?"

"I suppose it could be Lesley." I rake an anxious hand through the tangled strands of my towel-dried hair. "She knows what time I get ready for work."

His shoulders stiffen, and he turns to stalk down the hall.

"Wait." I rush after him, catching up at the entry to the open living area. "What are you going to say to her? You need to be careful. She won't hesitate in calling the cops again."

"Let me handle it."

"But—"

"I thought you'd learned to follow instructions." He stops and swings around to face me.

I bristle.

The loud knock sounds again.

"Do you seriously think that's the noise a decrepit old lady makes when she raps arthritic knuckles on a door?" He speaks low, his face hard. "Stay where you are, and keep your mouth shut. You hear me?"

My pulse quickens, the thought of a threat rooting me in place as I nod.

He continues his adamant stride across the room. One hand reaches beneath the back of his suit jacket, giving a glimpse of dark metal that makes my stomach drop as he yanks open the door.

There's a moment of silence.

A temperamental pause as Remy's back snaps rigid.

"What the fuck are you doing here?" he snarls.

My skin prickles at the sinister chuckle that carries from my front porch.

"Is that any way to greet your brother?" comes the smooth reply.

Brother?

Oh goddamn fucking shit.

A chill sweeps through me, the icy freeze settling in the pit of my stomach.

"What a coincidence your weekend bender brought you to a familiar home," the brother drawls.

I'm not sure which one it is—the guy from the phone call in the car or the so-called butcher.

I don't know which I'd prefer. But the door opens wider as if pushed from the outside and a man steps in, barging past Remy. Tall. Broad. Dark suit. Darker soul.

I recognize him. He's the guy from the dive bar. The one who met with my father the night this nightmare began.

Salvatore.

I inch backward, creeping toward the hall. His gaze snaps in my direction, his savage focus skewering me in place.

"There she is." He grins, the expression far from friendly. "Ms. Pelosi. Finally, we meet."

All the moisture leaves my mouth, the recollection of Saturday morning's conversation about Remy's brother hitting me right in the chest.

"Will he kill me?"

"Only if he finds out about you."

Remy slams my front door, stealing my attention, his gaze lethal as he mouths, *"Don't panic,"* behind his brother's back. "Go get ready for work, Olivia." He exudes violence as he strides forward, yet the anger seems different from when it's directed at me. There's a temperamental edge to it. A deep-seated volatility. "I'll come get you in a minute."

I don't know what's more terrifying—his abnormal use of my proper name or how Salvatore stares at me like I'm his next meal, and not of the pleasurable variety.

The fear I've battled all weekend transforms, no longer tingling kinetic energy. It's now bone-chilling. Bile-producing.

I retreat another step, my palms sweating.

"No. Stay." Salvatore increases his grin, flashing perfectly predatory teeth. "I'd like a proper introduction."

"Don't play games." Remy rounds his brother to stand between us. "Why the fuck are you here?"

"Why the hell are you?" Salvatore's expression transforms from fraudulent kindness to ominous anger in the blink of dark eyes. "And why the fuck have you been lying to me?"

This is bad. Super-dooper, I've-just-started-an-underworld-family-rivalry bad.

I take another retreating step.

"I said *stay*." Salvatore jabs an enraged finger in my direction while his hate-filled glare remains on his brother.

They face off as I stand frozen. Unblinking. Barely breathing.

"That's enough," Remy snarls.

"Not until I get answers. Why the hell have you been lying to me?"

"Because you're a hot-headed fucking moron." Remy leans to the left as if deliberately cutting off my line of sight to his brother. Or vice versa. "There was a complication Friday night. I'm taking care of it."

"Does she know?" Salvatore sneers.

I hold my breath, every fiber of my being a brittle thread. I should run while I can. Escape out the laundry door.

"Does she fucking know?" he repeats.

"She knows enough."

Salvatore curses under his breath, the oath burrowing beneath my skin. "Big mistake, baby brother."

"It was out of my control."

"But extinguishing the liability wasn't? You should've dealt with this already."

Oh, God. Oh, God. Oh, God.

Remy stands taller, seeming to grow an inch. "I've got it under control."

"That's not what I've heard."

"From *who*?" Remy gets in his brother's face. *Right* in his face.

A chuckle huffs from Salvatore. Vindictive. Terrifying.

"Don't push me." Remy clenches a fist. "You may be older, but you've sat behind a desk for a year while I was out breaking bones and spilling blood. Who do you think would win this fight?"

"You want to fight me, brother?"

"What I want is for you to get the fuck out of here and let me handle my business."

"*My* business," Salvatore corrects. "This is soon to be *my* organization. *My* empire."

"But it isn't *yet*."

Another sickening chuckle taints the air. "You're right. That's why this little interlude was sponsored by our uncle. He's requested your presence at the penthouse." Salvatore takes a casual retreating step, his eyes meeting mine. "*Both* of you."

I stop breathing, each chaotic heartbeat acting like a tightening noose around my neck.

Remy shoots me a glance over his shoulder as if sensing how close I am to running. To passing out.

"*Don't panic*," he mouths again, this time with vehemence.

"He's requested an introduction." Salvatore's grin returns, his gaze playful.

Fear has been my constant companion since early Saturday morning. But with Remy it was different. Wild and rampant. I could think while under the spell of his tyranny.

Not now though.

The fear that consumes me is cold and isolating. The icy tendrils of horror make it impossible to function.

"That isn't necessary," Remy grates.

Salvatore smirks at me. "I assure you it is. Right now in fact."

I shake my head, my throat so dry it throbs.

I'm not meeting anyone. I can't. I have an important funeral to prepare. Being late isn't an option. Ivy and Allison would ask a million questions, and my failing brain isn't capable of giving birth to the insurmountable lies necessary to appease their curiosity.

"I said *no*." Remy sidesteps, breaking his brother's line of vision with mine again. "I'm handling this."

"And what is *this* exactly?"

"A minor inconvenience."

I hold in a squeak.

"Seems like more of a security risk, brother. One that comes in a tempting package."

"I'm *handling it*," Remy snaps.

"Not anymore you're not. Lorenzo's orders."

I keep shaking my head. "I need to get to work. Being late will—"

"Make her understand." Salvatore claps his brother on the shoulders. "Articulate the importance of the meeting on your drive to his penthouse." He turns and starts toward the front door. "I expect you to be no more than five minutes behind me."

Remy doesn't voice another protest.

Why? Why doesn't he scream that we're not going?

"I look forward to getting to know you better, Olivia." Salvatore grabs the door handle and yanks it open. "See you both soon."

He claps the door shut behind him.

Silence rings in my ears.

Remy doesn't fill the void.

"This is bad, isn't it?" I whisper over the ache in my throat.

He shoves a hand through his hair.

"They're going to kill me, aren't they?" I wrap my arms around my middle, clinging tight.

"No." Remy swings around to face me, his expression pinched with turmoil.

"You're lying." I force myself to stand tall. To be strong.

His eyes harden as he bridges the space between us in thunderous steps. "They're not going to fucking touch you. You have my word."

I don't believe him.

I know what this is. The whole tell-her-what-she-needs-to-hear stitch.

Guilt already swims in his dark irises. Guilt I never would've thought capable of existing, but it's definitely there.

"I need my phone back." I hold out a hand. "I have to message my dad. If I go missing—"

"You're not going missing. I'll protect you."

A laugh bubbles past my lips.

He's going to protect me? *Him?* The guy who's been a revolving door of threats and intimidation all weekend?

I want to believe him though. *God,* how I want to sink into the deceptive support and make it my home.

I step back, distancing myself from the idiotic weakness.

"I *will* protect you." He straightens his shoulders as if repelling my rejection. "This is a slight complication, that's all."

No, it's not.

Otherwise he wouldn't need to protect me. He wouldn't be looking at me with that remorse-riddled pity.

I mistakenly thought I'd waded through the worst of this situation. That somehow, getting to work and being away from Remy would be the beginning of the end to all this.

"Believe me, Ollie." He stands proud. "You expected me to trust in you after what went down with the cops. So trust me with this. Everything will be okay."

"How?" I look at him like he's a lifeline, my nightmare having become my only savior. "It's clear your brother wants me to disappear."

"Because you're a liability. I've told you that from the start." His dark eyes flash with sincerity as he runs a hand through his hair. "We just need to persuade them otherwise."

16

REMY

"We have to get going." I curse my idiotic need to console her. "It won't work in our favor to keep Lorenzo waiting."

"But I'm not ready. I'm barely even dressed, and Alexandra's funeral is this morning. If I'm late—"

"I think tardiness can be bumped down the list of concerns when a bullet through the brain is a possible alternative."

It was meant as a joke. One I immediately regret.

Her eyes widen. Her tempting lips part.

Fuck.

"Ollie, listen." I step into her, cupping her cheeks, thankful she doesn't balk in revulsion. "I will *not* let anything happen to you. Do you hear me?"

She stares up at me, hazel eyes glassy, skin pale, breathing labored.

"Your father is a valued asset. Our arrangement is priceless."

She winces.

"We just need to convince my brother and Lorenzo you're on board."

"How can I convince them when I'm struggling to convince myself?" She pulls away. "I'm not built for this."

"None of us are." I drop my hands to my sides. "Do you think I was born into this role?"

"I don't know. I don't know anything about you."

"This hasn't always been my life. I had a heart once."

She looks away, focusing on the blank television screen. "It's all too much. What if I say the wrong thing? What if I—"

"You thought on your feet last night. You strategized. You got those cops to leave."

"No, I didn't." She shakes her head. "That was you and your *guy on the payroll*."

"There's no time to question yourself. You can do this." She's convinced she's going to die. I'm not entirely sure she won't. "You *have* to do this." I lead the way toward the front door. "Come on. Let's go."

She glances to the hall behind her, her damp hair tangled in clumps around her cheeks.

"Now, pyro."

Her posture slumps. "I don't like that nickname."

"I'm not overly fond of Grim either, but if the shoe fits..." I stop before her hat rack and grab her thick brown coat.

She approaches, stride short, feet dragging. She stops before me, not protesting when I drape the heavy material over her shoulders.

Her eyes never leave mine, the pleading hazel depths stirring emotions in me I never thought I had.

Why the fuck do I care so much?

Why do I care at all?

I shouldn't give a shit about taking her to Lorenzo. Shouldn't mind that she'll be spending more time in Salvatore's presence. But both those things have my rage on a low simmer.

Denying them isn't an option. My brother would only find her as soon as my back was turned. At least this way I can be there. Can do the talking.

I pull open the door, and the cold wind slaps my face as I stride for the Bentley still parked across the street. The crunch of her footsteps follow behind me. We both climb into the car although clearly, neither one of us wants to leave.

"My phone?" she asks while I start the ignition.

I pull it from my jacket pocket, having dumped the rest of her surrendered electronics on her dining table first thing this morning.

I should outline rules and regulations with the device. How she shouldn't complicate matters by telling her father of this morning's situation. How any calls for help will be intercepted. Instead, I hold tight to the cell as she grasps the other end, and level her with a warning look.

She remains silent, giving a solemn nod in understanding.

"We have to work together, Ollie. There's no point making this more painful than it needs to be."

"I know."

She drags on her seatbelt as I pull from the curb.

I keep one eye on her as I drive through the busy morning traffic, her focus intent on her screen.

"What is it?" I mutter, yet again giving too many shits about what's running through her head.

"Dad sent a heap of messages Saturday night. He must be worried sick."

"He's not." I force my attention on the road. "He called me when he didn't hear from you. I explained that it was best to give you a few days without the interference of Google swaying your perception of me and mine."

"What am I going to find online?"

I shrug. "Unsubstantiated stories and speculation."

"Are they though?" she whispers. "Speculation, I mean."

"Sometimes."

"Will you tell me why my father trusts you?"

"Our agreement couldn't work without trust. It's non-negotiable. And we've worked closely since the beginning. He showed me the ins and outs of your business. In return—apart from the money—I've helped where I can with his health issues. We may not have the same outlook on life, but we've learned to understand each other."

She focuses out her passenger window, as if trying to distance herself from me, her fingers self-consciously raking through her hair.

"Stop fidgeting. You look fine."

"I'm a wreck," she murmurs to the frosted glass. "And FYI—*fine* is never a comforting descriptor."

Does she want me to tell her she's mesmerizing? That the state of her hair doesn't mean shit when her gorgeous face has the ability to steal breath?

She continues finger-combing her damp strands, then starts fussing with her clothes. Her leg jostles, her jitters filling the car as I drive toward the city, her knee constantly bobbing, her hands a frenzy of agitated movement.

"You're going to need to get those nerves under control." I shoot her a glance.

She sighs. "Yeah, I'll get right on it."

Her knee continues to jolt. Up and down. Up and down. Faster and faster.

"I'm serious, Ollie. Lorenzo needs to know you have your shit together."

"I'm trying, but it doesn't help when I don't know what he's going to do to me."

My hands tighten around the steering wheel. I wish I could answer her with an impending Hallmark moment but the truth is, I don't know what to expect.

I've only had a relationship with my uncle for little over a year. Before that I barely knew he existed. I'm unsure how much influence I have.

What I do know is that he's smart, calculating, and risk averse. He's a powerful man with a hell of a lot to lose. He's also highly principled with a soft heart for those he cares about.

Too bad Ollie doesn't fall into that category.

It's all on me to sway his hand.

"You don't know, do you?" Her voice fills with sorrow. "You have no idea what I'm up against."

"*We*," I correct. "What *we're* up against."

I reach across the center console to slide a hand over her knee before I can think better of it. Before I can contemplate how fucking pathetic it is for the man who placed her in this situation to offer her comfort.

Her breathing hitches. The jolting stops. She turns rigid.

What the fuck are you doing?

I withdraw from the lenience—the stupidity—and reclaim the steering wheel. "Just pretend to be okay with the situation. He needs to trust you."

"Even though you don't?"

I'm not sure that's the case anymore. But exposing the truth is yet another mistake. "Yeah," I mutter. "Even though I don't."

I pull into the underground parking lot of my uncle's apartment building and take the reserved space between Salvatore's matte black Maserati GranTurismo and Lorenzo's silver Rolls-Royce Wraith.

I cut the ignition and turn to her. "My uncle values respect and self-control. Take your time before answering his questions. Don't get emotional. Show him you're not the type to buckle under pressure."

She swallows. Nods.

"You'll be okay." *Fingers crossed.* If history dictates, all it will take is one threat from Lorenzo and she'll bite back with a retort likely to get her throat slashed. Or worse, she'll attempt to knock him out with a blunt object and try to stuff him in the kitchen oven. "Let me do the talking."

She stares at me, those slaying eyes seeming to read me. "Are you really helping me? Or is this a trap?"

I'm definitely doing the former. But only time will tell if I'm unwittingly leading her into the latter.

"I'm doing everything I possibly can to get things back to the way they were." I lower my attention to the cell in her lap. "Have you messaged your dad yet?"

"Yes." She shucks the heavy coat, her expression somber. "I lied and told him everything is under control. If I'm being led to slaughter I don't want him to feel responsible."

"Good decision." I climb from the car, eat up the short path to the penthouse elevator, and wait for her to join me. "Whatever you feel in there, keep it locked tight. Whether it's fear or anger, push it to the back of your mind. You can take it out on me later."

"You might regret that when I'm wielding a baseball bat and swinging it toward that aesthetically faultless face of yours."

I slap my hand against the call button, holding in a grin. "I've talked you down from worse."

"Placing me in volatile situations isn't something to brag about."

I watch her in the reflection of the elevator doors as they open. Ignore the need to touch her again. "Be strong, Ollie. The weak don't survive here."

Her throat works over a heavy swallow, but she squares her shoulders and drags in a deep breath to follow me inside.

I enter the PIN code on the security panel, then press the lone button for the penthouse.

The ascent is quiet, the enclosed space suffocated with her turmoil.

"As soon as those doors open, we'll have eyes on us." I lean against the back wall, relieved when she stands taller, her chin high, but those delicate hands continue to fidget. "Your life is nothing more than a business decision for Lorenzo. Keep it simple. Don't create more complications."

She peers back at me with hopelessness. "My life is nothing more than a business decision?"

"Nobody's life is."

Her brow furrows. "Even yours?"

I shrug.

Did he take me in after my parents tried to have me killed? Yes.

Did he give me a home, money, a future? All of the above.

But will those luxuries disappear if I rub him the wrong way? Chances are.

If my own father can attempt to take my life, I don't hold much hope that a once-estranged uncle won't one day try to do the same.

"Great." Ollie pivots to the doors, turning away from me. "If you're not safe, what hope do I have?"

"You've got a retort and the means to effortlessly dispose of evidence. Lean into that."

She drags in a deep breath and lets it out in a rush.

The elevator opens and, as expected, one of Lorenzo's armed guards eyeballs us from his standing post beside the elegant white front doors of the penthouse.

He doesn't greet me. Doesn't pretend like he has permission to even utter my name. He rushes to clear our path, silently opening both doors and moving out of the way.

I stride inside the ostentatious bachelor pad with its excessive high ceiling, seemingly untouched furniture, and sparkling marble floor.

The far-off murmur of voices travels from the right of the building. I lead Ollie in that direction. Past the kitchen. Down the hall. Toward the open entry of Lorenzo's office where another guard stands in wait.

He doesn't make eye contact. Doesn't flinch from his soldier-like stance.

I shoot Ollie one last reassuring look, then continue inside.

"Remy." My uncle pushes to his feet from behind his meticulously crafted wooden desk, his Italian accent thick, his smile warm and almost believable. "Thank you for coming."

My brother stands by the floor-to-ceiling window, his back to me as he peers over the Baltimore skyline.

I keep my posture neutral, my expression edging toward boredom. "I'm a busy man. I could've done without the early morning summons."

Salvatore turns to me with a roll of his eyes.

"I'm sure you could've, *figlio*. But I wanted to meet your friend." Lorenzo takes in Ollie with a deceptively kind gaze. "Introductions are in order."

The hair on my nape tingles. I shut that down. Ignore it. "This is Olivia." I slide a palm around her back and guide her forward. "Carlo Pelosi's daughter, and the full-time mortician at her family's funeral home."

"Olivia, it's a pleasure to meet you." He makes his way around the desk, limping slightly, before stopping in front of her. "I met your father quite some years ago. He's a good man."

"Yes, he is." She offers her hand to shake, her trembling fingers her only tell. "You have a lovely home."

"Thank you." Lorenzo's smile deepens as he clasps her palm, shaking for longer than necessary. The first sign of subtle intimidation.

My hackles rise, my agitation increasing when Salvatore turns and prowls forward, staring down his nose at her.

"Please take a seat." Lorenzo releases her hand and indicates one of the two wingback armchairs in front of his desk.

Ollie glances at the chairs positioned within lunging distance of my brother, then to me, as if sensing the warranted threat of his close proximity.

"It's okay." I give a subtle jerk of my chin. "Salvo won't bite." I scowl at him in warning. "Will you?"

He raises a brow. "The jury's still out."

I glower, my temper locked and loaded.

He might hold more power than me in this organization, but when it comes to the sibling hierarchy I have no problem getting my point across with violence. Not even when the last fight I had with my brothers resulted in two of us being stabbed.

"In that case," I snarl through clenched teeth, "the jury might want to hurry up and learn some manners before the executioner loses his temper."

Salvatore throws his head back with an exaggerated laugh.

I want to fucking kill him.

"Ignore them." Lorenzo leans against his desk. "It always surprises me how grown men can revert to childish toddlers the moment a beautiful woman enters a room. Please—" he indicates toward the seats again. "—sit."

Ollie does as requested, scooting around the far side of the chair farthest from my brother before settling into the seat with her hands in her lap.

"I heard you had an eventful weekend." Lorenzo doesn't take his scrutinous eyes off her.

"Who told you that?" I step closer, standing like a sentry beside her chair.

"Wouldn't you like to know?" Salvatore smirks.

"Yeah, I would, asshole. If my men are going behind my back to report to you on things that don't require your involvement, I deserve to be informed."

"It wasn't your men." Lorenzo's focus turns to me, oddly reassuring. "I received a phone call from a police officer last night who wanted to make sure there was nothing he could do to help assist with the situation between my nephew and his girlfriend." His attention turns inquisitive. "Which was quite a surprise when I didn't know you were dating."

"It was even more surprising since the request came just a day after you called claiming you were out trolling to get laid," Salvatore adds.

"We're not dating. It was—"

Lorenzo raises a silencing finger. "Olivia is more than capable of informing me of how all this came to pass."

He's testing her. Sizing her up. Or at least determining the threat she poses.

But, unlike with her father, she can't lie to Lorenzo. Can't even manipulate the truth. Any hint of deceit will ensure this ends badly.

"Please, *mia cara*," he coaxes. "Tell me how you and my nephew came to be familiar."

She peers up at me, questioning.

Shit.

I try to convey my thoughts through a look of calm reassurance. "It's okay. You can—"

"*Remy*, enough," my uncle barks. "Allow my guest to speak."

Ollie's eyes widen on me, her fear showing. Then, in a blink, she reins it in and focuses on the man likely to order her death. "It's a long story…"

His smile returns. "Not to worry. I may be old, but I still have time."

She gives another swallow. Another glance in my direction for approval.

All I can do is incline my head.

She keeps her gaze on me as she speaks. "It started early Saturday morning. I was at work, having stayed late to try to get on top of my duties. I fell asleep in the break room." Those troubled eyes lose focus, lost in memory. "I woke to the sound of Remy and his men entering the building."

"That must have been quite the surprise," Salvatore drawls.

She blinks out of her daze and addresses Lorenzo. "I was scared, to say the least."

"Understandable." He winces with empathy.

I step forward. "I made sure—"

My uncle's glowering eyes snap to mine, one hard look of disapproval enough to force my mouth shut again. "If it's difficult for you to refrain from interrupting, it might be best if you wait in the living room."

My pulse becomes thunderous. "I'm not going anywhere."

His attention narrows. He's trying to figure out what she means to me.

I'd like to fucking understand that myself.

"Please continue, Olivia." He turns a softened parental gaze back to her. "He won't interfere again."

"I walked in on two men carrying the limp body of a middle-aged male." She clears her throat. "At the time, I wasn't aware he was dead, but it was obvious there was something illegal going on."

Lorenzo grasps the desk behind him on either side of his hips. Knuckles white. Annoyance evident. "And?"

"And after a temperamental—or more accurately, confrontational—conversation, I learned of the agreement that was made with my father."

The room falls quiet.

The prickle of foreboding grows.

I want to step in. Take over. Fix this.

"Did you also learn that the agreement had strict stipulations where your father was never to bear witness to our work while on your premises—for reasons of incrimination as well as safety?" Lorenzo asks.

"Yes." She sits taller in the face of danger. "I'm aware."

"And yet you seem to be taking this turn of events quite well." My uncle raises a brow. "Why is that?"

"I've had my moments. But I trust my father. Like you said, he's a good man. He wouldn't have walked into this without careful consideration. My faith is in his judgment."

For some fucked up reason her response fills me with pride. She's walking this tightrope with cautious precision. Perfectly drip-feeding the truth.

"And where was your father during this?" Salvatore asks. "Because, to me, this situation seems like a fucking red flag of mismanagement. Or maybe even a setup."

"He was in hospital." She takes my brother's stare head-on.

"Hospital?" Lorenzo directs at me.

"Yes. He had a fall after chemo treatment."

"So Olivia is now aware of his health situation?"

"I am," she answers.

"She knows he has cancer," I affirm. "I was there when he told her the news."

Lorenzo nods slowly, mulling over my response. "It must have been quite the night of revelations for you, *mia cara*." He pushes to stand, giving Ollie a slight squeeze to the shoulder before circling the desk and taking his office chair. "Is Carlo okay?"

"I'm not entirely sure." Her voice waivers. "I haven't spoken to him since Saturday afternoon."

"Because?" Salvatore prods.

"I gave Remy my phone so he knew I wouldn't call the cops."

Slow your roll, Ollie. Be fucking careful.

"That was necessary?" Lorenzo pins me with narrowed eyes.

"It was a precaution." I don't look away. Don't hint to my building unease.

"But the police showed anyway." Salvatore throws his hands skyward in theatrical mockery.

"Because of a nosy neighbor," I grate. "We shut it down without issue."

Salvatore scoffs and shares a glance with Lorenzo.

A knowing, ominous glance.

Not good. Not fucking good.

"What?" I sneer. "Spit it out."

Lorenzo raises an unimpressed brow. "Obviously this situation is concerning. She was never meant to find out."

"I won't talk," Olivia blurts. "I *can't*. Not only because I wouldn't risk my father's freedom, but because I've been implicated myself."

Salvatore cocks his head. "How?"

I clear my throat, hoping to get her to tap the brakes on the truth serum.

"I helped dispose of that man's body," she admits. "I was there. I flipped the switch on the retort."

"The plot thickens." Lorenzo leans back in his chair, entwining his fingers over his stomach. "I assume it was a forced action, though. Not something that would hold much weight in court."

"Maybe not," she continues. "But since then, I would've been seen driving your nephew's car to the hospital on my own. He's spent the weekend in my house. I even convinced my neighbor we're in a relationship. Those actions wouldn't be so easy to talk my way out of."

Fuck, Ollie.

I fight the need to clasp a hand over her mouth. To cut her off. To shut her the hell up.

"The mobster and the mortician having known ties." Lorenzo rocks gently in his chair, his agitation subtle. "What a juicy story for the tabloids."

Ollie snaps her panicked gaze to me.

Yes, pyro, you glitched.

I ignore her, refusing to meet those pleading hazel eyes. To weaken before the men looking for any excuse to be her executioner.

"The neighbor is no threat. She's older than time." I shrug off the skin-crawling apprehension. "And Olivia wouldn't have been noticed in my car."

"There's a difference between being noticed and having evidence readily available to find once the bloodhounds catch wind of this." Salvatore turns and walks for the window, disengaging from the conversation, his mind already made up.

Fuck. Fuck. Fuck.

I clench my molars. "I have this under control."

"Forgive me, *figlio*, but I lack your confidence." Lorenzo gives a somber smile. "Given the circumstances, I feel it necessary to spend a little more time with Olivia. Just the two of us."

"*No*," I demand. "That's not happening."

Salvatore doesn't turn back from the window.

They've both determined she's too much of a liability.

"Hear me on this, Lorenzo." I grate through gnashed teeth. "I said, no."

I'm punching above my weight. Pushing far beyond my boundaries. And still, I don't know why. Don't understand how this woman and her father became important.

"More consideration needs to be made." My uncle sits straight in his chair, all pretense of relaxation gone. "I'll chat further with Olivia and—"

"With all due respect, Mr. Cappelletti, I'm just as capable of reading between the lines as Remy," Ollie says with softened conviction. "I know my life is on the line. But I assure you, I'm not a liability. I may not have proven my willingness to keep my mouth shut yet, but I can promise there's nobody on this earth I love more than my father. I'm not going to do anything to jeopardize his freedom. I wouldn't have been able to do that even before I learned of the cancer, let alone now when I know he's suffering."

"It's too big a risk," Salvatore speaks to the Baltimore skyline, as if the *it* in question isn't Ollie keeping her life.

"I'm level-headed." She adds steal to her tone. "Death, murder, and the results of violence aren't new to me."

"That might be the case, crypt keeper, but I'm sure crime and danger are." Salvatore glances over his shoulder to Lorenzo. "We'd be placing unnecessary trust in someone who brings nothing to the table."

"She brings her father," I growl.

"He's already at the table, dickwad."

I chuckle, teeth gritted, fists clenched. I'm going to fucking kill him.

"He wasn't this weekend," Ollie argues. "All this came to pass because he was in hospital. Who knows if something similar will happen in the future? And if it'll be a staff member that learns incriminating information next time? But it doesn't have to be that way. I can be on the inside. I can help cover things up."

I glance from my brother to Lorenzo, waiting for one of them to be persuaded by her argument.

"I can't afford to lose access to that retort." I cross my arms over my chest. "Not when we're in the thick of it with the cartel. We need her. Do you think her father will work with us if we kill his daughter?"

I'm well aware I've just posed a question she threw at me only days earlier. A question that could easily be ignored if she were to simply disappear. But here I am, grasping at all the straws.

"Carlo has been fucking good to me. If you destroy that, I'm out," I vow. "I'll move to Washington with Matthew. You can find someone else to do your dirty work."

Salvatore rolls his eyes. "You don't have much leverage when Bishop is only a phone call away."

Not only is my brother a hothead, but he's a fucking moron. "Bishop would prefer a prostate exam from our mother than to receive orders from you."

"You feel that strongly, *figlio?*" Lorenzo asks me.

"Yes. I promised Carlo his interests would be kept safe under our agreement. I won't be like my father and betray him."

Salvatore turns back to the window, his chin raised.

If anything can sway him it's the thought of holding any similarity to the man who spawned us.

"And you." Lorenzo focuses on Ollie. "Do you understand the ramifications if anything goes wrong due to your involvement?"

She nods. "I think that's been made abundantly clear."

"No, child, it hasn't." He gives a sad smile. "The dissolution of this arrangement via problematic means would not simply end with the swift conclusion you may expect. It would be lengthy and exceptionally bothersome for both you and your father."

"She gets it," I growl.

"You would vow to be loyal to us?" he asks her.

A cold chill skitters down my spine as she nods.

"Your oath requires more than a simple head gesture, *mia cara.*"

"Yes," she promises. "I vow it."

His sad smile increases. "Unfortunately, it requires more than a verbal response, too."

"That isn't necessary." I inch closer.

Lorenzo opens his desk drawer, ignoring me as he scrounges around the contents until he pulls out a card similar to one found in a poker set.

Goddamnit. He pulled this stunt with me and Salvatore a year ago. I still bear the marks to prove it.

"Women aren't indoctrinated." I lower my hands to my sides.

"No, they are not." He pushes to his feet. "Instead, any woman outside the family who becomes a liability is silenced. Which would you prefer?"

I gnash my teeth. Glare my fury.

He remains paused behind his desk, unfazed by my animosity, waiting for a response.

"The ritual is pointless." I clench my fists.

"It's symbolic." He limps toward Ollie and holds out the saint card for her to take. "Although my time spent in prayer has dwindled over the years, my faith remains. I picked Saint Catherine of Siena for you, Olivia. She was a very determined, headstrong woman, much like I imagine you must be."

Ollie stares up at him, hands trembling.

I don't want this for her.

Not the fucking ceremony.

Not the fucking life.

"Salvatore." Lorenzo looks to my brother. "Do you have your switchblade?"

My brother turns from the window and stalks over as he digs in his pocket.

"I'll do it." I hold out a hand for his weapon.

"No need. I've got this." He attempts to step around me.

I block his path. *"I'll do it."*

He stares. Stares so long and hard I'm sure he knows that blade of his could soon be embedded in his abdomen if I don't get my way.

"Fine." He slaps the weapon into my palm. "It's your mess."

My mess. My mistake. My punishment.

I turn to Ollie, my gut heavy as I take in her barely masked fear. "Come here." I want to hold out a hand, help her to her feet. Instead, I keep my free arm at my side, my expression hard.

She licks her dried lips and slowly rises to stand before me.

I grab her wrist and take the saint card from her grip.

The slight tremor wracking through her fucking kills me, her trepidation like a lead weight in my gut.

"It's only the smallest cut," I vow.

She blinks up at me. Trusting. Unquestioning.

I hold her gaze as I pierce the blade into the pad of her pointer finger, her wince a knife through my chest. I squeeze her wrist tighter, forcing strength.

She smashes her lips tight. Breathes deep through her nose.

Such a phenomenal fucking woman.

Blood wells as I dump Salvatore's weapon on the desk, then guide her pierced finger to hover over the face of Saint Catherine, allowing the blood to drip to the card.

"As your blood mingles with the saint's grace," Lorenzo states, "so shall you bind your loyalty to our family." He pulls a cigarette lighter from his pocket.

"*No*," I snarl.

"It will be quick, *figlio.* Give her the card."

I can't fucking do it.

"*Figlio*," Lorenzo warns.

"It's okay." Ollie takes the card, holding it between her pierced pointer and thumb.

Her drops of blood slide down Saint Catherine's angelic face as Lorenzo leans in, igniting the lighter with a grated flick, then holds the flame to the bottom corner of the card, a mere inch from her fingertips, and waits too many fucking seconds for the blaze to take hold.

"Repeat after me." Lorenzo's accent lingers. "I swear allegiance to this family, with loyalty thicker than blood."

"I swear allegiance to this family." Her voice shakes as the flame builds, burning closer to her skin, the radiant heat no doubt scalding. "With loyalty thicker than blood."

"I am bound by silence and honor," Lorenzo continues.

She sucks in a breath. "I am bound by silence and honor."

"Until death claims me."

"Until death claims me," she whimpers.

With the last word of the oath I snatch the card, the flimsy board melting into my fingertips. I throw it to the large crystal ashtray on Lorenzo's desk, the flames flickering with the momentum.

"You're whipped and it shows," Salvatore mutters under his breath for only me to hear.

"*Grande.*" Lorenzo beams with false praise. "You are now part of the family, *mia cara*. You are one of us."

I breathe through the resentment as Ollie stares at the burns on her skin, no doubt a myriad of troubled thoughts hidden behind solemn eyes.

"Are we done?" I shove my hands in my pockets, fists clenched, knuckles aching.

"Almost. I have one more question." Lorenzo raises an aged finger, pointing it back and forth between us. "Is there something romantic going on here that I need to know about?"

"*No*." Ollie scrunches her nose. "Not at all."

Salvatore snorts, enjoying her exaggerated display of distaste.

"*Figlio?*" Lorenzo narrows his gaze on me. "Is that true?"

"Yes." Wanting to fuck her isn't romantic, right?

"You have not slept together?"

I don't blink. Don't even twitch. "No."

He leans against his desk, nodding. "Good." He returns his attention to Ollie. "I like you, Olivia."

I'm not stupid enough to be relieved by his statement, and being the incredibly smart woman Ollie is, she doesn't relax either.

"I'd hate for that to change," he adds.

A whisper of a chuckle escapes her lips. "Believe me. I don't want it to change either. I prefer being on the living side of my mortuary gurney if I can help it."

Lorenzo grins. An earnest, charm-fueled expression that quickly fades. "With that being said, I would feel more at ease if we had someone to keep a close eye on you for the time being. Someone that preferably isn't my nephew."

"It's already been taken care of." I jerk my head toward the hall, encouraging Ollie to get moving.

"How so?" Salvatore asks.

"I've arranged for a close contact I trust to gain employment at the funeral home. He met with Carlo yesterday. My expectation is that he'll be introduced to staff sometime this morning."

Olivia stiffens.

Lorenzo nods his approval. "And outside of work?"

"Spyware has been installed on her devices and men have been scheduled to keep watch."

Surprised hazel eyes turn my way, the heavy sense of betrayal eating up my periphery.

"Perfect." Lorenzo clasps his hands in appreciation. "Then please consider your time with Olivia now officially over. I want you to drive her wherever she needs to be, then leave her in peace. There's to be no further contact between you two unless an issue arises. Understood?"

OLIVIA

I stare at the reddened flesh of my fingertips, the first-degree burn throbbing as I'm driven toward the suburbs.

I don't know what to think. How to feel.

Every time I'm certain this situation can't get worse, the universe says, *"Hold my beer."*

"You did good," he murmurs from behind the wheel.

I'm not sure I agree. I was terrified, Lorenzo's faux charm having no calming effect on me.

"I've never been more scared in my life," I admit.

Remy hits me with a skeptical look. "Even with me?"

Yes. Even with you.

The realization is yet another unsettling part of this nightmare.

I'd been defiant with Remy. Combative. I even dared to shove him in the retort, for Christ's sake.

In contrast, I'd struggled to breathe through my terror while in the presence of Lorenzo and Salvatore.

It makes me wonder if I've truly feared Remy at all. If our brief moment at that dive bar may have frazzled my self-preservation where he's concerned.

Case in point, right this very moment, what I currently feel toward him holds no resemblance to apprehension and seems overwhelmingly like appreciation.

I'm grateful... to a murderer... who previously threatened to unalive me.

I return my attention to my throbbing fingers. "You inspire a different sort of fear." *One that mingles with attraction and dances freely with stupidity.*

"Well, given Lorenzo's dictate, you can rest easy knowing we never have to see each other again."

My stomach tumbles as I raise crossed fingers. "Here's hoping."

He snatches my wrist, frowning as he drags my hand toward him and inspects my damaged fingertips. "Have you got something for the burn?"

My breathing stutters, his hold sending a wave of tingles up my arm. "I'll be fine." I drag my wrist away.

"Just FYI," he drawls, "*fine* is never a comforting descriptor."

Why does he have to do that? To show just how much he listens to me. How intently he takes notice. I don't want to like him.

"Sorry. I should've said, 'Your concern is wasted on me when you're the reason I'm in this mess.'"

His hands tighten on the steering wheel.

I will *not* feel guilty for being a bitch.

Besides, there's no room for that emotion amongst all the adrenaline, fear, and gratitude flowing through my veins.

"Can I put some music on?" I reach for the display screen, my gaze catching on the digital clock.

Shit.

I'm so fucking late for work.

I yank my cell from my pants pocket, contemplating whether I should text Ivy when the screen alights with the notification of her six missed calls.

She's going to kill me. But not without interrogating me first.

"Problem?" Remy growls.

"I should've been at work forty-five minutes ago."

The car speeds up, the rapid acceleration thrusting me back into my seat.

"I'll get you there in fifteen." He weaves in and out of traffic, the psychotic killer doing me yet another favor.

I turn away from him, hating the renewed influx of appreciation.

"You're welcome," he mutters under his breath.

I double down, refusing to feel guilty over my lack of verbal recognition… but the remorse festers, eating me from the inside out.

He fought for me. Burned his hand. Threatened to walk away from whatever presumably lucrative position he has.

"I'm going to be asked where I've been. Why I'm late…" I talk to distract myself. To curb the urge to apologize. "What should I say?"

He takes a corner too fast, my body turning toward him with the momentum. "It's your job to figure it out. Lie like your life depends on it because I assure you it does."

"And if I can't come up with something believable?"

His eyes meet mine. "Tell them you got lucky. That you spent the night with a guy you met at a bar."

"I'd never do that."

"The Ollie I met six months ago would've. In fact, she begged for the privilege."

My cheeks heat, the warmth spreading down my neck. This is why I promised never to rile him again. He retaliates with sexual grenades that seem to detonate between my thighs.

"Keep it simple," he murmurs. "The less detail you give, the better. And if all else fails—gaslight."

My stomach sinks.

I'm not a gaslighter. Not a combatant. Well, not with anyone other than him.

"Your colleagues will pay the price if you fail." He continues dodging in and out of traffic with ease, as if the murder of my friends would be little more than an inconvenience. "Be cruel to be kind, pyro, otherwise that cremator of yours is going to be putting in some overtime."

I stare at my tangled hands in my lap. "Has anyone ever complimented you on your spectacular pep talks?"

He turns onto the street of the funeral home and pulls to the curb half a block from the parking lot, leaving the engine to idle. "Has anyone done the same with you and your abundant show of appreciation whenever someone saves your life?"

I wince, the guilt renewed.

I sit in silence, gratitude twisting my stomach.

He doesn't deserve to hear it. I can't soften to him. Can't crumble.

Goddamnit.

"I'm grateful," I whisper.

He doesn't respond. There's only the slightest squeak of his hands around the steering wheel.

"I know you're the only reason I'm still alive." I pick at the quick on my thumb. "How you fought for me in front of your uncle and brother was..." How do I describe it? Surprising? Oddly passionate? Confusing? "Appreciated."

I look to him, our gazes colliding for the briefest second before his jaw ticks and he turns his stare out the windshield. "You need to get going."

I know.

I shouldn't want to spend a minute more in his presence, but there's still so many questions.

I unclasp my belt. "Will I see you again?"

He huffs a sardonic laugh. "You've asked me that before. The answer hasn't changed."

Not if you're lucky.

The relief that takes over my chest feels different. Empty and cold. But it *is* relief. It has to be.

"You're still going to continue to use our equipment, though, right?" I ask.

"Right." He releases the steering wheel and inspects his palm. His own burns. The sacrifice he made for a stranger.

I want to see. To grab his wrist and drag his arm toward me so I can inspect the injury he received on my behalf.

Instead I return my hand to my lap and squeeze my fingers tight. "It's not comforting to feel appreciation toward a man who's forced you to do the worst—"

"*I've told you* that the alternative was—"

"I know." I raise my voice slightly, cutting him off. "I'm not trying to cause an argument," I say, softer. "I'm just…" I drag in a breath and let it out slowly. "Thank you, Remy. I have no idea what it cost you to fight for my life like you did, but I do appreciate it. More than I'm ever going to want you to know."

He returns his hand to the steering wheel, his knuckles white from the tight grip.

It's weird. Since the witching hour Saturday morning I've prayed to get away from this man. And now that the opportunity is here, I'm finding it hard to open the car door. "Will you tell me about this new guy? Is he actually going to do his job or is he merely there to—"

"Wesley will do his job, and he'll do it well. If he doesn't, I'll hear about it."

"Just not from me," I assume. "You and my father will continue to communicate behind my back."

He doesn't respond.

"What happens if I slip up? If I say something I shouldn't, or get caught in a lie?"

Hard eyes meet mine. "You won't."

"But—

"You *won't*." He returns his attention to the street, his jaw ticking. "If there's any chance of that happening, I have a responsibility to my family to turn this car around and take you back to Lorenzo."

My insides squeeze. "Right. Understood. No messing up allowed."

He sighs. "I don't enjoy scaring you, Ollie. But I'd hate killing you even more."

Squeeze. Squeeze. Squeeze.

"I get it." I push open the car door. "I'd wish you all the best with your future endeavors but that seems highly unethical, so…" I shrug. "I guess I'll just say goodbye."

Dark eyes turn to mine, his expression stark. "Goodbye, Ollie."

The finality stabs through me.

I swallow it down, grab my coat, and climb from the vehicle, not looking back in the fear my seesawing emotions will notch another confusing level of unhinged into my psyche.

I ignore the tingle up the back of my neck. The thoughts of Remy. The memory of his touch. Instead I focus on moving forward. On thinking about how my father might be feeling. On the importance of keeping my nose clean.

The frigid winter air chills my lungs as I finger-comb my hair one final time, then push through the front door of the funeral home.

I stop dead in my tracks at what looks to be an impromptu staff meeting in the reception area. Everyone turns to face me—Dad, Ivy, Allison, and a suit-clad man with warm brown skin, eyes dark as night, and a relaxed, carefree energy deceptive enough to momentarily make me forget he must be the one who's here to watch me on behalf of the mafia.

"Where the hell have you been?" Ivy gapes. "Alexandra's service starts in less than ninety minutes."

"It's okay." Dad holds up a placating hand, his skin pale, his hair styled to cover whatever is left of his forehead injury. "We've got it under control."

Allison grimaces. "*Now* we do. It didn't feel that way when Hugo came storming in."

"Hugo was here?" I walk farther inside, letting the door fall shut behind me.

"Don't worry. I spoke to him." Dad turns to the group. "Liv, come meet our newest employee."

It takes a conscious effort to drag my feet to my father's side as I pray my novice acting skills will see me through this mess. "New employee?" I assume ignorance is the best way to play this. "You found someone to replace Hugo already?"

"I did." Dad beams. "This is Wesley Robinson."

The clean-cut man steps forward to offer his hand. "Olivia." He eyes me with deceptive warmth, just like Lorenzo did. "It's nice to meet you."

"Likewise," I force out, sliding my palm over his. "I hope you're ready to hit the ground running. Today is one hell of a day to be introduced to the team."

"So I've heard." He inclines his head. "But don't worry. I'm here to do whatever's necessary."

I withdraw my hand, a chill sweeping through me at the subtle threat.

"Given our added duties today, we need to get back to work." Dad turns to Ivy. "Until we have time to go through day-to-day tasks, Wesley can help you with whatever has to be done."

"Sure." Ivy gives Wesley a flirty smile. "I'll keep him busy."

Jesus Christ. Not him, too. She really needs to start checking for red flags before gaining interest in a man.

"We'll be setting up the chapel if you need us." Ivy guides him toward the hall leading to the front of the building.

Allison walks around her desk to claim her chair.

My father starts for his office.

I'm stuck wading in existential dread. "Dad, wait." I follow him, entering his office and gently closing the door behind us.

As soon as we're alone, I want to crumple. The need only increases when he levels me with more remorse than what he'd shared in the hospital.

"I'm so sorry, Liv."

I stumble the few feet of space between us and wrap my arms around him. Cling tight. Breathe him deep.

He returns the hug with equal desperation. "Are you okay?"

I nod. "Are *you*?" I pull back, meeting his gaze.

"Yes, *fragolina*." He forces a smile. "I'm perfectly fine. There's no need to worry."

"You're so pale."

"Chemo hit a little harder this time." He offers a final squeeze before retreating. "And the fall didn't help. But I'm good. I promise. You don't need to worry."

Worry is all there is. All that exists. It's now my entire personality.

"Ivy's right, though." He rounds his desk to sit in his plush cream leather seat. "You're not looking your best. You didn't even braid your hair."

I slump into the armchair opposite him. "I didn't even *do* my hair. This morning got a bit hectic."

"What happened?" He inches forward to lean his elbows on the desk. "You messaged and said you were okay...I didn't know if I should panic."

I don't know how to tell him. If I even *should* tell him.

"Liv?" His brows knit. "Remy told me you agreed to a communication ban. That you willingly handed over devices as a sign of good faith."

It was a little more complicated than that, but... "Yeah, I did."

"But?" He eyes me, concern bleeding into his sickly features.

He's still extremely unwell. His posture lacks the usual professional confidence. His energy is at an all-time low.

"But nothing." I paste on a smile. He doesn't need the extra burden. "I wanted him to know there was no threat of me talking to anyone. So I gave him my phone and laptop."

"Good." He exhales with relief. "I wasn't sure what to think at first. Then he sent photos to prove you were okay and—"

"He sent photos? Of what?"

"You." He leans back in his chair and retrieves his cell from his pants pocket. "Here. I'll show you." He unlocks the phone screen and slides the device across his desk. "We chat through an encrypted messenger app. It's the one on the home screen with a big E."

I'm reluctant to see what else Remy has been doing without my knowledge. But curiosity gets the better of me.

I snatch up the phone, navigate to the app, and then open the only chat available.

A photo of me drinking tea in my backyard is the last thing that was shared late yesterday afternoon. I'm in sweats, my heavy black parka draped over my shoulders, the steam billowing from my mug as I take the much needed outside time to get away from Remy.

I scroll to the image before that—I'm in the kitchen unpacking the dishwasher.

And the next—I'm asleep in bed, the dim light from the hall casting a slight glow over my relaxed features.

It's a surprisingly favorable photo. Hair curtains one side of my face, my other cheek nestled into the pillow. And the front on view... He must've crouched down to my level to take the image head-on.

"I hope you don't mind," Dad murmurs. "I asked him to keep sending them just to make sure."

I can see that. Can read the conversation that accompanies the images.

CARLO

Is she still okay?

REMY

She's holding up well. Just finished eating.

Another image is shared, this one of me clearing the dinner table. I keep scrolling all the way back to the disastrous Saturday night.

He'd catered for me? Even when he suspected I'd deliberately tried to set him up in front of the cops?

"Liv, you told me that the worry you had for your mother during her cancer battle was a privilege."

I swallow over the ache in my throat and slide the phone back to him. "It was."

"Well, living a life on the right side of the law is also a privilege. One Remy wasn't afforded." He blinks pity-filled eyes at me. "His parents weren't kind to him, *fragolina*."

I swallow again. Swallow so hard it hurts. "What did they do?"

"I've spent six months learning what I can only assume is a fraction of the atrocities." He gives a sad smile. "But there's no time for that now. You need to prepare Alexandra. Just know, not everyone is afforded the benefit of morality."

But we were. We could've still been.

"I understand." I nod. "But Dad, about Wesley…"

"You don't need to worry about him." He waves me away. "Yes, he's here to keep an eye on things, but it's mainly to ease my workload in case I fail to keep up after future treatments. He's going to take over out-of-hours calls and pick up the slack when I fall short. Which will not only bring me some appreciated relief but also add a measure of freedom for the arrangements we have after-hours."

Scratch arrangements. Rephrase to criminal activity.

"It's going to be okay, Liv."

I keep nodding. Keep playing along. For now. "And these treatments, when are we going to discuss those in greater detail?"

"When the time is right."

I'm leveled with my third faux charming smile of the day, and this one scares me the most.

"Let's get over one hurdle before we take on the next."

OLIVIA

The next eight hours pass with a packed schedule that doesn't allow room for Allison or Ivy to grill me over being late and looking like a swamp monster.

They leave with cautious goodbyes as if waiting for me to explain myself, but I don't engage in anything other than a quick farewell and a half-hearted finger wave.

I escort Dad upstairs, making sure he's settled and has a fridge full of food. I don't pester him about the cancer. It's clear he's exhausted, and I can barely keep my eyes open so I kiss his cheek, tell him how much I love him, and catch an Uber home to a quiet house that still lingers with the woodsy scent of Remy.

Alexandra's service concluded without a hitch. The news coverage was respectful. The Pelosi Funeral Home was portrayed in an exceptionally professional and compassionate manner. So much so that I'm sure we'll see an increase in business over the coming months.

That thought alone should be enough to deplete what's left of my drained energy. But as soon as I enter my living room and catch sight of the devices I'd previously given Remy now sitting on my dining table, a resurgence of energy courses through me.

I don't care that the electronics supposedly have tracking software, or how my searches will be monitored. I grab my laptop, slump down on my sofa, and start an online search on Remy Costa.

Page upon page of results fill the screen, most dated prior to last year.

Playboy Fashion Heirs Release New Clothing Line
Style, Status, and Success: The Untold Story of a Fashion Prodigy

Tragedy Strikes as Alleya Warehouse Engulfed in Blaze: Remy Costa Speaks in Wake of Fire

The headlines don't track with the man I know.

Fashion heir? Prodigy? Playboy?

I dig deeper, adding keywords—*controversy, criminal, Baltimore.*

I find more recent articles: *Alleya Patriarch Found Dead*

Mass Exodus. Alleya Heirs Jump Ship

From Negligees to Night Clubs—Denver's Fashion Heirs Set Sights on Baltimore

I skim every write-up. Commit every image to memory. But whenever one of my questions is answered, ten more take its place.

I dive deep into the relatively recent and untimely death of Remy's father, Emmanuel. I learn about Lorenzo Cappelletti. His powerful connections. The investments worth millions. And still, it's not enough.

I read for hours, until my eyes burn and my head throbs. I begin to doze mid article, my head nodding, my laptop resting on my thighs, the living room lights still on. I drift into weightlessness. Soar. Then there he is, the infamous mafia man with tousled dark blond hair, stalking down a shadowed hall toward me in his impeccable suit, all calm and controlled.

My heart races as I backtrack into a heavy piece of furniture, the wickedly sinful man closing in on me, his hard thighs pressing into mine. I hold my breath, my focus trained on a dark gaze that makes my heart flutter. I don't understand his effect on me. I'm scared but excited. Terrified yet turned on. He leans closer. My mouth tingles. His scent envelopes me, his lips so tempting—

I startle awake, my pulse rampant, my breathing ragged.

I listen for noise. For movement. For Remy.

Why would he be here, idiot?

He's more likely to be out murdering the masses. Slaughtering civilians. Conquering my cremator.

Oh, shit. Could he be disposing of another body right now?

My breathing comes hard and fast, the witching hour paranoia gripping me by the throat. What if he's at work, leaving a trail of blood through the funeral home for someone to find? What if he makes another mistake and Hugo's no longer employed to take the fall?

I shove from the sofa, grab my car keys, coat, and phone, and rush from the house to my car.

He needs to be given more thorough instructions on when he can and can't use the retort. I have to outline how long it takes for the equipment to cool. To ensure he understands how to clean things properly so no trace of remains are left behind unlike the first time Hugo was suspected of using the equipment.

I'd call him if I had his number. But I don't. So instead, I drive toward work, stopping where Remy had yesterday, leaving half a block of space between me and the two-story building to make sure I don't unnecessarily wake my father by driving into the parking lot.

I focus on the chimney clinging to the side of the building. Squint at the very top.

The cremator is state-of-the-art, with the best afterburners to block any black smoke from entering the sky, but there's always a distortion of heated air as it enters the atmosphere.

I see no distortion now.

That could change though. Remy might show up later. He might have already been.

I stay in my freezing car for hours, my coat an unworthy opponent against the winter temperature while I curse this stupid arrangement and the heartbreaking circumstances that made it necessary. I shiver as I wait, my exhausted blinks slower than dripping molasses until the sun threatens to break past the horizon.

Only then do I give up and drive home, almost frozen solid, to get ready for work while battling a sleep deprivation headache from hell.

I arrive at the funeral home half an hour early so I can check on my dad, who proceeds to shoo me away from his apartment door with enough renewed energy to place my mind slightly at ease. He's regained his normal coloring. There's light in his eyes, too.

"Liv, stop worrying about me. I'm fine."

I stumble back down the outdoor stairs, my tired legs barely able to carry my weight, and sequester myself in the seclusion of my prep room, placing the do-not-disturb sign on the door.

Thankfully, Ivy and Allison heed the warning. They don't come to greet me when they arrive. There are no sassy quips, and there's no sexual innuendo about the new guy. More to the point, there's no grilling on why I pulled an eleventh-hour arrival yesterday looking like a bedraggled Komondor.

They know I don't often demand privacy unless I have a difficult decedent. Usually one with injuries that require meticulous concentration and long hours to finesse.

But I guess nobody told Wesley the drill, because midafternoon, a slight rap sounds at my door before it opens to showcase him standing on the other side in a black suit and polished leather shoes.

"Hey," he greets.

I shoot him a two-second glance from beneath my face shield, then return my attention to the deceased eighty-nine-year-old woman on the prep table before me. "I'm busy."

"I can see that. But we didn't get time to talk yesterday, and I wanted to make sure you know I'm here to help."

Help? No, he's here to spy. To do *whatever is necessary.*

"Are you helping me or *them*?" I mutter under my breath.

He falls quiet a moment. "I thought we were all on the same team."

Shit. We're supposed to be. I still have the raised flesh on my fingertips to prove it. I'm not playing my cards right.

"We are." I ignore the skitter of apprehension traveling down my spine and focus on smoothing out the sculpting clay filling the gash near Mrs. Clarke's temple after her life-ending fall down a flight of cement stairs. "I'm just tired. It's not easy trusting the process."

"That's understandable." He opens the door wider and leans against the doorjamb. "From what I'm told, your dad had a few teething problems with that, too."

"I'll have to take your word for it." I try not to be huffy. To bite my tongue. But it feels like the weight of the world is on my shoulders. My brain won't stop with the panicked thoughts. I've constantly got Dad running through my mind. His health secrets haunt me.

Then there's Remy, the man who helped and harassed me in equal measure. The same guy whose phantom scent still lingers in my lungs.

"If you ever need to talk, I'm here," Wesley offers.

"Sure." I keep smoothing out Mrs. Clarke's clay, hoping the whole ignore-him-and-he'll-go-away trick from prep school still works.

"No, honestly, I am. You guys seem like good people. If there's anything I can do to ease your mind or make this situation more tenable, let me know."

I pause, the thing I want most shoving to the forefront of my consciousness as I glance up at him. "Can I have his phone number?"

Wesley leans back to peer down the hall, then lowers his voice. "Remy's?"

I sure as hell have no interest in seeing or hearing from Lorenzo or Salvatore again, so, I reply, "Yeah. Remy's."

"I'm not sure I'm allowed to disclose that info, but I can pass on a message. What do you want me to tell him?"

I'm hit with another wave of apprehension, this one pummeling right into my chest. "Forget it."

I'm not supposed to have anything to do with the Grim Reaper— Lorenzo's orders. I can't risk rule-breaking so soon into this criminal agreement... at least not in such an obvious way.

I close my clay container and busy myself tidying up my work station.

"You sure there's nothing else?" Wesley pushes from the doorframe.

"Actually, there is one thing." I turn to face him, pulling off my latex gloves. "You can stay away from Ivy. She likes to flirt. Don't get any ideas."

He gives a subtle smirk, one Ivy would eat up like whipped cream on a chocolate sundae if given the chance. "I won't. In return, you should focus on making sleep a priority. I promise everything is under control."

There's something pointed about his dictate. As if he knows I spent half the night spying on the cremator.

"Yes, sir. I'd also appreciate if you paid more attention to the sign on my door. It's not there for decoration."

"Fair enough." He inclines his head and retreats. "But make sure you call out if you need anything." He closes the door with the softest, most respectful click.

I throw my gloves to the trash and clasp onto the edge of my prep table, leaning into the exhaustion for a few brief moments.

I need to get Remy's number. I won't sleep tonight without it. I probably won't sleep ever again unless I know more about his illegal activities whilst under my father's roof. And as horrible as it is to acknowledge, I can't trust my dad to tell me the truth.

"God, I hate this." I straighten and wash my hands, then pull on a new pair of gloves.

I don't get disturbed for the rest of the day. I'm not even approached when I creep into the break room for my lunch or the necessary double-strength afternoon coffees.

By the time I leave work, I'm a zombie. One who quickly rechecks my dad's fridge to make sure he's got enough food before being swatted out of his apartment. I drive home with the windows down in the hopes the winter air will keep me awake.

I buy dinner along the way, too focused on getting my hands back on my laptop to type in another online search about Remy to cook myself a proper meal. I eat the shrimp pad Thai from the takeout box as I scan the web, finding numerous photos of him at red-carpet fashion events where beautiful women cling to his arm, their besotted eyes fixated on his handsome face while he grins at the cameras.

How did he go from fashion to felonies? Mohair to murder?

I shower and contemplate going to bed, but instead drag my feet back to the sofa for more online stalking. Sleep claims me early enough, the brutal exhaustion throwing me into vivid dreams of warm, calloused hands sliding along the inside of my trembling legs. I'm clenching my thighs, whimpering for more when my head lulls forward, waking me abruptly.

I groan with the whiplash as my laptop teeters on the cushion then hits the floor, thudding on impact.

I close my eyes and scrub a hand down my face, but Remy's right there, staring back at me from every corner of my mind.

My heartbeat increases from its already quickened pace. The calloused fingers of unease claw at my stomach.

He could be at the funeral home. Could be creating another twenty-thousand-dollar paycheck for my father.

"Goddamnit." I shove to my feet and pace.

This panic isn't healthy. The constant fixation is going to produce an ulcer at best, and I don't want to contemplate the worst-case scenario. But I can't make the mindless churn stop.

A six-by-four prison cell isn't a place I aspire to live. Orange jumpsuits and being someone's bitch? Nope. No, thank you.

I can't leave my future in the hands of a man I barely know. A *criminal* I can't trust.

I stride for the kitchen counter, grab my keys, cell, and coat again, then return to my viewing point down the darkened street of the funeral home.

It becomes a vicious cycle—stalk the family business at night, pester my dad for health updates before work, ignore my friends during the day.

Does Remy know he has to check for pacemakers or radioactive implants in the people he kills? What happens if he blows up the retort and in the process blows his cover with the resulting explosion?

Or worse, his men could betray him. They could already be talking to the Feds without him knowing.

The paranoia builds. So do the bags under my eyes.

I work on autopilot while at the funeral home, the do-not-disturb sign now a permanent fixture on my door as I count down the hours until I can resume internet stalking.

I learn that Remy has been buying up local businesses like he's a teenage girl indulging in a shopping spree with Daddy's credit card. The most recent purchase was a popular nightclub he aptly renamed Smoke & Mirrors.

It isn't until Wednesday morning that Ivy crosses my path in the break room and gives me a lackluster smile coupled with a subdued greeting. Her low vibe gives me pause until I remember why I've endured days of radio silence.

"Hey." I grab my full coffee mug and walk for the hall. "Will this week never end? I'm so far behind schedule I can barely breathe."

The lie heats my cheeks, but I continue walking away from her in an effort to hide the fraudulence.

If anything I'm well ahead of schedule. Coming in a little earlier to check on Dad and withdraw into the mortuary before Ivy and Allison arrive has meant more time at the prep table.

"I bet." Her reply is solemn. "But you know where to find me when you're ready to talk."

I force myself to maintain my stride. She knows something's wrong. Of course she does. Nothing gets past Ivy.

"If only I had something great to talk about," I say over my shoulder. "Unfortunately there's nothing but work, work, work."

She doesn't call me on my bullshit.

Nobody does. All week.

Maybe Dad came up with a cover story to keep them at bay. Or they're distracted by the new suave employee. Either way, Friday arrives without me having to explain why I've been acting all kinds of dismissive. Problem is, sleep deprivation has me in a chokehold, my energy levels are nonexistent, and my cortisol is so messed up I'm on a constant anxiety spin cycle.

There's no maintaining the craziness.

I can't keep staking out the funeral home every night and acting like a hibernating bear all day. Falling asleep mid-embalm on Thursday was bad enough.

Then there's Dad, who has Monday rostered as another leave day, which I can only assume means more chemo. It makes perfect sense for me to take over his responsibilities to give him headspace to focus on recovery.

I'm the one Remy needs to liaise with.

I'm the paranoid perfectionist who can make sure we don't all end up with a relentless fear of dropping the soap in the shower.

I want to be on the inside. No, I *have* to be.

And if that means I have to steal my father's cell to get Remy's contact details, so be it.

It's not like he'd hand over the murderer's number if I asked when he won't even disclose his health status.

"Thankfully he hasn't changed his cell password in more than a decade," I murmur as I hose down my workstation. I just need to hope like hell I don't get caught because adding to my father's worries isn't an option.

"Are you talking to yourself?" Allison's voice carries from the hall.

I ignore it, ignore *her*, my friendship score card receiving a one-star rating for how deplorably I've acted this week.

I pray she ignores me too. There's only a few hours until the workday is over and then I can spend the entire weekend coming up with a foolproof plan to rewrite the train wreck of my life.

But the universe gives me the bird as Allison sneaks into my prep room and gently closes the door behind her.

"Hey." She levels me with a sad smile.

"Hey." I keep hosing, trying to pull off nonchalance that probably looks more like psychotic awkwardness. "Are you knocking off early?"

"No." Her eyes turn pleading. "I actually came to see if you're ready to discuss what's been going on."

I kill the water's spray and yank the hose so it retracts into its spool. "What do you mean?" I grab my antibacterial spray bottle and douse my workstation, not daring to look at her for more than a brief second.

"Liv." She sighs. "You know what I mean."

Fuck. I'm not equipped for this conversation, despite having had five days to prep for it.

I shake my head and scrub at a nonexistent mark on the stainless-steel slab. "I'm sorry, Al, but I'm completely clueless. I've been busy as hell this week."

"Don't give me that. Ivy and I know exactly what's going on, and we're both scared."

My hand pauses mid scrub, my pulse kicking into third gear.

She steps closer, lowering her voice. "We don't know what to do."

My skin breaks out in a wash of goose bumps.

They figured it out? *When?* More importantly, how am I going to hide their knowledge from Wesley so he doesn't relay their insight to Remy?

I swallow. Backtrack.

I meet her gaze, the color draining from my face at the look of apprehension that stares back at me. "Al..."

"*Please,*" she begs. "We thought we were doing the right thing. We only wanted to help."

I frown. Straighten.

"I swear it, Liv." Her eyes plead. "When Ivy suggested she handle last weekend's call-outs, I thought you'd appreciate it, despite your protests. I know better now. I should've listened to your instruction to divert the business line to your cell instead of going behind your back and transferring them to Ivy. Luckily, no calls came through, but still... It was the wrong thing to do."

I blink at her, the cogs of cerebral function taking forever to turn.

"It was a mistake." She steps closer. "And we're both truly sorry. We'll do whatever it takes to regain your trust and completely understand if we need to be given a formal reprimand. But please stop avoiding us. It's been bad enough with Carlo keeping his distance, but the thought of losing you as a friend is killing me."

They think my behavior is because of the whole on-call van thing?

I play it cool, bridging the space to my prep table to shoot it with another dose of antibacterial spray while I internally worship the universe for having my back after all. "We're not the type of business that can fly by the seat of our pants. There's insurance that needs to be in place, not to mention training and ethical protocols."

I should be consumed with guilt. Should be drowning in it. But the vibe coursing through my veins is euphoric relief.

"I know. And I should've known at the time, too." She throws her hands up at her sides. "Ivy and I just had one-track minds on trying to make things easier after the whole Hugo fiasco."

"It didn't make things easier." I keep scrubbing, hating myself for how I'm about to double-down and make this excuse seem legitimate. "I stayed here to work on Amisha and her baby until super-late Friday night. And when I attempted to leave at an ungodly hour, the only form of transportation I had was my bike."

Her jaw unhinges, her mouth gaping. "Oh, fuck."

I'm the biggest piece of shit. But still, *so unbelievably relieved.*

"Yeah." I nod. "I was stuck here. And calling an Uber to a funeral home at witching hour wasn't an option when the only drivers willing to do that type of pick-up are problematic men."

"So what did you do?"

"I slept on the break room sofa."

Her face falls, the weight of needless remorse staring back at me. "I'm so sorry."

I want to replicate the apology. To tell her *I'm* the one who needs forgiveness. For misleading. Misdirecting. Manipulating.

I never would've held the van debacle against her like this. I wouldn't have spared it a second thought if I didn't need to use it as an excuse to hide the criminal mess that's been compiling right under her nose.

I shrug. "It's okay."

"No, it's not. I messed up. Please tell me you'll forgive me."

"Of course I will. I'm just tired." I sprinkle some truth amongst the lies to soften my guilt. "I haven't been sleeping."

She cringes. "Yeah. I can kinda tell."

I huff a laugh.

"Do you want a hug?" She spreads her arms wide.

"Oh, hell no." I take a retreating step, the thought of comforting contact shooting my remorse skyward. "I'm fine. Honestly. It's just been one of those weeks."

"It must be contagious." She lowers her arms and cocks her hip against my prep table. "Ivy's had a tough break the last few days, too."

"Why?" The memory of her forlorn greeting Wednesday morning comes back to haunt me. "What happened?"

"I don't know." Allison scrunches her nose. "I caught her mid-breakdown in the catering kitchen a few days ago. She said it was family stuff but didn't elaborate. That's kinda why I'm here, breaking the do-not-disturb decree. I was hoping we could mend bridges for her sake, too. She needs you."

God, the guilt.

I'm such a horrible friend.

"I'm dragging her out tonight for booze and bad decisions." Allison bats her lashes. "Do you want in?"

I open my mouth, poised to relay my trademark emphatic refusal, but something niggles in the back of my mind, giving me pause.

Someone, to be more precise.

"Where are you headed?" I ask.

Allison's expression brightens. "I haven't picked a destination… but if you're on board, I'm happy to take suggestions."

I nod despite the alarm bells ringing in my sleep-deprived brain. Could this be what I need to get my life back on track? My opportunity to get Remy's number instead of stealing it from Dad's phone? To maybe even speak to Remy in person?

"I'd love to come," I lie. "As long as we can go to Smoke & Mirrors."

OLIVIA

I WANTED TO ARRIVE EARLY AND SCOPE MY SURROUNDINGS. BUT MAKING myself fit for visual consumption took ten times longer with the bags under my eyes now bigger than checked luggage for a three-month vacay.

Allison and Ivy are already waiting to get into the club, the line around the building packed with shivering women dressed in skimpy outfits as they cling to winter coats, my friends not immune to the scant dress code.

I scoot under the velvet rope to stand beside them, thankful I decided on my sleek black high-waisted skinny jeans, a bold red off-the-shoulder top, and my wool-lined leather jacket. With my hands shoved in my pockets, the only inch of space currently getting railed by the chill is between the top of my ankle boots and the hem of my pants.

"I'm so glad you showed." Allison engulfs me in a hug. "I wasn't sure you would."

"Thanks for the vote of confidence." I give her a quick squeeze and meet Ivy's gaze over Allison's shoulder as I ram my fists back into my jacket pockets. "Hey."

"Hey." Her mouth curves in a somber smile.

"Allison said you've had a tough week. I hope you're okay."

She shrugs and glances away. "It's nothing I can't handle."

I don't doubt it. She's always been tough as nails. Don't ask me how or why. She's a closed book when it comes to her upbringing. But the one thing Ivy never disappoints with is how she's always entirely on brand. If it isn't fun, flirty, or downright flamboyant, it's rarely part of her narrative.

"Are you sure?"

She plasters on a fake grin. "Are you kidding? It's Friday night and you're in line with us to go into a club. This is the highlight of my life." She meets my gaze, her eyes glassy as she snuggles farther into her white winter coat. "But for the record, I'm not a huge fan of the location."

"Why?" Allison rubs her gloved hands together in a vain attempt for warmth. "We come here all the time."

"We *used to* come here all the time." Ivy leans back against the building, cocking the sole of her thigh-high boot on the brickwork. "*Before* it changed owners."

My stomach does a sweeping role. "What's wrong with the new ownership?"

"I've heard he's not just shady, he's practically the king of shadows."

"Are you feeling okay?" Allison reaches out, placing a gloved palm to Ivy's forehead. "I thought bad boys were your vibe."

Ivy swats Allison's hand away. "From what I'm told he's not merely a bad boy. He's the type that gets his kicks by—" She makes a slashing gesture across her throat. "Now call me vanilla, but I prefer not to get laid while the life is draining from my body."

Allison screws up her nose. "No need to be so graphic."

I replicate the screwed face gesture, but for a different reason. Mainly because all those months of picturing me and Remy sleeping together climb up from the depths of my subconscious to plaster themselves to my frontal lobe… and they're nowhere near the gory scene Ivy depicts.

"Are you sure it's not a rumor?" I hedge. "Surely this place would be shut down if anything illegal was happening."

And I would've read about it, given my current fixation with consuming online Remy Costa content.

"Who knows?" Ivy shuffles farther along the building as more people are allowed entry inside the club. "But it's always good to be aware in case you see something out of the ordinary."

I shrug. "I don't plan on staying long enough to witness any illegal shenanigans."

I just need to find Remy. Get his number. Potentially renegotiate terms. Then flee. And if he's not here, I'll hit up his employees until one of them gives me his digits.

Ivy smirks. "What if you meet the man of your dreams?"

My face falls. "Please tell me you haven't set me up with someone."

She chuckles.

"*Ivy*," I warn. "You can't be serious."

She holds up her palm in surrender. "I didn't, I swear. But if I see someone looking at you like a snack, I'm not going to discourage a taste test."

"I'm no snack. I'm more like a street taco—sometimes a handful and usually falling apart. But I assure you, I'm not interested."

"Not even if it's your mystery man from the dive bar?" Allison waggles her brows.

I hunch my shoulders, crowding in on myself like I'm struggling for warmth instead of the reality of struggling to curb my panic. "Nope. Not even. And I promise I'll resent anyone who puts complicated men on my bingo card for this year, so you've both been warned."

"Understood." Ivy's expression turns grave. "I know I've got a lot to make up for after last weekend."

Her arrow slices me right through the heart.

"We both do." Allison cringes. "With Carlo, too. We need to do some sort of grand gesture to get him to soften the cold shoulder he's been giving us all week."

"That's not what he's been doing." The words vomit from my mouth without foresight.

"He definitely has." Ivy scoots farther along the building as Allison and I follow. "It gutted me when he handed over the call-out duties to Wesley but…" She shrugs. "I get it."

No she doesn't. *God*, how she doesn't.

"Wesley's a safer option, that's all. And Dad wouldn't want you out at all hours when you're so valuable in the office." I turn away, focusing on the bouncers at the front of the line, hoping dismissive body language is enough to change the conversation.

"I could be valuable on-call, too. But again." She gives another shrug. "The whole Wesley thing is understandable. I'll teach Daddy Pelosi I'm the right person for the job."

I groan.

Allison chuckles.

"You never did explain why you were late Monday morning." Ivy pulls her ID from her purse. "Please tell me you got laid."

I keep my focus on the front of the line. "Yeah. I got laid."

"Are you serious?" they both gasp in unison.

I glance at them with a roll of my eyes. "No. Who would I have slept with? The guy who delivers my groceries?"

"Why not?" Allison asks. "At least he's got a job, right?"

I feign a glower.

She snickers. "Okay. Fine. It was definitely an unlikely event, but just as plausible as you turning up late. Until Monday, you'd never done that either."

"And for it to have been on such an important day." Ivy's tone turns serious. "You knew camera crews would be there and still, you showed up looking like you'd just escaped a stylist session with an aggressive flock of seagulls."

My skin breaks out in goose bumps, their scrutiny making me unsettled.

"Everything has been so weird lately." Ivy sighs. "First the whole Hugo thing. Then Wesley shows up without notice to save the day. And then there's that black bump on Carlo's forehead that he so casually tried to hide."

"He told me he did it at the gym," Allison says with nonchalance. "He got up too quickly or something…"

"Since when has he ever gone to the gym?" Ivy raises her brows. "Believe me, I'd remember if he'd told me because I would've flashed my credit card to get a membership wherever that man went to pump iron."

I should gag theatrically. Playfully warn her to stop.

That's what I would've done last week before my simple life blew up in my face.

"I've got a feeling something else is going on." Ivy splays her left hand, using the corner of her ID to casually clean under one of her perfectly manicured nails. "My spidey senses are tingling."

Her spidey senses need to dial it down a notch.

"Don't you agree, Liv?" She cleans under another nail. "I'm thinking it has something to do with Hugo and the retort because—"

"Dad has cancer," I blurt.

Their eyes turn to me as I struggle to strategize.

It's not like I could let her obsess over the retort. Ivy's a smart woman. An intuitive one. Too many carefully pondered questions could get her killed.

"Cancer?" Allison whispers.

Their shocked gazes track me as I shuffle toward the club entrance, our place now third in the queue. "Yeah. The big C."

"I don't believe it." Ivy shakes her head. "When did you find out?"

"*I* found out last weekend." I hate how I've broken my father's trust but can't help feeling grateful for the diversion it's provided. "*He* received the news more than six months ago."

Allison balks. "He kept it from you?"

"Yep." I pop the P, hoping to keep the morbid topic as lighthearted as possible.

"So the dizzy spell after exercising…" Ivy's question trails.

"Had nothing to do with exercise and everything to do with the chemo treatment he had on Friday." I pull my ID from my phone case. "He was actually under medical supervision when he took the fall."

"I *knew* it." Ivy turns to Allison. "I told you he was hiding something."

"But why wouldn't he tell you?" Allison asks me.

"Because of what we went through with Mom. He doesn't want me knowing the ins and outs of his diagnosis."

"*Doesn't* want you to?" she repeats. "As in, current tense? Like he still doesn't want you to know?"

"Exactly. He's made it pretty clear I'm going to be kept at arm's length where his health issues are concerned. I only found out when the hospital called me about his admission. And if he figures out I told you both—"

"He won't," Ivy talks over me. "Will he, Al?"

"Of course not. My lips are sealed. I just…" Allison's brow furrows. "God, I feel so sick for you." She steps closer, spreading her arms for another hug.

"Please don't." I retreat into the velvet rope. "I'm a top-notch shit show on steroids underneath all this makeup. If I get emotional in public right now, I'll make the seagull stylists look like seasoned professionals."

Her arms fall to her sides. "I'm so sorry, Liv. If you ever need anything—"

"Anything at all," Ivy finishes for her. "Don't even ask. Just blink in our direction, and we'll take care of it. Okay?"

"Yeah," Allison agrees. "Speech is overrated. Just signal and we're on it. No questions asked."

I give an awkward chuckle as I blink back the unwanted burn from my eyes. "Thank you."

Allison clenches her hands and scrunches up her face. "What I wouldn't give to squish you right now."

"Don't you dare. I love you too much to blubber all over your pretty coat." I keep chuckling. Keep blinking back the threat of tears. "I bet you're both glad you invited me out though. My ability to set the mood is top tier."

"Pfft." Ivy waves me away. "We'd rather be with you on a bad day than anyone else on their best. You're our girl."

Their girl who lies. Schemes. Manipulates.

"What about your bad week?" I ask. "Are you sure you don't want to talk about it?"

"Absolutely." She steps closer, leaning in like she's about to drop a conspiracy theory. "What I would love to talk about, though, is the fresh batch of man candy now working under our roof. Isn't Wesley just the finest masculine specimen you've ever seen? And that jawline." She clasps at her chest. "I'd let that man crack me in half."

Allison snorts. "You're always on brand, Ive."

"Of course I am. What else are men good for?"

A barely legal guy encroaches behind us. "I'm happy to show you all the things back at my place."

"Aww." Ivy looks at him with puppy-dog eyes. "Aren't you just the sweetest for proving my point."

"There's no shame in a player's game, sweetheart." He turns to his posse of male friends with a smirk. "I'd be happy to crack you in half."

Someone clears their throat in front of us.

"*Next*," a deep voice grumbles.

We ignore the swarming testosterone behind us and step forward.

Two bouncers wait before the doors of Smoke & Mirrors. One is stereotypical—big, bulky, bald. The other is young. *Too* young, with shaggy blond hair and a baby face sprinkled with freckles. I'd bet my sanity that he's still in school—not that my failing mental health holds much merit these days. It seems odd, though, that Remy would employ a kid too young to work the club scene.

"Hello, gentlemen." Ivy saunters toward them, gaining a hungry stare from both man and child as she hands her ID to Mr. Big and Bulky.

"Ma'am." The big guy inclines his head and inspects her ID with practiced scrutiny, his expression remaining neutral before he indicates for her to step in front of his podium, directly in line with the club facial scanner.

Allison goes through the same procedure with the kid, sans flirtation, while I hang back, my nervousness building.

"Next." Big and Bulky looks at me, holding his hand out for my ID while Ivy climbs the few stairs to the club entry.

I freeze in place as Allison follows her onto the steps.

"Ma'am?" the guy asks, the younger male watching with curiosity.

"Sorry." I clear my throat. "Go ahead without me." I meet Ivy's gaze and wave my ID in the air toward the front doors of the club. "I'll be right behind you."

She frowns. Allison follows suit.

"*Please*." I clasp my hands in prayer. "I'm dying for a drink, and you both know how much I hate to line up. The thought of a packed bar, teeming with drunken extroverts, is enough to make me want to turn tail already."

"You *are not* going home." Ivy points a perfectly manicured finger at me.

"Then please go inside and get me something to bolster my confidence." I bat my lashes. "Pretty please."

"Fine." Allison rolls her eyes. "But I'm going to make it a double."

The bouncer clears his throat, impatiently waiting for me to hand over my ID.

"Given my upcoming level of discomfort, a double would be perfect." I wait until they swing around to the open doors to the club vestibule then continue inside before handing over my driver's license.

"It's not that crowded in there." The bouncer scans my ID and gets me to stand in front of the high-tech camera. "And the extroverts are usually too busy dry-humping on the dance floor to disturb the quiet ones."

"That makes sense." I force a chuckle. "But that wasn't really my concern." I smile sweetly. Well, I try at least. Fake expressions aren't my forte. "I actually wanted to speak to you… to ask if Remy's working tonight."

Big and Bulky's brow furrows as he focuses on his computer screen. "Why's a girl like you asking about a man like him?"

A girl like me? Do I seriously have 'virgin' tattooed on my forehead?

I give another awkward chuckle at the low-key insult. "We know each other, and I really need to speak to him."

"I'm sure if you know him well enough you already have his number. Give him a call or send a text. He'll message back if he's interested."

The kid discreetly pulls a cell from his bomber jacket and holds the screen at a weird angle. *Is he taking photos of me?*

"I lost his number." I shrug. "Is there anything I can tell you to prove I know him? I drove his Bentley on the weekend. He took me to his uncle's penthouse in the city. Salvatore even came to my house."

The bouncer sighs and waves forward the group of guys behind me. "Sweetheart, you're not dropping personal information about him that isn't already common knowledge. So unless you take the hint and drop the psycho stalker vibes, I'm going to have to ban you from the club."

I'm the psycho?

I swallow down my agitation and take the ID he hands me as the sleazy guys trample over my personal space in their race to see who can offer up their license first. "Will you at least tell him I'm here?"

Big and Burly continues with his job. Scanning the IDs. Instructing on the facial recognition process.

"Please," I beg. "It's important."

"Yeah, whatever. What's your name again?"

Shit.

Is it possible these men also answer to Lorenzo? Could Salvatore find out I'm disobeying him? I'm sure I could talk my way out of getting in trouble for being here and running into Remy by accident. But specifically asking for him?

"Umm… tell him it's Pyro."

Big bouncer guy shoots a look of mirth at the young guy, who's too busy typing into his cell to notice.

"Okay, *Pyro*. If I see the boss I'll tell him you're looking for him."

"Thank you." I'm nudged toward the club entrance by more of the encroaching assholes. "I really appreciate it."

Neither bouncer acknowledges me. They don't even look in my direction.

I walk into the enclosed entry, the thudding beat of music pounding harder as I continue into the hall, check my coat, and forge past the automatic doors into the darkened, sprawling interior. It's a kinetic playground of gyrating bodies on the dance floor in the middle of the room, with polished marble bars gleaming from either side of the building, a small crowd of people lined in wait as mixologists work their magic.

I stand on the tips of my slowly thawing toes and spy Ivy and Allison waiting to be served at the closest bar. I approach, waving until I gain Ivy's attention.

"*I'm going to take a look around,*" I mouth, twirling a finger rear my head in a circular motion.

She nods and holds up her phone in a gesture I assume means to keep my cell close in case I can't find her again.

I give two thumbs up, then revert back to mission mode.

I skirt the dance floor, the air around me filled with a blend of laughter, heavy bass, and impending drunken mistakes.

VIP sections line the perimeter of the room, shielded with draped deep purple curtains to offer secrecy for God knows what that happens behind them. Waitresses flitter around offering table service, the trays they carry ladled with glistening alcohol bottles.

I approach a beautiful blonde woman in a scantily clad club uniform and force myself to pretend I'm the most sociable person on the planet as I blink kind eyes at her. "*Excuse me,*" I yell over the music.

She pauses, beaming an I-work-for-tips smile.

"Is Remy working tonight?"

The warmth in her expression falters. "I don't know. You should ask one of the guys." She strides away, not forthcoming with what guys she's referring to.

I try another woman, and another, both giving equally dismissive responses before I resign myself to the daunting prospect of asking another male for help.

If I don't get Remy's number I'm going to be stuck on this neurotic, spying spin cycle until the sleep deprivation kills me.

I drag in a deep breath and stand taller to do another visual scan of the club. It's a mass of sensory overload. Multicolored lights dance across the walls, casting everyone in an ever-changing glow. A DJ stands on a raised platform in front of the moshing crowd, commanding his dancers with one hand tweaking his equipment while the other punches the air to the beat.

There are two alcoves along the back wall—darkened, shadowy spaces that each house a stone-faced, broody man who visually scours club-goers.

Bouncers.

They must be the men the waitress was referring to.

Dread churns in my gut.

If I were Ivy I'd already be all up in that man's daydreams, schmoozing my way through a conversation that would not only get Remy's cell number but also the bouncer's, along with his address and probably his social security number.

I focus on the one closest to me who has a faux-hawk, his muscled arms crossed over his chest as he leans against the right side of his brick enclosure.

I approach, hiding my nervousness behind a raised chin and a flirty smile.

I'm a few feet and closing in when the guy drags his attention from the dance floor and captures me in his sights.

He's a towering figure up close. Broad shoulders. A stern face that's softened only by the hint of curiosity in his eyes. He rakes his gaze over my body, his lips kicking slightly as he makes his way back up to my face.

"Hey, big guy." I fight a cringe. Holy hell, I'm awkward. "Have you seen Remy tonight?"

His chest jostles as if with a huffed laugh, but I can't hear it over the music.

"Who's asking, bright eyes?" He pushes off the wall of his alcove and inches closer.

"I'm a friend." I rake my teeth over my bottom lip and pray it looks teasing, not traumatizing.

He gives me another once-over. "You seem quite the friend. But not at all his usual type."

A thud of discomfort forms beneath my sternum. I'm not jealous of Remy's conquests. I'm *not*. I just don't like being referenced in the same sentence as them.

"I haven't seen him though." He shrugs. "He doesn't usually make an appearance."

My face falls, my positivity plummeting along with it. "Not at all?"

"He's more of an afternoon guy." He raises his voice to combat the new tech song with a heavier beat. "He prefers to punch numbers and direct staff when it's quiet. We run this place by ourselves most nights."

Shit. Fuck. *No.*

I need to talk to him.

I *need* sleep.

"Don't worry. He might show." The bouncer enters my personal space. He's so close I almost drown in his potent aftershave. "Want me to keep an eye out for you?" He places a hand on my hip.

I freeze.

What would Ivy do?

"That would be great." I swallow over my discomfort and tap a lone finger against his chest, dragging it over his pec a little as I struggle to hold his gaze. "I'll come back and check in later."

He smirks. "Don't wait too long."

I backtrack, his touch falling from my hip as I fight a shudder. "I won't."

I turn on my heels and flee, heaving a relieved sigh.

This is ridiculous. All I need is a phone number. One measly number. Why is that so hard to obtain?

I make my way back toward the bar, finding Ivy and Allison standing close by, a gaggle of sex-starved men circling Ivy like she's a meaty carcass they're salivating to devour.

I'd roll my eyes if I didn't get it. But she's stunning. Long sleek hair. Longer legs. Warm skin. Breasts worthy of a centerfold.

She gets attention for a reason, then that attention remains once the men gain the slightest insight to her personality.

"Thanks for the drinks, guys." She hands me a highball glass of clear, bubbled liquid. "*Gin and soda,*" she mouths.

"Thank you." I grasp the offering and take a gulp. The potency hits the back of my throat with a burn, and I splutter through a heavy swallow. "*Holy shit.* That's strong."

Allison laughs and leans close. "I told you it'd be a double. But I think the guys paid for top-shelf."

"Well I hope they're not expecting me to repay them with sexual favors because I'll do a lot of things for alcohol in a nightmare situation, but taking a guy home isn't one of them." I raise my glass in thanks and give a split-second glance of appreciation around the men.

They don't even notice. The four guys are too busy trying to charm Ivy.

"Fortunately for us, they only have eyes for her." Allison sips from her tumbler and peers over the rim at the mating ritual. "She's a crowd favorite on the nightclub scene. Most men appreciate the opportunity just to talk to her."

I blink in surprise.

I knew she was popular. Even Helen Keller could tell Ivy's something special. But I didn't realize she had a following.

The men linger, laughing and drinking, attempting to include Allison and I in on their jokes as the music thunders its way into my bones.

I feel like an outsider. The disconnect between the carefree chatter and my gnawing thoughts seems like a chasm between us.

The guys hang around through numerous songs. Allison and Ivy chat and flirt. I add a comment here and there to make sure I'm not being rude while my main focus is a constant low-key scan of the club.

I find more bouncers in discreet hiding places. One on the far end of the nearby bar. Another at the entrance to the VIP section.

"Let's dance." Ivy grabs my waist and attempts to drag me toward the dance floor. "I need to shake myself out of this funk."

Dread floods my veins.

"Wait. No." I twist from her grip. "I need to use the ladies first. Can I meet you out there?"

"You *do not* need to use the bathroom after one drink." She steps close, grabs my jaw, and playfully squishes my cheeks. "But I love you, so I'll let it slide." She bops me on the nose with her pointer finger, then starts sauntering backward toward the moshing bodies. "You should get another drink while I'm gone."

I nod, but there's no way more alcohol is entering my system. The double mixed with nonexistent sleep and a diet of anxiety already has me blitzed.

I turn to Allison, surprised to now find her up close and personal with a pretty, petite redhead, the fingers of their free hands entangled.

"I'm, um, going to go for a walk." I point aimlessly over my shoulder.

"Okay." Allison nods, still caught in a game of lock-eye with the beautiful woman. "I'm not going anywhere."

I circle back toward the handsy bouncer, dumping my glass on a passing table.

I seek him out across the dance floor, finding his gaze already on me. "*Shit.*"

The nervousness returns. The awkwardness, too.

I muster a smile, hoping it appears sultry, and approach. "Any news on Remy?"

"Maybe." He grins. "What's it worth to you?"

If intimacy is his currency, he's about to find out I'm flat broke.

"I don't know." I lean closer so he can hear me over the music. "Would my complete and utter gratitude be enough?"

He laughs. "I was kinda hoping for something more."

"I'm sorry." I pout. "I don't have much more to offer."

"That's a shame." He retreats back into his alcove, his attention turning to the dance floor.

"Please." I sidestep into his line of sight. "It's important. I..." *Come on, Liv. Come up with something to convince him.* "I, um..." *Fuck, why is this so hard?* "I just found out I'm pregnant with his baby."

The guy's eyes snap back to mine, his narrowed stare holding a hint of distaste.

Shit. For a smart woman, I can be so fucking dumb under pressure.

"I'm not after his money." I hold up my hands in surrender. "I'm not even after any sort of commitment. I don't need anything. I swear. I only want to tell him what's going on."

The bouncer contemplates me, the sliver of resentment slowly fading from his features. He gives me another once-over, his expression unreadable, the vibe temperamental.

"Fine." He shrugs. "I can take you to him."

My heart skitters around my chest. "Really?"

"Yes, really. He came in to do a liquor stock take. I'm not sure how long he'll stay."

"Thank you." I clasp my hands as if I'm a nun in prayer and glance over my shoulder, not seeing Ivy or Allison and hoping they don't see me either. "Thank you so much."

"Follow me."

He leads me away from the dance floor, behind a roped off area, past VIP booths, and through a staff-only door to an empty hall.

It's quieter back here. Marginally. But enough so I can finally hear myself think for the first time since stepping into the club.

Fluorescents beam down, the harsh light making me squint. We continue along the thoroughfare in silence until we reach an elevator at the end, the guy pressing the call button with the doors opening instantly.

"Ladies first." He indicates for me to step inside with a wave of his hand.

I hesitate, the hair on the back of my nape awakening.

I glance around for cameras. For surveillance.

There's a small round dome on the ceiling at the far end of the hall where we came in. Another inside the elevator. I slide a hand over my pants pocket, my cell giving me a renewed sense of safety.

"Are you sure Remy's still here?" I take a dubious step into the elevator.

"As far as I know." He follows and yanks at a fob attached to a retractable cord on his belt, scanning his security pass against the button panel.

My neck doesn't quit tingling as the doors close, but everything inside me has been off-kilter since last weekend. My nerves. Hormones. Sleep cycle. I've become super awkward. Majorly stressed. And impulsively paranoid. It's not the time to start listening to my body's messed up signals.

I lean against the back wall and brace to ascend, but the elevator goes down with a jolt.

I gasp as anxiety lodges itself in my throat. "Where are we going?"

He remains facing the button panel, his back to me. "All the liquor is kept downstairs."

I eye the security camera. Palm my phone. Question whether I should place a message in the group chat with Allison and Ivy to tell them where I am... but that would require an explanation of why I stepped into this shady situation and that isn't a favorable option unless I want more lives to be on the line.

In seconds the elevator comes to a stop and the doors open again, exposing a cement jungle.

The bouncer strolls out, then pauses to wait while I contemplate my existence. "You coming?"

I shouldn't. It's quiet down here apart from the muted thud of a far off base. But goddamnit, I need to speak to Remy.

"Look, lady. I've gotta get back to work. Do you want to see him or not?"

"Yeah. Okay." I nod and follow after him into an underground parking lot. SUVs and sedans sit amongst thick cement columns to my right. The closest spaces remain empty. There's no black Bentley in sight.

To the left is a chain-link-fenced enclosure. A storage area stacked with kegs three high and shelves with liquor bottles and cardboard boxes.

But it's still so quiet. Too quiet.

"Are you sure Remy's down here?" My voice betrays my skepticism as I slow my pace, gaining a few feet of space between me and the bouncer.

"That's what I said." He continues along the chain-link, jerking his head toward the storage area. "He's got an office in there behind all those boxes. There's a gate just around the corner."

I peer between the propped kegs, finding a path down the center of the enclosed area, either side banked with crates and liquor boxes.

Could there be an office behind all that liquid courage? Sure.

Would Remy—a stylish, rich, underworld murderer—choose to spend his time in there?

I guess it's away from the noise. Maybe there's some security reason too… but it still doesn't seem right.

"*Remy?*" I call out.

The bouncer shoots me a scowl over his shoulder. "Don't trust me?"

"Don't trust people in general," I hedge. Of course I don't trust him.

He chuckles and pauses. "Then why don't you go ahead and check it out for yourself. I'll wait here." He turns to me, his tall, bulking frame taking up the majority of the space between the chain-link and a silver hatchback to the right of the makeshift path.

The discomfort at the back of my neck skitters down my spine, raising every hair in its wake.

"*Remy?*" I call again, my voice echoing around the cement cave.

"He won't hear you." The bouncer jerks his chin in the direction we were heading. "Go on. The entrance is just up there."

Alcohol, sleep deprivation, and an unhealthy cortisol imbalance aren't enough to get me to maneuver around him. This was a mistake.

"I'll speak to him some other time." I backtrack with a smile, well aware I need the bouncer's security fob to be able to use the elevator. "I didn't mean to waste your time."

"You didn't, sweet cheeks." He smirks and lunges to grab my wrist. "We're just getting started."

OLIVIA

I FIGHT TO KEEP CALM. TO STAY IN CONTROL. BUT BEING EDGED BY ANXIETY all week makes it almost impossible.

"Please don't touch me." I twist my wrist to break his hold, only to have him grip tighter. "I'm sorry if you got the wrong impression, but—"

"Cut the crap." He closes in, and I'm forced to backtrack toward the fence to maintain the distance between us. "We both know you didn't follow me down here for my boss."

I twist my wrist harder. Tug my arm toward my chest. "I assure you I did."

"Because you're pregnant?" He scoffs and continues to prowl toward me. "Even if you are carrying his kid, he's not going to want to see you. The only good news is that I know you put out."

"He'll want to see me."

"Then you can go back to trying to find him after I'm done."

Panic siphons the alcohol from my system. I'm entirely sober, coherent, and terrified in the space of a few hammered heartbeats.

He releases my wrist, grabs my hips, and shoves me against the fence.

I gasp on impact, the hard, cold wire biting into my back. "*Stop.*" I push at his chest. "Let me go."

"Not until I'm finished, sweet cheeks." He leans in for a kiss.

I make a direct hit, slapping him across the face.

He flinches, leaning away slightly.

I take the opportunity to run, but I'm pulled back by my hair, searing pain lashing over my skull.

He shoves me against the chain-link again, pinning me with a forearm to the throat.

I scramble to gouge for his eyes. Attempt to knee him in the balls.

But he's too strong. Too big. The pressure on my throat becomes too much.

"Stop," I rasp, clawing at his forearm. "I can't breathe."

"Do you know how many women come sniffing around for the boss?" He sneers in my face. "All these pretty bitches after one guy, and do you want to know why?"

I shake my head. "It's not like that. I only want to speak to him."

"Money," he sneers in my face. "That's all women ever fucking want."

I claw harder. "Don't be stupid enough to think I won't go to the cops."

"Don't *you* be stupid enough to think the boss doesn't already have them in his pocket."

Shit. "You've done this before." I attempt to knee him again, but there's no space. No room to move. He's everywhere. All solid legs and meaty arms that make him impossible to move.

He snickers. "Just relax and let it happen."

I launch my mouth at his bicep, sinking my teeth into skin.

He roars, his arm loosening.

I shove him. Gain a breath of space to run.

Then his knuckles pound into my temple and my consciousness blackens for a second.

I sway, the pain howling through my brain, my vision coming back online in mottled colors.

My ears ring, the piercing tone drowning out my voice as I attempt to match the shrieking in my skull. I scream and scream and scream until a hand slaps over my mouth and I'm heaved against the fence.

He says something. Gets in my face with a threatening warning. But all I hear are bells.

I squeeze my eyes shut and slap. Claw. Pound.

It does nothing as a rough hand yanks at my waistband, viciously undoing my belt.

The noise grows. His words. The bells. My screams. Then rumbling, some kind of thunder, as if Mother Nature knows the severity of my situation.

They all mix into a tornado of havoc while he fumbles with his pants and I fight, fight, fight.

Then all of a sudden, he's gone.

There's no pressure against my chest. The cold air of the parking lot seeps into me as sharp, obscure shouts lash my ears.

I open my eyes to find the bouncer a few feet away, Remy in front of him, his mouth viciously moving as he holds my attacker by the throat of his collar.

"Remy." His name is whispered from my agonized throat, my voice not making sense.

I swallow and press at my ears, trying to re-right the sound.

"*Wha-wha, wha wha,*" Remy shouts in the guy's face. "*Wha wha wahwahwah.*" He releases him with a shove and storms in my direction, violent eyes turning soft as he stops before me.

"*Wha da de do do dou.*" He closes in exactly like the bouncer did, but there's no fear with his proximity—only the euphoric rush of relief. He takes off his suit jacket and drapes the silken warmth of the interior over my shoulders. Then his calloused palms cup my cheeks as he repeats the garbled words.

"I can't—" My throat burns as I speak. "I can't hear you."

I swallow again. Press my fingers to my ears.

When I pull them away the ringing lessens, a gentle hum taking its place.

"Ollie?" Remy's voice comes through in surround sound. "Are you okay? Did he—"

"No. He—" I shake my head, the movement threatening to unleash a migraine. I wince and gently prod at my temple. "He tried."

"But he hurt you." He gently tilts my head to the side, careful fingers providing the sweetest, most startling care. "He *hit* you?" One hand leaves my cheek to guide my arm away. "In the fucking head?"

I wince at the venom that chokes his tone, the pinched expression pulling at my battered flesh as I nod.

He releases me and swings around, stalking toward the bouncer who stumbles in retreat. Remy grabs him with a hasty yank by the shirtfront. Before I can gasp, his knuckles are pounding into my attacker's face. Once. Twice. Then Remy shoves him to the cement and reaches behind his back, retrieving a gun from his waistband to shove against the guy's forehead.

"*Remy, no.*" I rush for him on fumbling feet. "What are you doing?"

"Terminating his employment."

"*No.*" I tug his arm. "Don't."

"Listen to her." The bouncer cowers. "She followed me down here. She led me on."

He winds me with the lie, forcing all the air from my lungs.

How could he? How could this man attempt to rape me, then blame it on anything other than his own actions?

A car door opens nearby, and the sickening thought of another witness to my vulnerability has me snapping my gaze in the vehicle's direction. To Remy's Bentley parked in one of the empty spaces I passed at the height of my naivety, the hum I hear now recognized as the car's engine.

A woman climbs from the passenger seat.

A tall, blonde, beautiful woman with eyes as blue as the ocean.

"Remy…" She strides forward, her forehead wrinkled with concern, her long coat gaping to expose a tight black dress over an enviable body.

"Not now," he snarls at her. "Go upstairs."

"But—"

"I said, *not now.*" He snaps his attention to the woman. "Or so help me God, I'll—"

"Okay. I'm going," she soothes patiently. "Just keep your cool. This isn't about you." She meets my gaze with a wealth of sympathy. With kindness.

Inferiority washes over me.

Humiliation.

She gives me a sad smile, and in the frenzied aftermath of my attack, I find myself growing envious of her—her beauty, her composure, the connection she has with a man that confuses the life out of me.

She turns and walks toward the elevator. I'm about to yell out and tell her she'll need security access, my mind fixating on all the wrong things, when she diverts her path to a door marked *stairwell* and disappears inside.

The clang of the door closing echoes through the parking lot. The sound fades to leave nothing but the hum of the Bentley engine and the continued pounding of my pulse.

Remy stands there, looking down at the bouncer, his barrel still pressed to the guy's head. "Do you want the honors, Pyro?"

My breath clogs in my throat. "What I want is for you to put the gun down."

"Listen to her," my attacker begs. "Please, man. She—"

"He was about to rape you," Remy sneers. "Do you really want me to let him go so he can succeed with someone else?"

I don't know.

I can't think.

"I don't—" I push from the chain-link to stand on shaky feet. "I can't. I—"

I fumble with trembling hands to fix my pants, shame heating my cheeks at the sight of my lowered zipper and purple lace panties.

We don't cry.

We have to be strong.

Always.

I sniff back the threat of tears and clasp my belt.

"I can end him right now," Remy growls. "Just say the word."

"No," the bouncer pleads, blood oozing from a cut on his bottom lip. "It was a messed up mistake. I swear I'll never do it again. I don't know what I was thinking."

"Shut the fuck up." Remy's gun remains aimed to kill, but those eyes keep focus with mine. "Talk to me, Pyro. Tell me what you want done with him."

The bouncer scuffles backward on his hands and feet. "Please, boss. I swear, I barely touched her."

I don't notice my complete and utter exhaustion until I realize I'm too tired to even scoff. There's been one thing after another for an entire week. Death. Destruction. Lies. Complications. They have to stop.

"All I wanted was to talk to you." Fragility bleeds into my words. "That's all I came here for. And then I wind up down here, thinking he was taking me to see you and…"

Remy's jaw ticks. "Get in the car, Ollie."

"I can't. I came here with friends."

"So text them. Say you're not feeling well and had to bail. I'm taking you home."

Could I? *Should* I?

The thought of returning to the noisy club makes my head throb harder. And the prospect of facing Ivy and Allison after what I endured seems worse.

I'll break down. I'll finally let loose of family tradition and wither into a heap of pathetic sobs.

"Go on." He jerks his head toward the Bentley. "I'll join you in a minute."

"What will you do to him?"

He shrugs. "We're just going to chat."

With the barrel of his gun still firmly squared on the man's head, I'm not convinced.

"Remy," I whisper. "I don't—" *God*, I don't even know the guy's name. Don't know the first thing about him yet I followed him from a crowded place into a deserted parking lot, all because I wanted to negotiate with a murderer.

Ten out of ten for idiocy, Liv.

"Get in the car, Pyro." He breaks eye contact to stare at my attacker. "I've got this under control."

"Are you going to kill him?"

The bouncer whimpers.

"You've already made it clear that's not something you want to witness," Remy mutters.

I nod, numbly. Thankful, yet oddly hollow.

My attacker deserves something. Punishment. Revenge. Maybe a few broken fingers. But the thought of asking for that sits in a pool of rapidly building bile in the pit of my stomach.

I walk away, passing the cars I dawdled by on the way out of the elevator, back to the vacant spots where the Bentley idles at an odd angle between two parking spaces, as if Remy braked in a hurry.

His driver's door remains open—the one where the woman escaped from, too.

I take her place and pull the door shut behind me, my lungs filling with exquisite floral notes of jasmine.

I shove my trembling hands under my thighs to stop the chill from taking over, but also to stop myself from fidgeting as Remy pulls the bouncer to his feet and relays something I can only hear in partial snarls and biting tones.

I've made a huge mess into something bigger. Something more traumatic.

A lifetime's worth of therapy won't help to dig my way out of this.

I scoff.

Therapy isn't even an option with the list of illegal activities I'd need to lay bare.

Remy says something else to my attacker, then smirks, the expression sickeningly threatening. He returns his gun to the back of his waistband and stalks toward me, his temperamental composure seeming woven together with menacing danger and threatening volatility.

I hold my breath as he climbs into the car, the small space shrinking with his large frame, his presence taking up my entire world.

He turns on the ignition, shoves the car into reverse, then hits the gas hard enough to have me jolting forward as the vehicle lurches backward.

I cling to the sides of my seat as tires screech and the parking lot speed limit is ignored.

He's angry. His hostility clogs the air. Coats my skin.

I shudder with a violent shiver and finally the car slows, pulling onto the road outside in a somewhat normal pace.

"You're in shock." Remy reaches for the console and turns up the heat. "Let me know if it gets too hot in here."

I nod, and nod, and nod, the jerky movement on autopilot as the city street stretches in front of me. People continue to line up alongside the club, energetic, cheerful, and oblivious to my attack.

I've never felt more alone.

Remy takes a turn down a bustling road. Then another. Finally, he pulls to a stop behind traffic banked at a red light.

"You heard what Lorenzo said." His eyes turn to mine. "Why would you risk going to my club?"

"I needed to speak to you."

"Then speak," he demands. "What was so important that you'd follow a stranger into an isolated parking lot?"

"In all fairness, I didn't know he was taking me to the parking lot. He told me he was taking me to see you."

"And with everything you've learned about me, you still took in that information, digested it, and thought, yeah, this shady-as-fuck piece of shit sounds legit?"

Warmth blasts my cheeks, and it's not just from the heating system.

Sympathy no longer lingers in his expression. What stares back at me is something else. Something that feels a lot like wrath.

"I guess I was desperate."

His gaze snaps to the idle cars in front of us. "Why?"

The reasons seem pathetic now.

Because I'm tired.

Because I can't sleep.

"I need some amendments to the agreement," I whisper. "My father might be capable of letting you run unchecked through our business, but I don't know how. I need to be informed of what you're doing and when you're doing it so I can make sure there are no loose ends."

"There *are* no loose ends."

"But there was. Twice. Hugo had to take the fall both times."

His jaw ticks. Then the traffic light turns green and he takes off again, this time not as erratically.

"Look, I understand you don't want a witness to your handiwork, but I haven't slept for a week and—"

"I'm well aware of your nocturnal habits," he growls.

I raise my chin, defensive and unsure how I feel about the confirmation that someone has been spying on me. "Why are you angry at me?"

He slams on the brakes, the Bentley screeching to a stop in the middle of a suburban street. "Because you could've fucking died." He glares wild eyes at me. "Do you not understand that? Do you think he was going to let you walk away after he was done violently fucking you?"

I shrink at the image.

"If I would've shown up two minutes later or not checked my phone, how I found you would've been entirely different. You get that, right? You get that he was about to pull his dick from his pants and—"

"*I get it.*" I raise my voice yet shrink farther into myself.

I've never felt more shame.

More remorse.

Twice, Remy has saved me. Twice, I've owed him my life.

Finally, he sighs. "You heard my uncle, Ollie. We're not supposed to have anything to do with each other." He returns to driving, his temper mellowing if his smooth corners and slowed acceleration are anything to go by. "You need to figure out a way through this."

"You don't think I've tried?" I beg. "It's been a week, and I'm exhausted. The only thing I've achieved is heightened paranoia and potential psychosis."

"Don't forget the hours of intensive online research. You realize half of what you read online isn't real, right?"

"That's funny." I turn toward him, the passing streetlights casting his face in bursts of shadowed light. "Because most of what I found has been about a fashion heir whose favorite pastime is attending expensive publicity events. Yet here I sit before a mafia criminal who lives to increase his serial killer stats."

His nostrils flare, but he doesn't look at me.

He turns suburban corner after suburban corner before pulling into my drive and cutting the engine. The internal vehicle lights gradually illuminate the Bentley's interior as he stares at my tiny house, the dark of night seeming a mile away from our world inside his car.

"Remy, I'm destructively inquisitive. A perfectionist. I can be neurotic and overbearing and sickeningly hyper-focused. It's one of the reasons why I took the mortuary path instead of the funeral director role. I can't be the way I am with grieving people. I can't micromanage the way they mourn. But I can recreate someone's skull so it looks exactly the same way it did before they fell twenty feet down a mountain. Or reconstruct someone's facial features after massive trauma even though other morticians say it's impossible."

He keeps staring at the house. Keeps his mouth shut.

"I've been asked to speak at conferences because I'm a leader in my field on how to maintain the integrity of my decedents without always relying on embalming," I add.

Still, he doesn't speak.

"I'm an asset, Remy. I can help cover your tracks."

He doesn't quit the silence.

I sigh. "Please say something."

He swallows, his throat working over his Adam's apple in a way that shouldn't make me transfixed. "Wes said you've looked like hell all week. I assumed it was a trauma response from the weekend's events. I thought it would wear off."

"My problem is the future, not the past. Everything I hold dear is in the hands of people who consider my life expendable. Can't you understand how hard that is to ignore?"

The muscles in his jaw flicker as if he's actually taking in what I've said. Like he may even care.

Hope heats beneath my sternum, bringing energy to my limbs.

"What are you asking for exactly?" Dark eyes turn to mine.

"I don't know what I *can* ask for. But I guess what I want is a little control—*no*. Ignore that. It's not what I mean. I think the word that fits best is transparency. I want to know when you're using the retort. To be aware so I can double-check you didn't miss something."

His chin hitches.

The silence stretches, becoming uncomfortable as he stares at me. Then finally, he mutters, "I'll text you."

I blink in confusion.

"When I use the retort." He heaves a weary breath. "I'll send a random message. One that won't incriminate or allude to our agreement. Will that help you sleep?"

Yes. No… maybe.

A text would only give me the barest of details.

I'd be left to obsess over what type of killing it was. If I'd need to keep an eye out for blood. Bile. Body parts.

But it's enough for now.

I nod. "I'd appreciate it."

"Just be aware that if you—"

"I know." I hold up my hands in surrender. "You have the cops on your payroll and my death already planned."

"It's not planned, Ollie. The last thing I want to do is kill you."

But I will remains unspoken.

I keep nodding despite the thundering headache. "I understand." I grab the door handle before he has time to change his mind, only to have curiosity grab me by the throat. "One last thing…"

"Hmm?" He grunts.

"How did you know I was in trouble?"

He cringes, shame or maybe regret seeming to pinch his features. "I didn't. I was only told you were at my club."

"Who told you?"

"Someone working the door messaged to say you were asking about me."

"The kid." It's not a question. I'm certain now.

"Yeah. The little shit lives with me." A hint of pride gleams in his eyes before he turns to stare back out the windshield, making it obvious the *little shit* reference was made with affection. "He sent a photo. Then proceeded to tell me how you were out of my league and that he planned to set you up with the wealthiest bachelor in the club."

I sit straighter, my heart fluttering for unknown reasons. "But that's not why you showed up…" I hedge so damn hard and for such stupid reasons that I hate myself.

"You bet it is." He scowls. "The wealthiest bachelor tonight was Salvatore. I didn't want you two anywhere near each other."

Oh, shit.

"Yeah." He nods as if reading my mind. "It was another stupid call, Ollie. You need to stop making those."

The weight of regret crushes me.

I hate this—being wrong, feeling inadequate—even though that inadequacy revolves around my knowledge of criminal activity. I just hate everything about this entire situation… except maybe the man who has thrust me into it.

I don't know what it is about Remy. Why I hold his good deeds at the forefront of my mind and push the horror to the back. How his kind gestures hold so much more weight than his terror.

I struggle to see him as a killer even though I've come face-to-face with his handiwork. I can't align the criminal with the man who has run rings around my head from the first night we met.

It's all just senseless stupidity.

"I appreciate you agreeing to text me." I tug at the door handle. "And thank you for saving me again." I make to push from the Bentley.

He grabs my wrist, the jolt of contact threatening to shake his jacket from my shoulders. "We're not done."

I fall back into place to stare down at where he holds me, the rings on his fingers glinting against the car's soft interior light.

"Are you okay?" he asks.

My insides wage another war, fighting against the memories of what just happened and the idiotic lack of revulsion I feel toward his concern.

"Yes." My pulse thuds a heavier beat.

His patiently scrutinizing gaze folds me like a pretzel. So intense. So genuine.

I don't want to feel anything other than loathing for him. But I do.

I shouldn't welcome the contact. Shouldn't crave his care.

"I don't want you here alone." He keeps hold of me, the contact more than just a touch. "You should stay with a friend tonight."

I'm not going to tell him the only friends I have are currently back at his club, probably worrying about my whereabouts if the short, sharp vibrations from my cell are any indication.

Instead, I nod. "Maybe I will."

His fingers loosen, lingering on my arm like low-voltage live wires. "Want me to call them for you? Given the circumstances I should call your dad but—"

"No." I climb out of the car, the thought of my father hearing about this making my crummy dinner of stale crackers and sliced cheese threaten to evacuate my stomach. "I promise I'll be fine."

The slight hike of his brow is a glowing red flag that he doesn't believe the lie.

"You should return to the beautiful woman you were with." I strive for a distraction. "I'm sorry I ruined your date."

He stares at me, his expression unflinching. "You didn't."

Great. It's good to know my attack isn't going to sideline his sex life. It should be no surprise that he's confident the flawless woman is patiently waiting for him back in his den of criminality.

"Well, goodnight." I finger-wave like a loser. "Thanks for the memories."

His nostrils flare. "We're still not done." He reaches for his right hand and wiggles the ring from his index finger. "Do you have a chain?"

I frown. "A chain?"

He sighs. "Yeah. A necklace. Something discreet you can wear under your clothes."

"I'd have something inside. Why?"

He holds out the extravagant ring, the silver—or maybe white gold —centered with a band of glinting black. "I want you to wear this at all times."

I keep frowning, the confusion not dissipating as I take the thick weight from his palm. "I'm still caught up on why."

"As a form of protection. If someone attempts to hurt you again, show them this." He points to the words engraved around the inside of the band.

Property of Remy Costa.

"Are you implying *I'm* your property?" Incredulity attempts to enter the whirlpool of my emotions.

He rolls his eyes. "No, it states the *ring* is my property."

Why would he engrave his ring like that? Does he label all his property? Are his clothes tagged?

I itch to shuck his jacket to see if this is an entire wardrobe situation.

"Wearing it will give you protection. So as soon as you get inside, I want you to put it on a chain and wear it at all times."

"Protection from who?" I ask. "Your men?"

"That guy was a club employee, Ollie. Not one of my men. But yes, it will protect you from anyone in my employ, amongst others. Just wear it, okay? And if you get into trouble, use it."

"Is this like a *one ring* situation? Should I be worried about hobbits?"

His brow knits, this time in scathing confusion.

"Forget it." I shimmy his jacket from my shoulders.

"Keep it on," he warns.

"It's just a few steps to—"

"I said, keep it on. I don't want you freezing your ass off on top of everything else. I'll get it from you another day." He starts the ignition, finalizing the argument.

"Wait. I don't have your number."

"You'll get it soon enough." He grabs the steering wheel.

He doesn't say goodbye, but it's clear he's itching to leave. Probably in a hurry to get back to his non-virgin companion.

"Thanks again." I grab the door handle and push.

"You need to quit saying that," he mutters as the door clasps shut.

He reverses from my drive, then idles in the street, his body bathed in darkness as he stares at me through the passenger window, waiting for me to go inside like he's a concerned friend… Like some sort of hybrid murderous gentleman.

I give myself a mental shake and drag my ass up my front steps, his ring warm in my palm, my cell continuing its short, sharp vibrations in my pocket.

It's hard to leave him. To shut myself inside. All alone.

Reality hits as soon as I step foot into the entry. Flashbacks of the attack creep into my consciousness. The dull, lingering throb of injuries make themselves known.

I force myself to keep moving into the kitchen. To grab pain relief from my medicine cabinet. To wash the tablets down with water from the fridge to keep the nausea at bay.

I check my cell, opening up the group chat with Ivy and Allison.

IVY

Where is everyone?

Hello?

I'm thirsty. Who wants another drink?

Okay. Starting to freak. Are you guys still here?

ALLISON

I'm two feet behind you.

IVY

lmao… Liv?

They upload a selfie of both of them. Ivy's cleavage is smooshed together as she sticks her tongue out the side of her bright red lips, while Allison acts starstruck with a wide, gaping mouth and big bright eyes.

Guilt consumes me, devouring me from the inside out. I took them to a club with a bad reputation. I took them there knowing *I* was putting them in danger.

ALLISON

Paging Liv…

IVY

Seriously, where are you? I'm getting worried.

The last message came two minutes ago. They're going to kill me. I blink furiously through my blurring vision and start typing.

ME

Sorry. Had an embarrassing stomach bug issue in the bathroom. Had to leave in a hurry. Will chat tomorrow.

I don't wait for a reply.

I mute the conversation, already preempting their warranted responses of skepticism, and push to my feet.

The nausea grows with each blink. Each step. Each heartbeat.

We don't cry.

We have to be strong.

I focus on the good things. My *only* things—my job, my home, my dad. But the taint of the week's events only increases the churn in my gut.

Bile creeps up my throat.

The nausea wins.

I shove Remy's ring into my pocket and rush to the bathroom, drop to my hands and knees, then purge.

It's painful. My limited energy makes it a chore to even cling to the bowl. But at least I don't cry. I let the anguish leave my system in violent bouts of acidic regurgitation. The heaves come one after another until I'm left spent on the cold tile floor, missing my mother, anguished over my father, and unwillingly craving a dark-eyed, sinister man to take care of me.

You're losing your fucking mind.

I use the last of my strength to climb to my feet and brush my teeth, Remy's jacket still resting over my shoulders, his scent invading my lungs.

I'm not thinking about you anymore.

I repeat the promise like a chant inside my head.

I won't think of how protective you were.

Won't glorify how passionately you threatened to kill someone who hurt me.

I stumble to my bedroom, boots still on, and face-plant into the comforter, whimpering at the alternatives. If I don't distract myself with delusional thoughts of Remy, then I'll only relive the attack, stew on my stupid decisions, or catastrophize my father's cancer.

Glorifying the devil is the lesser of all those evils.

So that's what I do. I lie there, his ring in my pocket, his jacket warming my shoulders, and his image in my mind as I succumb to exhaustion. I fall into a cavernous sleep, falling, falling, falling, the descent heavy, consuming, and littered with all things Remy... only to be woken with a start what feels like seconds later from the sharp vibration of my cell in my hand.

I groan and drag my phone toward my face.

2:32 A.M. UNKNOWN NUMBER

You looked fucking beautiful tonight.

I snap upright, my brain protesting the harsh movement, my swollen temple throbbing.

It's Remy.

It has to be.

Vultures spawn in my belly, a million wings rapidly flapping to create a storm of conflicting emotion.

I shouldn't be thrilled by the compliment. I don't want to like him. Don't want to be attracted to—

Shit.

Icy dread punches me in the gut.

The message isn't a compliment.

It's the fucking fulfillment of our renegotiated terms—he just killed someone and plans to use the retort.

21

OLIVIA

I SCRAMBLE, RUNNING FOR THE DOOR ONLY TO SKITTER TO A HALT AND DASH back to my room.

I open my bedside drawer in the dark and feel around for the old chain I dropped inside years ago. I have no gun. No weapons. The only protection I have is the ring in my pocket that I hastily thread onto the thin silver necklace then clasp behind my neck.

Then I'm running for the door. Sprinting across my yard. Practically action-movie jumping into my car.

I make it to the funeral home in record time, my head fuzzy from sleep but my hectic pulse working to quickly rectify the lethargy.

I cut around to the rear of the two-story building to find Remy leaned against the back wall, his Bentley nosed up to the ten-foot high hedge, the overhead delivery room door open with his doppelgänger van parked inside.

My heart rate becomes erratic.

He's definitely killed someone.

He's taken those consoling hands, ended a life, and now stands unfazed against my childhood home in his black button-down and dress pants.

I park in the closest space, cut the engine, and climb out, his inscrutable gaze on me as I stride toward him, clutching the lapels of his jacket tight against my chest to fight the cold.

He takes in my attire with that indecipherable stare, lazily eying me up and down as grunts and groans carry from inside the building.

"Don't tell me you were still awake." He pushes from the brick wall, dragging the coat I'd left at the club out from behind his back.

I meet his gaze, struggling to understand him, fighting to make sense of my thoughts as I reach for my garment. "You killed someone?"

His eyes harden. "We tend not to verbalize things that could put us in prison."

I fill with dread, my mouth working over words I can't find. *Shit.* I'm so incredibly bad at this. Such a goddamn fucking liability. All I can do is nod in apology and hope he doesn't kill me. "Sorry."

"It's okay. You're still learning the ropes."

His words contradict the tightness of his features. The misstep was definitely *not* okay. Yet again, he's protecting me.

I shuck his suit jacket and hand it back, my gratitude—for his clothing, his patience, his everything—sucking me up in a convoluted vortex. I reclaim my coat, pull it on, and pretend I don't notice when his attention catches on the newest addition to my jewelry collection, his focus pinned at the top of my cleavage where his ring gently dangles.

I pretend and pretend. But those short seconds of his scrutiny on my chest make my cheeks flush with a rush of warmth. When his eyes finally raise to mine, I struggle against a wave of goose bumps taking over my body.

I swallow the discomfort and make to walk around him to enter the building.

"Hold up." He outstretches an arm, blocking my path. "Bearing witness wasn't in the agreement."

I pause, my lips stupidly moving without sound again. His proximity addles my thoughts. His entire existence does. "Wouldn't keeping me outside be more hazardous?" I lower my voice, trying to be cautious with the situation. "If I wait in my car I'm not part of the crime. I'm an outsider. Yet if I'm in the building, I'm an accomplice."

He stares down at me. Intense. Contemplative.

"I can handle it, Remy." I straighten my shoulders. "This is what I do."

"It'll change you," he warns.

I fight not to roll my eyes. Has he forgotten what I do for a living? What I've done for years?

"I assure you it won't." I continue forward, striding into his arm. Pushing past it.

I wait for him to stop me, almost aching for the possessive contact. But he makes no move to grab me so I keep moving, turning sideways to squeeze between the van and the brickwork.

He follows like a silent shadow into the brightly lit room, his presence a balm and a trigger all at once, until I reach the front of the vehicle and my feet root themselves to the floor.

The two threatening men from last weekend stand a few yards away, hunched over a male body on the floor, patting pockets and riffling through the victim's clothes.

"Is that…?" I heave a breath, all the blood in my face rushing to my feet. The decedent's face is mangled. Bruised. Bloodied. Misshapen. But I recognize the hair. The faux-hawk. "Did you…?"

Remy steps in front of me, blocking my view. "Yes."

I stare up at him in panic. "But you said…" I shake my head. "I thought…"

"I gave you the choice—to take his life or walk away. But he was never going to live after what he did."

My eyes search his, those calm, dark depths hiding such incredible violence as my breathing turns ragged.

"You deserved retribution. And he earned his punishment." He stares down at me, unapologetic in his callousness. "When I told you I'd protect you, I didn't just mean from my brother and Lorenzo. You're family now. Nobody touches you and gets away with it."

Oh, God.

I break eye contact and weave my arms around my middle, holding myself tight. "I don't want you killing people because of me."

"Then don't place yourself in situations that require my intervention."

I wince, the expression pulling at the tender skin of my temple while he continues to watch me. Scrutinize me. His gaze softens under mine, the slightest glimpse of empathy slipping through all his layers of malice.

I shouldn't see that in him. Shouldn't recognize his humanity.

But I do.

Oh, God, how I do.

He shoves his hands in his pockets, and I itch to do the same. To take the hands that cling so tightly around me and scrunch them out of view.

Shuffling and scuffed boots fill the silence, his men continuing to work behind him.

I picture them moving the body, lifting it without care as they grunt and mutter curses. The nauseating thud of what I assume to be the bouncer's skull against a hard surface makes my stomach roil.

I heave a breath and suck another back in.

This isn't right. None of it.

Not the murder and mayhem. Or the illegal arrangement.

And most of all, my attraction to an unrepentant murderer.

It's wrong. So mindlessly, reprehensibly wrong, and I don't know how to fix it.

"Come on." Remy's touch brushes my elbow. "It's time to go."

"No." I shake my head. "Give me a minute. I need to…" I keep trying to loosen the cement in my brain so I can strategize. "I want to…"

"What, Ollie?" He steps closer. "Tell me."

That nickname. His tone. It punctures me, stabbing me through the chest to slice me down the middle. "I need to figure out how I feel about this."

He stiffens, surprised somehow, but I don't care. I inch to the side to peer around his shoulder my nose scrunching at the heartless way his men carry the bouncer by his wrists and ankles.

"I…" I place a hand to the base of my throat, Remy's ring an unwanted reminder of his protection against the heel of my palm. "He…"

"Lacked remorse," Remy finishes for me. "He hurt you. Blamed you. And would've carried on doing the same thing to other innocent women. He doesn't deserve to hold space in your thoughts."

The internal doors squeak as the men carry the dead body into the hall, leaving me alone with the man who killed my attacker. Leaving me to drown in the heavy silence that's filled with emotions I don't want to feel.

"What did you do to him?" I ask, returning my gaze to Remy.

He considers me for long seconds. "I don't think knowing the details is—"

"What did you do?" I repeat with adamance.

His jaw ticks. "I hit him a couple times."

As far as under-exaggerations go, that one's a biggie.

He mutilated the man. Butchered.

"Is that how he died?" I swallow over the desert taking over my throat. "From being beaten?"

"I'm no coroner, but yeah, I'd conclude it was the rigorous blunt-force trauma."

Still there's no remorse. No hardship to the brutality. No anguished hindsight.

"But what if he had a family?" I whisper. "What if he had a wife? A child? A—"

"You think it would've been better for him to go home to a kid after what he attempted to do to you?" he grates. "Understand your value, Pyro."

He steps closer, consuming my personal space. "Nobody has the right to touch you." He reaches out, belying his own words by trailing his hands up my arms, my coat doing nothing to dull the heightened contact. "Your life is the most valuable thing you have. Nothing trumps it."

I peer up at him, falling victim to his intense gaze, becoming ensnared by the darkness.

"Do you think I'm wrong?" he asks. "Do you want to believe his time would've been better served in prison? Would you have preferred if your tax dollars funded a nonexistent rehabilitation? Because we both know he wouldn't have changed."

I know. I know. I know.

I cringe, hating his logic.

"I just…" A shiver runs down my back and I twitch, trying to get rid of the horrid sensation. "It's…" I glance away, still seeing Remy even though my attention is narrowed across the room. "It's like I said…" My voice becomes a pathetic plea. "I don't know how to feel."

"Yeah, you do. You just don't like that you feel relieved."

"I feel responsible," I bite back. "Because if I hadn't followed him into that elevator none of this would've happened."

"To you. It wouldn't have happened *to you*, Ollie. His victim would've been someone else."

My gaze snaps back to his, the truth in his words destroying me.

How can he be so callous and yet so logical? So vicious and then equally considerate?

I hate it. I still want to hate *him*.

But I don't.

There's no animosity at all.

Not even a smidge.

What consumes my insides is something different entirely. A longing. A hunger for understanding.

I scrunch my nose at the absurdity and whisper, "I should go."

I really should, yet my legs don't move. My brain won't send the signal to get my pins oscillating. There are too many questions. A wealth of knowledge I need to know. And he's right there, potentially an open book into an unknown world.

I remain in front of him, my hand falling to my side, my breaths heavy.

I allow myself one question. Just one. "Do you feel any guilt?"

"No." He doesn't pause for contemplation. "And you shouldn't either." He takes another step closer, the proximity tightening my lungs.

"That's easy to say, but—"

"There's no *but*." He leans in, getting in my face, forcing me to receive a front-row view of his sincerity. "The thing I need you to understand is that your world and mine aren't the same. His actions had consequences. And I enjoyed inflicting them." He raises a hand to my neck, and I hold my breath. "Nobody touches you. Do you understand?"

He does it again. Makes a demand, then breaks his own rules by guiding his calloused fingers delicately down my throat.

Everything inside me comes alive. Blood vessels. Nerves.

I'm a statue of conflicting warfare. All fractured heartbeats and heated veins.

"Breathe, Ollie. I'm not going to hurt you."

I acquiesce, the held air in my lungs shuddering from my lips.

He finds my necklace, lifting the delicate chain, dragging the threaded ring to sit atop the outside of my coat.

"Never take this off," he murmurs—at least I think that's what he says.

I'm too far gone, my sanity having fled the building. My self-preservation, *poof*—gone.

"Tell me you understand."

"I do," I lie, my voice smoky. Rasped.

His touch continues to linger.

It's ridiculous to want more. To fight hard not to lower my gaze to his mouth. It's the adrenaline. The tumultuous waves of shock.

"Never, Ollie."

"I promise I won't." My tongue swipes out to quickly lick my dried lips. "I don't want to be in this situation again."

He stiffens, and I struggle to understand what I said to flip his energy. But that's exactly what I've done.

"Good." He guides his hand to his side and steps back. "From now on you stay in your car while me and my men are here, okay?"

"But what about—"

"You know we're here. You know what we're doing. That's where this agreement of ours ends. So go home. Sleep. If you're worried about the skills of my cleaning crew, come back once we're gone. But otherwise, move on with your life. What's done is done."

I glance aimlessly over his shoulder as I struggle with whiplash. "How long until I hear from you again?"

"I don't know. But the timeline will be shortened if you go searching for trouble."

"I didn't go searching."

"Then I guess trouble just seems to find you, doesn't it, Pyro?"

I wince. I may not be able to hate him, yet somehow I find it incredibly easy to loathe him calling me that. "Only since you entered my life."

"Since you followed your father using a tracker app."

I grimace.

I don't need another reminder of that night. Or my father. Or Remy's heated hands.

"Are you still holding up okay?" He shoves his fists back into his pockets. "Do you need me to take you home?"

My heart squeezes. My nonexistent love life is to blame.

If only I'd dated a little more his attention wouldn't feel addictive. I'd have a better threshold for his concern. A stronger understanding of what this is.

"I..." I sigh, feeling so incredibly lost. "I can drive myself."

And that's what I do.

I don't say goodbye. Don't linger in this cloud of insanity. I turn tail and escape the building, hoping I never come face-to-face with him again... and lying to myself at the same time.

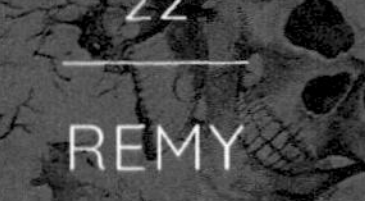

REMY

She turns and walks away, my gaze eating her up until she disappears around the van.

It takes everything in me not to follow. Not to chase after her and somehow rid her of the hollowness that seems to have carved its way inside her.

Instead I stand there, punishing myself with the what-ifs.

What if Flynn hadn't sent me a photo of Ollie at the front of the club?

What if I'd arrived at Smoke & Mirrors ten minutes later?

What if that piece of shit hadn't attempted to rape her and just went in for the kill?

I shove a hand through my hair, the rage reigniting. I wait until her engine purrs to life, until the low rumble disappears into the distance. Then I turn on my heel to find my men, and take pleasure in burning my employee's body to bone.

I spend days thinking about her. *Worrying* about her.

I picture her alone in that house, isolated with her struggles.

I should've done more to make sure she was okay. The only thing that stopped me was the threat of what would happen to her if I defied Lorenzo's orders. He's still too much of an unknown. A familial ally, yet potentially a patriarchal monster. Just like my father.

Once she's back at work, I demand updates from Wesley more frequently.

I hound him with questions.

Is she eating enough?

Ask her if she's sleeping.

Is she still wearing my ring?

None of his answers appease me. I want to hear them from her. Want to see for myself that the shadows under her eyes are gone. But cutting ties as much as our renegotiated terms will allow is for the best.

She said it herself: *"I don't want to be in this situation again."*

She doesn't want to be around me, surrounded by the aftermath of my brutality.

I don't text her again for weeks. But when I do, it's another painful truth—

ME

I've been thinking about you.

The aggravating mental gymnastics have been constant. Egregious. A dedicated, obnoxious train of thought that doesn't quit.

She's always on my mind. Those impassioned hazel eyes. The whimsically braided hair.

I hadn't thought the cartel would lay as low as they have. They're practically in hiding, with the whispers on the street being that there's a struggle to find a suitable replacement for their slaughtered leadership.

It's one of the bartenders at my brother's whiskey bar that triggers my reunion with lust-filled insanity, his stupidity at peddling drugs on family property ending his middle-aged life.

I would've spared him—sent him on his way with my personalized version of a slap on the wrist—if only I hadn't been informed of the transgression from a cop on the payroll who said the punk was willing to throw Salvatore under the bus to escape conviction.

This time when Ollie drives into the funeral home parking lot during the midnight hours, she remains in her car. Her vehicle is nowhere to be seen by the time the betrayer's body has been reduced to granulated bone.

And I, being the sick, pathetic fuck I am, miss her.

I'm frustrated that I don't get to speak to her. That she didn't break the rules so I could hear her voice.

More weeks pass. The cartel settles into new leadership, and Salvatore and I remain on alert for backlash that doesn't arise.

I contemplate killing a random just to see Ollie. For the mere excuse to be in her fucking presence.

Winter turns to spring, and I convince myself it'd be a good idea to meet with Carlo once a week to keep updated on his cancer status when what I'm really attempting to orchestrate is a dose of pretty little Pyro proximity.

Some weeks I'm successful because Ollie often works late.

One night I catch sight of her locking up as I drive around the back of the building to chat with her dad.

Weeks later, our cars pass in the drive, but when I hit the brakes and attempt to meet her gaze she speeds away.

Even when I do get to see her it's never enough.

But the visits aren't a hardship.

I appreciate Carlo.

He's a realist who holds a moral compass I admire. He's also the only father figure I've known who hasn't had homicidal tendencies. We chat about everything. Sometimes it's only for a few minutes. Other times it's for hours over coffee in his living room, the conversation flowing like we're old friends instead of mafia criminal and innocent business partner.

I tell Salvo the meetings are a necessity. That keeping an eye on Carlo's health means I'm keeping an eye on the stability of our contract, and my brother agrees with the logic.

But I'm yet to get what I really want. Time with *her*.

Everyone I come in contact with becomes a potential candidate to facilitate a pretty Pyro rendezvous. I think about killing twenty-four/seven just for the sake of being around her.

I end up getting lucky in the early days of March when I find two enemies tailing me around the city. Russo and Valenti torture them for info. Apparently the cartel aren't laying as low as they want us to believe, and my head is in their sights.

I'd probably give a shit if I wasn't so fucking pumped to have an excuse to message Ollie.

ME

I can't stop thinking about that night at the dive bar.
How you shuddered under my touch.

It wasn't the best message to send in the early morning hours after months of radio silence, but fuck, those thighs of hers have been playing on my mind to no end.

I even go to the extent of storing one of the dead cartel in our van overnight, risking life in prison, just so I have an excuse to go back to the funeral home two nights in a row.

ME

Do you remember how wet you got for me?

Again, it's not the most practical text, but I can't help it.

She's in my fucking head, constantly tinkering with my libido.

She doesn't message back. Those three dots of potential conversation don't appear. All I get is the update that the text has been *read*, and it's enough to get my blood pumping. To make my dick hard as I wait just inside the funeral home as she arrives to watch the building until she finally drives away.

The remainder of the month is slow. Carlo gets weaker with each visit, his jovial demeanor becoming tainted from the chemo. Then April hits, another cartel member takes a bullet, and I sit like a giddy schoolgirl behind the wheel of my Bentley, trying to think of the perfect line to text my obsession.

I dream about fucking you. About how gorgeous your face would look when I make you come.

No. Sex isn't an option, so texting it into existence is a monumental mistake.

I delete the message and try again.

I fantasize about tasting you. About gliding my tongue between your pussy —

Fuck. What is wrong with me?

Delete. Delete. Delete.

Would your panties get wet if my hand slid back between your thighs?

No. *Jesus Goddamn Christ.*

I clench my fists as Russo and Valenti stare at me through the windows of the van parked across the street, waiting for me to pull my shit together so we can hurry up and dispose of the evidence.

ME

> You mess with my head, Ollie… but for some reason I don't want you to stop.

I hit send before I can think too long about it, the *delivered* status turning to *read* in less than thirty seconds.

This time I wait, leaning against the outside of the building like I did the night she was attacked, while my men handle the disposal.

She reverses in to a spot across the opposite side of the lot, her car idling as she stares at me through the windshield, her wavy hair framing a hypnotizing face.

My dick stirs without my consent. My fucking limbs thrum.

I have to get closer. I *need* to talk to her.

Lorenzo and safety be damned.

I push from the wall and stride toward her but before I'm halfway across the lot she takes off, driving into the night with my goddamn fucking sanity.

Two days later I'm still reeling, my head distracted, my thoughts in the gutter as I enter my penthouse apartment early in the evening to a mass of Flynn's shoes scattered haphazardly in the foyer.

"Welcome home, boss," he calls from another room.

I scowl, hating how he refers to me in a business sense after months of us living under the same roof. "Hey." I dump my wallet and keys on the entry table and stroll into my open living area, the illuminated city skyline blinking its lights in the background.

"You're home early for a Monday." Flynn sits on my leather sofa, arms spread along the backrest, legs crossed and casual. "Do you want to join the party?"

Three white lines of powder sit on the glass coffee table, the display of drugs an obvious attempt to rile me.

All these months and I'm yet to raise my voice to this little fucker. But tonight might be the night.

The thought of him out on the streets buying coke, let alone touching it and spreading it into lines, has my animosity pulsing.

"Where'd you get that shit?" I keep my tone level. Measured.

His mouth kicks with a sardonic smirk. He's trying to get in trouble. To push me. To see if I'll push back, shoving him through the front doors, never to return.

The sad part is I get the psychology of it. The kid has a good thing here, but he doesn't think it'll last. He's trying to end it on his terms before it gets stolen from him.

He pulls this shit all the time. Pretends to be a rebel. Flirts with breaking the law. Attempts to get under my skin.

He even did a deep dive on Ollie after her stint at the club. He tried to taunt me with his underhanded knowledge of all things Olivia Pelosi. The little fucker then proceeded to print hundreds of online photos and plastered them over my bedroom wall.

The joke was on him though because I loved that shit. The kid constructed a shrine to my obsession without me having to lift a finger.

He shrugs, running a bank card along the outside of the white powder. "Here and there. I made more friends. They gave me a discount."

"Is that right?" I fail at keeping the snarl from my voice.

His lips kick higher.

Fucking masochist.

I clench my jaw, count to ten, and drag in a deep breath through my nose.

Do I smell baby powder?

That little fucking shit stain.

I'd laugh if the baggage from his childhood trauma didn't have him so messed up.

"Yeah." He kicks back, hefting his sock-covered heels onto the table beside the fake coke. "They seemed like good people."

"I'm sure they did." I discard my suit jacket and throw it over the back of the sofa. "You better not let it go to waste then."

He blinks in surprise. "What do you mean?"

"I mean snort that shit and then clean up your mess. I'm starving, and there's this place around the corner I want to try for dinner."

He sits taller, his feet thumping back down to the floor. "You want me to do drugs?"

"Well, I'm not going to encourage you to waste them, am I?" I start for the kitchen, desperate to hide a smile.

"But... you don't mind?"

I open the fridge. Grab a bottle of water. Crack the lid. "You know my work delves into some shady shit. Who am I to judge?" I watch him from the corner of my eye as I drink.

The poor kid is traumatized. Expression stark. Lips parted.

"Go on." I jerk my chin at him. "I'm getting hangry."

He glances from me to the baby powder lines then back again.

"You know how to do it, right?" I raise a condescending brow.

He cautiously scoots from the sofa to kneel before the table. "Yeah, of course."

Fucking liar.

"Go on then." I round the sofa to tower over him as he hesitantly leans toward the drugs.

He's about to take a reluctant sniff when I lightly tap him over the back of the head with an open hand. "Don't be a fucking moron. I know it's not coke."

He fumbles onto his haunches, remorse swimming in his usually playful eyes.

"You need to quit this testing-boundaries shit." I jab the water bottle in his direction. "I'm not going to kick you out."

He lowers his gaze to the table like a chastised puppy. "You will... eventually."

A part of me dies every time he says shit like that. Every time he thinks I'll give up on him. I may not be the best parental figure. I'm no Carlo Pelosi. But I'll do everything in my power to make sure I'm nothing like the man who raised me.

I can bite my tongue.

I can be patient.

"Then you don't know me very well, kid. I'm not the type to give up. I'm more likely to cuff you to your fucking bed and leave my men to guard your door until you wake up to yourself. Do you hear me?"

He keeps his gaze lowered with dejection.

"I said, *do you hear me?*" I jab the bottle into his shoulder.

"Yeah, I hear you."

"Good. Because your folks may have taught you that ditching parental responsibilities was easy, but mine gave me a thorough education on how to use and abuse minions until they're rung dry. You're a smart kid and a valued commodity. I won't be letting you walk out of here anytime soon."

He blinks up at me, his eyes wide with alarm.

"I'm joking, asshole." I reach out my free hand and help him to his feet. "You can leave whenever you like, but I'll never push you to go. I wasn't lying about you being valued. You've got a good head on your shoulders when you're not trying to shove the world away."

He relaxes. "But I don't even have an education."

"Yeah, you do. Yours was at the school of hard knocks. And as difficult as those lessons were, it will make you stronger. More adaptable." I clap him on the back. I'd pull the poor, dejected bastard in for a fucking hug if I didn't think he'd shove me away. "But you've gotta stop pushing against those who want to help you. Take what you can. Don't hold back. Be greedy with it."

He smirks. "Does that mean I should empty your safe and shit?"

"Nice try." I nudge him with my shoulder. "We don't bite the hand that feeds us."

He chuckles, but something niggles at me. Something that turns my thoughts to Lorenzo and how I'm being a hypocrite for biting his metaphorical hand due to the updated terms with Ollie.

"Well, then, let's get to feeding." Flynn starts for the entry. "What's this place you want to try for dinner?"

"It's a Teppanyaki restaurant." I walk around the sofa and grab my jacket. The temp outside is warm enough without it, but strolling around downtown Baltimore with a gun shoved into the back of my waistband isn't a look I want to attempt to pull off. "I hope you like Japanese."

He throws his hands up in the air, his expression light, as if we never even shared a heart-to-heart. "I don't even know what Teppanyaki is."

"Then I look forward to showing you."

He leads the way to the elevator, and we talk shit on the descent. He tells me how his greatest memory revolving around food was when his dad took him to Applebee's for his eighth birthday. But how they had to dine and ditch, only for Flynn to get caught by a security guard as he sprinted along the sidewalk while his dad took off.

It's an odd juxtaposition to the way I grew up, yet the kid still feels like a baby brother. The only thing seeming to separate us is that his parents were horrendously derelict while mine were egregiously conniving.

We step out into the tepid spring night, just two guys living carefree and laughing at each other's bullshit. I want him to have an easier life. To obtain the freedom I hadn't experienced until recently.

I'm determined to make it happen. To be some sort of fucked up mentor.

The advocate I never had.

"It's this way." I jerk my head toward the left of my apartment building while Flynn continues to talk shit, ribbing me about how I cut my hair and the 'pretty' cologne I wear.

I'm about to volley a slew of smack talk about his jeans that hang too low over his ass and how he needs to lay off the protein for global warming's sake when tires screech nearby.

I flinch, on alert, while Flynn laughs at his own joke.

An engine guns.

A woman screams.

My heart fucking plummets as I lunge toward him, the staccato thwack of bullets hitting the building behind us while a piercing pain stabs through my thigh.

He falls before I can lay hands on him. Eyes wide. Expression panicked.

He crumples to the cement and I follow, scrambling on top of him, covering his body as best I can.

But it's too late.

Blood already seeps into the chest of my button-down. His gurgled gasps for breath haunt my ears.

"Stay with me, Flynn." I shield his head with one arm and reach for my gun with the other. "Just fucking hang on."

23

OLIVIA

I frown at my cell screen.

His texts have always been elaborate. Downright flirty at times. This one hasn't even used autocorrect.

I grab a hair tie from the nightstand, throw back the covers, and snatch my car keys from the dining table as I pass.

I don't bother changing out of my pajamas. I won't be leaving the safety of my vehicle. I just want to see that he's at the funeral home. That things are under control like usual.

I eyeball the digital clock on my car's dash as I drive, the early hour seeming like another oddity to list next to the weird text.

Maybe it wasn't a kill confirmation.

Maybe he's tired of the sexual taunts and has switched to unintelligible gibberish for the sake of efficiency.

God, I hope not.

I can admit my body's response to his previous messages isn't healthy. That the way my blood automatically runs hot whenever I wake to a text in the middle of the night is majorly problematic.

But those messages have become a highlight to a dreary existence.

Even though Dad refuses to speak to me about his cancer, I know the chemo isn't working as well as it could. He's losing weight and energy. I can see it in his eyes despite his continued placations that he's doing well.

Ivy and Allison can see it too, especially after he confessed to being sick last week. Not that he could hide it anymore. There'd been too many days where he hadn't turned up to work until lunch only to leave a few hours later.

That devolved into my best friends acting differently. They now handle me with kiddie gloves. Like one wrong word or look will send me into an emotional spiral even though they've never seen me shed a tear.

It's only natural Remy has become a sickening thrill.

One I've vowed to experience from afar.

I drive into the funeral home parking lot and around the back of the building. But there's no other cars apart from my dad's Audi and the hearse. The delivery door is closed. The place is quiet.

Goddamnit.

I knew the timing was off. The message ridiculously uncharacteristic. I dragged my flimsy, satin-pajama-wearing ass out of bed for nothing.

I sigh and park in the spot opposite the overhead door, reversed in like usual, then reclaim my cell to stare at his message.

REMY

Tonigth

I keep staring for minutes that feel like hours, the heavy sense of disappointment making me hate myself because I can't even find the will to drive home. I want to wait. Just in case he's on the way.

"This is toxic." I lean back against the headrest and sigh.

I don't think I'm here because of safety and security anymore. I never go inside. Never step out of my vehicle. My only motivation is to watch Remy. To gain a glimpse of him.

It's sick.

But even acknowledging my illness doesn't make me inclined to leave.

Instead I sit wondering if my dad would know what's going on. I scrutinize the second-floor windows for movement. Contemplate whether tapping on his door and having the awkward conversation about why I'm here in the middle of the night is worth gaining information on Remy's whereabouts.

It's pathetic.

"To hell with this." I reach for the ignition, my finger almost poised to tap the button when the sound of another car approaches.

Headlights cut through the parking lot.

Remy's Bentley comes around the corner of the building faster than necessary, the familiar van carrying his men hot on his ass.

I remain in my car as the overhead door rises, but instead of Remy parking outside and the van driving into the building, the opposite happens.

I sit confused as the Bentley speeds inside, the van pulling into the closest parking space beside the delivery room door, then Remy's men rush out.

I don't like this.

It's frantic. Panicked. Nowhere near the calm control of the usual disposals.

I cling to my cell and keys then climb from my car to pad cautiously across the parking lot.

Shoes would've been helpful. A bra and underwear, too.

The cool spring night whispers over my arms and chest, but it's not the temperature that has my skin breaking out in goose bumps. It's the vibe. A sixth sense.

I reach the raised overhead door and stop to assess the situation.

Remy remains in the vehicle, his door open, his feet planted outside, elbows on knees, head hung.

He's usually flawless while doing the devil's work. Calm. Commanding. But tonight is different. He doesn't notice me in his periphery. Doesn't stop staring at the floor beneath his feet.

I can only see one of his men, the dark-haired guy reaching into the backseat of the Bentley to gently haul out a limp body. A limp *male* body. One far too lanky and lean to have reached adulthood.

"What the hell?" I whisper as blood drips to the floor.

The second man returns to the delivery room through the internal doors, hastily pushing my metal gurney toward the car.

They've never done that before, either. Never cared about using the gurney. From what I've seen, the cartage of dead bodies has only ever been done unceremoniously by grasped wrists and ankles.

"What's going on?" I add steel to my tone.

Remy's men ignore me.

Remy does, too.

I continue inside, transfixed as the men I've mostly known to be silent, threatening automatons place the body onto the metal transport with cautious, deliberate care.

"Is that a child?" I can't see the victim's face, but even the shaggy hairstyle speaks of a younger age.

The decedent can't be older than sixteen. Seventeen, max.

"You killed a child?" I can barely control my whisper-shouted tone.

I storm for Remy as his men pause at the double doors leading to the hall, their hate-filled eyes skewering me with warning.

I'm fueled by devastation. Empowered by disgust.

This can't be a part of the agreement. It's too much. Too immoral.

"You killed a child?" I repeat, stopping in front of his hunched form in the driver's seat.

He straightens, his face slowly raising to look up at mine with such devastatingly tortured eyes it steals my breath.

"Yes" is all he says.

One fractured, tormented word.

My stomach bottoms.

He holds my gaze, his posture lacking the usual authoritative command, his expression bleak.

"You killed a…" I can't repeat it this time. Can't finish the sentence.

His eyes swim with desolation. "Yes, Ollie. I killed a kid."

"*Bullshit*," one of his men snap. "You didn't do this. The blame is on the cartel. Working for you was the highlight of the boy's life."

It's as if a shovel plows into me, scooping out my insides.

I'm hollowed. Emptied.

I snap my gaze back to the gurney. To the boy. To the teenager I recognize from taking a photo of me outside Smoke & Mirrors. The same one who lives with Remy.

Oh, God. The cartel killed him, and Remy blames himself.

"Are you going to be okay while we take care of him?" one of the men asks.

Remy nods, looking straight through me, face pale, eyes bleak.

"You should leave and get stitched up," the other guy says. "We've got this covered."

"I'm fine." Remy raises a carnage-stained hand and scrubs it over his face, blood having dried into every crack and crevice of his fingers.

The guy scoffs and starts pushing the gurney into the hall. "The claret pooling at your feet says otherwise."

My gaze drops to the cement floor, the puddle of crimson stark beneath Remy's right thigh.

"What happened?" I gasp, rushing to do a visual search for injuries.

He stares at me. Stares right through me.

"Remy?" I grab his arm, my heart heavy, pulse intense. "Talk to me."

He shrugs off my hold. "It doesn't matter."

"Someone you care about is dead. And you're bleeding. It definitely matters." I drop to my knees before him, doing another visual scan of his clothes, finding two small holes close together in the upper right thigh of his dress pants. "You were shot?"

He falls silent, the bleak void of his mood sinking into me.

"Tell me what happened." I scan him for more bullet holes, fear and panic making my hands shake. "Is it just your leg?"

Again, nothing.

Goddamn him.

"Tell me." I reach for the bullet wound, pulling the wet, suctioned material away from his skin. "Now, Remy." I dig the tips of two fingers through the hole in his clothing and pull, tearing the fabric wider.

"Leave it," he murmurs. "This isn't an opportune time to take another stab at getting me out of my pants."

I sigh, understanding his need to deflect. "You can rest assured knowing that seduction is the furthest thing from my mind. I'm still a virgin, and we both know you don't mess with those."

"If only you didn't make me want to break my own rules."

My heart lodges in my throat.

Stupid, traitorous heart.

I focus on keeping my gaze on his leg. To not look up at him even though his eyes burn a heated trail over my face. "This is ridiculous." I pull harder, ripping the fabric barely half an inch. "I need to take you to a hospital."

"I don't do those either," he murmurs.

I purge a frustrated huff and drop my arms back to my sides. "So you plan on bleeding out?"

"If that's what karma dictates."

"Oh, okay." I roll my eyes and glare up at him, ignoring how his dejected stare makes me weak. "Just for clarity's sake, will disposing of you in the retort earn me another twenty grand, because if so, I might need you to call out to your men to return the gurney."

He doesn't laugh.

I guess the comedy festival is over.

"Come on. At least let me get you into the prep room." I grab his wrist. "I'm not a surgeon by any means but—"

"No." He drags his arm toward his chest, my grip on his wrist tugging me toward him. "I'm not spilling any more blood here for my men to take care of. I'll clean myself up at home."

I let go as he turns in his seat, raises his feet into the car, then grabs the steering wheel. But all he does is sit there, staring out the windshield to the closed double doors.

I've witnessed that far-off stare enough times to recognize it for what it is.

Grief has him by the throat.

"Why don't you let me drive you?" I whisper.

"Why not just wait to see if I die?"

Because the thought of losing him hurts for some reason.

Because he's made me grow attached to him, if even from a distance.

"You've saved my life twice already. And believe it or not, I don't necessarily enjoy being indebted to a murderous criminal."

He turns his head and meets my gaze, drowning me in his sorrow.

"Please, Remy."

His hands tighten around the steering wheel. "Don't fuckirg beg me, Pyro. I'm not in a state to deny you."

"Then don't. Let me drive you home. I'll help clean you up. I know a thing or two about stitching wounds."

He sighs, bone-weary and lax.

"Come on." I hold out a hand, praying he'll take it. "I'm itcking to slide behind the wheel of a luxury vehicle."

Those eyes search mine for long, silent seconds until finally he shifts.

He doesn't take my hand, but that's okay, because he climbs from the car, forcing me to sidestep as he unfurls his large frame to stand towering before me.

He reaches into his pocket, pops the trunk, then shuffles to the back of the car to retrieve a black blanket, returning moments later. "For the blood." He leans into the car to lay it down on the driver's seat. "I don't want you sitting in the mess I've made."

Forever the chivalrous murderous gentleman.

"Thank you." The appreciation is stupid. I'm thanking a criminal for sparing my clothes after a lethal encounter. *Stupid. Stupid. Stupid.* But that's what he does—makes me an idiot.

"Let's get out of here." He makes his way around the car, favoring his left leg.

My insides churn for him. For the teenage boy. For whatever they went through.

But I force myself away from the mental distraction and into the car. There's blood everywhere. On the steering wheel. Along the dash.

I don't dare to look in the backseat.

What the hell are you getting yourself into?

I close my door before I can contemplate fleeing, dump my cell and keys in the center console, then readjust my seat and drag on my belt.

Remy settles in beside me. "You're not even wearing shoes."

"Is that seriously a safety concern when you could be slowly dying?"

He glances out his side window. "I didn't take you for a catastrophizer."

"And I didn't take you for the type to go down without a fight, but here we are." I start the car, shift to reverse, and press the accelerator, the vehicle lurching backward fast enough to wrench a squeak from my throat.

"Sorry." I wince. "She's sensitive."

He drags on his seatbelt. "If memory serves, she's not the only one."

I ignore the innuendo. Completely disregard the heat that settles low in my belly as I continue to reverse, the bloody scene in the delivery room stretching out before me until I shift the car to drive and gently take us out onto the street. "You're going to have to give me directions, Swiss."

His brow hikes.

"Like the cheese." I smile.

"Yeah, I got it. I just didn't expect Little Miss Volatility to be cracking jokes." He jerks his chin at the road ahead. "Take a left at the intersection."

I follow his instructions. But apart from the simple left, right, keep going straight, he's uncomfortably silent for miles, which makes me uncomfortably concerned.

"You should really make a tourniquet for your leg. I'd offer my pajamas as a makeshift tie but..." I clear my throat, not bothering to finish the sentence.

It's obvious I have nothing on under my skimpy camisole.

"What?" He looks at me, deadpan, his gaze making the briefest journey to the ring that has found its home at the start of my cleavage. "Are you waiting for me to protest?"

I roll my eyes, hating the spark that shoots through me. "I'm sure you wouldn't. But seriously, you need to stem the bleeding." I glance down at his leg and the crimson painted across the car's cream leather seat. "Take your belt off and tighten it around your upper thigh."

"It's a through-and-through flesh wound. I'll live... Turn right at the next intersection."

I sigh, succumbing to his instructions.

I let panicked thoughts keep me company in between his murmured directions toward Harbor East—*what will happen if I'm pulled over? Should I take him to a hospital if he dies? Will his uncle and brother blame me?*

"This is it." He points a lazy finger toward a stylish apartment building on the corner of a harbor block, then deftly unfurls his belt from his pants. "Go around the back."

I chance continued glances toward him as I circle the glass tower to a parking garage door Remy opens with a remote. I drive up level after level while he wraps his upper thigh with the strap of leather and secures it tight with a wince.

"*Now* you make a tourniquet?" I ask.

"I don't want to trail blood through the parking lot." He jerks his chin at a space signposted *Reserved—Penthouse* right before the elevators. "Park there."

He climbs out as soon as the car comes to a stop.

I rush to cut the ignition, grab my cell, and then catch up to his uneven gait as he approaches the nearby elevators only to continue farther around the corner. "Wait. Where are you go…?" My question is cut short when he presses the call button to an elevator on the other side, the doors opening instantly.

The interior is luxuriously appointed, the walls covered in sparkling mirrors with subtle ambient lighting. There's not even a complete button panel. There are only three options. G - ground, P5 - parking, and P - penthouse, alongside some sort of scanner he places his fingertips against.

Of course he has a private elevator.

I ignore the obviously necessary security measures and wrap my arms around my middle as the doors close. "How are you feeling?"

"Peachy," he drawls, pulling out his cell to tap into the screen while we ascend. "You?"

My heart pangs at his dejection. "Remy, I…"

I don't know how to finish the sentence.

I'm sorry.

I wish I could make this better.

The doors open and he lumbers into a breathtaking apartment, the bird's eye view of the harbor stealing my breath.

I step inside only to stumble over something on the floor—a pile of sneakers haphazardly stacked in the entry, the hallmark sign of the teenage boy who once lived here.

My heart drops, but Remy ignores my stumbling. He's already walking ahead, hobbling through a magnificently opulent living room, the blood on the hem of his pants dripping on the polished tile floor.

What I imagined his home to be is nothing like the pristine

penthouse spread out before me. I think I anticipated a dark, sinister lair. Instead, everything is light—the cream walls, the tasteful white furniture. The space is welcoming—the stylish abstract art, the blanket draped over the closest arm of the plush sofa.

It's clean, professionally appointed, and tastefully lavish.

Remy continues to the kitchen and snatches a bottle of liquor from an overhead cupboard, screws off the lid, and gulps at the amber liquid.

I try not to fixate on him. On the bob of his throat. His perfectly chiseled jaw. The steely grip of his hand.

I turn back to the open space, occupying my eyes by cataloguing the luxury. A chandelier hangs over the glass dining table, the glistening glow reflecting in the floor-to-ceiling windows overlooking the Baltimore skyline.

"You have a nice home," I say lamely as I pad farther into the penthouse.

The hall to the left is long and wide, matching the one to the right. The television is huge. Over five times the size of mine. And there's a coffee table that…

I narrow my vision on the spectacular glass table with its thick gold trim. But the white lines of powder steal my attention.

My heart takes another sweeping dive, the reminder of Remy's career choice acting like a leash to my wonderment.

"The medical supplies are this way." He walks for the left hall, bottle in hand, only to pause when I don't follow. "Are you sure you still want to do this?"

I glance from him to the drugs then back again, my stomach churning.

The two don't add up. They're mismatched.

I can't entwine them. Can't make them fit into the same box. Only I need to. I have to remember he's a criminal. A brutal mafia murderer. Yet what stands before me is a man riddled with tightly wound emotion. The grief is easy enough to decipher, but there's so much more I want to discover.

"It's not that big a deal, Pyro." He continues on without me. "I can handle the wound on my own."

"I'm coming."

He walks away and I tag along.

Do I hate myself for it? Of course.

Could I stop myself? Not even if I wanted to.

I follow him halfway down the hall to a glistening bathroom bigger than any I've ever seen before. There's a lengthy vanity with polished tap ware. An open-ended shower. A standalone bathtub situated right beside the floor-to-ceiling glass with an immaculate view of the city.

It's the type of bathroom you'd see on Pinterest dream boards. On architectural websites.

I pause in the doorway as he yanks open vanity drawers, pulling out handful after handful of supplies.

"It's okay to have second thoughts." He diverts to the basin, his gaze meeting mine in the mirror's reflection while he cleans the blood from his hands.

I agree. But those thoughts should've taken place before I climbed behind the wheel of his car. Before I rushed from my house just to catch sight of him.

"I can handle it." I step inside the room, closing the door behind me.

He shoots me a curious look. "You caging me in?"

"I thought it best to have another barrier to the screams you're going to make once I start my handiwork. We wouldn't want your neighbors calling the cops."

He huffs a hollow laugh, the agony of it squeezing my insides. He shucks his jacket and throws it to drape over the edge of the extravagant bathtub, exposing a mass of dark blood stained into the front of his white shirt.

Panic floods my veins.

"You have other injuries." I rush forward, scanning the button-down, searching for more bullet holes. "Why the hell didn't you tell me?"

24

OLIVIA

I DUMP MY CELL ON THE VANITY AND REACH OUT, CAUTIOUSLY EXPLORING.

"No" is all he says.

"But the blood." I keep up the frenzied search as bile climbs my throat. There's no way I can fix a bullet to the chest. He could die. He *would* die.

His cool palms clasp my wrists. "It isn't mine."

My panic transforms to anguish at his guttural tone.

I stand straight, meeting his gaze.

This man is no heartless criminal. Pain swims in those eyes.

He must've held that boy while he died. Must've clung to him so tight.

"I'm sorry," I whisper.

He releases me with a wince and turns to the supplies. "How do you want to do this?"

By comforting you.

"I don't know." Nervousness bubbles in my belly as I move to the vanity and look through all the things he's pulled from the drawer. The sterile bandages. Tweezers. Staple gun. Antiseptic. Gauze. Cotton swabs. "You could start by showing me the wound."

I picture him lowering his zipper, removing his pants, exposing the outline of his crotch through whatever bloodstained underwear he must be wearing, and my heart palpitates.

Only that's not what he does.

He moves to sit on the vanity and grabs a pair of scissors to hack at his pants above the wound. The sound of grating material fills the room, fighting for dominance over the loud thunder of my pulse in my ears.

I don't look. Not yet. I clean my hands instead, working up a thick lather of his sandalwood-scented soap, making sure I scrub every nook and cranny meticulously.

I'd love to admit the impressive sanitation technique is only due to an enviable hygiene ethic, but the reality is that my fingers are trembling and I don't want him to notice.

He cuts off the entire right leg of his pants, then discards the scissors for the liquor bottle and takes a long pull. "If all this is too much I'll drive you home."

It is. Way too much. But I can't walk away. "Nothing inside those pants of yours has been, or ever will be, too much for me. I can handle it just fine."

From the corner of my eye I see his lips twitch, yet his gaze remains haunted.

"You can help by gently pouring antiseptic on the wound." I kill the water and pat my hands dry on a non-sterile towel, defeating the purpose of the last two minutes of scrubbing.

He does as I ask, opening the antiseptic to douse it excessively over his thigh.

I hiss in a breath, empathizing with the pain it must cause, but Remy doesn't react. "Go easy." I grab the bottle from him, my fingertips eliciting an unwanted tingle at our brief contact. "Let me handle it from here."

"This isn't my first rodeo."

"No?" I splash my hands with antiseptic, then focus on the bullet wound. "How many times have you been shot?"

"This is my maiden voyage in that regard, but my brother stabbed me in the opposite thigh not too long ago."

I pause, momentarily stunned at how casually he explains the familial violence. "Salvatore stabbed you?"

"No. It was Matthew. Don't worry though. I deserved it."

"I don't doubt it." I suck in a strengthening breath and creep closer, positioning myself between his spread knees, the proximity drying my mouth. "I'm going to touch you now."

I pause, anticipation thudding in my chest, butterflies erupting in my tummy.

He's so composed. Sedate.

I'm the opposite. Every nerve sensitive. Every heartbeat frantic.

I sweep my fingertips over antiseptic-covered skin, the contact tingling all the way up my arm.

His thigh tenses.

I snap my gaze to his. "If I hurt you—"

"You won't," he cuts me off.

"But if—"

"You won't, Ollie. Just do what needs to be done."

I swallow over the ache in my throat and nod.

I lean down, taking a closer look at the wound. The entry is almost perfectly circular. A small, round hole. The exit—a few inches around the side of his thigh—is slightly bigger, with ragged edges.

"I like that you don't get squeamish around blood," he murmurs.

"I don't think I was ever allowed the luxury, given my parents' work." I hold out a hand as I scan both wounds for debris. "Tweezers?"

He scrounges through his supplies and passes over a pair, his touch lingering in my palm until I drag my hand away.

He drinks liquor while I drag threads of material from inside his thigh. Not many. Just a few. And I ignore the way my neck tingles from his attention peering down at me.

"So tell me," I ask, "what actions were deserving of you being stabbed by your own brother?"

"None you'd find endearing."

I ignore the heat unfurling beneath my ribs, unsure if endearing himself to me is his aim, and equally uncertain if I want it to be. "I'm not surprised. If I was the gambling type I'd make a bet that you save all your charm for those random text messages you send me."

"The tone of the texts is necessary to create a plausible backstory for our contact."

"So they weren't true?" I try to sound casual. Flippant. I'm not sure I pull it off.

"I didn't say that." He falls silent, his attention confounding.

I grab the staple gun and confirm it's stocked. "You might want to take another drink before I do this next part."

"I'm good."

He doesn't sound like it. Not at all.

I cave and glance up to meet his gaze.

His head is slightly inclined toward mine, the wisps of his dark blond hair falling to frame tortured eyes.

I clear my throat and focus back on the exit wound, tackling the harder of the two injuries first. I pinch the skin around the opening, struggling to draw the flesh together at first. "Tell me about the boy." I poise the staple gun over the join I've created, my request probably not the best topic to distract from the impending pain. "What happened?"

He makes a noise. A low grumble.

"Come on. You don't have to tell me everything. Only what you're comfortable with." I press the trigger.

He flinches, but that's it. There's no hiss of breath. No curse. Just the slightest recoil as his skin is punctured. "There isn't much to tell. I was taking Flynn to get dinner."

I pinch more flesh together and prepare for another staple.

"We were walking from the building," he says on a rasp.

"This building?" I pull the trigger, inspiring another sedated flinch.

"Yeah. But don't worry. You're safe. I wouldn't have brought you here otherwise. I've got men on watch."

I nod away the fear, stowing it in the back of my mind to deal with later.

"We were side by side on the footpath," he continues. "One minute, he was cracking jokes about his latest prank—the next, bullets rain, and he's on the ground covered in blood."

I pull the staple trigger, hoping my attempt to distract him from physical pain isn't increasing his emotional suffering.

"They shot him in the chest." His voice cracks. "Twice. The kid didn't stand a chance."

I release the trigger one more time, closing the exit wound. "You did a good thing, letting him live with you."

He scoffs as I grab the middle of the entry wound to pull the skin together. "I told myself the same thing when I first invited him into my home. But I was kidding myself. I dragged him into a life far more dangerous than the one he had living on the street. If it wasn't for me he'd still be alive."

"You don't know that." I release another staple into his flesh while he takes a gulp of liquor. "Life is fickle. People die suddenly all the time. Healthy, happy people. From the most inane things. I see it every week. And that's for those lucky enough to have a roof over their head." I pinch more flesh. Repeat the same process. "Living on the street isn't something a lot of people survive. He could've starved. He could've frozen to death. He could've—"

"But he didn't. He was gunned down by my enemies. Because of my actions. This is on me."

I don't know what else to say to ease his guilt, so I focus on distraction. "Was he a drug user? I noticed the cocaine on the coffee table when I came in. Or maybe those lines are yours…"

He doesn't answer as I remain poised to inflict another staple.

I wait a few seconds, and still, nothing. There's only the feel of his gaze on the back of my neck, so deeply engrained the energy flutters all the way down my spine.

I don't want to look at him again, don't want to succumb.

But like always, I fall victim to Remy. I drag in a shallow breath and raise my gaze, immediately drowning in a sea of him.

"I don't do drugs," he murmurs. "Neither did Flynn. But I appreciate you being here even though you think I'm a monumental piece of shit."

I don't think that.

God, I wish I did.

I clear my throat and return my attention to the wound, pinching, stapling.

"The lines are baby powder," he continues. "It was Flynn's latest test to see if I'd kick him out. His parents did a number on him. They must've blown their lid at the slightest inconvenience, and he couldn't understand why I wasn't the same. He kept pushing to see when I'd kick him out."

I pinch, staple, wither toward heartbreak.

"It started with stupid things. He short-sheeted my bed. Poured pickle juice into the milk. Squeezed hair dye into my shampoo. I never told him, but I enjoyed it for the most part. He made it feel like I was back living with my brothers."

Pinch, staple, wither. "Back when you were playing sibling stabbing games?"

He huffs a strained laugh. "No, the stabbing was far more recent."

"It sounds like Flynn could've given me some lessons on how to rile you." I pull the trigger on the final staple, my fingertips lingering on his taut muscles for unnecessary seconds.

"Not a lot riles me these days, Pyro." He reaches under my chin and raises my face to his. "But rest assured you always will."

I stare into his sorrow, become consumed by it. "You seem okay to me."

"Look closer."

My pulse stutters.

My cheeks flush.

"You'd think losing Flynn, being punctured with a million fucking staples, and attempting to drown any ounce of emotion in liquor would've lessened your effect." His voice brushes over me in tempting strokes. "But I'm still fucking hard."

I pull back, my gaze instinctively snapping to the massive bulge of his crotch.

I suck in a breath and glance away as the flush takes over the rest of my body.

"It's sick, right?" he taunts.

I nod. Because it is. It's vile and shameless and so sickeningly problematic. But here I stand, guilty of the same lust.

I clear my throat. "You need to dress your wounds."

"You can do it for me."

No, I can't. I can't touch him knowing we both crave the same thing.

"Come on, Pyro. I like when you play nurse."

I glare at him. Glare so hard it hurts. It morphs. It transforms into a choking, needy ache in my throat.

He grabs the sterile bandages and holds them out. "You can't half finish the job."

I snatch the bandages and drop one back to the vanity before tearing open the other. "Too bad the cartel didn't have the same code of conduct."

His lips kick in a half-smile. "Don't pretend you wouldn't mourn my loss."

"Are you sure about that?" I remove the plastic from the adhesive edges then clap the bandage over the entry wound harder than necessary.

He jolts with a chuckle. "I like when you're fired up."

I grab the second bandage. "Do you want to do this yourself?"

"Not even a little bit."

"Then I suggest you start keeping your thoughts private." I rip open the packet, prepare the bandage, then place it over the exit wound, gentler this time, not daring to give him more angst. "If you're not going to see a doctor you should get a topical antibiotic to reduce the risk of infection."

"I'll get right on it," he drawls in a tone that implies he'll do the exact opposite.

"With people actively attempting to kill you, I'd do my best not to give them exactly what they want." I busy myself tidying up the surgical equipment, returning the staple gun to the drawer, balling up the empty bandage packaging, and throwing it to the waste bin beside the vanity. "You should also shower. You're covered in blood. The dressings are waterproof so don't worry about those."

"Do you help with patient bathing requirements?"

All my air congeals in my throat. I don't know why he's acting like this. Is it grief? Self-preservation after a life-threatening situation?

Whatever the cause, it can't be personal.

He's suffering and, proximity-wise, I'm currently his only outlet.

"Sorry, Grim. These hands are still virginal." I paste on a half-smile. "So I'm under qualified as far as your preferences are concerned."

25

REMY

THE REMINDER IS A SLAP ACROSS THE FACE. A NECESSARY ONE, BECAUSE while her hands have been on me, pinching my gaping flesh, stapling my wound, my dick has ignored the pain and the fucking sorrow to jut eagerly against the crotch of my tattered pants like an unleashable hound.

How the hell could I forget? *Hmm, I wonder.*

Maybe it's the softness of those careful fingers. The tempting sweetness of her strawberry scent. Or the unholy pajamas that would be entirely cookie-cutter on someone else, but on her? They're a wet dream waiting to fucking happen.

I avert my gaze and scoot from the vanity to shove a punishing hand through my hair.

"You *did* forget." Her tone holds surprise. "So that was legitimate flirting? And now this—" She waves a lazy hand in my direction. "—is genuine disgust at the reminder of my virginal status?"

"It's not disgust." It's self-loathing.

"Don't worry, Remy." She gives a sad smile. "I'll lose the V-card soon enough."

Anger floods my veins, my temples, my goddamn chest. "That's great, Ollie. Just make sure the guy knows that fucking you will be the last thing he does."

Shock slackens her features. "You're kidding, right?" She keeps her emotions in check, but I see the frustration bubbling to the surface. "You won't have sex with me but nobody else can either?"

Yep. That seems to be the way this unhinged situation is developing.

She snatches her cell from the counter and turns on her heel as she makes for the door. "You can be a real piece of work sometimes. But I'll let it slide because of what you've been through."

Each foot of space she places between us is like the shortening of a live fuse.

She's not the only one annoyed at my behavior. I'm fucking fuming —at the lust coursing through my veins, at how my feelings toward her are so mindless at a time when she shouldn't be smothering my thoughts.

"You're welcome for the staples though." She snatches the door handle. "I guess I'm not entirely useless."

"You're not fucking useless," I snarl.

"Actions speak louder…" She yanks the door open. "I'll find my own way home."

Like hell.

I lunge, the taut skin on my thigh pulling as I close in behind her, plastering my palm against the door to slam it shut.

I trap her in the cage of my arms, my chest pressing into her back, everywhere we touch awakening a monster inside me. "Rejecting you isn't effortless."

She stiffens.

"Watching you from inside the funeral home while you wait in your car is far from a cakewalk," I snarl into her hair. "Telling you how I feel through texts that you think are taunts isn't my idea of fun." I drag the delicious strawberry scent of her shampoo into my lungs. "And then having you in my home, with your hands all over me, while I force mine to remain at my side…*Fuck,* Ollie. You have no idea what you do to me."

She raises her chin. "You sure make it look easy."

Is she kidding?

I've lived for the thought of her for months. Been fucking blinded.

There's only Ollie. Only those beautifully emotional eyes. Those sweet, lush lips.

I lean into her ass, my cock hard against her softness. "Does this feel easy to you?" Her gasp sinks into me, waging war with my control. "Does any part of this feel like I wouldn't burn the world to the ground just for a few seconds between your fucking thighs?"

She remains facing the door, breaths increasing, body like a stretched rubber band about to snap.

How does she do this to me? Command me. *Control* me.

I'm a slave to her, every part of me bound and exposed.

"I want you," I growl in her ear. "I want you so fucking much it's more painful than a bullet wound." I nuzzle her neck, consumed by her.

I revel in the softness of her hair. The sweetness of her scent. The brutal rasps of her breath.

"But you still won't sleep with me," she whispers.

I tense. "No."

She yanks at the door again, opening it an inch.

I slam it shut with a snarl.

"Why are you doing this?" She turns, those deep hazel depths blinking up at me. "Is it the grief? The alcohol?"

I don't know. The only thing I understand is the mindless intensity thrumming through me. The need for her. I swear to God, I see it staring back at me, too. The illusion is a sickening punishment.

"You're driving me insane, Remy. I don't enjoy feeling like this. I don't like wanting you."

She wants me? Even after all she knows?

Fuck.

Just… *fuck.*

"I should hate you." She stares up at me, undaunted by my proximity. "Any stable-minded woman would want to take to your head with a two-by-four."

I huff a laugh. "Instead my girl prefers to shove me into a retort."

Her brows rise.

She heard it. I fucking did, too.

My girl.

The words may have only come out due to alcoholic lubrication, but it's true.

She's mine.

Having her might not be within my realm of reality, yet that doesn't mean I haven't claimed her.

She shakes her head, her nose scrunching. "I don't like how you make me feel."

The admission hits with the efficiency of a kick to the balls. "And how is that, Pyro?"

She winces. "Entirely out of control." She grabs at the chain around her neck as if the loose length chokes her. "Like your proximity has a direct link to my personal thermostat. My entire body feels in tune with yours. You make me think things that aren't healthy. It's not right."

My dick throbs back to life. "You've bewitched me, too, Pyro. Despite my shitty, godforsaken life, the hardest battle I've fought is trying to keep my hands off you."

"It's wrong. I don't understand it."

That makes two of us.

I shouldn't be drawn to a woman like her. Shouldn't be completely rattled by someone whose lithe body could be taken down by a rough gust of wind.

Her eyes turn pained. "The last thing we should have is chemistry."

"Yet here we are." Me with a raging hard-on, while her pebbled nipples press through the thin material of her camisole.

She stares and stares, unravelling me with each punishing pound of my pulse, her thoughts out of reach with the possibilities destroying me until she finally whispers, "My virginity isn't a big deal."

Fuck.

I grind my teeth. "It is to me." I want to spell it out. To force her to understand. "I won't make that memory with you."

She stands her ground. "I've been penetrated before. Maybe not by a man, but with toys. *Often.* You wouldn't hurt me."

Jesus Christ. The image is an onslaught. Her naked body. Her needy whimpers.

"This isn't about pain." It's about my fucked up childhood. About saving her from regret. About—*shit.*

Why do my reasons feel pathetic against the mesmerizing bat of those dark lashes?

I can't withstand it.

I'm too fucking weak.

My hand gains a mind of its own, lowering from the door to sweep down to her hip.

She sucks in a breath, as if the contact came with a jolt of electricity.

"Then tell me what the problem is," she rasps. "Tell me or I'm leaving."

That shouldn't be a threat. She's already dealt with my injury. Her work here is done.

But those eyes... Those tempting lips... Her goddamn fucking curves...

What I wouldn't give to grasp her chin and smash my mouth to hers.

"Tell me," she whispers. "*Please,* Remy."

My traitorous palm lowers to the hem of her tiny shorts, a lone finger sneaking a trail across her leg to her inner thigh. It's a mindless movement. A drunken one. But *God,* does it feel good.

"The reason doesn't matter." I run slow circles along the heated skin of her inner thigh, infatuated with how her heavy breaths match each rotation.

It's a simple touch.

The slightest fix for my addiction.

I'll stop soon.

"They matter to me." She squeezes her legs together, her eyes closing for brief seconds. "Especially when I want this." She tilts her hips toward me, my fingers traveling farther toward heaven.

Blood surges in my veins.

My dick fucking throbs.

I need to tell her to leave. To run.

Yet the thought of her not being here makes me livid. Makes me break out in a cold sweat.

"I'll never fuck you, Ollie." I succumb a little more to my addiction, sliding my hand higher, creeping closer toward that sweet spot I've jerked off thinking about for months on end, unable to stop myself. I need more. Need everything. But I'll settle for second best. "I can make you feel good though, if that's what you want."

She struggles through a heavy swallow. Nods.

Victory washes over me, the adrenaline in my veins so thick I can taste it. "Say the words, Pyro."

"Yes," she rasps. "Please."

Fuck.

My touch climbs higher, inch by agonizing inch as blood rushes straight to my dick.

I anticipate the feel of her underwear. Soft cotton or silken lace that I can tear right off of her. Only I don't come in contact with her panties. There's nothing. My fingers glide from toned thigh all the way to smooth, velvety sex.

She sucks in a shuddering breath, one hand holding her cell against the door, the other quickly moving to grasp the handle for support.

I swipe down her middle with a groan, my fingertips becoming drenched in her pleasure. "You're so fucking wet."

She whimpers. "When it comes to you I'm full of toxic responses."

"Is that right?" I circle her entrance, loving how her head falls back and bangs against the door.

"You make me crave unhealthy things, Remy."

"Like?"

She shakes her head.

"Tell me." I glide a finger inside her and she gulps in a sexy breath, increasing my pulse.

She's tight. Such a mind-numbingly perfect fit for my cock.

I'd have to prep her. Stretch her.

God, she'd feel me everywhere.

"I…" She moans, the sound rumbling off the walls. "I've been searching online for things that don't usually turn me on."

I keep my mouth shut as a sardonic laugh rumbles in my throat.

I've spent weeks reading her internet browser history thanks to the tracking software. But I thought all those porn searches were her fucking with me.

Rough.

Submission.

Breath play.

Sex with dangerous men.

"Do you think of me when you touch yourself?" All sense of playfulness is gone as I slide another finger inside her.

I don't want her to say yes. Don't think I can handle knowing we have something else in common.

"I'm not proud of it." She holds my gaze.

Goddamn.

"Do you want to know how many times I've fucked my hand thinking about you, my pretty little Pyro?"

She shakes her head. Adamant.

I lean close, my mouth near her ear. "Good. Because I've already lost count."

She shudders everywhere—shoulders. Thighs. Breath.

It's too much.

Too tempting.

If life were simple, I'd give her everything she wanted. Rough touches. Tangled, sweaty limbs. I'd show her the danger she craves, as long as I'd also be able to savor her. To cherish and revere.

I'd create the perfect balance. Make her scream and beg. Demand and plead.

She'd never leave the fucking bedroom.

If only she wasn't her and I wasn't me.

I curl my fingers inside her with each gentle intrusion, slowly increasing the pace.

Her lips part. Her inhale stutters.

I lean close, nuzzling into her neck. "Tell me how it feels."

"So good." Her moan is guttural. "God, I could come already."

"What's stopping you?"

"I don't want this to end."

"You might want to think twice about that. If this drags out much longer I'll have no choice but to palm my cock. I bet one stroke is all it will take to have me making a mess of you."

She falls quiet.

I pull back, meeting her wide eyes. But her expression isn't filled with disgusted shock. What's leveled on me is stunned curiosity. Bewildered enthusiasm.

Jesus fucking Christ, this woman.

I increase the pace of my fingers, her needy whimpers a torturous tease. "You're going to come for me." I place my hand atop her sternum, slowly sliding up her sweat-slicked skin over her necklace, all the way to her throat.

Her hips tilt farther, demanding more, her *gasp, gasp, gasps* rasping in my ears.

There's no way this woman wasn't made for me.

Made to torment me with temptation. To punish me for my sins.

"Be a good girl and show me how you get yourself off." I bury my face against her cheek, close my eyes, and concentrate every molecular cell of my being on keeping my dick in my pants. "Ride my hand, Ollie."

She does. Oh, *fuck*, how she goddamn does.

Those hips roll in the smoothest, rhythmic dance. Her legs grind against mine.

"Remy..." My name is a moan. A fucking delicious spell.

I squeeze her neck, scraping my teeth along her jaw. "Don't stop drenching my hand."

I want to taste her. To suffocate between those thighs and die a happy man.

She gasps. Harder. Faster.

"That's it." I apply pressure to her clit and she bucks toward me.

"Remy..."

My name has never been more melodic. A verbal narcotic.

"That's my good girl. Keep fucking me, Pyro. Give me what I want."

Her cell clatters to the ground and she grasps the wrist at her throat, her nails digging deep. I keep licking. Biting. Abstaining like a motherfucker.

"*Rem...*" This time her call is cut short, her lips falling open on a held breath.

Her pussy clamps around me. Her insides flutter.

I feel it all the way to my dick, the tortured organ seeping, jolting, fucking begging.

Her back arches off the door. Her tits thrust against my chest.

I'd give anything to cup them. Suck them. Lap at every sensitive, pebbled inch.

I lean back to watch the pleasure roll through her, a delicate hand strangling my wrist at her throat, the other clutching the door handle while her mouth gapes and her eyes close.

Nothing in this world has ever been more mesmerizing. More capable of bringing me to my knees.

But why? What the fuck is it about her that has me tied in knots?

This woman, with her painfully moral compass and subconscious death wish, has claimed victory over me while I wasn't even aware we were in battle.

Slowly, she turns lax, her pussy quitting its quivering death squeeze, her shoulders slumping back against the door with a soft thud.

She blinks her eyes open, her cheeks flushed with lust, her teeth dragging over her bottom lip.

Fuck she's beautiful.

A virginal seductress.

An innocent, naive goddess trapped against the bloodstained clothes of a loathsome murderer.

Shit.

The realization of how I've desecrated her hits like a physical blow. How I've contaminated someone entirely pure with my filth.

Then the memories of what brought us here wiggle their way back into my consciousness—*Flynn. Death. Destruction*—and my dick wilts.

I crossed a line.

I. Fucked. Up.

I release her throat, her fingertips gliding from my skin as she stares at me with building unease. "This was a mistake."

"Excuse me?" she whispers.

I took advantage of an adrenaline-fueled situation.

I risked our business arrangement.

I'm gambling with her life.

"For someone far more experienced than I am, I would've thought you'd remove your fingers from inside me before starting the cold-shoulder routine." She wiggles, dislodging my hand from between her legs. "But it's okay." She sidesteps, righting the hem of her shorts, smoothing out her camisole. "I get it. You've had a horrible night."

No, she doesn't have a fucking clue.

She doesn't realize that things have changed. How *I* will have to change.

That the monster I once was is nothing in comparison to who I'll become now that the cartel have made this personal.

They took someone from me. Someone I cared about.

And here I stand with my hand soaked in Ollie's pleasure while his body is being burned to nothingness.

I'm a piece of shit.

I turn and amble for the sink, then wash her gratification down the drain while she remains limp against the door.

"I'll call you a driver." I meet her gaze in the mirror.

She flinches, the rejection taking half a second to mask.

The thought of someone else taking her home sits like a lead weight in my gut, but the threats are stacking against her and I'm the one who keeps putting them there.

She needs to get away from me.

To quit asking for things that will get her killed.

"No." She pushes from the door to snatch her cell off the floor. "It's okay. I'll call my own."

"I want it to be *my* driver, Ollie. Someone I can trust with your safety." I switch off the water and face her.

She rolls her eyes. "Well, hold on tight, buddy, because you're about to be the poster child for not always getting what you want." She swings around to face the door, yanking it open.

"*Ollie,*" I warn.

She pauses.

"I'm not saying you're not allowed to be pissed at me," I growl. "But you don't get to put yourself in danger because of it."

Her posture loses its rigidity. "I'm not pissed at you."

"You sure about that?"

"Yes. This is on me. I'm the sober one. I'm not manipulated by grief. I never should've let things go as far as they did." She clears her throat. "I never should've let them go anywhere." She glances at me over her shoulder, her gorgeous features pinched. "I'm sorry."

Fucking hell.

Why is everything with her so fucking easy yet so excruciatingly hard all at the same damn time?

"Give me a minute to get some clothes." I walk toward her, needing to get to my bedroom. "I'll see that one of my men makes sure you—"

"Remy, I said I don't need a ride."

"I'm not budging on this." I step around her and try to lengthen my stride down the hall, but the pull of my staples fucks up my pace. I'm forced to limp, to fucking hobble while her footsteps retreat in the opposite direction.

"Don't defy me, Ollie." I enter my room and make a beeline for my walk-in closet to snatch a shirt from a hanger. "Give me two more minutes."

I yank the clothing over my head, but the only response is the faint whoosh of the elevator doors.

26

OLIVIA

"Don't defy me, Ollie," Remy calls down the hall. "Give me two more minutes."

The thought of leaving him at a time like this makes me ill. But it's nothing when pitted against the shame and humiliation that spurs my legs across the living room. I focus my sights on the elevator, the gentle whir of mechanics confusing me as the doors open before my eyes.

Salvatore strides into the penthouse, pausing in the entry to look back at Lorenzo who shuffles after him with the aid of a walking stick.

I freeze, clutching tight to my cell as I scan my surroundings in panic, for what I'm not sure—a weapon? An alternate escape route? An open window to yeet myself out of?

"*Ollie?*" Remy yells in the distance.

Salvatore swings toward me, a conniving smirk slowly tilting his lips. "Well, well, well. Look what we have here."

My breath clogs in my throat.

"Mind your manners, *figlio,*" Lorenzo chastises in accented English, his eyes scrutinizing me. "Are you okay, *mia cara?*"

My mouth dries.

Everything inside me feels like it's racing, yet my mind is entirely devoid of strategy.

He continues hobbling toward me. "I wasn't told you were with Remy when the shooting—"

"I wasn't." I swallow. "I ran into him at work. He was injured and refused to go to a hospital so I offered to tend to his wounds. I was just leave—"

"That's quite some work uniform you've got." Salvatore gives me a leering once-over. "You might want to readjust those silken boxers. Your lack of morals is showing."

My cheeks heat.

I can only imagine what I look like. The disheveled hair. The pleasure-stained pajamas. *Oh, God,* and Remy's ring. It sits in the crest of my cleavage like a glaring red flag of broken rules.

"Ignore him." Lorenzo whacks his nephew with the handle of his cane, then jabs it farther into Salvo's chest. "Hold this for me."

Salvatore takes the walking aid, still smirking while Lorenzo shuffles toward me.

I turn rigid waiting for the elderly man to threaten me for defying his orders. To hurt me. Maybe kill me.

He stops a few inches in front of me and shucks his jacket. "Here. Take this." He pauses for a moment of silent permission, then cautiously drapes the tailored material over my shoulders. "Please tell me you're not leaving on your own at this time of night."

"I—" My words vanish at Remy's uneven gait echoing down the hall.

Shit. Shit. Shit.

"I, um. Thank you for the jacket." I force a smile. "But I really need to go. I have work tomorrow…" I hesitate, unsure if I need permission, a permit, or a blood bond to get out of here.

But all Lorenzo does is peer at me with gentle consideration.

"Okay." He inclines his head and retreats a step. "I assume you have a car waiting."

My lips part, a lie poised on the tip of my tongue.

He raises a brow as if waiting for me to increase the defiance.

I snap my mouth shut.

"You will use my driver." He pulls a cell from his pants pocket. "He's already in the parking garage. It's safer than walking onto the street."

"Especially looking like that," Salvatore drawls.

"No. I…" I glance over my shoulder, Remy's broken footsteps growing louder.

"I insist, *mia cara.*" Lorenzo pats me reassuringly on the shoulder. At least I hope that's what the contact means. He could be sizing me up for a casket for all I know.

The problem is, my tattered pride and self-loathing won't allow me to stick around and weigh the odds.

I need to get out of here.

I nod as Remy enters my periphery, his posture stiffening. "Thank you, Lorenzo." I maneuver around the lethal monarch and stride for the elevator, ignoring Salvatore's low-key taunting snicker.

"Ollie," Remy warns.

My skin prickles as I keep walking. Keep defying.

I can't look him in the eye again. Not when he's drunk, distraught, and dangerously determined to make this situation worse.

"*Olivia*," he demands.

I flinch at his use of my actual name, and pause momentarily to poke the elevator call button.

This is all on me.

The mistakes. The carnality.

How could I have been so shortsighted? So self-absorbed? And with lust, of all things.

The doors open and I step inside, hoping this is the right choice, and the one with the least amount of disastrous aftermath.

I press the button for the parking garage and hate myself for chancing a glance back into the living room.

Everyone stares at me. Salvatore with his sickening smirk. Lorenzo with his cold, calm concern. And Remy, who scowls with what I assume is seething frustration.

"Don't forget the antibiotics," I murmur to fill the awkward silence. "I'm sorry for your loss."

The doors thud shut, trapping me in a confined space full of regret. A few seconds later I reach the parking garage, still barefoot and disgracefully disheveled while wearing a jacket big enough to fit two of me.

"Ms. Pelosi?" A large, suited man walks toward me from the open back door of a silver Rolls-Royce. "I've been told you require a ride."

I glance from the intimidating stranger, who does well to hide any judgement of my appearance, and take in the shadowed corners of our dimly lit cement jungle. Nobody else is down here. I could disappear and never be seen again.

Given my level of humiliation, maybe that'd be for the best.

"Yes." I'm too exhausted to keep wondering about threats, intimidation, and death. "A ride would be appreciated."

I get home shortly before two a.m, the silent thirty-minute car ride giving me a chance to detox the adrenaline but not the disgrace or concern.

I shower, scrubbing my skin of the dirty deeds, then crawl into bed, setting my alarm for a few hours later, only to toss and turn until sunrise.

Having left my car at the funeral home, I'm forced to ride my bike to work, each wiggle against the narrow seat punishing me with reminders of Remy. The way he consumed me. Unraveled me.

I feel like a loose ball of wool as I ride into the parking lot well before business hours, yet Wesley's Honda Accord is already here.

I enter through the delivery room, the pungent scent of cleaning chemicals poisoning my lungs as I lean my bike against the back wall.

There's no blood. No evidence of the night before.

From the amount of bleach in the air, I'm confident twenty years' worth of DNA has been stripped from the building. But I still complete my search for damning evidence, ending the ritual at the retort.

The room is slightly tepid, the machinery lukewarm from Flynn's cremation.

My heart pangs at the thought of the young man. It threatens to explode when my mind turns to Remy.

"I was told you were here last night," Wesley murmurs from behind me.

I don't bother responding.

Even though he's become a reliable member of the team—one that Ivy and Allison adore—I'll never be stupid enough to believe he has any loyalty toward me and my father.

"Everything has been cleaned and sterilized. And the temperature in the room is barely noticeable." His footsteps carry forward. "There's nothing for you to worry about."

Except how I gave aid to a criminal.

How I was driving a car that illegally transported a dead body.

And oh, maybe how the head of the East Coast mafia found me with the man I was told to stay away from.

That sounds like an anxiety cocktail to me.

"I plan to tell Ivy and Allison I spilled a bottle of bleach." He walks into my periphery, cocking his head. "Are you happy to go along with the story?"

"Yeah." I nod, the lies becoming easier to digest with how frequently they occur.

"Thanks. I'll leave you to it." He makes for the door.

"Wait." I swing around to face him, damning my concern to hell. "Is Remy okay?"

No matter how hard I try I can't stop thinking about him. His injury. His touch.

He gives a grave smile. "He'll survive."

"I meant emotionally as well as physically."

"So did I." He continues into the hall, leaving me with building unease.

I ditch my morning routine to help Ivy and Allison with their workload, mainly to distract them from going anywhere near the still-cooling cremator but also as a means of staying occupied.

Only my head doesn't quit fixating on all things Remy.

I eat lunch upstairs with Dad after he excused himself mid-morning to make some "private business calls"—aka he took a well needed nap.

I expect him to grill me on what happened last night. I'm sure he must've heard the commotion. But there are no questions. No unease.

Instead he brings up stories about my childhood, reminding me of the good old days when my life wasn't a complete mess.

The evening is spent staring at my phone, typing heartfelt messages of concern to a murderer only to delete them before sending because it still hurts to be labelled a mistake.

I arrive early again on Wednesday, wanting extra time to clear my head of all the criminal distractions, only to discover Wesley is already on site for the second day in a row with the cremation room tepid, and the retort warm to the touch.

I check my phone. How could I have missed a text from Remy?

It's clear the equipment has been used. Only there's no message. He didn't contact me.

The low simmer of my concern shifts to weighty apprehension.

This wasn't what we agreed on.

We had a deal.

But he's grieving. He's probably distracted… and I'm still a mistake.

Against the better judgement of the sixth sense tickling the hair on the back of my neck, I let it slide. I carry on with my duties, pretend the disposal didn't happen, and continue to ignore the red flags even though my thoughts are consumed with them… only to be kicked in the gut when Thursday morning is the same. Tepid room. Lukewarm retort. Wesley hovering.

This time when I pull out my phone, I don't bother searching for imaginary messages. I call Remy straight away.

He doesn't answer.

I try texting.

ME

What's going on? Are you okay?

Five minutes pass with no response.

ME

I thought we had a deal.

No reply.

ME

You lied to me.

The three dots of an impending reply blink on the screen.

REMY

I've never lied to you.

Bullshit. He said I'd be notified whenever he disposed of a body. He told me I'd be kept in the loop.

ME

You broke a promise.

The three dots flash on screen then disappear. Flash then disappear.

I stand staring at the screen, waiting, apprehensive anticipation chomping at my insides. But no new message pops up.

I'm left on read.

ME

We need to talk.

I fixate on the screen, impatient, restless.

He doesn't even read the message.

"Goddamn you." I smack my cell down on the transport gurney with a heavy *thunk.*

"Bad morning?" Ivy questions from the hall.

Shit.

"Hey." I swing around to face her. "I didn't know you were in already."

"Yeah." She eyes me dubiously. "Your dad has me doing some extra training so I wanted to get highly caffeinated before we start. What's with the colorful blasphemy?"

I school the guilt from my features. "Nothing major. I just forgot to get meat out of the freezer."

"How admirably domesticated of you." She chuckles. "I mean, at least it would've been if you hadn't forgotten. Want coffee?"

"Make me a double espresso and I'll give you my firstborn."

I have high hopes on Friday, because hope is all I have with the current radio silence. Problem is, as soon as I reach the parking lot and see Wesley's car I know the retort will be warm.

"Why isn't he returning my texts?" I announce loudly to the empty reception area.

Footsteps carry down the hall, Remy's lap dog walking into the room a few seconds later. "Did you say something?"

I clench my teeth. He knows exactly what I said. "You're obviously in direct communication with him."

"I'm only doing what I'm told."

"And what were you told, Wesley?"

He shrugs. "He said to come in early every morning and double check things were in order because it was going to be a big week."

A big week?

"That's it?" I scowl. "There was nothing else?"

Nothing about how I've been ostracized?

"He suggested I keep an eye on you. He mentioned you might be pissed."

"Smart man," I snip. "You might want to remind him that being kept in the dark doesn't work well for me. I won't stand for it."

"No?" He cocks his hip against Allison's desk. "Should I tell him you plan on doing something stupid?"

"Of course not," I seethe. "But I want answers. We had a deal."

I text Remy again.

ME

Call me.

After five minutes, the status doesn't change from *delivered*.

I call him. It goes straight to voicemail. Each call every hour on the hour thereafter has the same outcome.

I spend the in between moments embalming a grandmother of five who passed from an aneurysm. Lunch goes by. The afternoon hours stretch. Allison and Ivy give me their usual farewells at closing time, and I still remain there, my annoyance at Remy growing, my paranoia returning to the amped levels I rode before he agreed to grant me transparency.

I sleep in the break room. Then curse a blue streak when I wake the next morning without the Grim Reaper making an appearance.

I call his apartment building, but the concierge won't put me through. And nobody picks up when I dial the number for Smoke &

Mirrors.

I don't know what else to do.

I can't bring myself to talk to my dad about it because that would mean informing him of my updated agreement, and his health is temperamental enough due to the chemo without adding stress to the mix.

It's by sheer coincidence that I'm still at work two hours after closing the following Monday evening when the sound of a car pulls into the parking lot.

I yank off my face shield and mask and rush from my prep room. I cross the reception, catching a tiny glimpse of an unfamiliar black sports car as it drives into the parking lot.

I shove through the front door, trying to ignore how unprofessional it is to leave Mr. Armistead splayed on my prep bench as I jog around to the back of the building, my plastic clothes shield rustling between my legs.

Then there he is, stealing my breath through the darkness as he climbs from a sleek Aston Martin, his limp slightly noticeable on his walk toward my father's stairs illuminated by the second-story light.

"Hey," I call out, suddenly caught up on what to say. How to act.

He keeps walking, not bothering to glance in my direction.

God, it stings.

"Remy." I raise my voice. "Are you seriously ignoring me?"

I'm making more mistakes. Calling his name out loud. Creating too much noise. But I can't help it. I need to know what's going on. Why I suddenly no longer exist.

I run faster, my tiny heels clapping against the cement. I cut him off at the bottom step, blocking his path. "This is bullshit." I lower my voice. "You don't get to ignore me after I stapled your ass back together."

Hard eyes meet mine. "It was my *leg*—not my ass."

I balk at his venom, completely caught off-guard. "Don't be smart with me."

He releases a frustrated breath, acting as if I'm the most annoying inconvenience he's ever faced. Like he didn't touch me in the most intimate of ways. "I never asked you to stitch me up."

He inflicts the rejection with spectacular ease. It's top-tier excruciating. But I don't buy it. Not after all those guttural things he admitted in his penthouse.

Fuck, Ollie. You have no idea what you do to me.

"That's what you're running with?" I sidestep when he attempts to maneuver past me. "Well, do you remember what you *did* ask of me?" I lower my tone to a caustic whisper. "You asked me to tell you how it felt to have your fingers inside me." He scowls, but I ignore the warning. "You told me to come on your hand, and now you can't even return my texts?"

"You're the one who walked out on me when I begged you to stay."

"Begged? In what world?"

His nostrils flare.

"You didn't beg for anything, Remy. You *demanded* I take a driver *you* trusted after you called me a mistake."

His jaw tightens. "I didn't say *you* were a mistake. What I did to you was."

I glare. "I'm sorry, there's no nuance to the situation that makes your comment any less harsh."

"Then I guess we're done here." He grabs my waist, picks me up like I weigh nothing, and dumps me to the side of the steps.

Is he serious?

"Do you know how many times I've called you?" I remain in place as he labors up the staircase.

"No," he states simply. "I blocked your number."

My jaw unhinges as he continues upward, disappearing inside my father's apartment as if he didn't swing me a death blow.

We're *so not* done here.

Not even close…I just need to take care of Mr. Armistead before I can get to the bottom of what the hell is going on.

I run back inside the building, cover the decedent, and wheel him into the cooler, then remove the rest of my protective gear, grab my things, and lock up.

I expect to have to wait a while, but as I stalk around the corner of the building Remy is already halfway down the stairs, guiding my father to take cautious steps by his side.

"What's going on?" I increase my pace.

Remy shoots me a warning glower.

"Why are you still here, *fragolina?*" Dad's smile is tight. "You're spending too much time at work."

"I had a few loose ends I wanted to tie up. Where are you going?"

My dad focuses on his feet, taking each step with deliberate care.

"Dad?" I stop at the bottom of the stairs. "Please tell me what's going on."

He takes another step and another. "Remy's taking me for a drive. It's nothing for you to be concerned about."

Dread swallows me whole. "A drive? Where?"

He doesn't answer.

"A drive where, Remy?" I demand.

The sinful man continues to glower at me. "We've got a meeting."

Shit. Shit. Shit.

Is this because of me? Because I got caught at his penthouse?

"It's nothing to be concerned about." My dad grunts and groans his way down the final steps, then leans toward me, planting a smacking kiss to my forehead. "We'll be back soon."

Remy leads the way to his car.

Dad follows, slower, each step accompanied with a wince.

"Are you taking him to Lorenzo?" I ask.

Nobody answers.

"*Please,*" I plead. "*Remy,* can't you see he's struggling? He doesn't have the energy."

Remy reaches the passenger side and opens the door. "The meeting isn't with Lorenzo."

"I don't believe you."

"Liv, it's okay." My father pauses at Remy's side and glances over his shoulder at me. "We won't be long."

I don't believe him either—not when our relationship has become a breeding ground for lies.

"I'll come with you."

"Maybe next time." Dad descends into the car. "I'll see you tomorrow."

Remy closes the door as I approach, then starts for the back of the vehicle. I'm about to pass him when he swings an arm out, grabbing me around the waist to haul me behind the car.

"Get your hands off me," I snarl. "You're not taking him anywhere."

"Control yourself," he sneers against my ear, tightening his hold.

"Or what?" I shove at his chest, hating how my body instinctively molds to his. "What are you going to do?"

"Don't fuck with me, Pyro. You know what I'm capable of."

I should listen to the warning. But my body treats it like a thrill, awakening my limbs in a wash of tingling goose bumps.

"He's watching," he mutters. "Don't make this harder for him."

"Make *what* harder? Is your uncle threatening him? Why can't you take me instead?"

He grabs my chin, forcing me to hold his gaze. "I promise you, this *isn't* about Lorenzo."

I don't want to believe him, but those eyes, they charm me despite their ruthlessness. "Your words don't mean much these days."

"Jesus Christ, Ollie." Something flickers in his features. Something softer. Something real. "I'm trying my best to do right by you, and you're making it fucking difficult."

Do right by me?

My heart skips a beat. "What do you—"

"Listen." He releases my chin and steps back. "This isn't about Lorenzo and has nothing to do with our arrangement. I can't waste time placating you on this. I need to go."

"Remy." I grab his arm before he can leave. "We need to talk."

He stiffens. "This isn't the time or place." He shakes off my grip. "I'll get him to call you once he's back home."

I stand stunned. Hollow.

I hate that I believe him. Hate even more that through all the confusion I still trust him to bring home the man I care most about.

It's Lorenzo I have a problem with. "I'll be waiting here for his return."

Remy doesn't respond. Instead, he continues around the car with his uneven gait.

I pull out my cell and set a timer. "If you're not back in an hour I'm calling the cops."

He pauses in the middle of opening the driver's door, pinning me with a warning scowl. "Make it two."

I nod and retreat toward the building.

He climbs into the sports car, slams the door, and pulls from the parking lot, my father giving me a placating wave of farewell as they depart.

It's so stupid that my concern battles with an overwhelming sense of heartbreak. That Remy's cold shoulder is somehow in the same ballpark of consideration as my father's safety.

Then again, none of my reactions to that ruthless man have been filled with sanity.

I suppose I'm right on brand.

I sit on the stairs with my phone in hand. It doesn't fill me with giddy glee to navigate to the tracker app and revert to stalking again. But desperate times and all that.

I watch the little dot move away from the funeral home and across town to stop in the city.

I zoom in on the map, the sun slowly setting around me while I investigate their location—The Grand Windsor.

Why? What could they possibly be doing at a five-star hotel?

It takes two minutes of the dot idling for me to push from the stairs to pace. Another two minutes of manic contemplation before I go back inside and busy myself with work, my cell propped on my tool tray so I can constantly refresh the tracker.

They leave the hotel after half an hour. Make a detour on their return, the twenty-minute pause at a nearby suburban home. Then finally, they travel toward me.

I'm already waiting outside under the sensor light which beams down on the stairs, when the sports car pulls in, my father still in the passenger seat, a little red hatchback following them with a middle-aged woman behind the wheel.

They park side by side, Remy not glancing in my direction when he gets out and rounds the Aston Martin.

His expression lacks the harsh lines it did earlier. It's as if he's deliberately schooling his features. Not giving anything away.

I stride toward them, still eyeing Remy, waiting for him to give me a clue as to what's going on, but he remains focused on helping my dad to his feet.

"What happened?" I grasp Dad's elbow, my heart breaking at how much he leans against me for support.

"Nothing, *fragolina*." He pats my fingers and then shuffles to the end of the car while Remy hangs back. "But there's someone I'd like you to meet."

The woman stands in wait, her kind eyes taking me in with gentle appraisal.

"Liv, this is Lucy." My dad waves a tired hand between us. "Lucy, my daughter, Olivia."

The lines around the woman's eyes crinkle with warmth. "It's so lovely to meet you."

"Umm…you too?" I attempt to sound enthusiastic only for my tone to fall flat.

It's late evening, my father is clearly struggling, and this unfamiliar woman is lingering like she's got a job to do.

"Lucy will be hanging around for a while." Dad makes slow progress across the parking lot while I follow at his side. "Remy's been talking about getting me a home-care nurse for weeks, and I finally caved."

I stop, my heart halting along with my movement.

"It's okay, Liv." He pauses beside me. "I've been tired lately. The apartment is turning into a mess, and finding the energy to make dinner at the end of the day is becoming a struggle. She's here to—"

"Why didn't you ask me?" I turn into him, making sure he can see the pain his isolation inflicts. "*I* can make you dinner. *I* can clean."

"You're busy enough." Dad hobbles around me. "Luce, why don't you help me upstairs, and I can show you around before my body clocks off for the day."

"That sounds great." The woman takes my position, guiding her arm around my father's waist. "Don't worry, Olivia. I'll take great care of him."

I stand lost as they cross the parking lot without me and climb the stairs at a sloth's pace.

When's this going to end?

How long will I remain in the goddamn dark?

I peer over my shoulder to Remy who leans against the back of the Aston Martin, his indifference increasing my frustration.

I swing around to face him, ready to lash out, *needing* to fight.

"Don't," he warns under his breath.

The scolding riles me. *Infuriates* me.

Everything about this situation is one swift uppercut after another.

I only comply for my father's sake, biting my tongue until Dad blows me a kiss from the top step before disappearing inside.

As soon as the door closes behind him, I suck in a deep breath, ready to let loose the fury poised on the tip of my tongue.

"Get in the car." Remy cuts in before I get the chance. "We need to talk."

27

REMY

Her fury turns to trepidation, as if those few words or my dire tone are enough to instill the seriousness of our situation.

I push from the trunk and round the vehicle. "Come on."

"What's this about?"

"Get in the car and you'll find out." I glance over my shoulder to her father's apartment. I don't want him knowing we're leaving together, but Lucy would have him distracted by now.

I climb into the vehicle to stare through the windshield as Ollie swoops into the passenger seat, closes her door, and then drags on her belt.

She's composed, but even with her hands gently clasped in her lap I can tell she's wound tight. "Did something bad happen?"

"I'll get into specifics in a minute." I drive from the parking lot, my navigation aimless as I take random turns through suburban streets. There's no perfect place to do this, but I don't want to be behind the wheel when shit goes south. If I'm going to inflict a brutal blow, I'm doing it face-to-face.

She looks my way. "Remy, you're scaring me."

We haven't even gotten to the scary part yet.

"How am I scaring you, Pyro?"

"Your apathy after being so angry with me earlier. I can tell something's wrong."

I hadn't been angry, I'd been frustrated. Tempted. Fucking tortured.

She sighs dramatically. "At least tell me you don't have a shovel in the back of your car."

My lips twitch without my permission.

"There's no shovel." I shoot her a glance. "But I hope you know I wouldn't need one to make you disappear."

"Oh, I know." Her shoulders slump. "You're extremely resourceful."

I would've agreed weeks ago. Now, I'm not so sure.

"If you can't talk about where you took my dad, can you at least explain your comment about trying to do right by me?" Her attention haunts my periphery. "Why block my number? Why go back on our agreement?"

I tighten my hands around the steering wheel. "Why do you think?"

"Lorenzo."

Yeah, fucking Lorenzo.

After he ensured I wasn't at risk of keeling over from my bullet wound, and he delivered some fatherly words of condolence regarding Flynn, he started in on Ollie.

I warned you to keep your distance.

You're complicating an already risky situation.

In no uncertain terms he reaffirmed how easily bad things can happen to innocent people—aka how she will likely disappear if I don't cut ties.

But there are other reasons I should stay away from her too.

There always have been. Only now they're more adamant. So I tried to forget her. Tried like it was a fucking Olympic sport and I was itching for a medal, even though walking past my penthouse main bathroom was a constant reminder of what she felt like coming around my fucking fingers.

Then tonight happened.

"Am I in trouble?" she asks. "Is Lorenzo going to come after me? Or is that what you're here for?"

"We've always needed to maintain distance." I take the next left turn. "It was a mistake to act differently."

"Yet here I am, in your car."

Yet here she is, in my goddamn fucking car.

"Forget about Lorenzo for now." I take another left. A right. A left.

"Okay..." She cocks her head, clearly trying to lean farther toward my line of vision. "So what was at the hotel?"

Of course she reverted to stalking. This woman doesn't learn. "Remind me to tell Carlo to remove that app from his phone."

"I was worried. You can't fault me for that."

"You can trust me with your father." I reach the large expanse of Hillcrest Park, the dark of night making the deserted grassland seem inviting. I pull to the curb, dread poisoning my veins, and climb out before she can ask more questions.

I have two seconds of freedom from her sweet strawberry scent before she follows, her arms wrapped around her middle, her face shadowed as she stops before me, blinking those emotional eyes with the slightest furrow to her brow.

"Tell me," she begs.

"There was a medical conference in the city over the weekend." I walk past her, unable to withstand the shot of fear that crosses her features, and lead us along the trail into the moonlit park. "I called in some favors."

"What sort of favors?" She hustles to catch up, the maintained proximity making me thrum to do things I shouldn't.

"Ones that involve the best oncologist in the country."

She falls quiet.

Good.

It means she's changing gears, finally recognizing that this has nothing to do with my family or breaking the law and everything to do with her father's lacking health.

"I made sure Dr. Nguyen made time to see Carlo before he left town."

She remains silent, her head lowering as she frowns at the footpath.

I'm sure some would celebrate having access to the best medical professionals. But not Ollie—she's too busy putting the puzzle pieces together.

"Does my dad know you're telling me this?" she whispers.

"No." I turn to face her.

The glow from the streetlights doesn't reach us here. There's only the moon and stars left to illuminate her bleak expression as the slight breeze glides loose strands of hair from her braid.

"Then why tell me now when it sounds like you've kept his secrets all along?"

Because when it comes to her, my best skill is fucking up, and it seems I'm at the height of my career. "Things have changed."

She scans my face with hesitation, as if trying to find the answers before they're spoken. To read the truth in case she doesn't want to hear it out loud.

"Do you want to know, Ollie?"

"I..." She licks her lips and glances away. "Obviously it's bad news."

"I don't have to tell you if you don't want—"

"No. I need to know." Her voice breaks.

My fucking savagery does, too.

This wasn't meant to happen. Just like every other moment with Ollie should never have existed.

I planned to take Carlo to the oncologist, then deliver him home without drama.

I was supposed to maintain my distance from her for the sake of my family.

I should never have lied for her. *Killed* for her.

But when it comes to this woman I fail at every turn.

"His initial prognosis was never great, Pyro."

She flinches. Straightens. Nods. Such a tough, composed beauty.

But the next blow won't be as easy to withstand. "It's pancreatic cancer."

Her eyes flare. Her lips part. "No."

I give the information time to sink in. The severity. The well-known statistics. Then I reach for her, taking a hit of the drug I promised to steer clear of as I drag her into me.

"No." She shoves at my chest.

I clench my teeth against her misery, hating myself, hating the whole fucking situation. I drop my arm, determined to quickly tear off the remainder of the Band-Aid. "He's deteriorating."

She shakes her head and backtracks a little more. "What did your doctor say?"

I want to touch her again, to be holding her when I stab the final knife. "He agreed that Carlo's original prognosis was accurate. He's always been terminal. The chemo was only to buy him more time. But the benefits of treatment no longer outweigh the side-effects."

"Tell me you're lying," she rasps.

I continue toward her across the neatly clipped grass as she continues back. "I've never lied to you."

Withheld, for sure. But never lied.

Her face scrunches—her nose, her forehead. "How long does he have?"

She's still admirably poised. So controlled. I would've thought she'd be a blubbering mess by now. But no, not my Ollie. She keeps the agony trapped inside.

"How long, Remy?"

My pulse thunders in my ears as I reach for her, my fingers brushing her forearm before she inches away. "A few months."

Her face falls, her devastation increasing under the moonlight while she presses a splayed palm over her stomach.

"There's nothing more that can be done." I called all the doctors. Applied for all the trials. Even enlisted my sister to do holistic research.

Ollie's eyes fill with glassy desolation.

I reach out again. Always drawn to her. Always a fucking slave to this woman.

"Don't," she pleads. "I need space."

She turns to cross the lawn, her breaths growing louder, sharper.

I follow at a distance, waiting for a sob that never comes.

Instead, she jogs a few yards, making me lengthen my stride, only for her to collapse onto her knees on the grass.

She lurches forward on all fours.

"Ollie."

She retches.

Fuck.

I rush to her, the staples in my thigh threatening to tear as I drop down at her side.

"Please don't." She shoves at me. "Leave."

"I'm not going anywhere." I don't care if it's what she wants or not. What she thinks she needs. "I've got you."

She whimpers, her hands clawing into the lawn, her stomach viciously concaving with another retch.

"Please, Remy." Her shoulders slump, her arms wobbling.

"Just breathe." I rub slow circles on her back, cursing my inability to take her place. I'd willingly offer my only remaining parent to stand before death's door instead of hers. I'd pay good money to make it happen.

She retches again and again.

"Breathe, Ollie."

She sucks in deep breaths, her exhales huffing out on dry sobs.

Breath. Retch.. Breath…

I keep rubbing circles as her inhales lengthen, her lithe body incredibly fragile.

Sob… Breath…. Heave….

I want to kill someone. To fucking stab and torture.

That's what I'm good at. *All* I'm good for.

In this, I'm helpless. Worthless.

Breath… Breath… Breath…

She bows her head, the epitome of ruin. "I don't understand." She leans back on her haunches, then flops onto her ass on the damp grass. "He should've told me."

I agree, but there was no convincing him.

He didn't want Ollie to suffer for longer than necessary.

I admire him for that. For facing a death sentence on his own to save his daughter from heartache. But *damn it to hell*, I fucking hate him right now too.

"What am I going to do?" She drapes a loose hand over her face, shielding me from her sadness.

"We'll figure it out." I sit beside her, close enough for our arms to brush.

"What's to figure out? He's dying, and I won't be able to survive without him."

"You'll survive."

"I have no one." Her hand falls from her face and she meets my eyes, those shadowed depths tearing me the fuck apart. "My mom's gone. I don't have a close extended family. And I lie to Allison and Ivy so often that our friendship is tainted."

"You won't have to do that for much longer."

She winces. "His death is the end of your agreement?"

I nod, gliding her loose hair behind her ear.

Her brow furrows but she doesn't protest the touch. If anything she leans into it, her head tilting toward me, humbling me with yet another weakness toward temptation.

It's a mistake to want more. Always so many fucking mistakes with Ollie. But I test the boundaries of her tolerance, gliding my arm around her shoulders.

She continues to oblige the contact.

I continue to indulge in it.

I lower my arm to her waist. Her hip. She tenses yet there's no revolt, nothing at all to stop me dragging her onto my lap to cradle her against my chest—so I do it.

If I'm losing this battle, I might as well make it worthwhile.

I'll give her the comfort she craves and deal with the aftermath later.

She rests her head between my collarbone and chin, entirely pliant in my arms. Utterly perfect in her sorrow.

It was fucking futile thinking I could forget about her. No man could resist her gravitational pull.

She's faultless. Flawless. Forever mine.

I don't offer placations or talk for the sake of filling the void. I give her the peace to grieve what's to come. To become accustomed to the agony as the damp grass seeps into the ass of my suit pants and her strawberry scent stains my lungs.

"That woman…" she says softly. "She's a hospice nurse?"

I nod my chin against the top of her head. "The best in the city."

"So my dad has a hospice nurse, is only meant to survive a few more months, and yet still plans to keep pretending everything is fine? Where's the logic in that?"

"He doesn't want you to suffer."

"Remy, I've been suffering this whole time."

"I know. But there's a difference between the misery of speculation and the brutal reality of what's actually happening. He tried to save you from that. At least temporarily."

"All he did was steal time that could've been better spent. He wasted months. *Months* when we could've made memories. I would've taken him away—to the beach, to the mountains—while he was still in a state to handle travel."

"You have time."

"I have crumbs."

I close my eyes and press my face into her hair.

"I wish you would've told me sooner," she whispers.

Guilt strikes a punishing blow to my chest. "My loyalty—"

"Is to him," she cuts me off. "I know."

It *was*.

Carlo had my loyalty for more than six months.

He harbored my secrets and I, his.

But she changed everything.

She pulls back and meets my gaze, those beautifully troubled eyes wreaking havoc on my nervous system. "You care about him."

Yeah, too fucking much.

"He's a good man and a coveted father figure." I hold her stare, needing her to believe me. "I'll admit those attributes have been hard to come by."

"I bet your dad and Lorenzo would hate to hear you say that."

"I've known my uncle for less than two years, and the last thing my father did in this life was try to kill me. So no, neither one of them would be surprised that a well-mannered, morally driven funeral home director has become somewhat of an idol to me."

"That's how you see him?"

It's how I've always seen him, right from our first meeting when he shook my hand with a firm grip and a kind smile. He's never judged me. Never held my actions against me.

Carlo treats me as if I'm a man doing my best despite the shitty cards I've been dealt. Not as if I'm a rich boy with a silver spoon who's decided to forsake good over evil just for shits and giggles.

"I'll miss him, Ollie."

Her nose scrunches and she looks away, the pliancy of her body replaced with stiff sterility. "I hope you plan on elaborating on the whole father-attempting-to-kill-you comment." She pushes from my lap and stands above me. "You can't let a statement like that slide."

"We've had enough revelations for now." She's looking for a diversion and I don't blame her, but the topic of my dad always leaves an unfavorable aftertaste. "Let's save the legacy of Emmanuel Costa for another night."

I lead her back to the car, her frailty shadowing me one step behind.

I open her door. Watch as her devastation folds into the passenger seat. Then climb behind the wheel to drive her home.

She remains quiet. There's only her occasional sniffle to interrupt the faint hum of a forgotten playlist through the speakers.

She focuses out her window, her idle fingers tempting me to grab them to encase in mine. To do sweet, loving things instead of all the dark and twisted shit my hands are accustomed to.

"What happened to the Bentley?" she asks at a red light.

"I torched it." There was too much blood. Too many fucked up memories.

She drags a listless touch over the contoured leather of her seat. "I like this one."

Flynn would've too.

I imagine he would've begged me to drive it. Then pretended he gave it a thrashing while he barely nudged the needle past the speed limit.

I fucking miss that kid—his bullshit antics, his laughter. Even his goddamn scattered shoes at my penthouse door, but my housekeeper straightened them back into neat rows a few days ago, stealing his personality from the penthouse.

I pull into her drive and cut the ignition. "Let me walk you in."

"I don't think that's a good idea." She releases her belt. "You blocked my phone for a reason. I know you want to keep your distance."

"You're mistaking wants for needs. I don't want to stay away from you at all."

She contemplates me. *Reads* me. It's unnerving how easily she settles under my skin. "But you have to because of Lorenzo."

"He's an issue. But one of many." I unclasp my belt, the thought of letting her walk away irking the fuck out of me.

"Name the rest."

"We'd be here all night."

She sighs. "Then name the most important."

How the hell isn't it obvious? "I'm not someone you should want to be around."

She makes a slight sound of offense. The subtlest huff. "I can make my own informed choices."

"But you're not informed."

Her brows pull into a mini scowl, her grief still present in those sad hazel eyes. "I know what you do for your uncle."

"You don't know the half of it. You've been given broad strokes."

"Maybe, but I've seen your redeemable side. I've been a recipient of your compassion. You've protected me. *Defended* me." She pauses, as if realizing she's arguing the merits of a cold-blooded killer on the lowest night of her life. "All I'm saying is that you're more than what your job makes you."

"Do you know how many men I killed last week, Pyro?"

She lowers her gaze to her lap. "I'm no mathematician, but you used the retort three time—"

"Fourteen."

Her shoulders slump.

"First, I got my hands on one of the cartel. And with a little sulfuric acid influence, I got him to spill the names of all those involved in Flynn's drive-by."

She doesn't quit staring at her hands in her lap.

"I found the Cadillac they used. Kidnapped all four of the men that'd been in that car. Then doused the vehicle in gas and set it to flame while they burned to death inside."

She exhales a shuddering breath.

"Do you want to know about the others?" I wait for a refusal. Maybe even a naive dismissal of my actions. I get neither. "Number ten was the cartel soldier who gave the order. I slit his throat in a back alley. Nine interrupted the festivities so I took him out with a bullet. Eight, seven, and six were on Wednesday—all cartel members and extended family of those who took Flynn from me."

She shakes her head while it remains bowed.

Is my heartlessness finally sinking in, Pyro?

"I cremated them together—shoved them all in haphazardly at once."

Wild eyes turn to me. "Remy—"

"I repeated the process on Thursday with five, four, and three after I heard word they were about to shoot up my club. And two and one would've met with the same disposal but you decided to spend the night at the funeral home, and I couldn't risk seeing you in that state of mind. So my men ensured they had an ocean burial."

She holds my stare, brows furrowed, gaze beseeching—for what I don't know.

"I'm not the type of man you want returning your messages, Ollie. *That's* why last week was a mistake. Not for any fault of your own."

She keeps staring. Quiet. Concerned.

I can't fucking tolerate her silence anymore.

"Say something," I demand. "Tell me you understand."

She returns her attention to her lap.

"Tell me what you're thinking, Ollie."

She sighs. "I'm thinking that psychologists would have a field day analyzing the unhealthy thoughts running through my mind."

"Meaning?"

"Meaning I still don't see it. I can't picture you like that… or maybe I can. Maybe I'm so desensitized to death that I simply don't care. I just…" She heaves a frustrated breath. "I can't change the way I feel."

Annoyance thunders beneath my sternum.

Rumbling, explosive *need*.

"Make it make sense, Remy." Her eyes plead.

I can't.

I'm too fucking angry—at her for being so stupid. At me for being equally moronic.

Her ability to downplay the things I've done is as unhinged as me craving a woman who could put my entire family behind bars.

Yet the insanity continues to thrive.

Her voice is barely audible as she says, "I still want you."

I scrub a rough hand over my mouth and divert my gaze, focusing on the crone's house. At the frail silhouette that stands in the middle of the closest window, backlit by an orange glow.

Jesus Christ. That old bitch has sonar on my ass.

"I need to go." The option of walking Ollie to her door is dead and buried. In my current state I wouldn't be able to stop at her threshold. I'd follow her inside, drag her onto the nearest horizontal surface, then fuck her senseless, virginity be damned.

Ollie opens her door. "Why does it feel like I might not see you again?"

Because that's how it should be. How any motherfucker with two brain cells to rub together would act.

"I'm not messaging you about disposals anymore." It's not up for negotiation. "You should be confident in my process by now. And I'll make sure Wesley double-checks everything before your employees arrive at work. You've got more important things to concentrate on."

Dejection ebbs from her. "But I'll still see you?"

"Yeah, Pyro. You'll still see me."

"Okay." She climbs out and pauses to glance back inside. "Thank you for being honest. I understand how hard it must've been to betray my father's trust."

I suppress a flinch at the reminder. "Will you be all right on your own?"

"I'll be as all right as I can be given the circumstances."

I fight not to clench my fists. Not to shove from the car. To haul her into my arms and drag her back to my penthouse, giving her a Lorenzo Cappelletti death sentence at the same time.

"Call if you need anything." *Weak prick.* "I'll unblock your number." *Stupid fuck.*

"Is that a smart idea?"

No. It's the dumbest of dumb. But that's become my calling card where she's concerned. "If you need anything I can send Russo or Valenti."

She cringes, then quickly masks the distaste. "I'll be fine."

"A gorgeous woman once told me *fine* is never a comforting descriptor."

"I think that woman may have also thrown you in a working retort, so rest assured she can take care of herself."

28

———

OLIVIA

Monday night was hard.

Seeing Dad the next day and having to pretend I don't know he's dying is even harder. The only saving grace is my acclimation to dishonesty. I lean into our shared bond of mistruths and concoct a lie to excuse being melancholy. To warrant hugging him a little tighter. A little longer.

Apparently, one of my fictional high school friends died in a freak moped accident while in Thailand, so I'm super sad.

I give no names. No descriptive details. Dad's too busy pretending not to be exhausted to ask challenging questions. And I don't harbor any guilt because it gives me the excuse to be clingy.

I use getting to know Lucy as justification to have lunch upstairs with them every day. The problem is, with each shared meal, I notice how far my father's health has deteriorated.

Before Remy shared the truth, I'd thought Dad's symptoms were caused by chemo. That the treatments were making him lethargic, achy, and slightly jaundiced.

I know better now.

His pain is from the cancer, although he continues to try and hide it. He's barely eating. And rapidly losing weight. The yellow tinge to his skin only increases with the passing days. But I don't bring it up. I nod through the hypocrisy when he repeats how having Lucy around "*isn't a big deal*" or "*cause for concern*," hating all the mistruths, yet regretfully understanding them at the same time.

Mom's cancer battle was hard. By far the hardest thing I've ever endured—current underworld drama included.

I get why he doesn't want to tell me. It makes sense in a shitty kind of way.

So I let him think his secrets remain hidden. I'll give him that final wish—at least until the heartbreak wears me down.

"How are you and Remy getting along?" he asks Saturday morning after Lucy leaves to get coffee and donuts.

I focus on the picture of Mom framed and mounted on the wall, buying some time before another deceitful dance.

The truth is, I haven't spoken to Remy since Monday night. Five days without contact that feels more like five months.

The sick part is that I miss him.

"Don't worry, Liv. I know."

I struggle to keep my blank expression in check. "Hmm?" I feign indifference. "What do you know?"

"I'm sick. Not stupid. Whenever Remy has business to take care of I always try to glance out the window to make sure there are no issues, and numerous times I've seen your car in the parking lot with you sitting there, watching."

My stomach rolls. "Why didn't you say something?"

"I guess it brings me comfort to know he trusts you enough to have you hanging around."

I sit stunned, somehow still surprised by all the duplicitous cogs my father has spinning. "You weren't worried?"

"About you seeing a dead body?" He snorts. "Do they bother you all of a sudden?"

I'd been referring to the criminal implication. The threat to my existence.

"You're grown now, *fragolina*. Obviously you felt the need to be here and Remy allowed it, so who am I to stop you?"

I return my attention to Mom's picture as I blink the burn from my eyes. It's hard to understand how he can trust in my safety under these circumstances. But when I think about Remy, I guess I hold the same trust. There's something about him that makes me feel protected, and it's not only due to the ring dangling from my necklace that remains hidden under my clothes.

"With that same maturity and professionalism in mind," he continues, "I've decided I'm going to give you the opportunity to take over the business for a while."

I expected this, had predicted a rough timeline of events, but even with the foresight my throat tightens at the thought of working without him.

"Chemo is knocking me around this time, and I need a longer

recovery period." His smile is solemn. "The experience will do you good."

"But I don't know nearly enough about the ins and outs of your role. I wouldn't have a clue how to even pay our staff."

"Ivy knows the drill. I've been teaching her more about my job over the past few months."

Of course he has.

"You've got this all worked out, don't—"

A knock sounds at the front door, cutting me off.

"That must be Lucy back with brunch." Dad hesitantly shifts to raise from his recliner. "She mustn't feel comfortable using her key."

"Don't move." I quickly push to my feet. "I'll get it."

I don't want to get it. I don't appreciate having an audience to the dwindling amount of time we have left. But thankfully, Lucy has been great at busying herself when Dad and I are together.

It's not Lucy who steals the breath from my lungs when I open the door though.

"Ollie," Remy says in greeting against the backdrop of the mid-morning sun.

He looks entirely casual in faded grey jeans and a white T-shirt that clings to an impressive set of pecs, his hair mussed. It's the first time I've seen him in anything other than a designer suit, and I'm stunned.

"What are you doing here?" My stomach fills with ridiculous butterflies.

"I've got business with Carlo." He walks past me, his shoulder lightly brushing mine in the slightest tease of contact.

I rush to close the door and follow him into the living room.

"Hey, old-timer." He levels a sly grin on my father. "How are you feeling?"

Dad rolls his eyes with a hollow chuckle. "Don't start that old-timer crap with me."

"Then answer my question."

My heart clenches as they interact like seasoned friends.

"How much energy do you have today?" Remy slumps onto the sofa, kicking his legs out in front of him.

"Enough to take on the world," Dad drawls.

"Good because that's what we're about to do. I'm taking you somewhere."

My pulse kicks up speed.

"Are you talking about Taco Bell, son, or...?"

"I had somewhere more like Berkeley Springs in mind." Remy sits forward, dragging his legs in and resting his elbows on his knees.

"I've got us a house for the night. You and Ollie can relax by the pool with Lucy. If you're up for it, I even have dinner reservations on standby."

Dad's face lights up. "Are you serious?"

"One hundred percent." Remy's grin is subtle. Humbly proud. My stomach flutters at the handsomeness of the godforsaken expression, but my chest smothers the giddy sensation with foreboding. "My bag's packed and in the back of the car. I also prearranged this with Lucy, so she's already returning from getting some clothes."

I stride farther into the room. "He doesn't have the energy to travel."

"Sure I do." Dad repositions himself to sit more upright in his chair, trying to fake-smile his way through the discomfort movement must cause. "It's a great idea."

There's a jingle of keys from the outside stairs, then the front door opens to reveal Lucy holding a box of donuts in one hand and an overnight bag in the other.

She glances between us with hesitation. "Did I take too long? I wasn't sure what to pack."

"No. You're just in time." Remy pushes to his feet. "I'm going to take little Pelosi home to get her things and make sure she doesn't dawdle. You can help Carlo pack what he needs."

"Of course." She dumps her bag on the floor and hustles her way to my father, who stands with more energy and enthusiasm than I've seen in weeks.

But still… "I'm not sure I agree with this."

I can't ditch my apprehension.

Dad's explosion of excitement will result in a crash later—one that could be detrimental to his health. And then there's the whole laying-low-for-the-sake-of-our-lives stitch. Not to mention the lunacy of the four of us being tightly compacted into a tiny sports car for a drive likely to take more than ninety-minutes.

"It'll do Carlo a world of good." Lucy places the donut box on the coffee table and offers her arm to my father. "I'll make sure he's properly taken care of."

"I can handle it, Liv," Dad reiterates. "It's going to be great."

Nervousness eats at me, the anxiety warring with my quickly building excitement.

"Get moving, Ollie." Remy jerks his chin toward the door as he starts for the entry. "You're eating away at your dad's relaxation time."

The war continues, my insides being pulled in different directions.

I follow after Remy, catching up when he opens the door.

"Why are you doing this?" I keep my voice low and precede him outside.

"I feel like getting out of town." He closes the door behind him and maneuvers around me to descend the stairs.

"With *us*?" I follow, his sleek Aston Martin missing from the parking lot. Instead, a large black Cadillac Escalade sits in the shade of the towering hedge, its windows covered in dark tint. "Don't tell me you bought another car." I scamper down the remaining stairs, scurrying to catch up, his uneven gait still faster than my shorter stride.

"It's a rental." He continues his cool pace across the parking lot.

He rented a car… reserved a house… planned a night away…

I lunge the foot of space between us to grab his wrist. "Whose secrets are you hiding this time?"

He pauses, his gaze dipping to my hand circling the taut muscles of his forearm.

My body floods with warmth, the contact seeming far too forward after his warning to maintain distance.

"Sorry." I let go.

"There aren't any secrets. I want to get out of the city. All four of us wouldn't fit in the Aston, so I arranged the Escalade." He continues to the car.

I'm a step behind, climbing into the passenger seat, pulling on my belt. I stare at the man who warned me away less than a week ago while he reverses out of the parking space. "I thought we were keeping our distance."

He pulls onto the street and stares straight ahead as he drives toward my house.

"Isn't this risky?" I ask.

"I've taken precautions. We'll lay low."

"But it's still a risk…"

"Sometimes the risk is worth the reward."

Why is he being so painful?

I sigh. "And what's the reward?"

He shoots me a sidelong glance, then returns his attention to the road without answer. If he wasn't currently driving at speed, I'd shake him.

"What's the reward, Remy?"

His hands tighten on the wheel. "To give you more memories."

The answer blindsides me.

"To give me more memories?" I repeat his words, trying to get them to make sense.

This is for me?

Because I said I would've traveled with my father if I'd had prior knowledge of his prognosis? "Remy, that isn't necessa—"

"It's not a big deal. It's only one night."

It's a big deal to me. *Huge.* It's not like I have men waiting in line to spoil me with thoughtfulness. "What about Lorenzo?"

"What about him?"

"Did he suddenly decide it would be okay for the owners of a funeral home to start taking mini vacays with underworld figures?"

The muscles in his forearms flex. "It's twenty-four hours in a tiny-ass town. Don't make it an issue." He sounds confident.

I'm not convinced. "But you got Lorenzo's permission, right?"

"I don't need his permission."

Jesus Christ. "Remy..."

He falls silent.

"*Remy.*" Again he ignores me. Infuriates me.

Damn him.

I reach out, slamming my palm against the horn.

Remy's glaring eyes flash to mine at the resulting burst of sound.

"What the fuck is your problem?" he snaps.

"You." I turn to him, sitting at my full height, chin high, shoulders straight. "And I'm not afraid to say it. Unlike someone else, who spends half the time being cryptic just so he can pretend he's being honest. For once, just spit it out. Tell me why you're going against your uncle's wishes."

He glares at me, the anger in his gaze making me nervous before he returns his focus to the road. "Because I fucking left you on your own to grieve."

I blink in disbelief.

"If I would've told you about Carlo's prognosis earlier you could've taken him away yourself." His voice is bitter. Hoarsely guttural. "My omission hurt you, and although I'm a prick, your pain has stuck with me, making me feel like a top-tier piece of shit. So forgive me for making this small, selfish gesture to try to make things right."

And just like that, a little bit more of my heart gets lost to a man who kills for a living. The warmth, the butterflies, the pangs, they all meld together, creating a rampant storm in my stomach.

"You deserve this weekend." He lowers his voice. "I'll handle Lorenzo."

I settle back into my seat, lost to his generosity.

"I don't want you to worry." His tone is a subdued mutter as he turns onto my street. "I'm taking precautions."

"I trust you." The words are out before I can stop them.

I'm not surprised that he flinches.

He pulls into my drive, our arrival witnessed by Lesley, who's gardening in her front yard.

"What should I pack?" I open my door, preparing to make quick work of an overnight bag.

"Pajamas. Something to swim in if you think it's warm enough. And clothes for tomorrow."

I nod and jog for my house, waving a friendly hello to Lesley before racing inside.

I'm back within ten minutes, my belongings crammed into a suitcase small enough to rest on my lap.

I spend the return trip in an aggressively chaotic headspace, my thoughts caught between concern for my father and disturbing attraction for the surly man seated next to me.

By the time we arrive, Lucy and Dad are waiting on the stairs at the back of the building. Bags are shoved into the Escalade. Lucy climbs into the rear seat behind Remy. When I make to pull open the opposite door to join her, Dad waves me away.

"Not this time." He nudges in front of me. "You sit up front with Rem. Last night Lucy and I got started on a heated debate about pineapple on pizza that I'm eager to finish."

Lucy chuckles. "There's no debate. Pineapple does *not* go on pizza."

"Really?" I gape at her. "Dad, I don't think you need that negative influence in your life."

He laughs, and *damn*, the sound is heartwarming.

I'd give anything to hear it a million more times.

I ignore the pang in my chest and give the older generation what they want.

They continue their debate as Remy drives toward the mountains. Lucy argues culinary purity, how Italians never intended for pineapple to be on pizza, and advocates for preserving authenticity.

Dad has more of a creative expression approach. He says pizza making is often considered an art form and that shunning pineapple is disingenuous.

I listen with a smile while Remy remains quiet from the driver's seat, the slight quirk of his mouth doing things to me that it shouldn't.

Once the pizza debate reaches a stalemate, they turn to sports. How Dad loves the Ravens and Lucy wishes we had a local NHL team. But we've barely reached the outskirts of Baltimore when the chatter teeters to a stop and I glance behind me to see Dad fast asleep, his chin tucked against his chest.

"He didn't have the best rest last night," Lucy whispers.

I nod, feeling guilty for not realizing. I don't lose the smile though. I keep pretending everything is okay, just like my father has for months.

"Don't worry." She beams with reassurance. "I'll make sure he gets lots of relaxation while we're away."

"Thank you." I turn to Remy, leaning my cheek against my headrest. "So what are your thoughts regarding pineapple on pizza?"

He keeps his eyes on the road. "I prefer not to get involved in controversial conversations."

"Don't tell me a man as opinionated as yourself doesn't want to chime in with his thoughts."

"My choice is purely strategic. Your dad mentioned you being on the debate team in high school, and the only debating I've ever been good at is the mass kind."

I frown. "The mass kind?"

Lucy snorts as Remy shoots me a smug look.

I don't get it.

Mass kind? What the hell is a mass deba—

Oh, God.

My cheeks flame. "Very funny."

He releases a subtle snicker as I turn forward.

Picturing Remy masturbating is *not* on the approved weekend activities list. Picturing anything sexual while in his proximity deserves an almighty *hell no* when I still flush hot whenever I think about how he's touched me.

But even with that sensible, mature-ass outlook, I can't quit staring at him from the corner of my eye.

The corded forearms.

The muscled thighs.

Dear Lord, that chiseled jaw.

We reach Berkeley Springs in good time, the midday sun shining as we make our way through town, then continue out the other side.

We pass suburban houses and head into the quiet desolation of rural life, finally pulling into a winding dirt drive surrounded by lush trees and sweeping hills with no other houses in sight.

"It's gorgeous here," Lucy murmurs in awe.

My dad groans, rousing from sleep. "Have we arrived?"

"We have." Remy parks before a sprawling contemporary home with a wraparound porch.

It's massive, nestled beneath the shade of the treetops and surrounded by a bright floral garden.

A dark-haired, middle-aged man sits on a cement bench near the few stairs leading to the porch, eying us with interest.

Remy eyes him right back, making goose bumps of trepidation skitter down my back.

"Do you know him?" I ask.

"I assume he's the owner, but wait here while I check." He climbs out, all protective and dreamy.

The stranger pushes to his feet and strolls forward to exchange a handshake. Muffled words are spoken. Calm composure is maintained.

Everything looks aboveboard.

No threats sensed.

"I'm going to make a start on our luggage." I climb out of the car.

Remy's cold stare pins me.

Shit. Was I meant to wait for a signal?

I force a smile and walk toward them, preferring to be closer to Remy if a threat does exist.

"Good afternoon." I round the hood of the Escalade and step onto the grass. "You have a magnificent home."

The stranger nods in appreciation. "It's a blessing to have you here to share it."

Introductions are made and pleasantries are exchanged. But Remy remains tightly wound as he and Curt grab the luggage from the car while Lucy leads Dad inside.

I follow Curt to the door, Remy close behind me, and stop to take off my shoes when a strong arm weaves around my waist.

I gasp.

"Defy me again," Remy growls in my ear, "and I'll turn that ass red."

My lungs burn, every nerve in my body tingling.

"Being around me is dangerous enough without your inability to perceive possible threats." He holds me tighter, his body flush at my back. "Understood?"

I swallow. Nod.

"Perfect." He releases me and continues into the house. "I'd hate to have to make good on my promise."

29

REMY

It's no surprise I fuck up and lay hands on her before we even step foot inside the house.

I'm paranoid about her safety, and when she didn't stay in the car—like I fucking asked—I could barely resist the urge to drag her over my lap to make her see sense.

Now the feel of her is all caught up in my head, and I can't get it out.

It's not even like we're at high risk out here in the middle of absolute fucking nowhere.

I've taken a shit-load of unnecessary precautions.

But my continued stupidity has me spending hours holed up in one of the bedrooms, pretending I need to make important business calls. I only leave the isolation temporarily to allow entry to the chef I contracted days ago.

I give Ollie and Carlo the well-needed time together.

I reply to contractor emails concerning Smoke & Mirrors and sip the twenty-five-year-old Macallan whisky I asked the homeowner to procure, as if drinking expensive liquor will make the threat of Lorenzo finding out about this mini vacay any less of an issue.

Late afternoon a knock sounds at my door, raising my hackles. *If Ollie tempts me again…* But it's the middle-aged male chef who pokes his bearded face into my room.

"Sorry for the interruption, Mr. Costa. I'm about to serve antipasti to your guests beside the pool. Would you like me to bring a plate in here?"

I withhold a cringe, knowing I can't stay in here forever.

"No." I push from the bed. "I'll join them."

The man nods and backtracks, disappearing while I slide my cell into my pocket and ponder my pathetic weakness.

Carlo will seek me out if I don't show my face soon, and the truth is, I'm not as immune to his impending demise as I'd like to be. I want time with him too.

I leave the bedroom, Lucy's laughter carrying from the pool deck, Carlo's quickly following.

I walk outside, finding the two of them sitting side by side on cushioned loungers before I instinctively search for Ollie.

She breeches from beneath the pool's surface with a gasp, her hair loose around her shoulders. Her skin glistens as she begins to climb the steps like some otherworldly goddess in a skimpy black bikini that could potentially see me greeting Carlo in the fucking afterlife.

I don't know what I expected her to bathe in, but I wouldn't have dared to rent a place with a pool if the heavenly sight before me had crossed my mind for even the slightest of seconds.

She's a fantasy, the bikini bottom hugging the petite curves of her ass, the top molding to her tits to expose every inch of her cleavage and too fucking much of her side-boob.

I clear the tightness from my throat and turn away. My eyes catch on Carlo, whose gaze is narrowed on me with far too much scrutiny as he closes the paperback memoir in his hands.

Fuck.

"Did you decide to take a nanna nap, Costa?" he drawls.

I huff a laugh, pretending like his daughter isn't making my dick hard. "No, I thought I'd reserved those for the old man of the crew." I stroll toward him. "I've been working."

He raises his brows in disbelief.

Thankfully the chef approaches and places a tray of food at the end of Carlo's lounger.

"Sorry to interrupt, but I thought you might be hungry." The guy, who must've been a lumberjack in his past life, points to the delicacies displayed. "This is the *prosciutto e melone.* Then we have the arancini, bruschetta, olives and marinated mushrooms."

Ollie joins us mid report, her skin covered in goose bumps as she wrings water from her hair, seeming completely oblivious to her appeal. "It looks amazing."

He grins at her. "The mushrooms have been infused with balsamic vinegar, garlic, and parsley, but also have a dash of red peppers." His focus dips momentarily to her tits before snapping upward. "So be prepared for a slight kick."

The mushrooms won't provide the only motherfucking kick if this piece of shit doesn't mind his manners.

"I'm excited to see what you organize for dinner." She grabs one of the arancini balls and takes a bite.

"I'm actually not sure if I'm in charge of dinner." The fucker meets my glower, his eyes bugging slightly at my deathly expression. "Umm… have you decided if you're staying in or going out?"

"Not yet." I school my anger to address Carlo. "I made dinner reservations at Les Délices de Versailles. It's French cuisine, but we can stay in if you prefer."

"That sounds classy for Berkeley Springs," Lucy chirps.

It's not.

It's a small family-owned restaurant that I called in advance to make a few requests Lucy is already aware of. "It's black tie."

"*Black tie?*" Ollie almost chokes on her arancini. "But I didn't pack anything appropriate to wear."

"You'll find something." I don't chance glancing at her again, not when her cleavage is already fucking with me from the corner of my eye.

It also hasn't skipped my attention that she's not wearing my ring around her neck. I know why it's not there—wearing it visibly would inspire questions—but I don't appreciate her taking it off.

For protective reasons… as well as possessive.

"I was wondering why Lucy insisted on packing my tux," Carlo says. "French cuisine sounds perfect."

"Dad, are you sure you're up for—"

"*Fragolina*, relax. I'm living my best life."

Ollie sighs and reaches for an olive. "Of course you are."

"In that case… " I return my glower to the chef. "Your services shouldn't be needed until breakfast. Take the night off."

He inclines his head. "I'll put the snacks I prepared for later in the fridge, then tidy up and be on my way."

I don't fucking care, asshole. Just leave.

"It was nice meeting you, Nathan," Ollie offers softly. "I can't wait for breakfast."

Leave now, fucker, before you do it in a body bag.

The chef smirks. "I'll make sure I have something mouthwatering prepared."

The only thing he needs to prepare for is an early grave if he doesn't quit looking at Ollie like she's a fucking blow job waiting to happen.

"You're dismissed," I growl, instantly siphoning the companionable energy from the atmosphere.

Lucy balks.

Carlo stares at me.

And Ollie? She pops another olive in her mouth with a condescending raised brow.

I'm going to kill that fucking chef.

Lucy clears her throat. "I guess I should iron my dress for tonight." She picks up some bruschetta and walks for the glass living room doors. "I'll come back for more food in a minute."

Ollie casually helps herself to another olive, her brow still raised. "You could've told me to pack something nice."

I ignore her words. Her expression. That fucking bikini.

I ignore everything as she turns on her heel and saunters inside. Everything *except* the pathetic jealousy coursing through my veins.

"You're attracted to my daughter," Carlo says without preamble.

I scoff. Mainly to brush him off, but also because attraction is far too weak of a word.

I'm not surprised it's written all over my face. "She's a beautiful woman."

"Is your interest merely physical?"

The question is laughable when my interest is manic on every level. There isn't anything about Ollie that doesn't fascinate me. But I'm sure pondering a murderer's fetish for his daughter isn't something Carlo needs to think about while approaching his deathbed.

"I thought so," he murmurs.

I shoot him an inquisitive look. "I didn't even answer your question, Pelosi."

"You didn't need to. I can see it. I see it in her, too."

I clamp my mouth shut and turn my stare to the pool.

My interest in her is one thing. The reciprocation is another.

Ollie doesn't understand who I am. *What* I am.

Despite trying to lay it out in brutal technicolor multiple times, she still looks at me through rose-tinted glasses.

"Are you waiting for me to kick the bucket before you make a move, son?"

"What?" I scowl at him. "No."

"Then what's the hold-up?"

I scrub a hand over the back of my neck. "You want me to be with your daughter, old-timer?"

He contemplates me with fatherly interest. "I didn't say that."

Exactly.

We don't need to take a poll to determine my worth when it comes to Ollie.

Money, power, and notoriety can't buy morality, integrity, and altruism.

"Olivia is a grown woman. She makes informed choices. If she thought you were the man for her, I could understand her decision." He pushes to his feet, the movement labored with a pained cringe. "I've always told you you're a good man, Remy."

He has, but this time there's skepticism in his tone.

"But?" I mutter.

"But if once I'm gone she decides you're the guy for her, then you'd better live up to my expectations." His fatherly gaze turns stern as he claps a hand on my shoulder. "Otherwise me and my wife are going to be busy haunting you in the afterlife."

30

OLIVIA

I step out of my private bathroom in my underwear after a luxurious shower that offered enough complimentary luxury products to have me smelling like a florist.

It's too bad that the waterfall showerhead wasn't enough to curb my annoyance with Remy.

He knew I'd need black-tie attire and didn't tell me.

It also doesn't help that I still harbor shell shock from him hauling me against him to growl a delicious threat in my ear. And the way he dared to act jealous toward the chef who happened to admire what Remy classifies as a mistake?

It's plain dumb… in the most tinglingly intoxicating way.

I walk hunched over, towel-drying my hair, before flipping back upright once I reach the massive king-sized bed.

A garment bag is laid across the coverings with a folded piece of paper sitting on top. A garment bag and folded piece of paper that weren't there before I got in the shower, along with a Jimmy Choo shoebox near the pillows.

Someone was in my room.

I glance toward the door, but it's closed. In the exact same state I left it.

I rest my towel over my shoulders and grab the piece of paper.

I told you you'd find something to wear.

x Rem

My stomach fills with static.

I drop the paper and rush to snatch at the top of the bag to lower the zipper, exposing an intricately plaited black satin bodice with a strapless sweetheart neckline.

My breath catches at the beauty. "Holy shit."

I wrap my arms delicately underneath the material, dragging out the billowing floor-length skirt.

"Oh, wow."

It's stunning and far too classy for someone like me.

I didn't go to prom. Hell, I don't even own a strapless bra. But *God*, it's so pretty.

I wish I could call Allison and Ivy and tell them all about it. They'd freak. Then they'd squeal. Then they'd gush about how the guy who'd bought it for me deserved to be deep-throated, or bukkake-d, or some other equally random sexual experience that I'd have no goddamn idea how to fulfill… at least until they found out who he was.

My cell vibrates with a text message from my bedside table.

I hold the dress against my half-naked body as I circle the bed to pick it up.

REMY

We leave for an early dinner in an hour.

He doesn't mention the dress. Just completely ignores yet another good deed.

I don't get it.

Why does he do nice things and pretend they don't exist?

I nibble my bottom lip, wanting to respond with gratitude. To tell him the dress is far too remarkable for someone who rarely steps foot in public. But all the gushing, grateful things I should say are smothered with the insurgent panic that I only have one hour to get myself into a state that will remotely do this phenomenal masterpiece justice.

So I drop my phone and flee to the bathroom, praying I don't have a meltdown.

Fifty-five minutes later my nerves are still jangling as I grip the bedroom door handle, my confidence nonexistent as the perfectly fitted bodice clings to my naked breasts.

The whole gown feels entirely foreign.

But I've put in the work. I've styled my hair with two loose braids over the front of my head that join into a messy boho braid styled to sit across my left shoulder. My makeup is simplistic with mascara and a light smoky eyeshadow, one—because I didn't bring my full makeup kit, but two—because I'm already nervous over the attention this dress will bring and don't want to do anything that may increase it.

I'm such an imposter, especially after looking up the description of the Jimmy Choos from the product tag and finding out that they cost more than my monthly rent.

For almost an hour I've told myself I'm doing this for Dad… It's only one night… A few hours max.

No matter what I tell myself, it doesn't make it easier to twist the door handle and step into the hall, but I do it anyway, the bile in my stomach threatening to escape up my throat.

Chatter carries from the living room—my dad's warm timbre, Lucy's playful prattle.

But it's Remy's smooth, confident tone that tears strips from my already lacking composure.

I keep my head down as I reach the end of the hall and pause, dying a little inside when the house falls quiet.

I don't need to glance up at them to determine they're staring at me. My sixth sense of impending doom already tells me they are, along with Dad's deeply indrawn breath.

I scrub my hands together, attempting to alleviate the palm sweat.

"Liv …" Dad murmurs, "you look …"

I chance a glance toward him on the sofa.

Big mistake.

He pushes to his feet in a tuxedo, blinking back tears through a bittersweet smile. "I wish your Mom was here to see you."

My heart pangs, but I keep my gaze on him, deliberately not chancing eye contact with the other tux-clad man who stands, sucking the entire world into his vortex.

"That dress is amazing." Lucy clasps a hand to her chest, the other reaching out to steady my father.

"Thank you." I blush, glancing nervously toward the far hall leading to the front door. "Are we ready to leave?"

"We sure are." Dad leads the way toward the entry, Lucy holding pace at his side.

I can't move. Especially not when Remy's massive frame haunts the corner of my vision.

He doesn't speak. Doesn't budge.

I itch to look at him to determine if his silence is for good reason. Does he think I look okay? Have I met his expectations?

"Everything okay?" he finally murmurs, his voice more roughened than usual.

I nod, suddenly mute.

From my periphery, I watch him round the sofa and come toward me.

Shit.

I can't do proximity. Not when I can already smell his delicious aftershave.

I kick my legs into first gear and start toward the entry.

It doesn't take long for him to close in behind me, his presence tickling every nerve down my spine.

"You sure know how to steal a man's attention." His words are so devastatingly low I question whether they're a figment of my imagination. "I've never seen anything more stunning."

My breath catches, clogging the back of my throat.

I shouldn't pause, not when Dad and Lucy are already outside, leaving the two of us alone, but curiosity digs its claws into me, forcing me to turn.

I become entranced by his unfathomable gorgeousness. I've seen him in what feels like a hundred different suits. All of them black. But tonight, in his tuxedo, his devastating handsomeness is beyond compare.

He's different.

No longer a criminal at work.

He's a man at play. An incredibly suave one, whose hungry eyes rake over me.

"It's a beautiful dress." I wipe a sweaty palm over the boning of my bodice.

In this moment, I could almost kid myself into believing that he's a normal guy, and I'm a normal girl, and a future between us would be far from a mistake.

"It has nothing on the woman wearing it." He weaves a hand around my back, raising the tiny hairs all over my body as he gently guides me toward the front door.

Every inch of my skin remains flushed and tingling for the twenty-minute drive into Berkeley Springs. Remy takes a turn off one of the main roads and parks in front of a small brick building, a chipped paint sign stating *Les Délices de Versailles* hanging above the awning.

It doesn't look like a black-tie restaurant.

If anything it seems more like an everyday eating house. One that locals know to steer clear of if the lack of cars out front is any indication.

"In all my years, I've never had French cuisine." Lucy opens her door in the back. "I'm so excited."

I hide a smile, her enthusiasm contagious.

"You ready?" Remy asks as Dad and Lucy climb out.

I nod, holding my focus on the restaurant.

I need to keep my wits about me—or maybe just wrangle my lust under some semblance of control—but my brain always wants to cut and run whenever I look at him.

We get out, all four of us walking toward the restaurant together—Remy in the lead, Lucy helping my dad in the middle, and me deliberately staying at the back.

The front door opens on our approach, a young woman in all black service-wear holding it ajar as she nervously balances a tray of bubbling champagne flutes.

"Mr. Costa?" She smiles at Remy.

He inclines his head.

"Welcome." She inches the tray forward for him to take a glass. "Please come in. Dinner is going to be amazing."

My heart rate increases as each of us claim a drink and follow the waitress inside.

It's kinda random.

Actually, it's top-notch weird.

The interior of the building is as 'black tie' as the outside. It's definitely nice, with a welcoming small-town vibe and cute wooden chairs that match the cute little vases filled with small fake flowers beside the table numbers. But Les Délices de Versailles is nothing more than a small-town family restaurant.

An *empty* small-town family restaurant.

There isn't a single soul dining here except us.

"Did you reserve the entire restaurant?" Lucy gushes.

What?

My gaze snaps to Remy for confirmation.

It's the waitress who nods with enthusiasm. "He even requested the live entertainment. We've never had a booking like this before. The chef is beyond excited."

On cue, a middle-aged woman walks through the swinging kitchen doors, raising a violin to her shoulder. She poises her bow against the strings as she moves to stand in the open floorspace near the small empty bar, then decimates my heart with a melodic rendition of a classic Ed Sheeran song.

I struggle to keep following everyone to the only table in the room covered with a crisp white tablecloth, the fake flowers replaced with red roses.

Remy arranged all of this? For me? For my dad?

The dress. The shoes. The extravagance.

How can he be so selfless yet still cast himself as the irredeemable villain?

The poor guy has more screws loose than I do.

"Come on, Liv." Dad waves me over to the table, his grin infectious.

"Coming." I down a large gulp of champagne and will the alcoholic goodness to suppress my growing attraction. All it does is awaken my mouth with tingles, making me wonder what it would be like to be kissed by someone brimming with confidence and charisma.

We're seated at a square table, Dad and Lucy side by side, grinning at each other in excitement, while Remy holds out my chair to help me into the place setting beside him.

We're offered water—sparkling, still, or tap. Tattered leather-bound menus are handed over.

"You can order from the menu," the waitress offers, "or choose to be surprised with what has already been prearranged."

"I want to be surprised," Lucy gushes.

"Me, too." Dad places his menu on the table without looking at it.

All eyes turn to me.

"A surprise would be nice," I lie.

I don't think I can handle more revelations. My bucket already overfloweth with praise for Remy. I'm not sure I'll even be able to hold a conversation with him after this—not with my ovaries in knots and my heart seriously entangled.

"Great. I'll let the chef know." The waitress retrieves the menus one by one, hugging them to her chest. "The first of your ten-course meal should be ready shortly." She turns on her heel, her ponytail swishing.

"*Ten.*" Lucy's eyes threaten to fall out of her head with how wide they stretch.

Dad chuckles. "I hope everyone is hungry."

"It's a tasting menu," Remy cuts in with refinement. "Each plate will be a small portion."

I nibble my bottom lip, staring absentmindedly at my sparkling cutlery.

I can't tell if this is common nature for someone with Remy's wealth, or if he's deliberately impressing me. Either way, someone has to tell him that continuing down the generous extravagance path is only making me want to experience all those dirty sex acts Ivy boasts about.

If he's not careful, I'll dock his brains out right here at the dinner table.

I reach for my champagne, only to turn rigid when Remy leans close.

"Are you okay?" His warm knuckles skate over the material of my skirt, pressing gently into my thigh.

"Mm-hmm." I take another gulp, emptying my glass.

I know alcohol isn't the answer, but I'm not sure what is when my body is filled with a demented level of thermonuclear energy.

"Just hungry." I tilt my legs away and lower the flute to the table, the base barely brushing against the tablecloth before the waitress hustles forward to fill it again.

"Did you hear a new Italian restaurant opened in Towson that has some sort of celebrity chef?" Dad asks.

I ignore him as I smile in thanks at the waitress, whispering my gratitude.

Remy and my dad chat about the restaurant, the conversation soon evolving into the topic of nightclubs, and then government rules and regulations.

I don't expect them to get along so well. But they talk without pause, one discussion rolling into another, with fun quips and taunting sarcasm that makes Lucy laugh while I pretend to be enamored by the violinist and not their bond.

It isn't long before the waitress returns with a team of staff trailing behind her, all four of them exuding some form of nervousness as they position themselves behind each of us to synchronize the placing of our meals.

"This is the *amuse-bouche*." Our main waitress moves to stand tall before me and my father. "It's a *petite gougère* filled with truffle-infused *béchame*."

I'm pretty sure she's butchered a few of the pronunciations but it's incredibly endearing.

Remy inclines his head in gratitude while the rest of us sit in awe as the staff scuffle away.

It's so strange—us dressed like royalty in a family diner, the waitstaff equally out of sorts with the fine-dining experience.

I don't even know how I'm supposed to eat the pastry. With my fingers? A knife and fork?

I focus on Dad, waiting to see how he handles the situation, and find him staring at the tiny morsel of artistically displayed food in confoundment.

This is ridiculous—the clothes, the restaurant, the misplaced luxury.

I can't help the laugh that bursts from my lips.

There's never been a situation more out of my comfort zone, but I love it.

Dad's gaze snaps to me. Lucy's, too.

"It's not funny." My dad smiles through the concern. "I have no idea how I'm supposed to eat this without being rude."

"Just use your fingers." Remy picks up the *gougère* and demonstrates, my laughter snuffed as his mouth wraps around the circular pastry.

I salivate.

I'd give anything to know what it's like to be kissed by him. *Devoured.* It's becoming the entirety of my bucket list.

Dad and Lucy follow suit. I choose to nibble mine through the nausea-inducing infatuation.

Our plates are cleared. Our drinks refilled. Then the appetizer arrives—a salmon tartare with avocado, caviar, and yuzu dressing, which we eat through a debate over the best ice cream flavors.

The soup course is a creamy chestnut with an extravagant French name. The hot appetizer is seared *foie gras* on brioche with apple compote and sauternes reduction.

It's all breathtakingly incredible, each bite a mouthwatering surprise as the champagne begins to soothe my frazzled energy into something warm and comforting.

Dad brings up the topic of most memorable childhood moments as the fish course is served. I smile as he revisits a story I've already heard a million times about how my late grandmother would scream bloody murder if anyone dared to tackle him while playing school football.

There's a palate cleanser. A meat course. Then a platter of cheeses. And a pre-dessert before an *actual* dessert.

It's ridiculously lavish and the absolute best food I've eaten in my entire life.

By the time we're finished, my belly is bursting and my skin flushed from more than one too many champagnes.

I've grown high on the classical music, the violin notes dancing in my ears and vibrating into my chest.

I begin to feel at home, even though I'm miles from Baltimore in a dress that's fit for royalty, while seated in front of my dying father and adjacent to a brutal murderer.

"Remy, do a sick man a favor and ask my daughter to dance," my dad says, pulling me out of the mental calm to drop me straight into a pot of *what-the-absolute-fuck?*

Dad meets my gaze with a snicker. "Don't look so surprised. You love dancing."

"I loved it when I was five. Things change."

He returns his attention to Remy. "Come on, Costa. It would mean the world to me to see her live a little."

"*Dad*," I scold.

Is he trying to play Cupid?

He doesn't acknowledge the reprimand. He gives literally no shits as he blinks at Remy with overexaggerated puppy-dog eyes.

Oh. God.

What's worse is that I can't tell what Remy's thinking as he focuses on me with indifference. If he's trying to come up with an excuse, or attempting to distinguish whether my protests are earnest or just to save face from an inevitable rejection.

It's both.

I don't want to recreate the first time I was turned down by the man of my fantasies. And even if he does want to dance, I don't think I can when my renewed nervousness will undoubtedly cause me to regurgitate each and every one of those ten courses in front of my dad, Lucy, and the restaurant staff.

So I scowl at Remy in warning.

Scowl so hard I'm sure the resulting wrinkles will become a permanent fixture.

His lips twitch, his unreadable expression quickly filling with deviousness.

"Don't do it," I whisper.

Don't do it. Don't do it. Don't do it.

He pushes to his feet, towering above me with smug superiority as he holds out a hand. "May I have this dance?"

Bastard.

Lucy squeaks with joy.

I don't move. I can't. My legs are lead weights while my stomach twists in knots.

"Are you going to turn me down, Ollie?" Remy's slight curve of lips transforms into a full-blown, panty-melting grin.

"Of course she won't." My dad tugs at my wrist. "She wants nothing more than to make her father happy."

I groan. "Talk about emotional blackmail." I grab the starched white napkin from my lap and dump it on the table. "It's not a vibe, Dad."

He snickers. Lucy giggles.

It's a ripe ol' comedy fest, but I'm not laughing because as soon as I slide my fingers over Remy's calloused palm I struggle to do anything other than hide my increased need for oxygen.

He guides me to my feet and leads me past empty tables as the musician glances up from her violin, playing one final note of her song before stopping, the result filling the room with awkward silence.

I slow my pace. "I think she wants to have a break."

"She's waiting for us to take our place," Remy corrects.

I wince, the expression lasting the briefest second as he drags me into the open space beside the bar then turns to face me.

I stiffen as our eyes meet—all dreamy confidence versus pained hesitation.

He tugs me forward, guiding me against him, my hands instinctively raising to palm his chest for stability.

It's too much. Too close.

I lower my gaze, pretending to focus on foot placement while butterflies launch an internal assault against me. The sweet melodic notes of a new song begin to play as Remy palms my hip and entwines our right hands. Then we're swaying, barely dancing, his pulse beating beneath my fingers.

"Your dad is playing matchmaker," he murmurs under his breath.

I'd already assumed as much, but the confirmation is unsettling.

"He gave me *the talk* this afternoon," he adds.

I pull back to look at him. "The talk?"

"He asked about my intentions."

Dear fucking Lord.

"What did you say?" I choke out.

"I admitted I'm attracted to you, but apparently that's already common knowledge."

My butterflies morph into vultures. "I hope you explained that I'm a pitifully inept virgin that you gave a hard pass. I'm sure he would've offered his sincerest condolences."

Without warning I'm dragged backward into an extravagant dip. I gasp in mortification as Lucy gasps in excitement across the other side of the room.

I glower as I'm pulled back upright, my eyes pinning his in fury.

"Don't look at me like that, Pyro." He growls under his breath. "I assure you your anger doesn't have the wanted effect."

"And what effect does it have, *Reaper*?"

He strengthens his grip on my hip and drags me tighter against him, the hard length of his cock pressing into my pubic bone. "Does that answer your question?"

My feet flounder against his until he loosens his hold, allowing me the freedom not to be edged by his dick.

"I'd apologize for being crass if I didn't know that you love what you do to me." His fingers entwine with mine, making the hand contact more intimate.

"You're wrong." I lean into his shoulder, hiding my face from view.

"I could never love knowing we both want something you won't allow us to have."

His shoulders tighten. It's the only sign I've hit a sensitive target.

I quickly flounder to change the subject. "I can't believe you booked an entire restaurant."

"We needed to lay low."

"Yeah, but an *entire* restaurant?"

I can sense his self-satisfied smile without having to see it. "Why not?"

"It must be nice to be able to hemorrhage money on a whim." I huff.

"I guess it is. I've never done it before."

"Remy, you're constantly in designer suits."

"They were gifts from Lorenzo."

"What about the cars?"

"Rentals."

I push back from his shoulders to stare at his earnest expression. "The penthouse?"

"Is owned by Matthew."

My dance movements slow. "You're telling me you've never splurged like this before? Not ever? Not even when you were making stacks of cash with your fashion label and walking red carpet events?"

"There were no stacks of cash. We weren't paid for our work. Instead, me and my siblings were manipulated into believing our parents were investing in our future by withholding funds when what they were really doing was denying our ability to escape."

"Remy, I'm so sorry. I assumed—"

"It's okay." He tugs me back into him, making it seem so natural for me to rest my head between his jaw and shoulder. "I'm well aware you know very little about me."

"I don't know your stories, but I know what type of man you are."

A low rumble of disagreement emanates from his chest. "At least you think you do."

I'm not going to ruin the moment by arguing. It's clear neither of us will be swayed on our opinion.

"I've thought about you all week," he admits quietly into my hair. "I didn't know if you were all right."

"I was."

His thumb strokes my hip, lazy and smooth. "You didn't cry. Not when I told you the news. And not at work all week."

I sigh. "Please tell Wesley the whistleblower I don't appreciate him being a snitch."

That thumb continues to stroke back and forth, back and forth, coaxing me into a dreamy existence.

"You can cry in front of me, Ollie. I won't hold it against you."

I drag his scent deeper into my lungs. "I'm not sure I know how anymore."

"Why is that?"

I shrug, my feet shuffling in incremental movements. "Growing up surrounded by death made for some pretty emotional times. I'd finish school only to return home to a place filled with mourning."

It was hard. I couldn't burst through the front doors of my parents' work with news of good grades or achievement awards in case they were consoling someone. On the flip side, I couldn't get upset when they were organizing a funeral that I found devastating—like that of a young mother, or a kid my age. Having some random girl blubber about a stranger's hardships would only make things harder for clients.

"I had to learn how to mask sadness," I admit.

He continues to rub comforting strokes with his thumb, swaying us gently.

"My mom told me the most important role of the family business was not only to provide an honorable farewell to our decedents, but to provide comfort to those who were suffering... *We don't cry.*" I repeat the words she spoke so many times. "*We have to be strong. Always.*"

I can still hear her voice in my head. The soft cadence. The compassionate tone.

"I wanted so badly to become an unbreakable force of nature like her that I stopped crying altogether. I can't remember shedding a single tear during my teenage years. And my most recent case wasn't even an emotional reaction. It was when I moved houses and tripped while holding a thin glass vase. It shattered and stabbed me straight in the chest."

I lean back and make the mistake of pointing to the small, faded scar above my left breast.

His attention follows my finger, the hard flex of his jaw making my skin burn.

He clears his throat. "That tracks. You're pretty lethal with a vase."

I grin. "You should see me with a scalpel."

"No, thanks. I'm already having a hard time controlling my lust." He leans in, surprising me with a chaste kiss to my forehead. A chaste kiss that sizzles right through me, scorching every organ I possess. "Your mom sounds like a wonderful woman."

"She was." I breathe through all the sizzling. The heart palpitations and undeniable chemistry, too. "Do you speak to yours often? I know the relationship with your dad was... troubled, but what about your mom?"

He pivots us slightly, sending us swaying in the opposite direction. "We're not much for talking. Her teaming up with my father in the whole offspring murder plot kinda put a dampener on our relationship. And besides, she hasn't been allowed a lot of call time since being imprisoned in the basement of one of Lorenzo's mansions."

I stop moving, shock rendering me immobile.

"Keep dancing, Ollie." He guides me back into movement. "It's not a big deal."

"Not a big deal?" I struggle to fathom the complexity of his life. "Every time you talk about your family I don't think it can get any worse."

"It's not my family—only my parents. My siblings and I stuck together as best we could."

"Remy, your brother stabbed you."

He hits me with a devilish grin. "Yeah, but I did have a gun held to the woman he loves."

"What?" I gape. "Why?"

"It's a long story. One that isn't meant for a night like this."

I nod, appreciating that he's shared insight into his life at all. "Isn't it dangerous for you to tell me as much as you do? It's incriminating."

"It is. So do me a solid and quit being someone I want to share my secrets with."

My breath stalls in my lungs, my vulnerability toward his statement cut short by a chair scraping behind us.

I glance to my right, finding Dad and Lucy climbing from their seats.

I tense. "What are they doing?"

Dad reaches into his suit jacket, pulling out his wallet.

"It looks like Carlo is about to offend me." Remy releases my hip. "Do you mind if we cut the dance short?"

"Not at all."

He gives my hand one final squeeze then maneuvers around me, leaving me cold as I follow his long stride back to the table.

"What's going on, Pelosi?" Remy glowers at the credit card my father places atop the tablecloth.

"Lucy and I are going to call it a night and let the two of you continue alone."

"Dad, no." I step forward. "If you're leaving so am I."

"Please don't." His eyes plead. "Today has been the best I've had since before your mother died. But I'm tired, *fragolina.* New meds are making me sleepy. I won't leave if you plan on coming, too."

I open my mouth to protest but pause at his beseeching expression.

He truly wants me to stay.

I think I might want it, too.

"All I'm doing is going back to the house to sleep." He shuffles closer to wrap an arm around my shoulders. "Please stay and have fun for me."

"What do you say, little Pelosi?" Remy grabs the credit card and slips it into my father's chest pocket before looking at me. "Do you think you can handle one more drink?"

31

REMY

I help Carlo into the waiting Uber. Then it's just me and Ollie in the empty parking lot, the streetlight gleaming down on her dark hair.

"Where do you want to go from here?" I ask, pretending I'll be satisfied with a response that doesn't involve my hands all over her body.

"I'm not sure." She shrugs one perfectly bare shoulder. "I haven't been to Berkeley Springs in years."

"We drove past a bar on the way in. It's only around the block."

"That sounds nice."

I make my way toward the Escalade.

"Wait," she blurts. "We're not walking? I've got ten courses I need to help metabolize."

I pause, the hair on the back of my neck rising. We may be in the middle of nowhere, but it doesn't mean I'm any less inclined to minimize our exposure to the world. "Are you sure your feet are up for it in those heels?"

"I can handle the shoes you bought me, Remy." She shoots me a shy grin. "Along with anything else you have to offer."

My cock stirs. I force myself to ignore it. "It's safer in the car."

"Safer from who?" She twists her hips playfully, making the skirt of her dress swish. "Name one person who would target a woman dressed like a fairy tale princess?"

"When that woman is you, my answer is—literally any red-blooded male in a twenty-mile radius." I jerk my head back toward the car. "Come on. I'll drive us there. If you're still eager for exercise after our drink I'll make you walk home."

She chuckles, her eyes gleaming with a reserved smile.

I fucking love the curve of her lips.

I don't see it often enough.

I doubt I ever will.

We climb into the Escalade and as she settles into the seat beside me I'm well aware it doesn't take a genius to determine I'm messing with trouble.

Things between us feel different after that dance. Kinetic. Or maybe that's just the thrill of the looming death sentence hovering over our heads. We're teasing the mouth of the mouse trap. One wrong move and the trigger will snap.

I have to force myself to reverse out of the car space before I'm tempted to touch her again.

"I haven't had a chance to thank you for my dress." Her fingers dance over the satin fabric covering her thighs. "Is it another rental?"

"No, it's yours."

"Where did you get it?" Her lashes lift, those curious eyes eating up my periphery.

"It was something the family fashion label produced a few months before we sold the company. The new buyer wasn't interested in releasing the line, so there's a warehouse full of them back in Denver, none having seen the light of day until now."

"This is an Alleya exclusive all the way from Denver?" She gapes.

I shoot her a knowing grin, surprised she remembers the name of my family business.

She rolls her eyes. "You're aware of my google stalking, Remy. I don't cut corners when it comes to research."

"Your memory is pristine."

"Yep. I bet I can recall more names of women you've dated than you can."

"That wouldn't be hard." I can't recall another woman existing before Ollie.

I turn my attention to the empty parking lot and drive out onto the street, preferring not to encourage a deep dive into my past.

"How did the dress get here?" she asks.

"I had it couriered."

"When? How long have you been planning this trip?"

From the moment she walked away from me Monday night, heartbroken and alone. Mere minutes after I told her we need to keep our distance. "A few days."

"But you'd been so adamant that we needed—"

"I know what I said, and nothing has changed except my lack of restraint where you're concerned."

She pauses a moment, her attention feeling like a physical caress across the side of my face. "Well, thank you. It's the nicest gift anyone has ever given me. I'll never forget it."

Neither will I.

Not the look. Not the feel. Not even the fantasy of stripping it from her body.

I'm a fucking sucker for this woman.

"I'm glad you like it." I turn the corner, taking us down a quiet side street. "But next time I'll think twice about giving you something that means you can no longer wear my ring."

"I'm still wearing it."

I pause at the intersection, taking the opportunity to scrutinize her again—her delicate collarbone… the elegant hands… her slender wrists.

There's no ring. And no pockets on the dress.

She didn't even bring a purse or phone.

"Where?" I frown.

She grabs the bottom of her thick braid, tapping a finger against the elastic holding it together, and there, glinting in the soft light of the dash, is a tiny slither of white gold. "Most of it is hidden in my hair. But I made sure it was tied to the elastic so I don't lose it. Apart from when I was in the pool I haven't taken it off."

Something potent and possessive pulses inside me.

"Will you tell me why you engraved it with *Property of Remy Costa*?" She releases the braid, her hands falling to her lap. "Does it have a hidden meaning?"

I shrug, taking the next left to drive onto the main road through town.

"Tell me." She shifts her body to face me, her cheek nestled against the headrest in that cute way she did on the way here from Baltimore. It makes me feel like I'm the center of her attention. Her entire world, if only for a moment. "Are you concerned about dementia and want all your possessions properly labelled?"

I snort.

"Is it a security measure so nobody steals it?" she asks.

I roll my eyes. "No."

"Do you give your rings as keepsakes to all the women you've shared memorable moments—"

"*No*," I answer too quickly. Too gruffly. "There are no other women." I temper my tone, and this time my voice comes out quieter.

Like I'm a fucking pussy. There's no goddamn balance when it comes to my response to her. "The ring is engraved because when I was given access to unmanaged funds for the first time in my life, I guess I wanted something to mark the occasion. It felt like the ownership of something was a *fuck you* to my parents."

"You hadn't owned anything before this ring?"

"Nothing that hadn't required their permission."

She keeps her fingers pressed against my ring, gently rubbing them back and forth. "And then you gave it to me."

And then I gave it to her.

"Don't worry. I've got backups." I wiggle my fingers against the steering wheel, the streetlights glinting off the five rings still adorning my hands.

She keeps her eyes on me, increasing that kinetic energy as the car falls quiet. I'd give anything to careen into the closest parking space and slam my mouth against hers.

It would be the biggest mistake of all. Pulling her close. Breathing her in.

The memory of sliding my hand between her thighs is unignorable. But kissing her, *tasting* her… that shit would haunt me like the plague.

There'd be no going back from that.

"Quit staring at me, Pyro. You'll only stir up trouble."

She sighs, shifting her body back to face the street.

We approach the bright green building we passed on the way to dinner, the bar teeming with cars parked out the front.

I pull into a space at the far end of the row, cut the ignition, and sit staring at the outline of a martini glass illuminated in fluorescent light in the front window.

I should've taken her home with Carlo.

It's too tempting being here alone with her.

"What happens once my father passes?" she murmurs. "With the agreement, I mean. Does it really just end or…"

"It ends."

"You won't want to use the retort anymore?"

"I'll figure out an alternative. But Baltimore was never meant to be a home base. We're only here to reassert authority. I'll be gone soon enough."

"Gone?" She sits straighter. "You're leaving?"

"Eventually." I drag my gaze to hers, wanting to know what my departure means to her. If she's relieved. Excited.

It's worse. Disappointment stares back at me.

Fuck, Ollie. Don't do this to me.

"It's a good thing, Pyro. I'll be out of your hair, and you won't have to be an accomplice anymore."

"But you enjoy being in my hair."

I fucking love her gall. She doesn't shy away from me. My compliments, maybe. But not this shit between us.

"Your hair is an enjoyable place to be. But we both know I was never meant to be there." I unclasp my belt and climb from the car, absolutely fucking hating myself when I decide it's a great idea to round the hood to open her door.

I'm no gentleman.

This *isn't* a fucking fairy tale.

Yet she climbs from the Escalade like an ethereal goddess. The right dose of poise. The perfect hint of insecurity.

She's fiction. Far too perfect to be real.

"One drink," I mutter. "Then we're going home."

I close her door and make for the sidewalk.

"Wait." Her heels tap as she hustles to maneuver around me, blocking my path. "Let's play a game."

Warning bells blare in my fucking ears.

"A game?" I glower.

"Mm-hmm." She nods. "We've been doing it all day—actually, we've been doing it for months—so it's only an extension of our current reality."

"That doesn't sound like my type of—"

"Come on." Her eyes beg. "It's simple. Haven't you noticed how often we play pretend? We do it with my father's health, faking our way through conversations as if he's not dying. Then we pretend you're not a wanted criminal in front of Lucy. I even pretended not to notice when you got jealous in front of the chef."

My nostrils flare at the reminder of that asshole.

"Just for one night, why not play the game a little harder and pretend there's no external influences keeping us apart?" She blinks at me through dark lashes. "No defiant uncles or homicidal enemies. It's just us. Two random people who get along seriously well despite the crazy world around them."

Wouldn't that be fucking nice.

No chains holding me back.

No fear of her winding up in a pool of blood at my feet, bullet ridden and begging for help.

"That's not a good idea." I walk around her, pausing when both her hands wrap around my wrist.

"Why?"

Why?

I scoff. *Fucking why?*

Does she not understand how much self-restraint it takes to keep things platonic? Doesn't she have the faintest fucking clue what the temptation of her does to me?

I turn back to her with a cruel smirk, stepping close, leaning in.

She stiffens as I bring my mouth within an inch of her ear and inhale the unrecognizable floral fragrance that catches me by surprise. It's not as sweet as her strawberry scent, but it still hits me right in the dick.

"Because if I had a night to play pretend, Pyro, I'd have you on your back in a heartbeat with your legs spread and my mouth between your thighs. And I'm pretty sure people around these parts wouldn't appreciate me doing that in public."

Her breath catches.

I swear to God, I feel the hitch of it in my own throat.

"Now do you have any more fun suggestions or are you ready for that drin—"

A passing car beeps its horn, cutting me short.

It's an anomaly in the abnormally quiet town, the noise pollution stealing my attention.

I track the black sedan as it passes, the tinted windows obscuring some of the male passengers' features but not enough to hide the driver staring directly at me.

The hair on the back of my neck rises again.

Twice in one night.

Not a good omen.

Ollie's hands slide from my wrist as she follows my gaze. "Do you know them?"

"I doubt it." I step into her, guiding an arm around her back. "But a lot of people know me."

"Should I be worried?"

"Always." I won't sugarcoat it. That dress may turn her into a princess but I'm far from a white knight. "Being around me means constantly looking over your shoulder, especially in public."

"I realize that. But if you're using this as another excuse to push me away then the joke's on you because I'd happily never step out in public again."

I scoff a laugh, unable to help frothing at her enthusiasm to get entangled with a death wish. "You're something else, Ollie."

She grins. "Yeah, I am. And you're currently missing out." She walks around me, leading the way into the bar.

Like always, I follow. I'm a dog on a leash for this woman.

I pause inside the door to scan the street one last time, watching as the black sedan turns the corner and disappears from view.

One drink, then we're gone.

Nothing good can come from giving her more alcohol.

She isn't drunk, but a tipsy Ollie with lowered inhibitions isn't helping with my restraint.

She's already at the bar by the time I catch up, ordering an apple martini, while I opt for necessary sobriety and ask for a soda. I lead her to the booth in the far corner, acting unfazed by the extra attention the patrons give us. But it's our clothes that draw their focus. Not my reputation.

I sit with my back against the wall, my eyes on the room, and Ollie painfully right in front of me.

"You're on edge." She sips her martini, looking fucking edible as she meets my gaze over the glass rim. "Is it about those men in the car?"

That, and the fact I want to plow her into next week. "I don't enjoy being exposed."

"That's understandable." She nods thoughtfully, taking another sip of her martini. "Just out of curiosity though…" She cocks her head, studying me. "What would it take for you to kiss me?"

"Jesus fucking Christ." I snap my attention to the other side of the room.

Soda isn't going to cut it.

Scotch wouldn't even do the trick.

She needs to stop drinking, and I need to find a hole to crawl into.

She chuckles. "I think I like riling you."

"Yeah?" I snarl. "I think I liked it more when you were scared of me."

"I was never scared of you."

"No?" I spear my eyes back to hers, regretting the moment those humor-filled depths drag me under. "I recall history differently."

"Well, obviously I was scared the first night at the funeral home. But it was nothing in comparison to coming face-to-face with Lorenzo and Salvatore. It's always been different with you."

Because she knows I could never hurt her.

At least not physically.

My fingers tighten around my glass. "So you have fully functioning self-preservation when it comes to them, but not with me?"

"It's been fully functioning across the board for the most part." Her lips twitch. "But then you said you wanted to spread my legs and place your mouth between my thighs, and now all bets are off."

32

REMY

I stare at her, the restraint I've been battling for months being chipped away with each bat of her lashes.

I'm about to throw caution to the fucking wind and drag her out of here when the front door of the bar opens and two men walk in.

Maybe I wouldn't have recognized them from the shadowed car if they'd headed straight for the bar and casually ordered a drink, but they hover in the doorway, scoping the room, both of them pausing their visual sweep once they reach me.

Fuck.

It's nothing more than a brief moment of hesitation. Yet it's enough.

They know me, and they're not showing interest because they want to buy me a beer.

"Ollie, I need you to come sit next to me." I keep my gaze on them as they exchange words then walk to the bar pretending they're not shady as fuck.

She straightens but doesn't ask questions. She's smart enough not to even look over her shoulder as she climbs from her side of the booth to slide into mine.

"Is that them?" she whispers.

I give a subtle nod while the shorter of the two men hands money to the bartender, cocking his elbow casually against the counter.

They're not familiar. Both have fair skin, blue eyes, and light red hair, making them seem like descendants from the land of the Leprechauns.

Not the usual characteristics of my enemies, but that doesn't mean shit.

I reach under the table and untuck my shirt from my pants to retrieve my gun from the waistband holster.

"Is that necessary?" Ollie chokes.

"Everything's fine." I rest the gun against my upper thigh, keeping it hidden beneath the table as I drag her closer into my side.

"Can we please cut that word from our vocabulary? This really doesn't feel like a *fine* type of situation."

"I'll handle it."

The men grab two beers off the bartender, then make a show of looking for somewhere to sit, as if they don't already plan to walk in our direction.

"I need you to listen to me carefully, Pyro."

"Okay," she says with hesitation.

"Finish your drink." I want the liquor to help ease her anxiety.

She reaches trembling fingers toward her martini glass and takes a sip.

"Good girl." I release her waist and slide my free hand over her wrist in a vain attempt at comfort.

"Please don't say that right now." Pink floods her cheeks.

I smirk, the expression short-lived as the men approach. "They're going to sit near us. They might even start a conversation. But I want you to remain quiet and relaxed. Can you do that for me?"

She nods, short and sharp.

The men close in, eying the empty booth adjoining ours.

I slide my finger over the trigger of my gun, my pulse increasing, the demand to protect Ollie becoming a living, breathing thing inside my chest.

They get within five feet… four… three…

Then the taller of the two—the driver—pauses at the neighboring booth, his eyes narrowing on mine in fake scrutiny.

"Hey." His voice holds a slight Irish lilt as he jerks his chin in my direction. "Do I know you?"

"I don't know." I glower. "Do you?"

He's obviously not Mexican. Not cartel.

But he's something.

A definite threat.

His companion attempts the same feigned scrutiny, eyeing me and Ollie.

"If you don't mind, I'm trying to share a private drink with a friend." I continue with the death stare, my trigger finger getting itchy.

They exchange a glance. A nod. Then lower into their booth, the driver facing me while the other slides in the closest side and moves all the way across to lean against the wall.

"What's going on?" Ollie whispers.

"I'm not sure. But I need you to dig into my pocket and get my car fob."

She swallows heavily as her hand lowers beneath the table, brushing my thigh, her fingertips skimming my dick.

I fucking flinch.

"Sorry," she rasps, her expression full of horror.

I'd laugh if it wasn't the most inopportune moment to be distracted by my hardening cock.

"Stay focused, Ollie. Now's not the time to be offering hand jobs." I shift slightly, helping her dig into my pocket and retrieve the fob. "I'm going to need you to excuse yourself to use the ladies. Announce it casually, but loud enough for our friends to hear."

"Okay."

"Once you're out of view, I want you to find a back or side exit. Try the kitchen—"

Her eyes widen. "I'm not leaving you."

"It's only temporary. I'll follow as soon as I can. I just need you to escape without causing suspicion, then get in the Escalade and be prepared to drive away from here as soon as I walk out the front doors."

"Remy, I can't." Her touch lingers on my pants, her fingers latching around my pocket. "I've been drinking."

"The least of our worries is a drunk-driving charge. I want you to focus on listening to me so I can get you out of here."

Her teeth dig into her bottom lip. Biting. Gnawing. "I'm nervous."

"That's a healthy response. But all you have to do is follow instructions. I know what I'm doing."

She sucks in a deep breath and sits taller. "Okay. I'll be waiting." She scooches an inch away. "I need to use the bathroom," she announces at the perfect volume. Casual, yet loud enough to have the closest threat cock his ear in our direction.

"Get me a scotch on your way back?" I ask.

"Sure." Ollie nods without retreating any farther. Instead, she hovers there, posture tight, eyes pained, gaze lowering to my mouth.

Is she seriously contemplating kissing me? Right fucking now?

I can't unsee it. The yearning. The concern.

And goddamnit to hell, I can't help craving it, too.

"This is a mistake," I mutter as I grab her wrist and tug her back to me, smashing my mouth against hers.

It's a swift press of lips.

Hard. Fast. Fierce.

But fuck, even with the complications currently sitting in the next booth, it makes my dick pound.

She barely has time to release the softest of whimpers before I pull back and scowl through my lacking restraint, struggling to keep my breathing under control.

It takes a few seconds for her to blink the daze from her eyes, then she slides out of the booth. "Scotch on the rocks?"

I nod, proud of her for continuing the drink charade.

"I won't be long." She turns on her heel, her dress dancing around her ankles, then heads for the signposted hall leading to the bathroom across the other side of the room.

As soon as she's out of view, I pull out my phone and type a text to Valenti.

ME

> I've got trouble. Any ideas why I'm on the Irish radar?

I press send and place the cell down on the table, my attention moving to the guy closest to me who turns to meet my eyes.

"I swear I've seen you before." He squints. "What's your name?"

I raise my gun under the table, aligning it with his back. "Who's asking?"

"I dunno, maybe an old friend. Who knows where we've met?"

I smile with menace. "We're not friends."

"Well, we've definitely seen you around." The other guy pulls out his phone, taps the screen, then holds it up in my direction. Staring back at me is a recent surveillance photo taken out the front of my Baltimore apartment building, with my dashing face taking center stage. "Congratulations, you've got a price on your head, Costa."

Fuck.

It's one thing to be at war with the cartel, but for them to outsource my demise takes it to a whole new level.

I huff a laugh as my cell buzzes short and sharp against the table. "Don't get shy now, boys. Tell me what the Rodriguez family are offering."

"One fifty," the guy closest responds with a grin.

One hundred and fifty grand?

"Wow." I raise a brow. "That's insulting. Give me a week and I bet they'll be far more generous in their attempts to get rid of me."

Phone guy shrugs. "We're happy with the current terms."

"Really?" I position the pad of my finger over my gun's trigger, so fucking tempted to squeeze. "You think attempting to kill Lorenzo Cappelletti's nephew is a smart decision?"

He lowers his cell and takes a sip of beer. "It would seem like an insult to fate not to at least try. We weren't even in town because of you. Now look at us."

His companion chuckles. "You're the easiest stroke of good luck we've had in a long time."

"The result of the Irish getting involved in Italian business won't resemble anything remotely close to luck," I drawl.

"We're not affiliated with the mafia. We're merely contractors looking for a payday. But don't worry, Costa—we won't do it here." The guy closest waves a lazy hand toward the rest of the room. "Too many witnesses."

They're serious.

They actually plan on killing me.

"Well, I wish you all the best." I slide from the booth, keeping my gun hidden inside my jacket. "But you won't succeed. All you've done is piss me off and scare my girl. And while I could ignore the former offense, I assure you I won't let the latter slide." I tip my head in farewell. "I hope you enjoy your final moments."

I stalk toward the bar, daring to turn my back on them.

I have no doubt they'll attempt to kill me, but like they said, they won't do it here.

There are too many repercussions for lone contractors who don't have the backing of a big organization to keep them out of prison.

I head for the far end of the bar to the two older men talking casually with the bartender.

"Excuse me," I interrupt their conversation, the three of them turning to face me with varying degrees of annoyance. "I'm not usually one to cause trouble, but I thought it might be best to inform you that those two Irishmen over my left shoulder are trading kiddie porn while under your roof. Do with that what you will."

I take a second to watch their expressions morph into rage as the bartender grabs a wooden bat from under the counter. Then I head for the front door, shooting my Irish buddies a smirk as they begin sliding from their booth.

I won't have much time, but I shouldn't need it. A few seconds head start is enough to get me into the Escalade.

Shouts ring out behind me, the men from the bar calling for blood as I push through the exit and stride onto the sidewalk.

The Escalade is right where I left it, Ollie behind the wheel like I instructed, the engine purring.

I keep my pace in check, not wanting to scare her as she swivels a finger back and forth between us, silently asking if I want the driver's seat.

I shake my head and round the hood, climbing in the passenger side to fasten my belt. "Drive, Pyro."

"Are you sure you don't want to switch spots?" she asks in panic.

"There's no time."

The Irish duo flee the bar, the older men, the bartender, and a few random crusaders chasing after them while shouting obscenities.

"Step on it, Ollie."

She squeaks and guns the engine, shooting backward. "Which way am I going?"

"It doesn't matter. Just get out of town as fast as you can."

"Oh, God." Her hands scramble as she turns the steering wheel and pulls out onto the road in the direction of our rental property. Then she shifts to drive and plasters her foot to the floor.

I hold tight to my gun, watching my side mirror as Ollie speeds down the block, racking up a list of traffic violations while she chews her bottom lip.

"Who are they?" she asks.

"Hitmen looking to bag a whale."

"What?" She shoots me a frantic look. "Are you the whale?"

"Unfortunately."

I check my cell and tap on the unread text.

VALENTI

Apparently congratulations are in order. You've earned a bigger target on your back.

ME

So it seems. A little help would be appreciated.

Ollie releases a tortured breath. "Are you texting while I'm fleeing from hitmen?"

"No. Just checking Insta notifications. It isn't often that I don't have to drive."

Wild eyes meet mine.

"I'm joking, Ollie. Relax. You're doing great."

"Tell that to my erratic pulse. I think I'm going to throw up." She indicates to illegally overtake a Honda CR-V across double yellow lines. "Shouldn't I take back roads in an attempt to hide?"

"We don't want to hide."

Those fear-filled eyes meet mine again. "We don't?"

"Not yet."

"I seriously don't know if I can do this, Remy. You should be driving."

I turn in my seat, glancing through the back window as the black sedan pulls into traffic. "I wouldn't want anyone else behind the wheel."

"Yeah?" she scoffs. "Not even those two men who are always following you around?"

"Russo and Valenti?" The Irish trail in our direction. "Don't get me wrong. They're the best at having my back, but neither one of them can pull off a bikini like you can."

"*Oh, God.*" Her hands twist against the steering wheel. "Please don't talk like that while I'm trying to concentrate."

"No problem." The aim is to distract her. Keep her calm. "Just continue following instructions like a good little girl and—"

"*Don't say that either,*" she shrieks.

I turn back to face oncoming traffic with a smirk. "Why? I was under the impression you enjoyed praise."

"Unless you want to be wrapped around a power pole at a hundred miles an hour *please* drop the subject."

"Fine. We'll reconvene on the topic later."

"No, we won't."

I open the map app on my phone and start scanning for an escape route. "I assure you we will."

She huffs a frustrated breath and illegally overtakes a white minivan. "Shit. There are traffic lights up ahead. What do I do?"

"If it's red, slow, but don't stop. We need to keep moving."

The light remains green as we approach. Then turns yellow.

She increases our speed instead of slowing. "*Shit. Shit. Shit.*"

"Keep going."

The light turns red when we're still yards away. A blue hatchback edges into traffic from a side street.

Ollie blasts the horn, swerving slightly as we hit the intersection. The hatchback slams on its brakes, the elderly driver giving us the bird as we fly past.

"Goddamn fucking shit," Ollie cries. "What the hell am I doing?"

"We had more than a few feet between us. You're doing fine."

"If you say *fine* one more time, Remy fucking Costa, I swear to God—"

"Damn, Ollie. How did you know dirty-mouthed good girls are my kryptonite?"

She blows out a harsh breath, her gaze remaining on the road. "I'm going to kill him. If I don't kill myself at the same time."

"Just keep driving." I check behind us, the black sedan stuck on the other side of the intersection. "They're caught at the lights."

She nods to herself. "Okay. I can do this. It's just like riding my bike through peak-hour traffic."

We pass small-town stores and cafes.

The local cemetery on our left.

A large pharmacy on our right.

She speeds through Berryville while I keep watch for the sedan, only catching glimpses when it cuts in and out of traffic in the distance.

"Do you still want me to stay on this road?" She scans her rearview as the buildings space out, making way for hills, trees, and vacant land.

"For now."

The town lights disappear, darkening everything around us into a sea of black. The only way I can tell the Irish are gaining on us are the headlights that keep darting onto the wrong side of the road every time we reach a stretch of highway.

I check the map again. "I'm going to need you to slow down."

"Slow down? Why?"

"Because I can't risk them finding us later."

Her questioning gaze snaps to mine. "What does that—" Her words cut short as horror dawns across her features. "Remy, No. They'll kill you first."

"I won't let that happen."

She returns her attention to the road, wincing against the blinding beam from an oncoming truck.

"You've trusted me far more than anyone should, Pyro. Don't quit on me now."

Her wince increases. "What's your plan?"

"I'll talk you through each step as it comes. But for the moment, you need to slow down and let them catch up."

She blows out a shaky breath.

I fucking hate this for her. That I can't pull her away from danger without dragging her through it first.

"Slow, Ollie."

I'd always thought I wanted her to see the side of me that's about to be exposed—the tyrant, the murderer. Her forgiveness of my sins is probably her only flaw. Yet now that I sit poised with a plan that will place her in close proximity to bloodshed, I can't stand picturing how she'll react.

If only she could remain ignorant.

"Ollie," I warn.

She whimpers, her shoulders slumping as the car slows.

I turn to look out the back window, the headlights of the trailing vehicle approaching at speed.

I double-check the map on my phone. "Take the next left."

"Off the main road?"

"Don't think; just act."

She sucks in a deep breath and activates her turn signal.

I fight a laugh. "We want them to follow, but indicating that we're about to turn is making it a little too obvious."

"*Oh, God.*" She flicks off the turn signal. "I did it out of habit. Have I ruined everything?"

"Not at all." I keep watching our back as she nears the adjoining road. "You're going to have to pump the brakes though. You can't hit the corner at this speed."

She doesn't respond. She doesn't slow either.

"Ollie?"

"I can't do this," she pleads. "It's too much."

"Yes, you can. Take the turn."

She scrunches her face, tapping the brakes hard before steering sharply toward the side street.

It's too fast.

The tires screech. The vehicle lurches sideways. We fishtail.

"*Remy,*" she cries.

"Don't brake." I lunge for the wheel, helping correct the skid. "Ease off the accelerator."

She complies, the car wobbling before regaining its tread.

"*Oh, God, oh, God, oh, God,*" she chants.

I dump my cell in my lap and reach out, gliding my palm around her neck, rubbing a gentle thumb across her jawline. "You're doing such a good job, Ollie. I'm so fucking proud of you."

She whimpers, leaning into the contact, melting into the praise. "What happens next?"

"Just pay attention and keep driving, sweetheart. This should be a quiet road that leads us back toward Berkeley Springs, but we're going to detour up the mountain."

She nods, concentration tightening her jaw as we approach a hard left turn. She takes the corner like a rally driver, crossing both lanes to speed into the straight.

For a few silent moments we could almost pretend we're not being followed. There are no other cars in sight. The mass of trees surrounding us blocks out any other sign of life.

But then her gaze shifts to the rearview. "Remy, there's more of them."

I check the side mirror, seeing our tail, along with an additional set of headlights. "It's okay."

"How is it okay?" She sits taller, the panic returning. "There are two cars following us now. How can we handle both?"

"We don't need to." I dial Valenti's number, the connection going through the car's Bluetooth, the ringtone loud before the call cuts in.

"Lovely night for a high-speed car chase," he drawls in greeting.

"I could've done without it," I mutter. "But let's get this over and done with. Ollie's not a huge fan of her introduction into street racing."

"That's a shame. She's doing a great job."

She scoffs. "I'm going to projectile vomit any minute now."

"Right." Valenti clears his throat. "Want us to give them a friendly high-speed nudge toward a tree?"

I watch Ollie, waiting for her to protest the crime.

She doesn't react. There's only ongoing trepidation.

"Yeah." I keep my eyes on her. "That sounds like a plan. Just wait until we take another turn. I want us as far away from homes as possible. When I'm ready, I'll distract them with a few tire shots."

"Understood."

Ollie breathes out a measured breath.

"Let's get it done." I mute the call, still staring at her. "You okay?"

"Yeah. I'm great. Apart from being manic with fear, irrationally turned on by your good girl references, and extremely nauseous with my inability to handle emotion." She gives me a sarcastic thumbs-up before clasping her hand back against the wheel and leaning into the next bend. "Couldn't be better."

I grin. "Would it help if I told you I'm also irrationally turned—"

"*No*," she growls.

I snicker. "Okay, Pyro. No more fun and games. It's time to end this." I unmute the call and refresh the map to check our surroundings. There's nothing but dense trees and stretching land to hide the isolated houses, rental cabins, and vacation properties nestled into the mountain. "We're aiming for Spring Brook Drive. It's roughly two and a half miles ahead."

Ollie nods.

"Got it," Valenti replies.

We're barely around the next bend when Ollie's gaze shoots back to the rearview.

"They're closing in," Russo warns.

I glance through the rear window, the headlights behind us fast approaching. *Shit.* They're going to ram us before Valenti gets the chance to act. "Take a hard right."

"*What?*" Ollie squeals.

"*Hard right.*"

"*Fuck,*" Valenti mutters.

Ollie slams on the brakes, clenching the wheel as our tires screech.

The sedan closes in, hitting its brakes a second later, skidding uncontrollably toward us.

"*Brace,*" I shout, thrusting a protective arm across her chest.

But she plants her foot against the accelerator, taking off down the gravel lane as our enemies overshoot the turn, Russo and Valenti following them.

"Jesus Christ, Pyro." I lower my arm. "You missed your calling as a stunt driver."

"Less praise. More direction." She inches closer to the steering wheel, peering into the stretching canopy created by the overbearing trees as tiny stones clink against the car undercarriage.

"They overshot the lane," Russo shouts. "But they're turning back to follow you."

"Good. We've bought ourselves some time." I point at the bend up ahead. "Keep going, Ollie. This road meets up with the one we were just on."

She squeezes the wheel tighter, seeming more determined now than nervous. She eases off the gas as she approaches a sharp curve, then speeds through it.

I keep eying the back window, dust and dirt kicking up behind us. "We're clear for now."

She accelerates hard, the Escalade's engine revving.

"The intersection is right up ahead."

She nods. "I see it."

We remain on our own as she slows, hard turns, then accelerates back onto the road.

"What's happening, Valenti?" I demand.

"We're still on their ass. We can't be too far behind you."

Ollie pushes the needle to the limit down a long straight. The world is empty out here. No cars. No visible houses. But if one forest animal bounds across the road, we're going to be mixing DNA with a tree trunk.

"Goddamnit." She glances to the rear view. "How can they drive so fast?" She hogs the road, speeding through bends.

"Don't worry about them. Just concentrate. The turn is up ahead."

Her gaze darts from the asphalt to the speedometer. Back and forth. "They're gaining on us again."

I check my side mirror. "Good. We still need them to know where we're going. You've got time."

She slows on the approach to Spring Brook Drive, the light behind us growing. "It's more gravel." She takes the corner and zooms onto the uneven road, passing long, stretching driveways that lead to darkness. "I'm going to get us killed, Remy."

"No, you're not. This is almost over." I recheck the map. "There are a few bends up ahead. Then an intersection leading onto a lane. We want to have these guys handled before that intersection. It's the farthest we're going to get from nearby houses."

"There's an ammunitions store hidden down one of these side lanes," Valenti adds. "Hopefully any loud noise will be attributed to their business and not ours."

That's what I'd been hoping for.

"We're going to pass five tiny off-roads. That's the first." I point to one on our right. "Once we reach the fifth I want you to slow down." I lower my window and double-check my gun's magazine. "It's going to get loud, Pyro. But you've got this."

She nods, sucking in a strengthening breath.

"Ready, Valenti?" I ask.

"Born ready."

"Four," Ollie whispers as we pass another off-road, then leans into the bend. "Three."

I hold tight to my gun, staring through the swirling dust and debris kicking up behind us. The Irish aren't on our ass, but their headlights carry through the trees.

"Two." Ollie straightens her shoulders, sitting tall. "One."

"Slow right down. We want to catch them off-guard." I lean the top half of my body out the window as she rounds the final bend, decreasing speed. "Be prepared to take off if this doesn't work."

"It'll work," Valenti vows. "These assholes are too cocky."

"Here's hoping." I track the slithers of light through the trees, the acceleration of oncoming vehicles approaching fast.

Ollie slows to a crawl in the middle of the road.

"We're almost there," Russo announces. "Get ready."

A heartbeat later the Irish come into view, their bright lights threatening to blind me.

I aim low and squeeze the trigger. *Pop. Pop. Pop.*

They hit the brakes in a grate of swirling gravel. The car careens to the left, tires spinning. Dust flying.

"I'm going in," Valenti shouts, slamming the nose of his Audi into the back of the sedan to make our enemies spin.

Through the darkened interior I meet the eyes of the Irish passenger, his gun raising to aim at me through his open side window. He fires as the vehicle speeds toward the trees, the *pop* followed closely by the unmistakable sound of shattering glass as the bullet hits a taillight of the Escalade.

"Get down," I shout.

Ollie hunches on command.

But it doesn't matter. There's no stopping the sedan as it rockets uncontrollably toward the trees, launching into a trunk with a deafening crack.

"Oh, God," she whimpers.

"It's okay." I eye the car, watching for movement. "It's almost over."

The headlights died on impact, the angle of the vehicle hiding my view of the occupants. But I clearly see the passenger door as I wait for it to open.

"I'm going to check it out," Russo says.

I unclasp my belt and disconnect the call, not wanting Ollie to overhear anything upsetting. "I need you to stay here. Turn off the lights but don't get out."

"Remy—"

"I'll be back soon." I climb from the Escalade, close the door behind me, and stalk for the sedan.

Russo is already jogging toward the mangled car as hissing steam billows from the hood while Valenti cuts the lights to his Audi, plunging us into darkness.

It takes a few blinks for my eyes to adjust to the moonlight as I approach, my Walther palmed at my side.

"They're alive." Russo yanks open the driver's door on the far side of the car, his gun aimed inside. "But pretty fucked up."

I close in, striding from the gravel road onto the dense wild grass.

Russo meets me at the trunk, yanking off his leather gloves. "Here. Have these. I assume you want the honors."

I take the offering and put them on, eying the interior through the back window.

"The driver's belt is stuck. He's not going anywhere." Russo jerks his chin toward the other side of the car. "And the dumb fuck in the passenger seat wasn't wearing a seatbelt."

I step around him to continue toward the driver.

"I'm going to go help Valenti organize the tarp and siphon some gas." Russo walks backward toward the road. "If we can't find somewhere nearby to dump the bodies, I'll drive them to Baltimore and get Wesley to help with the usual disposal while Valenti stays to keep watch."

I nod and keep striding for the open door, the hiss of the billowing steam deafening.

The driver remains behind the wheel, the deflated airbag spewed out before him. He frantically pads his palms around his lap, waist, and down the sides of his seat, searching for something, but his belt must be restricting his movements because the pathetic bastard remains ramrod straight.

I close in, placing the barrel of my gun to his temple. "Is this what you're looking for?"

He stiffens. Freezes.

I jab the barrel harder against him. "Do you still think the hundred and fifty grand was worth it?"

"*Please.*" He raises his hands in surrender. "We were just looking for a payday. It wasn't personal."

"This won't be personal either. I'll tell the cartel you said hi." I pull the trigger, the blast echoing through the canopy.

Skull fragments and blood splatter the interior as his head flops forward and his body slumps.

He deserved to suffer, but dragging out this situation isn't an option when Ollie is involved.

I don't want her to be tainted any more by this.

By *me*.

A faint whimper sounds from the passenger, his body out of his seat, his torso and arms speared through the windshield.

I stalk to his side of the car, passing his door to stop in line with his head slumped against the hood. This part of the vehicle isn't under the tree canopy, allowing the moonlight to stream down on the macabre scene before me.

"Things didn't turn out as planned, did they?" I slide my gun into the waistband holster and retrieve a shard of the windshield from the grass beside my feet.

He garbles in reply, the words unintelligible.

"What did I say would happen?" I grab his hair and yank his head up, the faint *drip, drip, drip* of blood from his hairline tapping against shiny black metal.

His eyes roll as a barely heard keening noise reverberates over the slowly decreasing radiator steam.

I thrum with adrenaline. With fucking victory. Murder has never felt so good because the death of this piece of shit means Ollie will remain safe.

"I told you you'd die if you came after me." I lightly tease a sharp edge of the glass across his neck. "But to do it while I was with Ollie?" I cluck my tongue. "That's unforgivable."

33

OLIVIA

REMY'S EXPRESSION IS FERAL AS HE SHOVES THE JAGGED PIECE OF GLASS INTO the man's throat, his victim choking and gurgling after impact.

I gasp, trying to reconcile what I'm seeing.

I'd stayed in the car like he'd asked.

I'd stalked the rearview and side mirrors, trying to gain a glimpse of him while I panicked over what might be happening. Then the gunshot sounded and I freaked.

I turned off the car's interior light and used every ounce of stealth I had to slowly and carefully climb from the car without making a sound. And now I stand in the middle of the gravel road, frozen as Remy's gaze snaps to mine.

"Ollie…" His voice is raw.

I can't speak.

Beneath the glow of the moonlight, I see it all—his gloved hand, the pooling blood.

I've tried to imagine him like this so many times. To envision the brutality. The confident ease with which he takes a life.

For some reason, I could never fully craft the image.

Yet now it's here. In dark and sinister shades under the glow of a late spring moon.

I wait for disgust to grip me by the throat. For horror to take hold.

Nothing latches its claws around me. At least nothing malevolent.

There's only overwhelming relief.

He's alive.

I'm alive.

"It's okay." He slowly lowers the dead man's head and retreats from the sedan, holding his gloved hands up in surrender. "You can take the car. I won't chase you. I just want you to think rationally and get somewhere safe."

Take the car? Chase me?

"I don't understand," I whisper.

"They had to die, Pyro."

I shake my head. That's not what I meant.

I understand that he did what was needed. I'm not naive. This is who he is. How he works.

"Go." He juts his chin toward the Escalade. "Get back to your dad. I won't follow."

He won't follow? He thinks I want to run from him?

"I'm not going anywhere." I start forward, slowly at first, but with each step the compounding waves of adrenaline build.

I need to touch him. Hold him.

I want to feel with my own hands that he's all right. That there are no bullet holes or stab wounds.

"What are you doing?" He yanks off his gloves and throws them against the sedan's hood, then hesitantly walks for me.

I'm jogging in my Jimmy Choos by the time he reaches the road, my dress swishing around my ankles, my heart clogging my throat.

"Ollie, no," he warns. "There's glass."

I don't care. I don't give a damn if there are nails or spikes or lava. I keep running for him, and he keeps striding toward me until we're feet apart and I'm launching myself at his chest.

He catches me, his strong hands gripping my hips as I wrap my legs around his waist, a mass of dress material pooled between us.

He'd been hesitant to kiss me in the bar, but I no longer have the sense to consider his reluctance. I palm his jaw and slam my mouth to his, all smashed lips and gasped breaths.

He doesn't deny me.

Instead he groans into the contact, his fingers digging at the flesh of my hips, his tongue demands entry to my mouth.

I can't get enough.

Not of the kiss. Not of his touch. Not of him.

I clench my thighs tighter around him as he walks us toward the Escalade, his men making rustling noises and murmuring in the distance.

"You're safe." He speaks against my lips. "I've got you."

"I was worried." I glide my fingers into his hair. "I heard the gunshot and—"

His tongue rakes over mine, deepening the kiss, increasing the relief.

I match him stroke for stroke, raking my fingers through his hair, tightening my hold around him.

But I still need more.

"Are you hurt?" I ask.

He takes us to the passenger side of his car, pressing me back against the cool metal of the door. "There's only one part of me that's aching, and it's got nothing to do with the Irish."

I lean into the Escalade and tilt my pelvis against him with a groan.

I can feel the length of where he aches. So incredibly hard and big beneath his pants.

He grinds into me with a moan, the sound of his need undoing me.

"You should've stayed in the car," he mutters into my mouth.

"I couldn't see you." I inch my head back to meet his gaze, but he shifts his mouth to my cheek, starting a trail of heated kisses toward my neck. "I didn't know what to think."

Instead of leaning down, he grabs my waist, hitching me higher against the side of the car so his lips can continue the heavenly path lower, over my collarbone, across my sternum.

My thighs burn with the tight grip around him. I didn't know if we'd ever get here again. Heated and panting. But this is a million times hotter than my daydreams.

He's hungered and rabid. All hard muscle, hummed groans, and possessive hands, his kisses scorching, his touch electric.

He finds the small scar on my chest, licking, nipping. "You're going to have to stop me, Ollie. I can't do it on my own."

I moan at the tingles invading my body. "Never."

He hitches me higher, his face coming in line with the top of my bodice. I straddle his ribs as he tugs at the neckline of my dress, his heavy body holding me in place.

He bends the boning, exposing my naked breasts, palming them gently.

"*Fuck.*" He stares at me like I'm a wonder of the world. "No bra."

"I didn't have one appropriate for the dress."

"And for that I'm thankful." The words barely reach my ears before his mouth is back on me, those pleasuring lips scorching a trail from my cleavage to my nipple, sucking the tightened flesh until it burns.

I cry out, my hips bucking into him.

"You're so fucking beautiful," he murmurs between licks. "I've dreamed of this. I haven't stopped."

"Me, too." I'm already incredibly wet and achy. I don't know how I'll ever get enough.

"Stop me, Ollie." He releases my bodice and hitches me higher, his face in line with my stomach, then my abdomen, his nose nuzzling along the fabric as if he's entranced.

"I wouldn't dare."

He lifts me high enough that I can rest my elbows against the roof of the car for support, his palm sliding beneath my dress to guide one leg, then the other, over his shoulders.

"Hold the material." He kisses the inside of each thigh, the contact scorching as he palms my ass. "I want to see you."

I comply with a shudder, teetering on my elbows, caught between manic lust and tumultuous nerves as I raise the heavy skirt to pool at my stomach.

He plants another press of lips to one inner thigh, then the other, his predatory gaze staring between my legs.

"I can fucking smell your lust." He groans.

My breath catches as his thumbs skim the elastic crotch of my panties, then shift straight down my center.

I whimper, arching into him.

His stubble scrapes my sensitive skin as he slowly creeps his mouth toward my core, planting more kisses, inching my legs apart.

My pulse thunders in my throat, the anticipation creating an inferno in my veins until the hot heat of his breath is tormenting me through the lace. He pauses, his eyes meeting mine.

"Stop me, Pyro."

I stare at him, his gaze wild yet slightly pleading. "I'll never want to stop you."

Viciousness takes over his features. Then his mouth is on me, his hot tongue licking through the lace.

"Fuck," he groans. "I can already taste you."

My pussy flutters. The rest of my body follows suit.

I pant as he laps at me through my underwear, the strokes of his tongue coming harder, faster.

"Remy, please." I rake a hand into his hair, pulling at the strands.

I need more.

He inches back, and I almost cry in protest. But then his fingers grip the lace at my crotch and savagely rip the thin material apart.

I jolt with the brutality. Whimper with renewed greed.

He looks at my pussy through the moonlight. Stares intently.

I've never been so vulnerable, and alive, and mindless, and obsessed.

"You fucking glisten, Ollie." He strokes a thumb down my core, making me feel how incredibly wet I am.

Then his mouth is on me. His tongue *in* me.

"Oh, God." I throw my head back, closing my eyes to the blissful onslaught.

He growls, kissing, lapping, sucking.

His tongue is everywhere, raking over my clit, sliding down my core.

He feasts and I savor the devouring, his jaw scratching responsive skin, his lips destroying my virtue.

I don't care that we're at a crime scene. That his men are yards away. Or how dead bodies litter the outskirts of this fantasy.

All I care about is him.

That he's mine.

"I want to feel you come on my face." He speaks against my pussy. "Make me a happy man, Pyro."

"Then keep going." My fingers claw into the material around my waist as I relax my arms and rest back against the roof. "I'm already close."

He kisses my mound, ending the sweetness with a harsh scrape of teeth. "That's my good girl."

Oh, God.

I shudder, the vibration turning into a tremor as he swoops back in and sucks harshly on my clit.

I cry out. Shocked. Stunned.

It feels so good.

I'm senseless from the onslaught when something presses against my opening. A thumb? A finger?

He pushes it inside me, my pussy instantly clamping down on the penetration with greedy want.

"You're fucking tight." He keeps sucking on my clit as the intrusion creeps farther inside me, pressing down, slowly circling.

I can't stop the sounds that escape me. The needy sighs. The hungry mewls.

"Does that feel good?" The vibration of his voice only adds to the deliciousness.

I moan in answer.

"How good?" He sucks harder, making me squirm.

"I'm… dying." My voice is barely audible. Nothing but a panting, breathy rasp.

His thumb retracts. Two fingers take its place.

I moan, squeezing my thighs around his neck.

"Rock your hips, Ollie. Ride my fucking mouth."

I release one hand from the pool of material and reach between my thighs to snatch at his hair, grinding, riding.

He groans. "Don't stop."

I whimper at the tightening build of my core. "I'm close." My voice is frantic, foreign to my own ears.

He curls his fingers inside me, hitting a spot I've never felt before.

It's raw and blinding. A burst of exquisite delight.

My back arches as my core spasms, the tingling euphoria expanding through my abdomen.

"That's it," he coaxes against my clit. "Come around my fingers."

I whimper with the waves of pleasure. Shuddering. Unravelling. It's burst after burst of paradise, the rapture numbing my fingers and curling my toes until the orgasmic clenching begins to lessen.

I slowly float down from the high, my body spent and lax. I release his hair, my legs losing their death grip around his neck.

Then I'm sliding. Descending.

He gently guides me back down the side of the car, his body pressed close to mine to keep me upright.

He peers at me with hunger. With awe. "You taste like the sweetest sin, Pyro." He leans in, nuzzling my neck, the scent of my pleasure on his skin sinking into my lungs as he helps to right the long lengths of my dress.

All I can do is smile into the bliss.

I understand adrenaline is playing its part. That I'll look back on this in a different light. But for now I'm putty in his hands. A slave at his alter.

"You were right," I whisper, gliding my fingers to his waistband. "The locals wouldn't have appreciated you doing that in front of the bar."

His snicker brushes my skin, lightly tickling.

I still want more.

I glide my hands to the buckle of his belt and tug at the leather strap.

"No." He stiffens, his fingers clamping tight around mine. "We need to get out of here in case the cops are on the way."

The rejection is more subtle than it was the first time in his penthouse, but it hurts all the same.

The giddy perfection flees my body.

He weaves an arm around my waist, inching me sideways, allowing him the room to open the passenger door.

"I have to speak to my men." He guides me inside, helping to drag on my seat belt as if I'm a child in need of parental assistance, or more accurately—a virgin he's now placing a barrier in front of. "I won't take long."

I remain stunned as he closes the door, leaving me to pick up the pieces of my tattered pride in private.

I don't understand. Why can he go down on me on the side of a back road with his men nearby, but me reaching for his belt buckle goes against some sick sort of terms of service?

It doesn't make sense.

I *want* this.

Want *him*.

It's not fair.

Minutes later, he climbs into the driver's seat while I try not to sulk.

I remain stiffly defiant while he does a three-point turn and travels back past the car wreck where his men carry the driver's limp body from the vehicle.

"What will happen to the crime scene?" I murmur.

"Russo and Valenti will make sure the bodies disappear."

"And the car?"

"They'll torch it."

The flame reference takes me back to the way his mouth felt between my thighs. How my body burned.

We fit perfectly.

No one could convince me otherwise.

"How did they get here so fast?" I breathe through the building sadness, trying to distract myself.

"They followed us from Baltimore. They've been here the whole time." He shoots me a glance. "I wouldn't leave you unprotected."

Merely unsatisfied.

I sigh, hating the animosity that festers. "Tell me why I can't touch you."

He returns his attention to the road. "You want to talk about this now, while we're trying to dodge the authorities?"

"Yes."

His jaw clenches, and for a few silent moments I think he's going to deny me. "Ollie, I had you pressed up against a dirty car after I'd just killed two men while my employees were nearby, organizing how to dispose of the bodies. Is that really how you want to lose your virginity?"

"So given different circumstances you would've slept with me?"

His nostrils flare.

"Remy?"

He doesn't answer.

"Goddamn you." I don't know if it's the adrenaline, the rejection, or the culmination of the last few months catching up with me, but I'm done with undisclosed information. "I can't keep doing this. You reel me in only to spit me out. Why are you so offended by my virginity?"

His fingers flex against the steering wheel as he speeds along the darkened road. "Nothing about you offends me. Never has. Never will."

"Is it because you think I won't be any good at it?"

"No," he snarls. "I already know you'll be equally flawless in fucking me as you are in everything else you do. But wanting you is dangerous. I'm teetering on the edge of my restraint when it comes to us."

"Why restrain yourself at all? It's obvious we both want this."

"Why?" He huffs a faint laugh. "Because in that bar, when you were about to walk away, I fucking kissed you." His eyes turn to mine in annoyance. "There was a threat in the next booth. I knew they wanted to kill me, and still I turned my back to the danger because you make me so messed up I was willing to pay the price."

I stare, humbled and heartbroken.

I understand what he's saying. I can even agree with it. But there has to be more.

"Then why kiss me again?" I ask. "Why do what you did against the car?"

I find it hard to say it—*he went down on me.*

He placed his mouth between my thighs and unraveled my soul one tightly wound string at a time.

"I know there's more to it," I whisper. "You have a problem with my virginity. You've said it before. You can't deal with my lack of experience."

He pauses at the intersection leading onto the highway, his eyes cutting to mine for a hard glance before he takes the turn. "It's not you."

"Do you expect me to believe that when—"

"Yes, I expect you to fucking believe it because it's the truth." His voice raises. "Your virginity isn't the issue. It's *me* being the one claiming it. I won't take that from you. Not after what my parents did to me."

My heart stutters. Falters. "What they did?"

"Yes. They fucked me up more than you can imagine. So believe me when I say I'm the one who holds all the blame."

A lump builds in my throat. "Will you tell me?"

"I've already told you enough about my genetic contributors to leave you scarred for life."

"Yet I'm still here, begging for more. Doesn't that mean something?"

He huffs an indignant breath.

"Please, Remy. I hold so many of your secrets—why not this one?"

He swipes a rough hand over his five o'clock shadow while the headlights of an oncoming car approach and then pass. "I'm protective of your virginity, Ollie, because the reminder of losing mine makes me fucking ill."

I turn cold.

"It's not that big a deal." His demeanor says otherwise. "Dear ol' dad wanted to make a man out of me, and given his lacking parenting skills he thought making his fifteen-year-old sleep with a stripper was a great idea."

My hand climbs to my throat. "He forced you?"

"I was a teenage boy. It's not like I wasn't itching to get laid, but—"

"But he forced you."

His fingers squeak against the steering wheel. "It wouldn't have been so bad if it were at night when all the young, pretty college students are out working the clubs, but I'd cut school because I didn't study for an English exam, and the only women taking stage during those hours were middle-aged and strung out."

I cover my mouth with my hand, fighting to keep my horror contained.

"Your first time sticks with you. You'll look back on it. You'll remember it for the rest of your life. And sharing that moment with someone like me, in my line of work—" He shakes his head with adamance. "I won't do that to you."

Air hits my lungs with a bite of pain.

Why didn't I already assume his restraint was for my benefit?

It's always been for me.

When he threatened to leave Lorenzo's employ. When he broke my father's trust. When he arranged this weekend away with the impressive house, the beautiful dress, and a fully booked restaurant.

All. For. Me.

"I'm sorry I pushed for that information." My voice is brittle. "I can't imagine—"

"Christ, don't fucking imagine it. It's bad enough that the memory won't fade." He stares at me, my pulse faltering as the darkness stretches out the window. "The only reason I'm telling you this is because I don't want you to think I'm holding back because you're lacking in any way. It's the opposite. You've got no idea how hard it is not to surrender to you."

I force a pained smile. "I've got a pretty good idea."

"Then make it easier on both of us and quit tempting me. I'll hate myself if I succumb."

I wince as he returns his focus to the highway, the miles between us and the intimacy we shared growing wide.

"Okay," I whisper. "I won't tempt you to sleep with me again."

His chin raises in acknowledgement, but he doesn't respond.

"I mean it, Remy. I won't."

"Good. Then we're done discussing it." He continues driving toward the vacation home, the silence dragging.

I sit there mulling over the conversation—what his parents put him through, what I promised, and how we can work around it.

I'm not giving up.

Sex or not, I refuse to believe we can't have something. *Anything.*

He's grown to mean too much to me to simply let go.

The car slows as we approach the familiar drive. He turns onto the property, the tires grating against the coarse path until he stops before the shadowed home with the lone entry light shining from behind the front door.

He cuts the engine, his gaze remaining out the windshield. "Are you all right after what happened with the Irish?"

I nod. "I think so."

"Do you need me to do anything for you?"

"No. I'm okay."

"Good." His voice loses all strength as he unclasps his belt and opens his door. "I'm going to want to leave as soon as your dad wakes in the morning. So we should get some rest while we can."

I follow him from the car, but like a gentleman, he rounds the hood, helping me gain my footing in the unfamiliar heels.

He remains at my side as we walk to the house. I keep close, not sure how I'm going to handle space between us while he places the PIN code into the security lock, then holds open the front door.

"Go ahead." He jerks his chin toward the bedrooms. "I'll stay here and turn off the entry light once you reach your room so we don't have to illuminate the hall and risk waking your dad."

I can't bring myself to walk away from him. I already know tomorrow will come with him having erected walls to keep me out. I need the few more moments we have left.

"I can handle the dark." I wait, expecting him to protest.

Instead, he stares at me, seeming to war with the simple decision to accompany me toward my room, the seconds passing, the tension building.

He flicks off the light, bathing us in shadow. He's nothing more than a silhouette as he continues toward me, murmuring a quiet, "Come on," as he passes.

My heels click against the tile while I follow, the *tap, tap, tap* increasing my anxiety over the thought of saying goodnight.

He slows as we approach my door. "I'll see you in the morning." Then he continues, taking a step away.

My heart screams, the tortured organ curling in on itself.

I can't help it. I reach through the darkness to claim his hand. To hold tight.

He stops.

Everything does.

All thought. All sound. All movement.

There's nothing but silence between us. Palpable and foreboding.

"Bed, Ollie." It's a growl. A low, delicious grumble.

I swallow over my tightening throat, unable to obey.

The heat I'd felt while pressed into him against the Escalade returns with vengeance.

"Bed," he repeats.

Bed is exactly what I want as long as he's in it.

His fingers twitch, and through the darkness he stands taller, growing more commanding. More fierce.

God, it's a turn-on.

Then he swings around to face me, abruptly stalking the foot of distance between us, his chest grazing mine, intimidating me back against the doorjamb, his body a dark intimidating force.

"Breaking your promises already?" he snarls in my face, and *holy fuck*, it's exquisite.

His praise is heaven. But his waning tortured restraint could be bottled and sold for the addictive thrill of it.

"No," I whisper. "I'm not going to tempt you to sleep with me."

"Then what is this?" He closes in, his nose an inch from mine.

"I don't like being indebted."

Through the low light I can just make out the confused narrowing of his eyes.

"You've made me come twice." I curl my fingers in his shirt. "Let me return the favor."

A heavy huff of breath leaves his nose.

I grow emboldened, undoing one of his buttons.

"Do you want me to hate myself?" he snarls. "Is that it?"

"That's not going to happen. You're not going to sleep with me."

"You think you could hold me back?" He grinds the hardness of his dick against me.

I smother a whimper. "I know I can," I lie. I have no clue what I'm capable of when it comes to resisting him. But I have to try. "You won't force me. And I'm telling you now, sex isn't on the table."

"Is that right?" He weaves a hand around my waist, roughly yanking me harder against his cock. "So what is on the table?"

I release another button and raise on the tips of my toes, leaning into him, my lips a breath from his ear. "I want your cock in my mouth."

His low rumble of laughter is menacing. Fucking dark and electrifying.

"You want me to fuck that gorgeous face in a shadowed hall while your dad sleeps a few rooms away?"

I nod, breathless.

He hauls me into my bedroom and closes the door behind us. "That's not how this works, my pretty little Pyro." He flicks on the light, blinding me.

I snap my eyes closed and hide my face against his neck.

"If you want to open the floodgates—" His voice rumbles. "—then you do it while I can see those plush lips stretched around my cock."

Holy. Hell.

I bite my lower lip, fighting to contain my lust.

"Get on your knees," he demands.

I clench my core, breathing through the crazy amount of adrenaline coursing through me as I lower in front of him.

"Have you done this before?" He stares down at me, gaze intense, his body practically thrumming with desire.

"No."

His nostrils flare. He may not enjoy the prospect of my virginity, but he wants this. *Needs* it. "Are you sure about this?"

I nod, nervous and wildly excited at the same time.

He's quiet a moment, watching, scrutinizing. "Then undo my belt and lower my zipper."

I reach out trembling hands, unclasping the leather belt, my heart thumping with the grate of the zipper.

"Pull out my cock."

I do that, too, releasing the massive length of him from his boxer briefs to take in the sight of him.

He's beautiful, all thick and engorged, his pubic hair trimmed.

He drags his hand over my jaw, his thumb delicately grazing my cheek. "Good girl."

I shudder.

Surrender.

"See?" He palms my chin, making me look up at him. "Your body hums when I praise you."

"I love it," I admit. "Just not when we're in the middle of a high-speed car chase."

"Duly noted." He grins, the smug expression quickly fading. "Now spread those lips around my cock, Ollie. I want inside that pretty mouth."

I swallow over the dryness taking over my throat and shuffle closer.

I'm tentative, moving forward slowly, watching him as he watches me. I swear to God he holds his breath.

Then I lick my lips and spread my mouth around him.

He tenses, those eyes silently praising as he allows me to get used to the novelty.

He's hard, yet so velvety soft.

I've barely touched him, yet now he's against my tongue, the liquid seeping from his tip leaving an unfamiliar taste. I hesitantly glide back and forth, each assault taking him farther, deeper, until I gag slightly.

He moans. "You don't know what you're doing, Pyro."

I stiffen, my cheeks heating with embarrassment.

"Don't misinterpret me," he warns. "I'm not talking about the way you take my dick, 'cause God fucking knows you've already got me on the precipice." He runs a soothing hand over the crown of my braid. "I'm talking about what you're doing with us. You're starting something that will never end."

Good.

I continue sliding my mouth over him, humming my approval.

I can live without sex. I already have for this long. But I can't live without him.

"You want more?" He eyes me with heated reverence.

I nod.

He growls his approval, his hand fisting my hair. "Then let me guide you." He holds my head in place and slowly inches himself inside me. Little by little. Getting deeper. Stretching my lips farther. "Breathe through your nose."

I do as he asks, loving the way he leads me.

He starts to fuck my mouth, the grind of his hips smooth and measured. He's holding back. Taking it slow.

I palm the back of his thighs, digging my nails into his muscles, silently begging for more.

"*Jesus,*" he groans.

This time it's me guiding him to move faster. Harder. The deep rumble emanating from his chest makes me all kinds of crazy while he thrusts with more force. Using me. *Enjoying* me.

"Enough." He quits moving. "Get off your knees."

I ignore him, sucking, licking, starved for more.

He tightens his hold on my hair. "Don't worry, I'm not finished with your mouth. I just need to get my hands on that sweet pussy."

Heat floods my core and I pull back, yet still I can't quit kissing his length, licking the distended veins until his palms wrap around my upper arms and he hauls me to my feet.

He turns me to face the bed, inching close against my back. "Such a greedy little Pyro." He unzips my dress, the heavy weight falling to pool at my feet. "What did I do to deserve you?"

I wish I knew so I could make sure we stay like this. In tune and fated.

"Do you still think you can stop me from fucking you?" He grinds his dick between my thighs, sliding along the slick ridge of my pussy.

I close my eyes, hating myself for the promise.

"Yes," I breathe, the feel of him already coaxing me toward climax.

A few more strokes and I'll be done for.

It's ridiculous. I'm a mess.

"Good." He nuzzles my neck, scraping his teeth along my carotid. "Because I'm free-falling. I'm relying on you." He smacks my ass. "Now get on the bed."

My skin breaks out in goose bumps as I step away to sit on the comforter.

"Hands and knees, Ollie, and stay close to the edge of the mattress. I want access to the heaven between your thighs while you suck my cock."

My limbs tremble with the compliance then he's right there, his legs leaning into the side of the bedframe as he palms his dick and guides it toward me.

"Take it slow." He slides his free hand down my back, over my ass. "I'm not ready for this to end."

I nod, my tongue lapping at his slit, but then his fingertips brush my clit through the opening of my ravaged panties and I can't stop myself from taking him to the back of my throat with a needy groan.

"*Shit.*" He fists my hair as his fingers plunge inside me, controlling me while he works me up.

But it's no use. I can't stop rocking back and forth, already a greedy mess for the friction between my thighs.

"*Ollie.*"

The masculine warning does nothing to ease my craving.

I squeeze my core around him, my cheeks hollowing with my rabid suction.

"*Fuck*," he snarls. "You feel so good."

I whimper around him, releasing him momentarily to tell him, "I'm so close to coming it's insane."

He groans, edging another finger inside me. "Do it." He pistons his digits. "Show me how you take my dick while you lose control."

I suck on him like my life depends on it for no reason other than I fucking love it—the excitement it brings, the power I hold.

I come undone, crying out my pleasure around his cock, grinding wildly against his hand.

"That's my girl." He keeps working me over the crest, extending the pleasure as he continues to fuck my mouth.

I'm breathless by the time the clenching inside me fades.

"My turn." He pulls back, dragging his length from my mouth and hand from my core.

I whimper at the loss but watch in fascination as he coats his dick with the slickness on his fingers, then jerks the head of his shaft in fast, commanding strokes.

He stares down at me with heated longing, face pinched, breaths panting. "You did this." He grabs my jaw with his free hand, dragging me upright, slamming his mouth on mine as he groans so deep and low.

Then I feel it, his cum purged against my stomach, over and over again.

Dear Lord, I could climax again from the mere sensation of him marking me.

It's too soon when he breaks the kiss, pressing his forehead to mine, his heated breaths brushing my lips. "You've got no business being this perfect."

I chuckle and fall back onto my ass, glancing down at where he's branded me. "I could say the same about you."

He eyes me as I trail a finger through the fluid on my belly and raise it to my mouth, curious for a taste.

"Jesus fucking Christ." He shoves a rough hand through his hair. "You're going to be the fucking death of me."

34

REMY

She leads me to her private bathroom, then allows me the honor of stripping her out of those white shredded panties. It takes another two-second glance at my filth still sliding down her body for my dick to perk up in search of round three.

"You're hard again." She walks into the open-ended shower, eyeing my cock over her shoulder as she turns on the water. "Does that mean I didn't do a good enough job?"

"No, Pyro." I follow, closing in at her back, wrapping my arms around her waist to splay my hands over her hips. "My dick is rarely soft around you."

I nuzzle my face into her neck, hating the weakness she creates in me and fucking loving it at the same time.

I can't keep denying her. The sex—yes. This thing between us— hell no.

Somehow I have to figure out how to make this work. How to keep her safe. How to muzzle the head of the East Coast mafia so I can have free rein with my girl.

I wash her, falling victim to the gentle way she leans back against my chest, her head resting against my shoulder as I run soap over her skin. She returns the favor, paying extra attention to the parts of me that enjoy her the most, along with the healing bullet wound on my leg.

I let her get to know my body without judgment, despite the act of Herculean strength it takes to stop my own hands from wandering. I don't even utter a word of protest when her fingertips graze teasingly over my balls, making me want to bite my fist.

Her shy, inquisitive nature undoes me.

And I fucking adore that I get to claim so many of her firsts.

All except the one I'm not willing to comprehend.

When she asks me to sleep in her bed, I don't bother fighting it. If I returned to my own room, I'd only lie there thinking about being beside her. And I'd rather sport a hard dick while in bed with a beautiful woman than be alone while the female in question runs rings around my head.

It isn't until she falls asleep that I grab my cell from the bedside table, dim the screen light, then open a text to my oldest brother.

ME

> What would you do if you fell for someone Lorenzo warned you away from?

The message turns from delivered to read almost instantly.

Two seconds later my cell vibrates with an incoming call from Matthew.

Fuck.

I rush to reject the call, then start typing again.

ME

> She's asleep beside me. Don't want to wake her.

MATTHEW

> Fucking hell, Rem. What have you gotten yourself into?

I scrub a hand down my face, asking myself the same question.

MATTHEW

> Going behind Lorenzo's back is never a good idea. I've been ordered to handle men for far less than getting their dick wet in the wrong place.

Handle aka kill.

Fan-fucking-tastic.

ME

> What would you do if it was Layla?

The three dots of impending reply appear, then vanish. Appear then vanish.

MATTHEW

> Nothing and no one could keep me from her. Not in this lifetime or the next.

> Layla means everything to me. But the problem is
> what this woman means to you.

I glance to Ollie peacefully sleeping at my side, her hair still braided, her bare shoulders begging to be kissed.

I'd like to think it's too soon to tell what she means. That there's no way of knowing how I'll feel for her in a few days, let alone a few weeks.

But that's a lie.

I already know.

The problem is the heavy weight that forms in my gut at the thought of what's to come in the future.

It's close to eight in the morning when I carefully climb out of bed, trying not to wake Ollie as the sound of clattering pots and pans echo from the kitchen.

I can already smell bacon. I'd be surprised if Carlo can't, too.

"Are you trying to sneak out before the awkward morning-after conversation?" Ollie mumbles into her pillow.

I grin, enjoying the rasp of her morning voice while I pull on my pants sans underwear. "No. I'm trying to sneak out before your father wakes up and finds me walking from his daughter's room in last night's clothes."

"Smart thinking." She lazily turns onto her back, hauling the sheet high to cover her nakedness while she unabashedly ogles my ass.

"At least one of us is being smart." I raise a warning brow. "If you keep staring at me like that the sounds that come from this room will be far worse for Carlo to deal with."

"I can't help it."

"I'm sure you've seen your fair share of the male anatomy."

Her brows furrow in the cutest frown of contemplation. "Does it count if all those males were dead at the time?"

I suppress a laugh. "Have I told you how much I love how morbid you are?"

The tops of her cheeks darken.

It's a strange comment to inspire shyness but I'll take it.

"I also love how you blush." I yank up my zipper before my dick can get any harder. "The drive home is going to be torture."

"Will it make it more difficult if I tell you I forgot to pack enough panties?" She bats her lashes. "And you kinda destroyed the ones I had on last night. I'm going to have to go without all day."

I latch onto the button of my pants, my grip painfully tight. "You're playing with fire, Pyro."

She gives a wickedly shy grin. "Really? That's my favorite pastime."

I lower my gaze and readjust the growing tent in my pants. As much as I'd like to flirt with her all day, there are repercussions from last night to deal with. "We need to start making tracks."

She sits up, positioning herself against the headboard. "Did something else happen?"

"No." I grab my shirt and jacket off the floor. "But I don't want to risk being caught unaware. Russo and Valenti stayed up all night disposing of issues and watching the house. I want them back in Baltimore so they can get some sleep."

"Okay." She climbs out of bed, dragging the sheet with her. "I'll shower and be ready as soon as I can."

I pull on my shirt while she heads toward the bathroom, the white sheet trailing behind her like a sordid wedding gown. "Remy..." She pauses at the open door and glances over her shoulder to look at me. "What is this?"

I frown. "What is what?"

"This." She turns back, waving a hand toward me. "Us."

I tense.

"Actually—" She holds the sheet to her chest as she continues inside the bathroom. "—don't answer that. Your face already holds a familiar expression, and I didn't appreciate where the conversation led last time."

I clench my jaw. "I can't give you a label right now, Ollie."

"Fair enough."

No, it's not fair enough.

She gave me an all-access pass to her body and I can't even give her reassurance. All I need is fucking time.

"I won't take long in the shower. I'll see you in the kitchen for breakfast." She closes herself into the bathroom, the click of the lock a deafening shun.

I curse myself as I leave her room and return to mine, then shower, change, and pack my shit.

Ollie is already seated at the breakfast counter, talking to the chef when I enter the open living area with my duffle bag, their far-too-friendly conversation raising the hair on the back of my neck.

She looks fucking gorgeous in short shorts and a flowing long-sleeve white linen top, her twin braids begging to be tugged.

"Are you seeing someone?" the chef asks while cracking an egg.

I clench a fist around my bag handle, biting my tongue while I wait for her response.

She shakes her head. "I thought I was, but there's no label, so I assume it was a fling."

I drop my duffle to the tile, the heavy weight falling with a booming *thud.*

They both glance toward me, the chef with wide-eyed surprise, and Ollie with taunting sass. She knew I was standing there when she answered him.

"She's seeing someone," I snarl.

The chef glances between us, an *oh, shit* look crossing his face.

"Am I?" Ollie swivels her stool to face me, casually forking a bite of bacon into her mouth. "That's confusing."

The chef turns away, busying himself with something in the fridge.

"Can I have a moment in private, *Olivia?*" I ask through clenched teeth.

Her lips quirk.

She's loving this, and yeah, I don't fucking blame her, but she needs to be careful. I have a short fuse when it comes to the thought of losing her.

"Of course, Remington." She slides from her stool to pad toward me.

That is *not* my fucking name, and given her extensive googling, she goddamn knows it. But it looks like she woke up and chose violence this morning.

"Your room," I growl. "*Now.*"

She smirks—*fucking* smirks—then saunters that heavenly ass to the hall and into her room.

"What are you playing at?" I close the door behind us, the wood hitting the threshold with a *thwack.*

"I'm not playing. You said no labels, so I'm single, aren't I?" She frowns in mock confusion. "That's how math maths, right?"

She pivots and walks for the bed.

I grab her wrist, tugging her back to me, her toes stumbling across my shoes, our mouths an inch apart. "That's not how my math fucking maths, Pyro, and you know it. You don't get to flirt with other men unless you want them dead."

She stares up at me, her inhales increasing. "Is that a two-way street?"

"You bet your fucking ass it is." I weave my arm around her waist, dragging her into my hips. "If you want a label so badly, take whatever you need. You want to be my lover, Pyro? Fine. You want to be my spouse? My girlfriend? My fucking wife?" I lean in so our noses are almost touching. "I. Don't. Fucking. Care. They're just words, Ollie. You can take them all."

She frowns. "You don't care?"

"No, I don't."

She flinches and pushes against my chest.

"What have I done now?" I tighten my hold. "Didn't I just give you what you want?"

"No." She wiggles, trying to calmly escape.

"Then what is it?"

"I want to know you care about me."

"You're all I fucking care about. How do you not know that?"

She pauses, her brow furrowed, her insecurities clearly warring with what's right in front of her.

"You want proof that I'm in this but you've had it the whole time." I drag a finger under the collar of her shirt and drag out her necklace. "You wear my ring, Ollie. I've been yours for months."

A breath shudders from her.

God, I want to taste her again. To make her come.

"But we need to keep this quiet for a while." I nuzzle my nose against hers, fighting temptation like a motherfucker. "At least until I figure out how I'm going to deal with Lorenzo."

"I can prove myself to him," she whispers against my lips. "Just tell me how."

"You'll do nothing. Leave me to handle it. Okay?"

She swallows. Nods.

I return the necklace to its hiding place beneath her shirt. "Now get that tight little ass back out in the kitchen and welcome your father to breakfast before I bend you over the bed and make the drive home incredibly awkward."

She grins, then slays me with a hard, deep kiss, before walking from the room.

I have to remain in place for a good five minutes to get my dick under control.

The drive home isn't any better. Not with Ollie seated beside me, her fingers constantly playing with the frayed hem of those short shorts while I question whether or not the whole no-panty situation was real or just a fucking cruel punishment.

I drop her father and Lucy off at the funeral home first, even though Ollie's house is closer. I fucking fly up those stairs to dump Carlo and Lucy's bags in the living room.

"In a hurry to get somewhere?" Ollie taunts as I climb back in the car.

"Watch your mouth. If you're not careful, I'll fill it."

She chuckles, her grin wide.

Does she think I'm joking?

The damn woman has broken me. I can't quit picturing what I want to do to her.

"Out of curiosity…" she muses, resting her cheek against the headrest to stare at me. "What would you fill it with?"

My muscles tense. "Don't fuck with me, Pyro. I may not be in a hurry to take your virtue, but there are a hell of a lot of things I can do within my parameters."

"Like what?" she purrs.

Son of a goddamn bitch. "You want to know what I've been thinking about the whole car ride?"

She nods, her teeth dragging against her bottom lip.

"I was thinking about how pretty you'd look on top of me, riding my face while you sucked my cock."

She clenches her thighs together.

"I want to watch you touch yourself," I grate. "I want to learn how you've made yourself feel good all these years. With toys and without."

I fight a groan at the image of her fingers inside her pussy while my cock glides in and out of her mouth.

It's slow and brutal torture.

She whimpers. "I really should've worn underwear."

I scowl at the traffic ahead, forcing my hands to remain on the steering wheel.

Indulging in her while in Baltimore is too risky. I need to work out a plan first—not only with Lorenzo, but the cartel and their outsourced contract regarding my existence.

"Yes, you fucking should've," I mutter. "We can't mess around for a while. It's not safe."

"How long is a while?"

A week. A fucking month. "I don't know."

"I can handle it." Her tone falls quiet. "We both can, right?"

I turn onto her street, the answer to her question remaining to be seen. "If you're asking if I can be faithful, that's not something you need to worry about."

"Then what should be worrying me?"

Literally everything else—Lorenzo, the cartel, the cops.

I could write a list but that would take a rather large notebook and more free hours than I have at my disposal.

"Just lay low." I pull into her drive, deliberately keeping the engine running as I shift into park. "Don't draw unnecessary attention."

"That's my life motto." She reaches into the back of the car, her ass poking up in the air, those tiny shorts doing exactly what sexualized fashion marketing intended as she drags her tiny suitcase and dress bag from the backseat. "Are you going to come in?"

"Not this time. We don't know who's watching."

Well, we definitely know the nosey old bat next door would be, but apart from her, the list of witnesses is unknown.

Ollie sighs, her shoulders slumping as she wrangles her belongings in her lap. "Will you call me?"

"More often than you'll appreciate."

She smiles, her eyes dancing with infinite beauty. "I'd like to see you try."

God, she astounds me.

Confuses me.

Fucking destroys me.

Her gaze lowers to my mouth, that look of hers transforming to the wanton yearning she had back in the bar when I almost bartered my life for a kiss.

Then in a blink it's gone. She snaps out of it, leaving me to be the dazed horny fuck itching to break the rules.

She climbs from the car. "I'll speak to you later."

I reach to unclasp my belt, already succumbing just a little. "I'll help with your bags."

"No, it's okay. If you follow I'll struggle not to break the rules, so it's better if I go on my own."

I clench my teeth, hating that she's stronger than I am.

She closes the door and crosses the yard then climbs the few steps to her porch.

I scrutinize each step. The flex of her toned calves. The glide of her smooth thighs.

She drops her belongings to the floor, shoves her key into the front door to push it wide, then bends over to reclaim her bags.

The thoughts that pummel me are fucking filthy. So gloriously wicked and vile.

I can't take it.

I cut the engine, shove from the car, and stalk toward her.

She turns to me in confusion as my steps thunder across her porch, then I'm shoving her bags inside the house and dragging her across the threshold.

"Remy?"

I kick the door shut with my foot as her hands grasp my shoulders. A few fumbled steps later I have her backed against the cushioned armrest of her sofa, thankful for all the drawn curtains that hide what I'm about to do to her.

"You better not have lied about not wearing panties." I yank at her zipper, shove my hand beneath her shorts, then *fucking groan* at the skin on skin when my fingertips glide to her bare mound.

"Do I meet your expectations?" she rasps, curling her legs around me.

"You've always blown them out of the water." I slam my lips against hers, my tongue seeking immediate entry.

She moans into me, arching her hips as I slide my fingers lower.

"Already wet," I growl.

"It's a given, especially after learning what that mouth can do."

A throat clears across the opposite side of the room, startling the fuck out of me.

I yank Ollie off the sofa and shove her behind me, grabbing my gun from my waistband with my other hand to point toward the intruder.

"Calm down, brother." Salvatore drawls from the far shadowed end of the dining table. "I apologize for interrupting, but I wasn't sure how long I could control my gag reflex."

My pulse thunders with rage as I keep my gun trained on him. "What the fuck are you doing here?"

Ollie's fingers dig into my hips, her panicked breathing brushing my ears.

"Apparently, I'm catching you in the act of defiance, am I not?" He pushes to his feet, his chair scraping loudly against the tile. "Lorenzo wants to see you."

"*Oh, God,*" Ollie whispers behind me.

"Don't worry, sweetheart," he drawls. "Lorenzo wants to see you, too."

"Over my dead body," I snarl.

My brother snickers. "I was joking. He doesn't want her. *Yet.* So you can lower your weapon. There's no need to be hostile."

I glare. "You're such a fucking dick, Salvo."

"It's in the genes." He strides toward us, Ollie's fingers clutching at my shirt. "I'll wait for you outside."

I tense as he passes, my gun following his every step until he's on the other side of the front door.

"Should I panic?" she asks, the question redundant when her tone suggests she already is. She never should've stopped panicking.

Neither of us should've, because this is exactly what I was worried about.

"I'll handle it." I turn to her.

"Should I come with you?"

Yes. I don't want her out of my fucking sight. But I also don't want her in the vicinity of Lorenzo and his guards. "It's best if you stay here."

Her eyes plead with me. It's fucking torture.

"Do you still want this?" I cup her jaw, hating the fear that stares back at me.

She swallows. Nods. "Yes."

I shouldn't be relieved.

It's selfish, and careless, and fucking asinine. It's the opposite of what's best for her. But I'm too far gone. Letting her go isn't an option when she's just as caught up in this madness as I am.

"I need you to take this." I grab her wrist and place my gun in her palm.

"What?" Her eyes bug as she tugs her arm away. "No."

"If you want me, Pyro, you also want this lifestyle. So you'll take the fucking gun." I grab her again, forcing the Walther back into her hand. "You need to be able to protect yourself."

I wait for her to retreat. To change her mind and make the safer choice.

Instead, her delicate fingers wrap around the weapon, her gaze focused on it with trepidation. "What do I do with it?"

"The safety's off. If anyone unfamiliar gets within five feet of you, pull the trigger. Ask questions later."

She glances from me to the gun and back again. "Do you really think I'll need it?"

"I'm not taking any chances, and neither should you." I wrap my fingers around her neck and kiss her. Hard.

She clings to my shirt with her free hand, tugging, yanking.

"I've gotta go." I pull back.

She keeps clinging to me. "I'm sorry, Remy."

I grab her chin and stare into those slaying eyes. "Don't be. This was bound to happen when I lack the restraint to stay away from you. I just need to figure out a way to get us through it."

A bang rattles the front window.

"Come on, dickhead," Salvo shouts. "I have better things to police than your love life."

I snarl. "I'm going to kill him."

Ollie pulls a half-hearted smile. "Can I watch?"

"No, Pyro, you can participate."

Ollie chuckles, the cadence spiritless.

I hope it's not the last sound I hear from her.

"Be safe," she whispers. "I'll be waiting."

I place a kiss to her hairline and force myself to stride for the door, not looking back as I walk outside.

Salvo waits against the railing of her porch, arms crossed over his chest, brows raised and mocking.

I don't say a word. I keep my animosity locked tight and stalk for the Escalade.

He follows, climbing into the passenger seat.

"Where the fuck is your car?" I growl.

"I was dropped here. I didn't want to spoil the surprise. And the hag next door is nosey as fuck."

I shoot a glance toward the neighbor's house, my gaze colliding with Lesley's as she stares at me through her front window.

Inquisitive old bat.

"Head to my townhouse," Salvo instructs.

I reverse out of Ollie's drive, stopping short of squealing the tires as I take off down the road.

We're a few blocks into the trip when he opens his mouth again. "What the fuck were you thinking?"

I keep my focus on upcoming traffic, knowing transparency won't work in my favor. He won't understand. He's never loved anyone other than our mother. Not our dad. Not high school sweethearts. He's always been a cold, heartless bastard like that.

"Why would you go against Lorenzo?" His tone becomes subdued, no longer edged with ego. "Why willingly give yourself a weakness?"

I lock my jaw and pretend I don't hear the concern in his voice.

"I thought we had a good thing here," he says. "We have freedom, and money, and fucking power. We've never had any of that before. And you're out here risking it all, for what?"

For her.

For Ollie.

For a relationship that may undermine all those things Salvo boasts about, but somehow gives me so much more.

"I didn't exactly plan for any of this," I mutter.

"I fucking hope not, otherwise you're dumber than the dumbass I already thought you were."

"Fuck you, Salvo."

"Fuck you, too, you deadass dumb shit. I can't believe I spent my Sunday morning in your mistress's fucking house, waiting for you to return home from some tawdry weekend love fest. What a goddamn joke."

"It wasn't a tawdry love fest, you Gucci-wearing, frappe-drinking, mother-loving asshole."

He scowls at me with a raised brow. "You're seriously throwing drink choices at me while you fuck up all our lives?"

"This has nothing to do with you."

"Like hell it doesn't. I've covered for you. I've *lied* for you. To fucking Lorenzo—who happens to be the only good fortune we've had our whole godforsaken lives. And here you are, pissing it away because of a pretty face and a mediocre set of tits."

"Speak about her like that one more time and I'll—" I clench my teeth, cutting off the threat.

"Seriously?" He glares at me. "That's how it is now? You threatening me? You pointing a goddamn gun in my face because of a woman?"

My forearms throb from my tight grip around the steering wheel.

He scoffs. "You're all I've got left, you self-centered motherfucker."

"Oh, fuck off, Salvo. Like you give a shit."

"Are you fucking with me right now?" He deadpans. "Dad's dead. Mom's imprisoned. And Matthew and Abri are in Washington, living their best lives. I thought we were in this together."

Guilt chips away at my anger. I don't fucking appreciate that he's making sense for the first time in his life.

"Like I said," I mutter, "I didn't plan for this to happen."

"It must be serious. She wears your ring."

"It's as serious as it gets as far as I'm concerned."

He drags in a long breath, then lets it out on a sigh. "You do realize she can throw us under the bus."

"So can Valenti or Russo, along with any of your men or Lorenzo's. What's the difference between her and them?"

"For a start, you're not sticking your dick in Valenti and growing attached." He narrows his eyes on me. "Or are you?"

My nostrils flare as I take the next turn harder than necessary.

"They're disposable," he grates. "That's the fucking difference. If they mess up, they're gone. *Poof.* Vanished. How the hell are you going to act if she does something wrong and we're forced to silence her?"

"She won't," I bite out.

"Says your dick. Maybe let your other brain function for a little while."

"Both brains are fully functioning and equally enthusiastic to fuck your shit up right now," I snarl.

"That's disturbing. Maybe, in future, don't reference your dick brain and fucking me up in the same sentence."

"I hate you, Salvo."

"I love you, too, brother." He messes with the buttons on my dash, turning on the radio.

We remain quiet for the next fifteen minutes, the low hum of music echoing from the speakers.

I don't know what the fuck I'm meant to do or if I should've left Ollie unsupervised. I don't know a damn thing apart from how messed up I'll be if something happens to her. And the farther I drive, the faster my thoughts race in panic.

"So what's our plan?" Salvo asks once we're a few blocks from his townhouse.

"*Our* plan?"

"Yes, *our plan*. Why else do you think I'm here?"

"I dunno, maybe to rub my face in my mistakes, because that's what it feels like." I force my gaze out my side window, trying and failing to lessen my annoyance. "Do you have any suggestions?"

He falls quiet for a moment, the silent contemplation making me uncomfortable. He usually acts as if he knows everything. Without pause or need for reflection.

"I'm honestly fresh out of ideas," he mutters. "Lorenzo is hard to read sometimes. Matthew thinks the sun shines out of the old man's ass, but I'm yet to see the glow."

I grunt, despising the visual.

"I've got your back, though." He unclasps his belt as I pull up to his drive. "Whatever your dumb ass needs, I'll help fight for."

"Thanks, asshole."

"You're welcome, Casanova."

He pulls out his phone, using an app to open the head-high metal gate leading into his courtyard. I park beside Lorenzo's Rolls-Royce.

It's Matthew's black BMW that raises my hackles.

"Our brother is here?" I cut the engine, my pulse increasing with foreboding.

"Yeah." Salvo opens his door. "I didn't know he was in town until Lorenzo gave the order to find you."

Matthew must have ratted on me.

Fucking snake.

I shove from the car and stalk to the house, passing Lorenzo's guard to let myself into Salvatore's foyer.

I hear them talking—my backstabbing brother and our controlling uncle— the murmured words trailing from the far end of the house.

I can't fucking believe this.

My relationship with Matthew may have been distant over the years, but I thought we were closing the gap. Instead, he decided to throw me under the bus to climb farther up Lorenzo's ass.

I storm down the hall, clenching my fists, wishing I still had my gun as Salvo enters the house.

"Take your shoes off," Salvo yells. "I just had the tile polished, you fucking Neanderthal."

I keep storming, keep raging, keep trying to hold my fucking temper but at this point, there's no escaping the detonation.

I walk into Salvatore's library, finding Matthew seated on one of the caramel leather sofas, an ankle kicked over his opposite knee, his arm lazily stretched against the shoulder-high back rest while our uncle stands in front of the bay windows facing the view of Inner Harbor.

"What the hell are you doing here?" I snarl, charging forward.

Matthew's gaze cuts to me, his expression mildly curious instead of guilt-ridden. "Good morning, brother. It's a fine day we're hav—"

"Fuck you." I stop in front of him, kicking his planted shoe to send his resting foot falling to the floor. "Get up."

He eyes me with tired disinterest. "I suggest you take a seat and bite your tongue."

Like fuck. "You think I won't hit you while you're seated?"

"I think you're letting emotion get the better of you. *Unnecessarily.*" A sneer enters his tone. "So, like I said, take a fucking seat, and bite your goddamn tongue."

There's no way I'm doing either. Instead, I keep glaring at him as Salvatore enters the room.

"What did I miss?" he asks.

"Nothing, *figlio*." Lorenzo turns to face us, his fatherly gaze resting on me. "Take a seat. We have a lot to discuss."

I cross my arms over my chest. "I'll stand."

He sighs, plodding forward with the aid of his walking stick. "Of all Emmanuel's sons, I have to admit, I didn't think you would be the most defiant."

"Well, hold onto your fucking pants, Grandpa. You ain't seen nothing yet."

"*Remy*," Matthew warns. "Know your place."

"Do you know yours? Because it sure as shit isn't at my side where a brother should be."

"Enough." Lorenzo continues forward to claim the leather armchair seated between the two sofas that face each other. "I called a family meeting because we have a problem."

I scoff. "She's—"

"Shut the fuck up," Matthew growls. "I won't tell you again."

My nostrils flare, the vehemence pumping so hard through me that I can barely see straight.

"You called a family meeting because...?" Salvatore takes a seat opposite Matthew.

Lorenzo doesn't take his gaze off me. "I've learned that the cartel have increased their efforts to protect themselves."

I scowl, confused.

"They have a hit out on Remy. It's barely enough to claim the interest of any serious threats, but there will be small fish who seek to claim the money, without thought of our family's wrath."

"My bad..." Salvatore shoots me an apologetic grimace. "I thought this meeting was about something else."

"Hmm?" Lorenzo raises a brow.

"It's nothing." Salvo waves him away. "I just thought when you asked for someone to look for him this morning that he'd fucked up like usual. But alas, my baby brother's notoriety has stolen center stage."

I glower at him, sending a silent warning to shut his goddamn mouth.

If this isn't about Ollie, I still have time to strategize.

"Given the increased threat, I'll stay in town." Matthew relaxes into his seat, kicking his foot back onto his knee. "I'll call Bishop. We can wipe the slate clean with the cartel if need be."

"No." Lorenzo gives a dismissive shake of his head. "Although remaining in Baltimore temporarily is why I asked you here, more violence is not the answer I'm looking for. I've already spoken to Gabriel Rodriguez. He's the new appointed head of the cartel's operations since we had his brother killed. He's a mean son of a bitch, but thankfully, he's smarter than Javier was."

"And why are we thankful for that?" Matthew asks.

"Because he listened to my warning not to escalate our conflict and agreed to return to the cartel's regular business dealings instead of trying to undermine ours."

Salvo raises a skeptical brow. "So the hit is no longer in play?"

"It doesn't matter," Matthew interjects. "Even if the hit has been retracted, it'll take a while for news to spread. Especially to the bottom feeders who would've taken up the offer."

Lorenzo nods. "Matthew is right. It would be wise for all of us to take extra precautions until further notice. Even though I've told our own messengers to spread the word, these things take time."

My brothers seem appeased while I remain skeptical that this is the only reason we're all here.

"You don't seem surprised, *figlio*." Lorenzo cocks his head, scrutinizing me. "Were you already aware of the increased threat?"

I shrug. "There may have been a hint or two."

"Mmm." He nods thoughtfully.

It's so aggravatingly fake. He definitely knows about Ollie. He's fucking with me.

The three of them chat strategy and precautions while I remain standing, quietly simmering in animosity until Salvo rises to his feet.

"I need a coffee," he declares as if everyone should give a shit.

"Good idea." Lorenzo looks between my brothers. "Why don't you two go for a drive and get us all something to eat and drink?"

"I'll order it online and have it delivered." Matthew pulls out his cell.

"I'm afraid I insist." Lorenzo juts his chin toward the hall. "Remy and I have private matters to discuss."

All eyes turn to me, my brothers with barely hidden apprehension, Lorenzo with no emotion at all.

"Why don't we both just hang out in the kitchen while you two talk?" Salvo suggests. "I've got that fancy-ass coffee machine, and the housekeeper always has snacks in—"

"I won't ask again." Lorenzo's tone hardens.

Matthew turns his attention to our uncle, the two of them engaging in an impassive stare-off.

"Fine." Matthew pushes to his feet. "We won't be long."

"You won't return until instructed," Lorenzo corrects.

Matthew's fingers twitch at his sides, then he turns to maneuver around the sofa, clapping me on the shoulder as he passes. "Don't torch a bridge before it needs to be burned," he murmurs. "Whatever happens, we'll work it out."

He continues from the room as Salvatore stands.

"What's this about?" Salvo asks.

"It's not your concern just yet, *figlio*. Go on." Lorenzo jerks his chin toward the hall again. "I'll have someone call you when we're ready for your return."

My brother pauses, the hesitance more clear in his hardened expression than in his lack of movement.

"It's okay," I say. "I can handle this."

"You sure?"

"He's sure," Lorenzo answers for me.

Salvatore's jaw tightens, but he casually strolls from the room, his footsteps retreating down the hall along with Matthew's until the front door closes, leaving me and my uncle in silence.

"Are you ready to take a seat?" Lorenzo indicates the sofa in front of him with the gentlest of hand movements.

He's always so sickeningly serene.

In the year we've worked together I've never seen him lose his shit. He's given kill orders while holding that caring, fatherly smile. He's learned of the murder of people in his organization and taken the news without a flinch.

He's emotionless.

Possibly heartless.

I lean my ass against the far armrest. "I'm good here."

He sighs. "Okay, let's get this over and done with."

My pulse beats harder in my throat.

"You left town for the weekend." He cocks his head, eyeing me intently.

"Yes," I answer through clenched teeth.

"You weren't alone." He continues with the cool, calm voice beneath the cool, calm exterior, and it fucking drives me insane.

"You can quit the lead up to the dramatic reveal." I shove back to my feet, no longer capable of remaining seated. "I assume you're well informed. Was it Matthew who snitched on me?"

"No snitch was necessary, *figlio*. Sometimes a hunch is enough." One side of his mouth kicks upward in subtle charm that doesn't hit its mark. "But I'm surprised he didn't warn you that nothing gets past me.

I pride myself on caring for my nearest and dearest. I do whatever it takes to keep them safe."

"You do whatever it takes to assert control." I glower. "And I get it. You need a certain level of transparency in this line of work. But I'm done being handled by family members who claim to be doing their best by me when their interests are far from altruistic."

His smile fades, but the calm remains.

He doesn't speak, only sits there staring, lazily scrutinizing.

It fucking irks me. Being away from Ollie while she's susceptible irks me even more.

I clench my hands into fists and fight to keep my breathing level. "Look, Lorenzo, despite us working together since my father died, we're not all that familiar with one another. You spend most of your time with Salvatore while I do your dirty work, so I'm going to do you a solid and give you some free insight into the man I am."

He continues to stare with undaunted interest.

"The funeral home is *my* project." I raise a hand to stab a finger at my chest. "My brother may have negotiated terms, but *I* set up the working arrangements, *I* learned the funeral business, *I've* handled every part of this venture for almost a year now. And I did it fucking well despite the curve balls that were thrown."

He remains quiet, contemplative.

The hair on the back of my neck rises. I'm going to fucking lose it.

"I don't like being micromanaged," I snarl. "I don't like being followed or watched or whatever the fuck you've been doing to get insight on my whereabouts. And I certainly don't like my personal activities examined."

He steeples his hands in his lap. "Are you finished?"

Barely.

"Ollie is not to be touched." My tone spits venom. "She isn't to be threatened. Or antagonized. Or fucking intimidated. Not by you, your men, or my fucking brothers. I will die on that hill and take down anyone who dares to defy me."

He raises a brow.

"If anything happens to her," I sneer. "If someone so much as looks in her direction without my approval, I'll make what I've done to the cartel look fucking dull in comparison."

I wait a beat, expecting him to reply.

He doesn't.

My uncle just sits there, serene, relaxed, maybe even entertained, his gentle smile returning. "Now are you done, *figlio*?"

Fuck. Him.

This sadistic motherfucker gives no shits. Not about me. Not about Ollie.

He's a fucking psychopath.

He drags in a deep breath and spreads his legs out before him, crossing them at the ankles. "Can I tell you something I've learned along the years?"

"I assume that's a rhetorical question."

"I guess it is." He chuckles. "What I've learned is that the older you get, the more your vision fails. But the funny thing is, despite the limiting eyesight, you end up seeing more than you already had."

What in the Dr. fucking Zeus is this shit?

"I understand Olivia is important to you, Remy. I had an inkling from the first night Salvatore met with Carlo. Not that it was hard to determine. You both reported back—your brother with smug superiority over securing the retort deal, and you with your far-off stare and distracted thoughts as you muttered about a woman who brought complications."

"And?"

"And I knew she would become a problem—"

"She's not a fucking problem."

"*Figlio*, I allowed you your time to talk." His eyes harden. "Now you will grant me the same respect as I have mine."

I clench my teeth, my blood rampant in my veins.

"I knew she would become a problem," he repeats, "*for you to protect.*"

I stiffen.

"Do you know why my sons don't work in the family business?" he asks.

I barely know anything about his sons—my cousins. "No." Apart from their names and a rough estimation of their ages, I don't have the faintest idea about the three brothers.

"Their mother was taken from them when they were young. She was a beautiful woman. Much like your Ollie. But blonde and blue-eyed. A gorgeous anomaly in our Italian ethnicity."

"And?" I pace out the steps to the next sofa, unable to remain still.

He gives me a sad smile. "And she was tortured horrifically. Her fingers removed one by one. Followed by her teeth. Then those beautiful eyes. Until finally she was sliced open from throat to groin and left to die."

My stomach roils, not only at the image, but at the thought of a similar fate happening to Ollie.

"She was the love of my life," he states simply. "The mother of my children and the keeper of my heart. But I couldn't protect her from my enemies." He fiddles with the curved handle of his walking stick in an uncharacteristic sign of vulnerability. "I refused to fail in the same way with my sons. No matter how much I wanted to keep them close, I made the decision to send them home to the motherland."

I grow impatient, the trip down history lane only increasing my agitation.

"I changed their names and gave them new lives." He holds my stare. "We may have kept in touch and I travelled to see them often, but I didn't allow them to return to the States until after they were twenty-one and had a full understanding of what they would be returning to."

He breaks eye contact to stare at his walking stick. "I'd planned for them to take over my legacy. To learn the ropes and become accustomed to the organization, but once they were back under my supervision, I admit I feared too much for their safety to allow them anywhere near the family business. I am weak in that regard. Not even Matthew knows the truth." He raises his eyes to mine. "Your brother is one of my most trusted confidants and I made him believe my sons were too selfish to consider taking over for my retirement when the truth is I shunned them for their own safety."

I scrub a hand over my mouth, my rings scratching flesh. "What's this got to do with me and Ollie?"

"I harbor guilt, *figlio*. In protecting my children, I've forsaken my nephews and sent you down a path far too similar to my own." He drags in a weary breath. "From the moment you brought Olivia into my penthouse I understood she could be for you what my wife once was for me, and that filled me with fear. I didn't want you repeating my mistakes. So I thought it best to keep you apart."

My nostrils flare.

"I tried to scare her away that day, but it only seemed to forge your bond. Which is why I instructed you two to separate yourselves."

"You threatened to fucking kill her," I grate.

He flashes a half-hearted smile. "I merely alluded. And yet the way you stood up to me in the name of protecting her was enviable. I wish I would've been that possessive with my wife when she was alive."

"Where the hell is this going, Lorenzo?"

He sighs. "Nowhere, *figlio*. It never was."

"I'm going to need you to be a little more clear than that because I don't fucking follow."

"What I'm saying is that my request for you two to remain apart was merely due to my own trauma. Yes, there are issues that may arise if she makes a costly mistake, but you were already smart enough to understand that. My actions were a safety measure for her as much as for your heart. But I see now that there's no separating the two of you, so I'm here to grant you my blessing."

I stare. Numb with shock. "Are you fucking with me? This was all a hoax?"

"Not a hoax. A learned experience without the heartache."

I scrutinize him. I stare so fucking hard, trying to read him, that my temples throb. "You're serious… You made me think you would order her death if I so much as touched her."

"Mmm." He nods. "Which was problematic in itself. And probably a subconscious act of rebellion to my own actions, because historically, what does one usually do when told not to do something?"

What the absolute fuck?

"I wanted to ensure you didn't make a decision you would regret later," he continues. "But it's obvious now you've made your choice."

"There was no choice." I raise my voice. "I tried walking away. *Numerous* times. I would've fucking ignored her existence if any part of me felt that was even slightly possible. But she's always there—in my fucking head, her voice in my ears, her scent in my godforsaken lungs. She's just—" I cut myself off, not wanting to admit I'm out of control because of this woman.

Lorenzo's smile is forlorn. "She's your heart's choice. Logic doesn't have any say in it."

I gape. I can't fucking help it.

I'd thought he was psychotic. Reality is, he's a lovesick romantic.

"Does she feel the same about you?" he asks.

"Yes." I nod. "I wish she didn't but she does."

"And will she continue to feel the same once the full terms of the current agreement come to completion?"

A knife twists into my stomach, the pain unignorable. "I don't know."

His expression softens. "Her father's death will be hard."

I raise my chin, taking the reminder head-on. "It will."

"I'm sure you'll figure it out." He grabs his walking stick and pushes to his feet. "And now I'll leave you to curse my actions in private."

"Wait. Did you pull this shit with Matthew and Bishop? Why didn't I hear about them having to endure your meddling?"

He hobbles around the closest sofa toward the hall. "Because they have spent more than a decade in the lifestyle. They entered their relationships knowing the risks. You're still green, my boy."

And I've never felt the color more adamantly than I do now.

"But please take my warnings to heart." Lorenzo pauses in the doorway. "You need to keep your distance from her until news of the rescinded hit has spread. It doesn't need to be too long. But the next few days are imperative."

I nod, the sweetest adrenaline flooding my veins. "I will."

And then it's going to be a free-for-all.

11:45 A.M. ME

Any news? I'm worried.

11:50 A.M. ME

Please tell me you're okay.

12:01 P.M. ME

Should I prepare to flee the country?

12:17 P.M. ME

I can't believe I didn't thank you for the weekend. It was incredible… The perfect last hurrah—or so it seems.

12:17 P.M. ME

Not gonna lie, I probably would've preferred to lose my virginity before I died, but 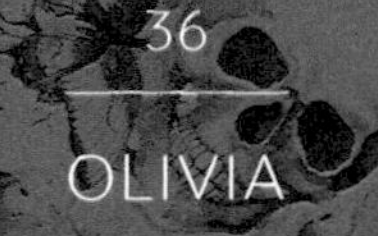

12:38 P.M. ME

If you can't already tell, I'm panicking. I should've downloaded a tracker app to your phone.

12:39 P.M. ME

If we survive your uncle, would a tracker be a realistic request?

12:39 P.M. ME

Just a tiny little one. You wouldn't even know it was there.

You're fucking adorable.

I'm fine. You're fine. There's nothing to worry about.
The Lorenzo situation has been sorted.

1:06 P.M. ME

He knows and doesn't care?

1:06 P.M. ME

That doesn't seem like a Lorenzo kind of reaction...

1:08 P.M. REMY

I promise everything is okay. We just need to lay low
for a while until external issues die down. You've got
roughly a week, then you're all mine.

Monday

6:03 A.M. ME

Despite your reassurance I'm kinda surprised I lived
through the night. I kept one eye open and everything.

6:07 A.M. REMY

Pyro, there's nothing to worry about. And even if there
was, I'd never let anything happen to you. Get some
sleep tonight, and I'll see you soon.

Tuesday

11:21 A.M. ME

But what if you're already dead and I'm currently
texting with one of your uncle's men? What if I'm
actually having this conversation with Salvatore?

11:39 A.M. REMY

[photo upload of Remy's unimpressed glower, his lips
kicked slightly in mirth]

11:39 A.M. ME

That could be an old image.

11:40 A.M. REMY

I can send you a pic of something very few people
would recognize if you prefer.

11:41 A.M. ME

11:41 A.M. ME

Are you talking about the scar on your leg or…?

11: 43 A.M. REMY

Definitely not my scar, Pyro. And don't forget that
spanking is still on the table if you continue with the
sass.

Wednesday

2:49 P.M. ME

My dad hasn't worked much this week. Instead he's
been visiting with friends and relatives. It's like he's on
a farewell tour. I hate it.

3:05 P.M. REMY

Maybe you should take some time off too. Want me to
find someone else to help with the workload?

3:33 P.M. ME

No thanks. Your recruitment of Wesley was bad
enough. I'm pretty sure he's already slept with Ivy,
despite me warning him not to. When can I set him on
fire?

3:33 P.M. ME

I mean—when can I fire him?

3:35 P.M. REMY

Why do I suddenly feel like the least psychotic person
in this conversation?

Thursday

5:57 P.M. ME

Thanks for the flowers. They almost made me cry.

6:25 P.M. REMY

Flowers? What flowers?

6:34 P.M. ME

I know it was you. Who else would send me fifty red roses with a card that says—I can't wait to see you again?

6:36 P.M. REMY

Salvatore, for starters. Expect the unexpected, Pyro.

6:38 P.M. ME

😳

6:38 P.M. ME

So was it you or him?

6:38 P.M. ME

Remy??? Do I have a house full of roses sent from your unhinged brother?

6:38 P.M. ME

You're fucking with me, right?

6:38 P.M. ME

REMY???

6:39 P.M. REMY

Yes, I'm fucking with you. I'm glad they only almost made you cry.

6:40 P.M. ME

When will I get to see you again?

6:42 P.M. REMY

Your dad said you're having dinner with him Friday night. I'll see you then.

Well, you best be prepared for your own spanking because that whole Salvatore-stalker joke wasn't funny.

FRIDAY NIGHT ROLLS AROUND FASTER THAN I COULD'VE ANTICIPATED, GIVEN my excitement.

It also helps that managing the funeral home—with Ivy's assistance—has meant every waking moment is spent with new and inspiring distractions.

But now I sit in my father's living room, the television softly playing an old season of *Below Deck* while I nervously gnaw on my bottom lip in anticipation.

"Have I told you how much I loved last weekend?" Dad lays back in his outstretched recliner, his eyes closed, his smile bright.

"Yeah." I nod. "Maybe once or twice."

Fifty-five thousand times would be more accurate, but I can't get enough of his joy.

Despite his packed social calendar, and the extra hours he's needed for rest, we've made time to share at least one meal every day this week.

Today's was an early dinner of Caesar salad with grilled chicken that Lucy organized. She even insisted on cleaning up to give Dad and I more alone time, while she remains in the kitchen stacking plates into the dishwasher, the music from her online playlist giving us an added sense of privacy.

"If you're up for it, we could go away again," I hedge. "I have the savings to splurge on a mini vacation. Not to the extent of formal attire and private chefs, but enough for something nice and simple. We could get a beach house and relax by the ocean."

Any other day this week I wouldn't have suggested it, but today he's been better. Full of energy and taunting wisecracks. I've also been trying to focus more on the positives instead of the increased jaundice of his skin, and how he now rattles when he walks due to the bottle of pain meds that permanently live in his pocket.

"I'd love that," he murmurs. "We could watch the sunset over the water. Maybe read a good book or two."

"Sounds perfect." I smile. "I can check out vacation rental websites tomorrow."

He opens one eye to peer at me. "In the meantime, will you do me a favor?"

I purse my lips. "That depends on what it is. You're now a man with a track record of choice decisions. You no longer have the green light for favors."

"But this one is important." He drags in a long, contented breath. "I've had a great week, *fragolina*. I couldn't have asked for better. The only thing that could top it off would be knowing you're out kicking up your heels with Allison and Ivy tonight."

I shoot him an overly dramatic scowl. "You're guilting me into going dancing again?"

"Last weekend's installment was a great success, was it not?"

My face heats.

Thankfully he's yet to ask any more questions about me and Remy. But maybe he hasn't needed to. I'm sure the chemistry between us in that French restaurant was hard to deny.

"Please, Liv." He leans forward, tilting his recliner back into the upright position to punish me with a hopeful smile. "Go out with Ivy and Allison. Let your hair down. Drink. Be merry. Shake your—"

I sigh. "Dad, you know I don't like the club scene."

"But the girls need it. They're itching to have a wild night but won't go out anymore because they think it's in bad taste to be enjoying themselves while I'm sick." He clasps his hands in prayer. "Pretty please. Be their leader and show them it's okay. Teach them that they shouldn't put their lives on hold for anyone. Especially not an employer."

The downplaying of his role in their lives hits me with a pang in the chest. "You're more than their boss."

"I know." His expression turns somber. "But you understand where I'm coming from, don't you? They can't hit pause because of my struggles. If anything, they should be grasping life tighter around the neck and wringing it for all it's worth."

I agree. I just wish I didn't have to be involved in the wringing.

"I want to end tonight knowing you're out there living your life." He smiles fondly to himself. "I want to picture you dancing again, your anxieties eased with a few cheap club drinks. It'll be fun. But more importantly, it'll be for me, which is all that matters."

I roll my eyes. "If only they gave Olympic medals for emotional manipulation."

He grins. "It's the skill I never knew I had."

I chuckle. "Fine. I promise to text the girls and see if they want to go out for a little while. But if they aren't interested, I'm not forcing them."

"You won't need to." His widening smile crinkles the skin around his eyes. "Because they're already preparing. You've got—" He checks his watch. "—roughly an hour before a car will be at your house to pick you up."

My face slackens. "What?"

His expression brightens with deviousness. "I leveled them with a similar dose of emotional manipulation this morning. They agreed and said they'd pick you up around nine."

"*Dad.*"

"You're welcome."

I push to my feet. "No. It's not enough time." And I've waited all week to see Remy.

He chuckles as I panic. "You'll be fine. You've never been someone who takes three hours to get ready." He struggles to rise from his chair, and I quickly rush to help. "You're beautiful without all the accessories and makeup. Just like your mother was."

"They do say a father's love is blind."

"Don't be like that." His humor fades with each passing breath. "You're a blessing, Liv. In every way imaginable. Never forget that."

My skin prickles at the detour into sentimental territory.

I've waited a long time for the opportunity to bring up the truth, but it never seems like the right moment to drop the bombshell. Now is no different.

I'd prefer him to remain blissfully unaware of my knowledge. To rest easier, thinking he's done his best to shelter me in that protective, fatherly way of his.

He cups my cheeks and places a kiss to my brow. "Promise me you'll have a good time."

I sigh with exaggeration. "It's not exactly an easy promise given my aversion to crowds."

"And people in general," he snickers, his hands falling to his sides.

"You're only cementing your cruelty."

"And you're only cementing how you're the best daughter in the entire world." He peers at me with beaming pride. "You've grown into such an amazing woman. Please take tonight to celebrate yourself. If not for you, then for me."

Oh, God. Please don't get sad. *Please. Please. Please.*

"Fine." I nod. "But if I'm doing tonight for you, then you and Lucy need to supply the perfect Saturday morning hangover brunch for me tomorrow. Your shout."

"I want nothing more than to have brunch with you tomorrow." He gives my hand a squeeze. "I love you, *fragolina.*"

I swallow the emotion scrambling up my throat and wrap my arms around him. "I love you, too, Dad."

He kisses my hairline. "Take on the world for me."

"I'll take on one club. For a few hours. Nothing more."

His laughter rumbles into me before he ends the hug. "Okay."

I grab my phone and keys from the coffee table, then shout a quick goodbye to Lucy before hustling out the door.

I'm already three steps down the staircase when I raise my gaze to see Remy strolling across the parking lot, hands in pockets, grin devastatingly handsome as he peers up at me.

My heart thunders to a stop, my feet almost tripping over themselves.

"Hey." I slow my pace, fearing a misstep that will cause me to break my neck before I have the opportunity to touch him again.

"Hey, yourself."

We meet at the bottom of the staircase, his aftershave making me high as I admire yet another crisp, stunning suit, the top two buttons of his matching collared black shirt undone.

"Long time no see, Pyro." Those dark eyes take me in, his lips lazily kicked at one side in subtle flirtation.

The bastard seems completely unfazed by our reunion while I'm over here begging for my ovaries to stop screaming at me to climb him like the God of Pleasure he so clearly is.

"Yeah. Long time." I shrug, attempting to match his demeanor. Two can play at this game.

He grins, slow and methodic.

My stomach launches itself into my throat.

Okay, so maybe two *can't* play at this game because that cocky curve of lips has me *dying*.

He inches closer, his fingers brushing mine in the slightest breath of teasing contact. "I've missed you."

"Are you sure?"

He seems to ponder my question with annoyingly exaggerated consideration.

"You're so mean." I shove at his chest, only endeavoring to make him laugh as he snatches my wrists and drags me into him.

"I'm not mean, Pyro. At least not to you." He releases a wrist and wraps a hand around my neck, his rings scraping my sensitive skin as his lips press against my forehead. "I'm just trying to stay under control."

I sink into him, fighting a groan, loving the familiarity of his hold. It feels like forever since we've touched. A lifetime in the space of five days.

"Did you enjoy dinner with your dad?" he asks.

I nod. "He's in good spirits." I take one more deep breath of his deliciousness then lean back to meet his eyes. "What are you here to discuss?"

"Nothing. I'm only making a quick trip to drop something off."

I raise a brow, glancing down to his arms that are filled with a whole heap of me and nothing else. "Did you forget to bring it?"

He squeezes me. "Do I look like the careless type?"

"No, but it'd be nice if thoughts of seeing me again had even the slightest capacity to distract you into forgetting your purpose."

"You distract me more than enough." He retreats, his arms falling to his sides. "Did he convince you to go out?"

"Why am I still surprised that he tells you more than me? That man is like a strategic mastermind, and you're his little co-conspirator."

"I prefer partner-in-crime." He winks and maneuvers around me to take the first step. "I'd better let you go and get ready. I'll see you later."

"You will?" My heart threatens to explode.

He smirks at me over his shoulder. "I suddenly feel like a night out."

"Should I expect another painfully underwhelming reunion like this one?"

"I've waited all week to see you. I promise there's nothing underwhelming about what I plan to do once we're no longer standing under the full view of your father's window."

Heat filters through my chest, the deliciousness spreading to parts down south.

"Convince your friends to go to my club." He continues up the stairs. "Your names are already on the VIP list."

"What a gentleman," I coo.

His smirk increases. "I promise I won't be later."

Holy hell.

Damn every single perfect, pretentious inch of him.

I've fallen for this man. Head over heels. Heart over mind.

"Goodbye, Remy." I force my smile under control as I rush across the parking lot.

"Bye, Pyro."

He stares down at me from the top landing as I climb into my car, his wicked grin stalking me until I accelerate out of view.

I've never driven so fast through the Baltimore suburbs in my life.

Last weekend did a number on me. I've also never showered, shaved, and scrubbed my body all at the same time.

I'm in the middle of simultaneously applying ruby red lipstick to match my silken slip dress while yanking on my stiletto heels when a car horn beeps from my drive.

"Shit." I slide a hand over the way-too-short hem that sits higher up my thighs than commonsense demands while inwardly cursing myself for dressing in something to impress Remy as I hop toward the front door, my other hand trying to secure the strap of my shoe around my ankle.

"Look at you." Ivy wolf whistles from the open back window of the ride share. "Someone's getting eaten tonight."

Oh, my fucking god.

I shrink with embarrassment, knowing Lesley's super spy senses would've overheard as I finally secure my shoe strap.

I glare at the car with my approach, mouthing, *"I'll kill you"* to my best friend.

Ivy cackles as Allison's laughter carries from the far side of the backseat.

"Not funny." I yank open the door, forcing Ivy to scoot into the middle seat with a wave of my hand.

"You look incredible." Allison stares at my dress as if it's from another planet, because given my usual laid-back style, it practically is. "I've never seen you in anything like that before."

"And you probably never will again. Lesley's granddaughter gave it to me a year ago because it didn't fit her anymore. I'm surprised I didn't throw it out." I slide inside feeling all kinds of uncomfortable, dump my clutch into my lap, and then yank on my belt.

"Okay, ladies." The female driver eyes us from the rearview mirror. "Where are we headed?"

"Smoke & Mirrors." I pop my lips together, hoping my lipstick is okay seeing I didn't have time to check.

Allison squeals. "I love that place."

"Wait. Why?" Ivy grumbles. "Can't we go somewhere else this time?"

"Nope. If you get to announce to my entire neighborhood that I'm getting eaten tonight, I'm calling dibs on our location." I grab my cell from my clutch and look up the club's address to show it to the driver. "Take us here please."

"Liv," Ivy sighs. "That place is—"

"It's the only club I know. And I feel comfortable there. *Please,* Ivy, just one more time," I beg. "Would it help if I told you our names are on the VIP list?"

"Are you serious?" Allison clasps her hand around Ivy's thigh with another squeal. "How the hell did that happen?"

"I guess Dad knows a friend of a friend."

Ivy continues to vibrate with skepticism, the disparaging mood not budging even after I nudge my arm against hers.

"Pretty please, Ive." I place a smacking red kiss to her bare shoulder. "With sprinkles on top?"

"Okay. Fine. Whatever you want. I just don't like what I keep hearing about the place."

I try not to feel offended. Really, I do. But I want her to like Remy's club, especially when one day I'm hoping she'll like Remy, too.

"So… Smoke & Mirrors?" the driver asks.

"Hell yeah." Allison bounces in her seat. "Let's do this."

I RECEIVE A TEXT FROM THE BOUNCER THE MOMENT OLLIE ENTERS MY CLUB.

I tell myself I need to give her time to be with her friends. But it takes twenty-eight agitated minutes of restraint before I stalk from my office and make my way downstairs to the main club area with Valenti and Russo tailing me.

I find her in seconds, my eyes calibrated to her beauty as she sways on the far side of the half-filled dance floor in a dress made for sin.

She's here later than I'd anticipated.

I assume they must've gone somewhere else for pre-drinks. But it's still too early to be crowded in here. The bars aren't packed. The VIP booths are relatively quiet.

She doesn't have a drink in hand, only her clutch, but it's clear her night hasn't been spent concentrating on sobriety.

Her hair is down. Her body sways with carefree abandon. And that smile.

Fuck.

How can one curve of lips possess such power?

She's wearing a bare slip of a dress, deep red, low at the neckline, and from the few glimpses I've caught sight of between the movement of bodies, it also rides cock-numbingly high on those toned thighs.

She's a walking wet dream, and I'm not the only one to notice.

I scan the clubgoers lining the dance floor, taking note of all the men who ogle her as I remain in the shadows near one of the bouncer alcoves.

"I didn't pick her as the type to draw attention," Valenti says over the music.

She's not. That dress is for me, and the knowledge makes my dick uncomfortably hard.

The leggy brunette she works with shimmies a few feet tc Ollie's left, attracting just as much male interest, while the other woman—Amy? Allison?—has her hands all over a blonde in thigh-high stiletto boots to the right.

"Your usual, boss." A waitress stops in front of me, her serving tray empty apart from the lone whiskey tumbler filled with amber liquid.

"Thanks." I take the drink without making eye contact.

"Do you think it's going to be busy tonight?" she purrs.

I glower, my scrutiny remaining on Ollie as she sways to the beat.

"Only time will tell, sweetheart," Russo answers for me, jerking his chin at her in silent dismissal.

Her shoulders slump and she walks away, metaphorical tail between her legs.

"She was on the prowl." Valenti states the obvious.

"They always are," Russo mutters. "If only we had a boss who thought to make introductions."

I shoot him a glance and raise the glass of scotch to my lips. "If you want to mix business with pleasure, by all means, go for it. You both deserve the night off."

He screws up his nose. "Nah. Not tonight. I'm too curious to see what happens with you and your little lady."

"Shit," Valenti curses under his breath.

"What?" Russo stiffens in alert as both of us return our attention to the dance floor.

My pulse rushes in my ears at the sight of the spiky-haired guy closing in behind Ollie.

He says something in her ear. Something that makes her laugh and turn in his direction.

I clench my teeth.

I thought she hated people.

"What do you want us to do, boss?" Russo asks.

I scrub a rough hand over my mouth, forcing patience. "Nothing." *Yet.*

She's allowed to dance with other men.

I may not like it. I may even hate it so much I'm contemplating my club's downfall with a brutal murder in front of all my patrons. But if there's anything I've learned this week, it's to bite my tongue.

The song ends and another begins, this one a techno remix of a classic love song.

To my fucking horror, Ollie steps closer to the walking death wish and places her hands on the guy's shoulders. I can only assume his hands are somewhere far lower. I can't see a damn thing through the throng of bodies.

I take another sip of scotch.

Then another.

Fuck. I down the remainder of the liquid and squeeze the tumbler tight, my grip threatening to shatter glass.

"Here." I shove the tumbler at Russo's chest and pull out my cell.

ME

You're becoming quite the black widow. What's his name and how do you think he'd prefer to die?

My gaze remains riveted on her as she breaks away from the embrace to retrieve her cell from her clutch. She smiles as she focuses on the screen.

Fucking smiles.

I inch backward into one of the bouncer alcoves as she raises her gaze and scans the club, not finding me. Then she's tapping out a reply, the buzz of my cell coming seconds later.

OLIVIA

Was attempting to find a taker for the V-card. Do you think he's the one?

Jealousy punches through me. So does an electric thrill.

She wants to play.

Game on, Ollie.

She scans the crowd again, and then hesitantly returns her attention to the man whose life is shortening by the minute.

ME

I don't know, Pyro. Ask if he's willing to die for the cause and see what he says.

While you're at it, I'd appreciate a height and weight guesstimation so I don't have to waste time during disposal.

She checks her phone again, the laughter on her face doing things to me that the guy quickly eviscerates when he leans too close and says something in her ear.

I shove my clenched fists into my pockets. "Take care of him."

Russo and Valenti shoot me questioning looks.

"Permanently?" Valenti asks.

I gnash my molars.

She'd hate me for the death sentence.

Would the animosity last forever? Maybe not.

But would it delay our forthcoming gratification? Undoubtably.

"No." I growl. "Bring him to me."

"Sure thing." Valenti approaches the dance floor, entering the slew of gyrating bodies to make his way to the man who'll soon learn a valuable lesson, while Russo remains at my side.

Ollie stiffens, but keeps swaying as Valenti leans into her dance partner, saying something in his ear that has the man jerking back theatrically to clasp a hand to his chest.

I scowl, not expecting the dramatic response.

Valenti shoots me a glance, whatever silent message he's trying to convey across the room not hitting its mark as he makes his way back toward me with the guy in question following a step behind.

It isn't until they're a few feet away that I see what he's wearing—a skin-tight, fishnet tank top with equally tight baby-pink shorts.

Russo snorts.

Jesus fucking Christ.

The guy I wanted dead practically skips toward me, sizing me up with enough carnal interest to convey Ollie isn't his usual demographic.

"Hey, daddy." He bites his bottom lip. "I heard you wanted to see me."

She set me up.

I want to be pissed, but a grin pulls at my lips, my enjoyment of this game making me crave her even more.

"There's been a misunderstanding." I give him a dismissive stare. "Enjoy your night."

"Oh." Lover boy pouts. "But you're just my type."

"Maybe some other time."

Russo chokes on a laugh, attempting to hide it over the clearing of his throat.

I return my attention to Ollie on the dance floor who now stares directly at me with a shit-eating grin.

"Are you serious?" My potential lover's voice brims with excitement.

"No." Valenti advances in threat. "He's not fucking serious, now scram."

Ollie holds my gaze, making the rest of the world disappear as she moves her body to the beat, her hand gliding seductively over her chest, up her neck, then into her hair.

I don't know what's gotten into her tonight, but I'd like to add to it.

I pull my cell back out of my pocket.

ME

> Not nice, Ollie. You almost sentenced an underserving man to death.

OLIVIA

ME

> Keep laughing. But as soon as you step foot from view of your friends, you're mine.

I watch with predatory intent as she remains transfixed on her screen.

OLIVIA

Is that supposed to be a threat?

A sexual one?

You do realize I've been trying to get in your pants for weeks, right?

Have I not made that blindingly obvious?

Should I start stripping on the dance floor to make it abundantly clear?

I smirk at my cell like a kid on crack.

I'm in love with this woman. There's no doubt about it.

"I need you two to create a diversion." I shove my cell back in my pocket and focus on Valenti. "One that keeps Ollie's friends occupied while I kidnap their favorite troublemaker."

He jerks his chin in understanding. "I'll organize some shots. Free alcohol will do the trick."

"It could also induce a stampede," Russo mutters.

"I don't care." Anticipation thrums through me. "Do it."

My men head toward the closest bar while Ollie continues to eye-fuck me from across the room.

I can already feel her. Smell her. Fucking taste her as she dances for me and only me.

She's going to come so hard tonight she'll feel it for days.

We both will.

I remain in the shadows, watching my own private dance until Russo and Valenti catch my attention on their way to the DJ stand, two bottle service waitresses with full trays of shots following behind them.

Russo talks to the DJ, grabs the guy's microphone, then announces an impromptu dance competition with free drinks for patrons with the best moves.

Cheers of excitement pierce my ears as people flood the dance floor, the music switching to a more frenzied techno beat.

I stalk forward while Ollie is distracted, her gaze frantically scanning for her friends as they're pushed apart by the growing crowd.

"Big mistake, baby girl." I stop in front of her, not waiting for a response before hauling her over my shoulder.

She squeals, the noise smothered beneath the frenzy.

"Text your friends and tell them you're using the bathroom," I demand.

"How?" She wiggles. "I'm upside down."

"Don't pretend those hands aren't skillful."

Her laughter vibrates into my shoulder as I carry her to the staff only door and slam it shut with my foot once we're in the empty hall.

"I get the distinct impression you enjoy playing with me." I place her on her feet, not giving her time to find her footing before I walk into her, backing her against the brick wall. "Did you enjoy taunting me?"

She rolls her lips together, fighting a smile as her clutch falls to the floor. "I'm not sure why you'd get that impression." Her cheeks lift. Her eyes gleam. She fights so hard to contain that smile, but it breaks free to slam right through me. Ruthlessly.

I've been attracted to her fear. Her tenacity. Her lust.

But this—her happiness—it's the holy fucking grail.

I cage her against the wall, my predatory eyes taking liberties with the raised view. The thin spaghetti straps. The gaping neckline. "What the fuck are you wearing, Pyro?"

She flinches. "You don't approve?"

"Oh, I fucking approve. Every man under this roof does." I meet her gaze, our proximity making every inch of me thrum.

Her brow furrows. "I wore it for you… but now I can't tell if I should've chosen something more subdued."

"You can't tell because I'm so fucking hard it's difficult to convey appreciation." I palm her waist, the warmth of her curves sinking into my blood. "I'd never police your wardrobe. I'm far more inclined to cut out the eyes of the men who don't deserve to look at you."

Her smile returns, the effect even more detrimental to my composure when it's timid. "I like that answer."

I inch closer, teasing us both with the breath of space between our lips. "I hope I'm equally impressed with yours when you tell me why you're not wearing my ring."

That curve of lips turns sinful. "Who says I'm not wearing it?"

I lower my gaze again, taking in the wealth of cleavage, the mass of skin on display. It's not in her hair because her locks are loose and tangled around her shoulders. "Where?"

She licks her bottom lip with a nervous flick of her tongue. "Maybe you should search and find out."

I growl, unable to withstand the torture any longer.

I swoop in, slamming my mouth to hers.

She melts into the contact, opening for me, deepening the kiss on impact.

I grind into her, my dick desperate for the friction while a needy sound escapes her throat.

"Find it," she rasps against my mouth, raising a leg to wrap around my hip.

I groan, clasping a hand to her elevated knee, my palm burning as I skate a trail toward the apex of her thighs. I'm inches away from heaven, so fucking ready to get my hands on her panties and tear them to shreds when something foreign brushes my fingertips.

I glance down, finding a thick band of black elastic wrapped around her upper thigh, my ring tied to it with a tiny red ribbon.

My cock jolts with appreciation.

"I told you I was wearing it." She looks up at me through hooded lashes. So coy. So undeniably stunning.

"Good fucking girl." I smash my mouth back on hers, one hand gliding into her hair to command the tilt of her chin while the other continues to slide along her thigh, over her smooth hip, to her bare ass.

Don't tell me she's not wearing any panties.

I'd hauled her over my shoulder. Her pretty pussy would've been on display.

A growl rumbles in my throat as I splay my hand, my fingers brushing fabric.

My virgin minx is wearing the tiniest silken G-string.

"You have no idea what you do to me." I lower my hand from her hair, my touch skimming her jaw to gently palm her throat. "I'm a slave to you. I always have been."

"I feel the same way," she whispers into my mouth. "From the first moment we met, I've been yours."

Fuck.

I can't take the perfection.

The serendipity.

I drag my hand from her ass to slide between us, gliding over the slip of material covering her crotch. "Then show me." I rake my tongue against hers. "Burn for me, Pyro."

She shudders as I find her clit through the slippery fabric, rubbing gently back and forth.

She grabs for my shirt, her greedy fingers tugging, pulling.

"Do you like that?" I grind my throbbing cock into her hip as our mouths dance. "Do you enjoy me touching you?"

"Yes." Her lips are frantic against mine. Her nails scratch into my chest. "You drive me wild. Every time I think of you I…"

I pull back, meeting her eyes. "You what?"

She pants, her chest rising and falling with heavy breaths. "I .." She bites her bottom lip, gliding an arm between us, her hand finding mine between her thighs. She tentatively clasps my fingers, guiding them beneath the elastic of her panties, and smooths them over the warmest, wettest honey pot. "I get like this."

I tense. Every muscle. Every limb.

There isn't a part of me that isn't screaming with the need to shove my cock inside her and claim what no man has taken before.

"You're so fucking wet for me." My voice is a guttural growl.

"Always." She tilts her hips toward me, trying to gain penetration. "Please touch me." She wraps a hand around my neck, clawing my skin. "I need you."

I salivate. Loving her need. Thriving on it. "Such a greedy little girl." I rub two fingers along her slit, back and forth, teasing her entrance.

She cries. "*Please, Remy.*"

"Don't worry. I have something better for you." I drag my hand from her hair and shove it into my jacket pocket, pulling out the bullet vibrator that's haunted me all fucking night. "I've dreamed about touching you with this."

She eyes the tiny device as I turn it on with a press of my thumb, the muted hum of vibration barely heard over the bass music thudding through the walls.

I glide it into her panties for my soaked hand to take charge. "You told me you've got experience with toys, and I swear to God the image hasn't left my mind." I place it against her clit, my chest tightening with reverence as her lips part and her back arches off the wall.

I pulse with appreciation.

With fucking awe.

She closes her eyes, her thigh clamping around my hip. "Remy."

My name is a whisper. A goddamn prayer to the devil.

I lean close, my mouth brushing her ear. "I'm going to watch you come, Pyro. I'm going to watch you come so fucking hard, then I'm going to spend the rest of my life religiously rewatching the security video until I die a happy man."

She stiffens, her eyes snapping open.

Shit.

My pretty girl isn't comfortable being recorded.

"Nobody else has access to the files." I circle the vibrator, rounding her clit.

She doesn't relax. "Remy, I—"

"It's okay. You can turn off the security system. Just slide your hand into my pocket and take out my phone."

She shakes her head. "No...I..."

"I'm not taking my hands off of this flawless body, so you either grab my phone or I get to rub my cock raw as I relive this moment over and over and fucking over again, habitually, for the rest of my goddamn life."

She trembles. "I..." She gasps for air. "I don't care about the camera... Oh, God, Remy, I'm already so close."

I pause. "You're not panicking?"

"No," she pants. "The thought... of you... watching me like this..." Her hips arc higher. "It makes me so fucking hot."

Adrenaline pours through me. Pride. Possession. "You're fucking perfect."

She whimpers. "Remy..."

I bury my face in her hair, breathing in the sweetness, trying to distract myself from the lust. "Tell me where you want your toy." I add pressure to her clit. "Here?" I slide it lower, teasing her entrance. "Or in that slick and needy cunt?"

She gasps. "Inside." She shoves a hand around my nape, tugging my hair, clawing my scalp.

I groan. "Do you know how hard you make me?"

She mewls, her hips rocking harder.

"Do you know how badly I want to palm my dick and slide deep into this virginal pussy?"

"Do it," she begs.

I clench my jaw, fighting temptation. "Not tonight."

She turns her face to mine, her eyes glazed with hunger. "But you will? Eventually?"

There's no denying it.

I no longer possess the willpower to do the right thing.

I'm going to fuck her. Just not here. Not now.

When I finally succumb she'll be sober, and we'll be some place better than against a seedy behind-the-scenes wall of a club.

"Yes." I hold her gaze as I glide the vibrator inside her. "I'm definitely going to fuck you. That tight pussy will feel so fucking good around my cock."

Her eyes widen, her breath hitching once, twice.

"*Remy*." She comes undone, lips parted, neck arching.

The beauty of it steals my sanity.

She's a fucking mirage. Too exquisite to be mine.

I slide my hand up her throat, over her chin. Without being coaxed, she tilts her head forward, moaning as she wraps her mouth around two of my fingers, her cheeks hollowing with unholy suction.

I snarl. Dick throbbing. Reality spiraling. "You're such a good fucking girl."

She's everything.

My pleasure. My pain. My suffering.

I drag my fingers from her lips and claim her mouth with my own, reveling in her groans, drowning in her bliss.

I need more of her.

All of her.

I kiss her as her crest peaks, her nails gradually losing the bite of ferocity, her limbs slowly softening with pliancy.

She hums with contentment, and I inch back to see her blissed out and glowing.

"You're crazy," she rasps.

I incline my head and retract the vibrator from inside her. "Crazy for you, my pretty little Pyro."

She smiles, the expression blindingly infectious.

"You know you used to flinch when I called you that." I remove the device from her panties and turn it off.

"I didn't like it before." Her body turns to putty against mine.

"And now?"

She blinks up at me in a lust-drunk haze. "Now it makes me feel closer to you. Like we're not so different."

We *are* different.

Good and bad. Light and dark. Innocence and guilt. But there's no denying the selfish part of me that purrs in contentment at her admission.

"You make me feel alive, Remy."

That contentment fractures. She has no clue how close I am to fucking this all up. "I'm glad I've done something right."

I wrap my hand around the vibrator and slide it into my pocket, suppressing my apprehension with the sickening thrill of how her pleasure coats my palm.

Her smile sobers. "I wish you could see yourself through my eyes."

And I hope to hell she never sees me through mine.

My cell vibrates in my pants.

Ollie raises a taunting brow. "Another toy?"

I smirk through my annoyance at the interruption. My phone is silenced to all but a few numbers. The only calls able to come through are usually important.

I drag my cell from my pocket and stare at Lucy's name illuminated on screen.

"Is that Dad's Lucy?" Ollie swipes at the errant strands of hair clinging to her cheeks.

"Yeah." An unwanted sense of foreboding skitters down my spine.

"Are you going to answer it?"

"No." Carlo's nurse hasn't called me before. Apart from a few short texts prior to her employment, and another few to arrange the trip to Berkeley Springs, our communication has been limited. But that won't always be the case.

"Why not?" Ollie asks.

The call ends. The cell screen turns dark.

I raise my attention to her. "I'm sure whatever it is can wait." I don't want to speak to Lucy in front of Ollie. "And besides, I've got more important people to concentrate on right now."

The tops of her cheeks turn a rosier shade of pink.

It's crazy, the things that make her blush.

"I'll call her back later." I pocket the device and glide my hand over Ollie's jaw, stealing another kiss. "I've barely started making my way through the list of things I want to do to you."

38

OLIVIA

I'M ABOUT TO WHIMPER IN RENEWED YEARNING WHEN HIS PHONE VIBRATES again.

He tenses.

It's only slight. The barest of movements. But enough to cement the uncomfortable feeling in my gut.

He releases me to retrieve his cell.

Lucy remains illuminated on the screen.

"I need to take this." He fixates on the phone as he walks farther down the hall, swiping to connect the call. "Lucy?"

He falls quiet, raking a rough hand through his hair.

I swallow the dryness taking over my throat, all the tingling lust previously coursing through my body now deadweight in my gut.

"*Fuck*," Remy whispers a curse.

I turn to ice. "What's wrong?" I snatch my clutch off the floor and start toward him, his eyes meeting mine over his shoulder, the starkness of his expression making me want to throw up.

"I'm with her now." He holds my gaze. "We'll be right there."

My heart races as I approach.

Something happened to Dad.

Did he have another dizzy spell? Maybe a fall? Did he—I scrunch my nose, refusing to think the worst. We still have months.

"We need to go?" I ask.

He nods, every inch of him tense.

I focus on levelling my breathing, my heels clicking against the cement floor as I claim my cell from my clutch and open the group chat to Ivy and Allison.

Sorry. I had to leave. Dad stuff. Will speak to you tomorrow.

I turn my phone to silent, too frazzled to handle any concern they might volley back at me, and follow Remy to the elevator.

I don't ask questions while he drives us toward the suburbs in his Aston Martin, too scared my voice will break and trigger a meltdown. Instead, I pick at the quicks of my fingers and force myself to remain positive.

A million things could've happened to require our attention, and a lot of them don't necessarily need to revolve around my father's health. There might have been a blackout. Lucy could've fallen down the stairs.

I'm clutching at straws. I know I am, but Dad was in a great mood when I left. There's no need to catastrophize.

Remy turns onto my father's street, the lights of the lower level of the funeral home shining as we approach.

Hope sparks to life beneath my tightened ribs. Could Lucy's call have been about the business? Was there a break-in? Maybe a retort gas leak.

Oh, fuck. Did someone find out about the illegal disposals?

I shoot Remy a glance, but there's no panic in his features, only bottled concern.

He pulls into the parking lot, passing numerous cars I'm not familiar with. A white Chrysler. A grey pickup.

I undo the straps of my heels as he drives past Lucy's hatchback and the hearse, my door in line with my father's stairs.

"Stop the car." I unclasp my belt as Remy continues toward the empty parking spaces. *"Please stop."*

I open my door, needing to move, to run, to sprint.

He mutters a curse and hits the brakes.

I'm out of there in seconds.

I hop across the asphalt, kicking off one shoe before starting on the next. Once both feet are free I take the stairs two at a time, my breathing erratic.

I reach the landing, my chest aching from the exertion. Then the door opens and Lucy stands before me, no smile, no heartfelt greeting, no slither of positivity to cling to as tears dance in her eyes.

"I'm so sorry, Olivia." Her words stab through me.

"No." The denial slips free, the single syllable leaving a chemical burn down my throat.

I squeeze past her to scan the living room.

Dad's not there.

I scramble along the hall, rushing toward the place I've found parental sanctuary my entire life and skitter to a stop at my father's bedroom doorway.

The familiar sight of him peacefully resting in the hospital bed brings another burst of hope. "Dad?"

He's still wearing the clothes I left him in, his cheek snuggled against a pillow, his hands gently placed atop the comforter.

"Dad?" I swallow over razor blades.

He doesn't stir. Doesn't blink. Doesn't move.

"Dad?"

Footsteps approach behind me, Remy's tentative grip coming to rest on my shoulders as I fight to keep my breathing level. "I'm sorry, Ollie."

The pained sorrow in his voice breaks me.

I choke on a sob and hurry to clasp a hand over my mouth, forcing the weakness to remain inside.

We don't cry.

The memory of my mother's voice has never been more punishing. It squeezes at my heart without mercy.

This isn't right. I was supposed to have more time.

"I don't understand." My voice breaks as I pad forward, unable to drag my gaze off my father.

I thought my job would've better prepared me for this. The years of intrenched sterility. The constant chill that accompanies death. But it's never felt this way before. Not even with my mother's passing. It's as if the devil's claws are tearing my father's soul from mine, leaving me raw and ravaged.

"I thought we had months." I pause beside the clinical single bed, my stomach twisted in churning knots.

"I thought we did, too." Remy follows, rounding the opposite side of the bed as I grasp my father's fingers.

He's still warm. Still flexible. Without rigor.

"It doesn't make sense." I scrunch my nose to combat the burn blurring my vision. "We saw him a few hours ago. He was fine. There were no signs… right?" I glance to Remy, finding him hunched over, picking up something from the floor.

I blink through my foggy vision as he gracefully straightens to his full height, casually sliding his hands into his pockets. "Remy?"

"No, Pyro." He approaches my father's side, his movements measured. "There were no signs."

My throat tightens with unease.

Something about Remy doesn't sit right with me. I sense more than grief from him. There's trepidation, too.

"Did you pick something up off the floor?" I sniff back the tingle in my nose.

"Hmm?" His brow furrows as he breaks our gaze to focus on my father. "Do you want me to give you space? I can wait in the living room."

I keep staring at him. Scrutinizing.

Why did he ignore my question?

"What was on the floor?" I guide my dad's hand back to the comforter, fixated on Remy's haunted expression. He continues to deny me eye contact, intensifying my anxiety, making it swirl with overwhelming despair.

"Why are you ignoring me?" I beg.

His stark gaze turns to mine, but he remains silent.

"What was it?" I swallow against the need to throw up.

He keeps staring, those beautiful lips clasped shut.

Panic creeps in, slow at first, the tingle of it climbing the back of my neck. I round the bed, my ability to think positive well and truly gone with the foreboding that strangles the room.

"Show me." I hold out a palm.

He stands tall, his hands still firmly planted in those pockets.

I storm forward, decimating the few feet of space between us to grab his wrist and yank it upward, ignoring the remorse etched across his face. "*Show me.*"

His fingers remain curled tight around whatever is hidden in his grip. "Let it go, Ollie."

Let *what* go?

I dig my nails into his skin. Claw at his hand. Pry his fingers open.

His posture loses the confident rigidity as he opens his palm, allowing me to snatch the tiny vial with a black lid.

"What is this?" The smallest drop of clear liquid remains trapped inside the glass. "Did you give him something?"

He doesn't deny the accusation. Doesn't do anything other than watch me suffer with pained eyes.

"*Talk to me,*" I scream.

He winces, raising his chin.

What is this? His dismissive demeanor. The pained silence.

I unscrew the lid and hold it to my nose, taking a sniff of the faint chemical odor. "Is it drugs?"

He remains mute.

"*Is it drugs?*" Panic consumes me, sharp and excruciating. I shove at his chest, causing him to stumble back. "*Why won't you tell me?*"

"Ollie…" His eyes beseech.

"Ollie, what?" I can't take the secrecy anymore. I *won't*. Months of stacking concealments have towered over me. Now, they've fallen and buried me beneath the rubble. "Why are you doing this?" I turn away, shoving my pinkie into the vial. I touch my finger to the liquid, then raise it to my mouth.

"*No.*" Remy grabs my wrist, stopping me before I can taste. "Don't fucking do that."

I freeze. The slowly creeping panic plunders me like a tidal wave.

I can't breathe. Can't compute. There's only pain and agonizingly thick guilt that stares down at me.

"What did you do?" I plead.

I left my dad with him. I left him alive and well.

"Did you kill him?" I maintain eye contact as I blurt the outrageous accusation, his hand still wrapped around my wrist.

The words seem to strike him like physical blows.

His tormented expression intensifies.

But he isn't offended by the allegation. He doesn't even deny it.

All he does is stand there, peering down at me, his answer silent yet so deafeningly loud.

"No." I yank my arm away.

He didn't.

He couldn't.

He idolizes my father.

Idolized.

"Tell me you didn't do this." My voice trembles. "Please, Remy."

His eyes implore me, wordlessly asking forgiveness.

"*Please,*" I beg.

"This isn't how it was supposed to end." His tone is roughened.

I shake my head. "Then tell me what *was* supposed to happen. What did you give him?"

"Pento."

"Pentobarbital?" I gape. *The euthanasia drug?* "That's what you delivered earlier?" When he'd smiled his gorgeous smile as he arrived while the cause of my father's premature death rested in his pocket.

"It was part of the agreement, Ollie. Right from the start. He wanted to end his life on a high. On his own terms. He didn't want to slowly deteriorate while you watched him suffer. But he promised he'd tell me first." He reaches for me again, the gentle scrape of his rings over my forearm a sickeningly torturous form of comfort. "I fucking swear to you he promised he'd let me know when the time came."

I retreat a step, my lower lip trembling, and the bile, oh *God*, it threatens to rocket from my throat.

He killed my father.

The man I adore—the one I trusted—stole my only surviving parent without cause or warning.

"Wow." I choke on a sob. "I guess you got what you wanted."

"What?" His face blanches. "*How?*"

"You said I couldn't see you for who you are." I slide a hand over my stomach, begging the nausea to remain at bay. "I do now. I finally understand what you've been trying to tell me all along."

"Ollie, please." The agony in his voice destroys me. The utter devastation of it all.

I back away, fighting against my body's senseless urge to remain close to him. "I need you to leave."

He straightens. Stiffens. "I can give you space, Pyro, but I won't—"

"You'll go or I'll call the cops." I cross my arms over my middle, fighting to remain composed. "The agreement is over. Your work here is done. I never want to see you again."

39

REMY

I STARE AT HER, DRINKING IN HER PAIN, PUNISHING MYSELF WITH HER despair. "I can—"

"Leave." Her arms tighten around her middle, like they've done so many times before. It's different now. The sight of it destroys me.

I wish I could touch her. Comfort her.

But if I get the chance to do that again it won't be anytime soon.

I bridge the space between me and the bedside table where two envelopes are propped against the stack of paperback memoirs Carlo had been reading.

I take the one with my name written on the front, my gaze casting over the man I admired, and even now, can't find the will to condemn.

Ollie doesn't say a word as I walk for the hall, her hard sniffs marking my path toward destruction.

It kills me to leave her.

I pause in the doorway and turn back to face the pale starkness of her beauty. "You know I love you, right?"

Her expression crumples, her lips trembling, eyes watering.

I fight to remain in place, waiting for her to forgive me, even if only slightly.

But she locks down the heartache, my pretty little Pyro clutching the unraveled threads of her composure to reel them back in. "Please, Remy, just leave."

I would've preferred her anger. For her to scream and slap and shriek. Hell, I'd settle for her knocking me out and throwing me back in the retort. I'd even let her follow through with the cremation.

But this? The mature composure and brutal vulnerability?

It only makes me love her more.

I incline my head and force myself to walk away.

For her sake.

For Carlo's.

I could've fabricated the truth and made up an excuse for the vial. But despite all the nails hammered into my conscience, I couldn't stand bearing that one, too.

I'm responsible for her father's death. Just like I was with Flynn's.

I arranged the pento. I handed it over. And I believed Carlo when he promised he wouldn't take the lethal dose until we both agreed it was time.

Son, I just want to have it here so I know you won't back out of the agreement.

After all the lies he told his daughter, why did I think I'd be spared?

Lucy looks up to greet me from her seat on the top step of the external stairs. "Is she okay?" She pushes to her feet. "I heard raised voices."

"She's definitely not okay. You should go back inside and wait in the living room just in case she needs someone."

She nods. "How are you holding up?"

I ignore the misery decimating my chest and slide Carlo's envelope into my jacket pocket. "I'll be good once I know you're close by to help her." I descend the stairs, skirt the building, and make my way through the unlocked front doors of the funeral home.

Voices carry down the hall, and I continue to the break room where two men turn from the coffee maker to greet me with forlorn expressions.

Stanley Flores, the older of the two and the replacement mortician Carlo hired, who stands beside John Welch, the taller, skinnier assistant.

"Mr. Costa." Stanley places his mug on the counter and strides toward me, offering his hand. "I'm sorry we're meeting again so soon."

I clasp his palm and shake it numbly. "So am I."

John strides forward and does the same, killing me with the menial gesture in the midst of devastation. "I'm sorry for your loss."

"Thanks," I mutter.

"As previously discussed with you and Carlo, we will give Olivia the time she needs to be with her father, then we'll safely transport him downstairs and fulfill his wishes regarding his after-life care." Stanley raises a brow. "Now, I know you're well aware of what will happen moving forward, but has Olivia been brought up to speed on who will be preparing Carlo for the funeral?"

"No. And I don't think she's going to appreciate being kept out of it."

He winces. "I understand. I'll show her the notes he left, and hopefully it will help to ease the situation. It really isn't wise for close family to handle the preparation of a loved one."

I scrub a hand down my face.

"I want you to know everything else is in safe hands," he continues. "John and I have been familiarizing ourselves with the current decedents in the funeral home's care, and additional staff will be here first thing Monday morning to assist with all ongoing duties until Carlo's employees feel they're able to return to work."

Speaking to a man who has already slipped so easily into Carlo's shoes feels fucking heartless.

I hate this.

One minute Carlo is here; the next, he's been replaced.

"Great." I make for the door, desperate for fresh air. "You've got my number if you need it."

"And you've got mine," Stanley calls as I stride down the hall. "If you have any concerns at all, please reach out."

My concerns for Carlo are over.

I'd spent months dreading his death, visualizing the unwelcome conversation when he would tell me he'd decided his time was up, and how I'd comfort Ollie when she learned the news. I was meant to be by her side *and* his when he took his last breath. She was meant to say goodbye.

He stole those moments from us.

He bailed early, like a fucking coward.

I stalk around the building, my ability to breathe getting harder with the increased tightness in my chest. I stop at the back of my car, plant my palms against the trunk, and bow my head as I take in gulps of air.

I didn't bat an eye when my own father died.

I could get a call right now that my own mother had passed and not give one flying fuck.

But Carlo?

His death has sliced me open and left the vultures to tear at my insides. I'm wrecked. Fucking shattered.

I yank at the top button of my shirt, the restriction making it harder to breathe.

Fuck his promises. His friendship.

He left me.

I ball my hands into fists and squeeze my eyes shut.

He left Ollie.

I choke on my anger. On the suffering.

I can't believe he did this.

I drag the envelope from my pocket and tear it open, unable to fathom what the hell he could have to say for himself.

What could you possibly have written to explain or excuse your actions?

I yank out the folded piece of plain white cardstock and spread it open.

Forgive me.

xoxo Carlo

The agony beneath my ribs explodes, spreading through my limbs.

I scrunch the card and launch it across the parking lot, my eyes burning as I glare at the brickwork of the building.

Fuck. Him.

Fuck everything.

I pace.

I curse.

I stare at the upstairs window, despising that I can't be in there. That I don't know how Ollie's coping. *If* she's coping.

It takes a fucking lifetime to regain some semblance of calm, which is when I call Wesley and tell him to get his ass to the funeral home.

He arrives fifteen minutes later and takes the news with a solemn nod.

"I want you to drive Ollie home when she's ready," I mutter under my breath.

"Me?" He frowns.

"Yes. She needs her space from me."

His expression fills with pity. "Sure thing."

"Call me as soon as it's done."

I text Lucy, letting her know a car is waiting to take Ollie home whenever she's ready.

Then I leave.

I drive away from the place of grief that brought me so much fucking life.

I aimlessly pass through the suburbs, the image of Carlo on that bed haunting me. I do it for hours, keeping myself behind the wheel and occupied because being back in my penthouse where the pain of Flynn's death already lingers would only send me on a bender I wouldn't recover from.

It's two in the morning when I get the call from Wesley.

"She's safe at home," he says.

"Did she say anything?"

"Not a single word."

The weight in my gut grows heavier. "Was she crying?"

"Not a single tear."

I disconnect the call and check my GPS. I'm a few blocks from Ollie's house. I'm pretty sure I've been subconsciously circling the vicinity, unable to stray too far from her.

I take the next turn, driving a familiar path until I'm parked on the street opposite her darkened house, then climb out to stare at the place where she remains hidden from me.

I've dragged her through hell.

She's struggled with fear—from me *and* the thought of conviction.

She was assaulted by one of my staff members and almost raped.

Then the Irish could've killed her if given the chance.

I've hurt her so much.

I'm still doing it.

A twig snaps nearby. Normally I'd flinch, maybe pull my gun, or make some effort to protect myself. But I don't bother as the old crone walks barefoot from the darkness of her front yard in an ankle-length nightdress, her long grey hair loose around her shoulders. She comes to stand before me, undaunted and curious.

"I see you're back to your stalker routine." She sidles up to me and leans back against my car to mimic my interest with Ollie's house. "What happened this time?"

"Her dad died."

She releases a weary sigh. "I didn't expect that so soon."

"None of us did," I grate.

"That explains why I woke up to her vomiting a little while ago. That girl's bathroom window is in line with my bedroom. I can always tell when she's upset."

"I think you're going to be hearing a lot more of it in the days to come."

She nods, and for quiet moments we stand there, side by side, staring at the house I should be in.

"Well, I'm very sorry this has happened," she finally murmurs. "I'm also very sorry that I'm getting the distinct impression you have no intention of leaving your stalking post. You know, back in my day, it wasn't polite to loiter on the street in front of someone's home like a thief waiting for an opportunity."

I drag in a frustrated breath.

I'm so fucking exhausted, annoyed, and completely over this shit.

I'm tempted to kill the old witch just for the spike of adrenaline. It wouldn't take much. A belt. Maybe a pillow. I could make it relatively painless… if I wanted.

"Lesley," I say patiently, "you're currently leaning against a car that's worth more than Ollie's house. Do you really think my intention is to steal?"

"Maybe not any earthly possessions. Her heart, on the other hand…" She pushes from the Aston Martin and stands up straight. "Look, I'm going to be honest with you."

"How refreshing." I glower.

"Olivia has had a lot more bounce in her step since you've been snooping around."

"Is that so?" I cross my arms over my chest, regretting the happiness I brought her because now it only means more suffering.

"Mmm." She nods. "She's also been checking in on me more often, and that music she blares from her living room on the weekends hasn't been the depressing, moody garbage she usually listens to. She even seems to have more energy, despite rushing from the house at all hours of the night—I assume to see you."

I scoff a laugh. "Now I understand why you don't like me. Your position as neighborhood stalker must feel threatened."

"Maybe." She shrugs. "It's obvious you're the reason for the positive change in her. But do you want to know what I really think?"

Fuck, no.

Not even a tiny bit.

Not even if I was on fire and her thoughts were the only thing capable of extinguishing the flames.

"I truly believe, that despite the positive change in her, the best thing you can do for that girl is stay away."

The words repeat in my head, the message an agonizing echo.

Stay away.

Leave.

I never want to see you again.

It's time to quit ignoring how truly destructive my presence is in Ollie's life.

It's selfish to want her.

It always has been.

"You know what, Lesley?" I push from the car and swing around to open the driver's door. "I think you're right."

40

REMY

I DO AS THE OLD BAT INSTRUCTS AND STAY AWAY FOR DAYS DESPITE HOW THE retreat from Ollie makes my veins itch.

No physical contact is one thing. But no texts or phone calls is a cruel form of withdrawal I struggle to endure.

I've instructed everyone I know, numerous times, to keep me updated on Ollie's movements and temperament as often as possible—Wesley, Lucy, Russo, and Valenti as well as Carlo's temporary appointed staff.

I even bribed her grocery delivery driver to inform me if any concerning changes are made to her eating habits because even the slightest insight into her suffering is a balm to my guilt.

My only solace is that her two best friends barely leave her alone. They're always at her house for hours on end. They bring food and coffee. I'm pretty sure they carried in a box of liquor, too.

And when they're not there, Lesley takes their place.

I wake on my sofa the morning of Carlo's funeral, in old gym shorts and not much else. Three empty bottles of Jack sit on my coffee table, along with a stack of take-out food containers.

Sobriety had been the plan at the start of the week. But as the days passed, intoxicated oblivion became the goal, and there's no getting through today without backing up on the inebriation train.

I shove from the sofa and drag my ass to the kitchen in search of a fresh bottle of whiskey.

I rummage through the alcohol cabinet above the fridge when the whir of my private elevator alerts me to an unwanted visitor, the slide of the opening doors followed by the clap of heels.

I close my eyes and bow my head as a weary female sigh carries from behind me.

I'd recognize that judgmental tone anywhere.

"What are you doing here, Abri?" I turn to face my sister.

Her eyes widen as she takes me in.

Okay, so maybe I haven't shaved in a while, and personal grooming hasn't really been a priority, but that expression is overly dramatic.

"Actually, don't answer that." I pivot back to the liquor cupboard and reach into the far corner to claim the last bottle of Jack. "Whatever your reason, I'm not interested."

"I'm sorry to hear that." Her heels continue to tap across the tile as she approaches the island counter. "But I didn't endure drunken late-night phone calls and early morning D.C. traffic to take no for an answer. So hurry up and get dressed. We have a funeral to attend."

I ignore her and crack the lid of the whiskey.

"Put the bottle down, Rem. You're better than this."

I turn to her with a derisive laugh. "I assure you I'm not."

"Well, for today you're going to pretend to be." She shrugs. "By free will or force, I don't care."

I scowl, not only at the statement but her outfit. "Why are you wearing that?"

She's dressed for a funeral. In all black. Conventional heels. Conservative dress.

"I guess you missed the first time I said it, so I'll repeat it slowly—we have a funeral to attend." She enunciates the words as if I've got a learning disability.

With the way her presence and appearance doesn't make sense, I'm beginning to think I do.

"I'm pretty sure the person who killed the victim isn't meant to attend the service, let alone his sister." I raise the bottle of Jack toward my mouth.

She launches her black clutch at me, hitting me in the face before I can take a mouthful.

"*Fuck.*" My head flings back on impact, the smack of pain striking the bridge of my nose. "*What the fucking hell, Abri?*"

The clutch falls to the floor, skittering across the tiles.

She bats her lashes. "Sorry, I should've calmly advised you how pathetic it is to be drinking before noon on a weekday, but you seem a little slow this morning. Shock therapy felt like the better option."

I rub a hand over my nose. "Do I need to call security?"

She barks a laugh. "I don't think Bishop would approve of me being escorted from the building."

"I'm sure he'd appreciate it more than having you thrown out the window, which is what I'm currently contemplating."

She sighs, her pristine posture slumping. "Rem, come on. You loved that man. And I'm pretty sure you loved his daughter, too. So you're going to that funeral. You need to pay your respects."

The throb across my face descends into my chest.

My love for both of them hasn't changed tense just because Carlo is dead. The emotion is still present. Not in the past. If anything, it's more adamant now than it ever was.

Abri rounds the island counter and gently takes the liquor bottle from me. "You need to say goodbye."

I scrunch my nose, fucking despising the thought. "And you need to go back to D.C. and mind your own business."

"I understand you're hungover, so I'm going to say this one more time with a little more context, just because God knows you're acting like you have half a brain right now." Her brow furrows in pity. "Bishop is currently double-parked out front. Matthew and Layla are in the car. We're all going to the funeral. That means Salvo and Lorenzo, too. And Valenti and Russo. Carlo was part of the family, and we support our own."

I pinch the bridge of my nose, the sting from her accessory abuse increasing instead of lessening. "She wouldn't want me there."

"Yes, she would. You've shared stories about her for months. I know what type of woman she is, and how much she cares about you."

"You don't know shit." I slam my palms down on the counter.

"No?" She cocks her head, undaunted. "I know you blame yourself. I know you're drinking to ease your pain. And I know that man was like the mentally stable father you never had."

"Get out, Abri." I growl.

"Sweetie." She gives a condescending smile and places the bottle on the counter. "Did you hear the part where I said Bishop is double-parked? If you make him wait much longer this uncomfortable conversation is going to be the least of your problems."

"You're threatening me with your husband?"

"Whatever works. But you know as well as I do that once he gets out of the car you'll be attending that funeral whether you like it or not. Probably whether you're conscious or not."

I glare.

I glare so fucking hard.

"Come on, Rem. This is important."

"Do you think I don't fucking know that?" I throw my arms out at my sides. "She fucking hates me, Abri. She knows I took her dad from her."

"Deep down I'm pretty sure you know that's not true. I get that you want to punish yourself—I've spent my fair share of months doing the same type of thing due to my own trauma. But you gave him pento, brother—you didn't make him take it."

"He was—"

"Utt." She raises a finger, imperious as she cuts me off. "We can do a deep dive on this later. I can even call my shrink and make you a virtual appointment—"

"I don't need a shrink, Abri."

"Let's agree to disagree. But for now, you need to go get ready. You've got fifteen minutes."

Nope.

Not going to happen.

Even if I didn't have a million reasons not to attend, it would take longer than fifteen minutes to shave my way out of looking like a yeti.

The family can all go without me.

Her clutch vibrates from its discarded place on the floor.

"You're running out of time." Abri holds up her arm, showing her watch that's illuminated with what I assume is a text. "Bishop just asked, 'Is that cock stain getting ready or do I need to make an appearance?'" She lowers her arm. "How would you like to proceed?"

"I'm not going." I'll die on this hill.

"So you're going to leave Ollie to handle Lorenzo and Salvatore on her own?"

Anger thrums through my limbs.

"My understanding was that she didn't feel comfortable around those two?" Abri wields the question with subtle satisfaction. "You know just as well as I do that Salvo won't be able to resist stirring the pot."

I open my mouth about to claim he won't, but there's no fucking denying he will. "I hate you."

She smiles. "Yes, and I'm sure I'll have sleepless nights until you love me again. But while we wait for that to happen, you need to go get ready."

I eye the whiskey bottle on the counter.

"Don't even think about it." She snatches at the alcohol and drags it behind her back. "I'll text Bishop while you're gone and let him know you're following the script."

I grind my molars as I stalk from the kitchen.

"Don't forget that shaving is the most important part," she calls after me. "Rugged looks more like homelessness on you."

It takes more than fifteen minutes to create some semblance of respectability, the forced shave, shower, and dress routine leaving me with a permanently embedded scowl.

The car ride toward the suburbs is painful as Matthew and Abri take turns making fun of me, the childhood trauma response not seeming as therapeutic as it once was.

As soon as we arrive at the funeral home, I slide out of the car and disappear into the inky sea of morbidly dressed mourners.

I search for Ollie despite every effort not to, but neither her nor her friends are anywhere to be seen.

"She's in her prep room." Wesley approaches to stand beside me. "I assume you're looking for Olivia."

I suppress a cringe, not appreciating my easily read thoughts. "How is she?"

"Enviably composed despite looking dead on her feet. Ivy and Allison are adamant she still hasn't cried, so they're worried. Justifiably."

That makes three of us.

If she's not crying, she's purging.

He steps closer. "I also don't know if it's cause for concern, but the guy I took over from—the one that left on bad terms—he's here."

I scan the crowd with more intent, trying to get eyes on Hugo. "Has he said anything to anyone?"

"No. He seems to be laying relatively low."

"Let me know if he becomes an issue."

"I will." He checks his watch and then focuses on the mourners making their way into the chapel. "I better check to make sure everything is in order for the service. I'll talk to you later."

I jerk my chin, remaining on the outskirts of the slowly moving crowd, the exodus giving view to Lorenzo, Salvo, and my men who wait near the side of the doors.

My uncle welcomes people as they pass, forever the charismatic businessman as he leans against his cane.

"Come on." Matthew walks past me with Layla by his side. "Let's get this over and done with."

I sigh and eye the parking lot.

"It's too late to run," he mutters. "I'll give chase, and we both know I'll catch you."

"Matthew," Layla chastises. "Don't taunt him."

My brother wraps an arm around her waist and tugs her close into his side. "It's what we do, *la mia stella polare.*" He steers her toward the building.

I follow begrudgingly, my eyes shooting daggers into the back of his head.

My family are the last of the crowd to enter the function room, Lorenzo leading the way, Valenti and Russo a step behind, while my siblings gather around me in support that I don't want or need.

We remain standing, taking our place at the back of the chapel in an act of fortitude and protection to the grieving. It's Lorenzo's weird take on family tradition, and right now, it beats sitting next to someone who's likely to sob and snivel their way through the proceedings.

I slide my fingers into my pockets, curling my hands into fists at the sight of the closed mahogany casket at the front of the room, the overhead lights beaming down on the shiny exterior with an ethereal glow.

Painfully melancholy music plays softly from overhead speakers as people chat quietly amongst themselves, waiting for Ollie to arrive.

"So this girl of yours…" Matthew bumps me with his shoulder. "I'm picturing full-blown Goth. Black hair. Dark makeup. Maybe a septum piercing."

"You're well off the mark," I mutter, wishing he'd ditch his role as distraction connoisseur. "I suggest you quit talking about her while you still have a fully functioning trachea."

"You can call this payback for how you acted when I got involved with Layla."

"How I acted?" I scoff. "I welcomed her to the family with open arms."

"Your welcome involved a gun being held against her fucking head." His tone gains a lethal edge.

"And I'll do it again if you don't stop pissing me off."

His chuckle is sinister. "That reminds me—I still haven't killed you for the transgression."

"Well, we're at the right place for disposal, so go ahead. I'm game."

"I'm not going to attack when you're acting like a sad sack and fucking begging for it, dickwad. But don't worry—I'll return the warm welcome."

"You already fucking stabbed me," I mutter.

"Mmm." He nods. "And I can still remember the feel of my blade slicing through your thigh. It's the stuff of wet dreams."

"You're sick."

"And you're pathetic. Get over yourself and reclaim your woman before someone else does."

Layla leans around him, placing a calming hand on his chest as she meets my gaze. "If you need tips on how to grovel, your brother could give lessons. He's had enough experience to be a pro."

"Hey." Matthew palms her wrist and gently raises her knuckles to his lips. "Don't share state secrets, *la mia ossessione.*"

She breathes a faint chuckle, her gaze turning doe-eyed as she stares at him. *Great.* Just what I fucking need—a cameo from the honeymoon phase.

"Take that shit somewhere else." I glare. "We're in a place of mourning."

The room falls quiet, the shift of attention moving to Allison and Ivy who enter the room, heads downcast, tissues in hand.

Ollie is a step behind, walking fearlessly on her own in her black knee-length pencil skirt, blouse, and blazer, her head high, her shoulders straight.

I stand taller, trying to gain a glimpse of her necklace. To see if she hates me enough to quit wearing my ring. But her collar is too high.

"Is she the bombshell in the front or the one at the back?" Matthew whispers.

"Shut the fuck up," I rage-whisper back.

The attention of numerous mourners shifts our way. Ivy glances up too, her bloodshot eyes widening in horror as she takes in my family line on her approach.

She knows who we are.

Fucking mint.

Her attention stops somewhere to my left, her eyes hardening, her horror turning to animosity.

I lean back to determine who she's fixated on and find Salvatore leering back at her with a menacing smirk.

They know each other?

Ivy scrunches her tissues in a tight fist and snaps her gaze back to the floor as she passes us, her spine ramrod, her anger obvious.

Then it's Ollie who steals my attention, her watery gaze meeting mine.

Time stops. My pulse and thoughts jump ship, too.

It's silent. Just me and her. Nothing but pain stands between us.

Her saddened composure fractures, her brow furrowing, her lower lip trembling. She stares at me in sorrow. In regret. Then she casts her gaze away, blinking rapidly as she plasters a hand over her stomach and continues down the aisle.

I glare through my desperation to follow her and dig my nails into my palms.

"She looks beautiful today, Remy," Abri murmurs. "And it's clear she still loves you."

I keep glaring. Keep digging.

Ollie and her friends reach the front row where they're greeted by a male celebrant. The women claim their seats. Then the celebrant takes his place in front of the wooden podium and greets everyone with a forlorn smile.

"Good afternoon, family and friends. We're gathered here today…"

I ignore the speech and stare at the braid exquisitely curled around the back of Ollie's head, feeling every time her shoulders hitch as if her sniffs are my own.

"…let us come together in love and support of one another…"

The words drone on, their weight meaningless when pitted against the memories of a man who showed me more fatherly guidance in twelve months than my father did in my entire life.

Carlo gave me his time, even given the little he had left. He trusted me with the one remaining family member he had. The woman he cherished the most.

"…I'd now like to share a reading that Carlo himself chose to be read before his passing. *Death is Nothing At All*, by Henry Scott Holland."

I lower my gaze to my loafers, struggling to withstand the emotional onslaught pulsing through the room. "*…Call me by my old familiar name…*" Struggling to face the loss after already losing Flynn. "*…Laugh as we always laughed at the little jokes we enjoyed together…*"

They both deserved better. Flynn and Carlo. Ollie and even me.

What the fuck did I do to deserve an upbringing sponsored by malice and psychotic oppression? What did any of my siblings do?

"*…I'm waiting for you…*"

"*Fuck,*" I curse under my breath.

Jesus Christ, Carlo. Could you have picked a more painful reading?

Abri's hand glides over my wrist, her fingers squeezing.

I bear my way through it—the reading, the continued diatribe from the celebrant, the sobs, and sniffs, and sorrow.

Then the celebrant moves away from the podium and Ollie gracefully takes his place.

Fuck. Fuck. Fuck.

I swipe a rough hand over my mouth, my chin, my neck. I deliberately dig my rings into my skin, distracting myself from the internal misery with the external torment.

Pull it together, you fucking piece of shit.

Her face remains unstained from tears.

She hasn't broken. Not yet. But the fissures of instability show in her hitched breathing and the growing paleness of her complexion.

She raises her gaze to the room, her eyes meeting mine. I hold my breath, the air burning in my lungs as the kaleidoscope of her emotions morphs.

There's desperation. Emptiness. Betrayal. Even a glimpse of acceptance.

The longer she stares, the more I see.

Fear. Hopelessness. Loss. Maybe even longing.

Then she winces and glances back down at her podium.

"You've got this." Abri squeezes my wrist again.

I shouldn't be here. Shouldn't have intruded.

I eye the exit and contemplate leaving for the sake of giving Ollie a few untainted moments to celebrate her father without me messing them up.

I shift, about to make an escape only to have Matthew counter my movement.

"Stay," he grates. "If she can endure this, so can you."

I huff a callous breath. "She doesn't want me here."

"I disagree, and the older sibling is always right. So shut up and listen to her eulogy."

"Please, Remy," Abri begs, not letting go of my wrist.

"My father was an incredible man." Ollie's voice drifts softly through the speakers, the tremble in her words the worst form of audible torture.

If I don't go, I don't know how I'm going to stop myself from going to her.

She needs to be held. She needs someone to help break down her fucking walls and let her goddamn grieve.

"I'm warning you," Matthew growls as Ollie describes her father's childhood. "If you make a move for the door I'll land the hardest NFL tackle you've ever seen, then Bishop will cable tie your hands and feet—"

"With pleasure," Bishop mutters beside Abri. "I've always got them on hand."

"—Then we'll place you next to Old Mother Hubbard in the second back row." Matthew jerks his chin to the crowd. "Because she looks like she wants to kick your ass more than I do."

I glance to the row he's referenced, finding the old woman in question. *Fucking Lesley.*

I sigh and return my attention to the podium despite the ache it brings.

"He had a way of turning things around," Ollie says with heartfelt poise. "He helped those who grieved to celebrate a life instead of focusing on their loss." This time when she raises her gaze, she stares at the ceiling, blinking rapidly. "He always seemed to find the light in the dark. In situations, as well as in people."

Jesus Christ.

She's talking about me.

"He tended to be conservative, but at times he liked to mix things up with a radical decision or two. He was fun, yet professional to a fault. And he loved with all of his heart. Always." She dabs her nose with a tissue. "My mother once claimed my father was the epitome of devotion and selfless sacrifice. Actually, it was a lecture she gave early one Saturday morning," Ollie continues in a lighter tone. "All I'd wanted to do was watch television but Mom kept nagging me to pick up the dirty clothes I'd left lying around. She told me Dad deserved a clean home after the long hours he'd worked all week. Then she went on to relay an extensive list of all the recent sacrifices he'd made."

She sniffs. "I wish I could remember even one of the sacrifices she mentioned, but in my defense, I was twelve, and the new season of *Brooklyn Nine-Nine* had been released, and anything outside of watching that show was static I didn't want to hear."

Abri chuckles, along with numerous other attendants throughout the room.

"But I get it now." Ollie pauses, dragging in a shaky breath before letting it out slowly. "It took my father's death for me to scrutinize his actions and find the multitude of sacrificial gems he left behind." Her shoulders curl and she wraps her arms around her waist, tormenting me with the distance between us. "I wish I could thank him for being my father, my mentor, and my greatest inspiration. And one day, I know I will. But until then—" She sucks in a sharp breath. "—take care, Dad, and give Mom a hug for me."

"Damn," Salvatore groans. "That was rough."

"Fucking brutal," Matthew adds.

"She's a strong woman." Abri's voice is barely audible as Ollie leaves center stage to reclaim her seat.

There's a moment of reflection where a fucking torturous a cappella version of "Hallelujah" fills the room while a montage of images are plastered onto an overhead screen above the podium. Ones of Carlo. Of him and Ollie. Then him with his wife. There are group photos. Those with what I assume are friends or colleagues.

Then the breath gets punched from my lungs when an image of me flicks on screen. One that must've been taken at Berkeley Springs without my knowledge.

We stand side by side on the deck of the vacation house, Carlo's hand on my shoulder, his fatherly eyes staring back at me.

It was when he'd asked me about my interest in Ollie.

Fuck.

I lower my gaze and pinch the bridge of my nose.

Goddamn you, Ollie.

Why include me? Why make me a part of this when it must have hurt her to acknowledge any role I've played in her father's life?

I keep my focus on the floor for the remainder of the song. I don't raise it for the entire conclusion of the ceremony. Not even when guests pass to exit the chapel.

I'm done.

Cooked.

Fucking fried.

Matthew leans close. "Do you remember when we were little and you wanted to ride your bike over the dirt jumps me and Salvo built in the back field, but it was already past your bedtime and Dad told you no?"

I raise my gaze with a scowl. "Yeah. Why?"

"Do you also remember how you did it anyway and bit the dust so hard you got a concussion and your face looked like a mangled piece of day-old meat?"

I scowl harder. "Yes, Matthew, I remember. Why the fuck are you asking?"

He shrugs. "I dunno. Was just thinking about it. It's a great memory."

Salvo, Bishop, and Abri chuckle. The rest of the entourage smirk.

"Get the fuck outta here." I jut my chin at the door. "Mom should've swallowed you."

He barks a laugh. "Well, she's certainly the type to eat her young."

41

OLIVIA

I stand in the courtyard, wishing the speed of time would increase so I could return home and stop pretending I'm holding my shit together when the truth is I'm the slightest nudge from mental breakdown.

I'm surprised I didn't succumb at the sight of Remy.

I force a smile as the afternoon sun warms my back and well-wishers form a line in front of me to pay their respects.

I've seen the tradition play out a million times. I even stood at my father's side for the very same procession after my mother's funeral.

But I never imagined the brutally hollow ache of doing it alone.

Distant relatives I haven't seen in years put their hands on me, offering hugs as if the embrace brings reassurance instead of uncomfortable contact.

Strangers exude pained grimaces and murmur numbing platitudes.

Then Lorenzo hobbles toward me, his walking stick lightly thudding against the cement on his approach.

I swallow, unsure if he's going to provide the final blow to my composure.

"*Mia cara ragazza.*" His mouth kicks in a sad smile.

I'm not sure what the greeting means. It could be a threat. A taunt. Who knows? But it sounds nice, and his eyes offer fatherly kindness I wish I didn't pine for.

"My sincerest condolences." He leans the walking aid against his hip and takes my hands. "Please know that the family stands by you in this time of loss. Whatever you need is yours. You only have to ask."

I nod, blinking back the burn. "Thank you. I received the food baskets you sent. They were appreciated." *At least for the few minutes the contents stayed in my stomach before being ejected into the toilet.*

"How are you holding up?" he asks.

I clear my throat, unsure if anyone seriously expects me to answer that with honesty. "I'm doing okay." I glance away, hating the vulnerability that edges its way up my arms. "We all know it takes time."

My gaze pauses on Remy resting against the building yards away, his foot kicked back against the brickwork, his eyes on mine.

My pulse falters, my heart breaking out in a mass of agonizing beats.

He's still the most beautiful man I've ever seen.

"Did you hear what I said, Olivia?" Lorenzo asks.

"I'm sorry." I blink back to the conversation. "What did you say?"

Lorenzo glances over his shoulder, tracing the path to where my attention had been. "You know he mourns for you as much as he does for your father." His kind expression returns to mine. "That boy has lost himself to you."

No. No. No. No. No.

Focus.

Breathe.

Relax.

I swallow the emotion-fueled bile that thickens at the back of my throat. "I'm glad he came" is all I can reply.

It's the truth.

Dad would've wanted him here.

I want him here. Well, I did, then I didn't, and then I did again.

My head is such a mess.

I lean forward, offering Lorenzo an awkward hug in the hopes of sending him on his way. "Thank you for your support. Maybe we'll talk again later."

"Of that I'm certain." He returns the embrace with one arm, then hobbles away, leaving Salvatore to approach.

The formidable man stares at me, then peers over his shoulder to Remy who pushes from the building, his brows creased in a severe frown. He seems poised to storm over here at any moment.

Please do.

"He's trying to kill me with his eyes," Salvo mutters. "I wonder if he knows he's not a Jedi."

My lips twitch with legitimate humor. "If only."

He snickers. "It'd take more than that to end me."

"I assumed as much." I keep my voice low, not wanting to destabilize the nausea.

His humor fades, his dark eyes gaining a surprising hint of hardened compassion. "Losing a parent is difficult. I assume it's even worse if they were worthy of the role. So my thoughts are with you, Liv. And like Lorenzo said, if you need anything, you'll be taken care of—in the near future and as the years pass."

I don't acknowledge the offer.

I pretend it doesn't exist.

I will *not* cling to comfort from Salvatore Costa. I'm not *that* unhinged.

"Now I'm choosing to retreat slowly." He backs away a step. "No sudden movement in case my brother has an itchy trigger finger."

My lips twitch again, and the warmth that invades my cold sterility at the thought of Remy's protection becomes a solace I yearn to drown in.

I glance back to where he stood against the building, no longer finding him there. I scan the courtyard, anxious at the thought of him leaving before we can talk.

"I'm so sorry, Olivia," an elderly voice offers.

I jolt against another unwelcome hug.

It's one of twelve more I receive until the line of mourners is gone, the crowd already moving on to the wake room for coffee and cake while I'm left to stand staring at my shoes.

If I was strong enough, I'd pull my father's letter from my blazer pocket to read his final words again, because apparently the three hundred and fifty-five thousand times I've already done it haven't been enough.

But reading his words is the only time I don't feel alone.

Completely isolated.

There's no Mom. No Dad. No Remy.

Footsteps approach and I tense, wondering if I've willed the keeper of my heart to come find me.

We need to talk. There are things I have to say.

"Liv," a male voice greets.

I raise my gaze to the man coming to stand before me. "Hugo." My voice is full of surprise, but I suppose it shouldn't be. He worked with my father for months before he was fired. "Thank you for coming."

He scoffs. "It wasn't for your benefit. I'm actually surprised you haven't had me escorted off premises."

I cringe. "We've had our differences but—"

"We've had more than differences. You cost me the only good job

I've ever had. I've been unemployed for months. I lost my fucking apartment because I couldn't pay rent."

The brain fog I've been in for days doesn't lessen. I'm devoid of words, unable to come up with something to fill the uncomfortable pause.

"Don't worry, Liv. I have a feeling I'm about to have a stroke of good fortune."

There's something conniving in his tone. The sound of it sends dread slithering down my spine.

"I'm sorry, Hugo, but can we discuss this later? My stomach is unsettled and—"

"I suggest you remain right where you are." He steps closer, leaning into my personal space. "We've got a lot to discuss about my unlawful dismissal, and something tells me it has a lot to do with the shady characters that seemed right at home at your father's funeral."

42

REMY

I chug instant coffee in a quiet corner of the wake room, vainly attempting to dilute my hangover.

What I really want is to get out of here, but Bishop refuses to give me a ride home until my sister approves of the departure, and said sister claims we all need to stay a while longer to show our support.

She even stole my fucking phone like a toddler and said I wouldn't get it back until I could be trusted not to escape in an Uber.

Matthew enters my line of vision, the crowd parting around him as if aware of his reputation. He catches sight of me and pivots in my direction. A man on a mission I don't have the faintest desire to be a part of.

He approaches and stands beside me, taking in the room with cautious eyes. "You've got a problem."

I tense, not only at his words but the exuded hostility. "What is it?"

"Some guy looked like he was threatening your woman."

My pulse increases, the need to act gripping me around the throat. "Where is she?"

"Sitting outside on a park bench, gently rocking back and forth like an escaped mental patient."

I press a clenched fist to my mouth. I don't have the strength for this. To stay away when she fucking needs me. "Is she safe?"

Matthew nods. "Lorenzo is keeping an eye on her."

"And the guy?"

He jerks his chin toward the restrooms where Bishop stands guard at the door, his expression characteristically hostile, the brutal scar across his right cheek not helping his unwelcoming demeanor. "He's using the facilities."

I dump my coffee cup on a nearby table.

Ollie might not want me getting involved, but if she doesn't know about it then no harm, no foul. Right?

"Wait." Matthew grabs the crook of my arm. "You might need this." He discreetly slides something metallic into my hand. "It beats firing a gun."

My pulse increases as I glide my thumb over one of his blades, the green light to violence making me feel somewhat whole again.

"Bishop and I can keep watch at the door." He jerks his chin toward the bathroom. "Go have some fun."

I slide the weapon into my pocket and stalk across the room, my anger volatile as I make my way around waitstaff and mourners.

Bishop eyes my approach. "I've been informed that the restrooms are about to have a plumbing issue. Nobody will be coming in or out."

I incline my head and shove into the male toilet, the door swinging shut behind me.

An elderly gentleman stands at the basins, washing his hands.

I take an educated guess that Father Time isn't the culprit and ignore him as he walks from the bathroom. Once the door shuts behind him I round the cubicles to find a guy a few inches shorter than me at the urinals, pulling up his fly.

A guy I recognize from his background check.

He hums a cheerful tune as he walks past without looking my way, then washes up.

"Hugo," I drawl in greeting.

He stiffens, the jovial hum cut short. He glances at me over his shoulder and slowly wrenches the tap. "Yeah?"

I offer a welcoming smile and casually stroll toward him. "We haven't met." I offer a hand. "I'm Remy Costa."

He turns to me, glancing from my face to my hand, then back again as he wipes his wet palms on his suit pants. "Hey." He takes my offering and squeezes my fingers—*hard*—as if trying to win an ego contest.

I can't help huffing a laugh.

First he threatens Ollie. Then he's humming. Now the disrespectful handshake.

I tighten my grip and step forward, slamming my free arm across his collarbone, adding pressure to force him scrambling backward.

"Wait. Stop. Hold up." He wrenches his hand free and grabs at my wrist. "What are you doing?"

"I heard we've got something in common." I slam him into the wall. "Ollie," I state simply. "It seems we both have a habit of upsetting her. But I'm told you chose to do it on purpose."

"We were just talking." He glares. "I didn't even touch her."

Didn't. Even. Touch. Her.

I cluck my tongue at his misplaced confidence. "Do you know who I am, Hugo?"

He's defiantly silent for long seconds. Then finally, he nods. "You're Remy Costa."

"And do you know *what* I am?"

He remains quiet, his nostrils flaring.

He knows.

"I'm glad you're familiar." I smile. "But do you want to know what's more important than my name, or even my reputation, at this point?"

His jaw hardens.

"It's my mental state, Hugo. And right now, I can feel myself nosediving toward horrifically violent psychosis. You see, I don't like when lowlife pieces of shit mess with those I care about." I inch closer. "And I assure you, I care about nobody more than Ollie."

"We've got history." He pushes at my arm. "I was only relaying a message."

I shove him harder against the wall. "What message?"

"That's between me and her."

I retrieve the blade from my pocket and press it to his abdomen, earning a hiss. "That's where you're wro—"

The bathroom door opens, and I stiffen.

Bishop strolls in, eyeing us with indifference as he continues past to the urinals.

Are you fucking kidding me?

There's a grate of a zipper, then the unmistakable sound of liquid splatter as he takes a piss.

I shoot a glare over my shoulder. "Seriously?"

"Nature calls." He shrugs. "Don't worry, princess, your brother is keeping watch."

I drag my attention back to Hugo's confused expression. "I'm afraid that nosedive of my mental state just gained some traction. If I were you, I'd hurry up and tell me what you said to her."

He glances from me to Bishop and back again. "Come on, man. I'm not scared of you. There's a room full of people on the other side of that door. One shout from me, and they'll come running."

I fake surprise, all raised brows and wide eyes. "Oh, shit. I should've thought of that. Please don't shout, Hugo. I wouldn't want to get caught."

"Don't listen to him, champ." Bishop's personal rendition of a waterfall trickles to a stop, followed by another grate of a zipper. "I'd be screaming for my life if I were you."

Hugo scoffs.

"Do it." Bishop approaches to stop beside me, giving Hugo a friendly pat on the cheek, and the guy winces away from his unwashed hands. "Scream like a little bitch while you still can." He maneuvers around me, making his way to the basins. "I love when they mistakenly have faith that the greater good will save them."

"I love when they don't waste my time." I add pressure to the blade at his abdomen, feeling the resistance of flesh against steel.

Hugo raises his chin and opens his mouth. "*Hel—*"

I cut off his shout with a left hook to the gut.

He doubles over, gasping for breath.

"I would've aimed for the throat," Bishop drawls. "But you do you, tiger."

I clench my teeth. "Can you fuck right off?"

"Throw a guy a bone." He cocks his hip against the basin, settling in. "This is the most action I've seen in months."

"*Fuck you,*" Hugo rasps. "You've got no idea what I know."

I turn back to him. "Exactly, asshole. That's why you're in this predicament."

His upper lip curls as he straightens, breaths wheezing from his lips. "I fucking own you, Costa. You and your little hypocritical whore."

"Oh, shit." Bishop snickers. "I do believe he just dug his own grave."

"I agree," I snarl.

"You can't kill me," Hugo brags. "I know too much. I've got an entire phone full of evidence—"

I launch a jab at his throat, feeling the crack of cartilage, gaining a hit of euphoria as his mouth widens in search of breath that can't be claimed. "I *can* and *will* kill you, motherfucker."

"See?" Bishop drawls. "I told you the throat was a better option."

I rummage through Hugo's pockets in search of his cell while he desperately claws at his throat. He doesn't protest when I retrieve it from the front of his pants, the struggle for breath consuming his attention.

"Why don't we trade?" Bishop pulls a filled syringe from the inside of his suit jacket, the needle covered with a bright orange protector. "I can handle his so-called evidence while you give him this."

I hold the cell up to Hugo's face until the screen unlocks. "What's in it?"

"Enough sedative to take down an elephant."

I raise my brows, impressed. "And you just happen to have this on you?" I hand the phone to Bishop and take the syringe, removing the plastic protector with my teeth.

"At all times. You never know when you'll get the opportunity to surprise a spaced prick who dares to play fuck-around-and-find-out."

I spit out the plastic and grab Hugo's jaw as he panics for breath, his face sickeningly pale. People will learn of what I'm about to do. They'll understand that I'd only known of a verbal threat to Ollie, and that slight intimidation was enough for this man to forfeit his life.

The world will hear how I protect her.

How I cherish her.

Even if she's not mine.

I stab the needle into Hugo's thigh and plunge the liquid into his system.

His eyes widen to saucers. His mouth continues to gape like he's a beached fish.

"Well," I drawl. "Consider this spaced prick well and truly surprised."

43

OLIVIA

Hugo's threat plays on a continuous loop in my head, the barrage only adding to the weight of instability surging through me.

He knows about the illegal misuse of the retort.

He might not have specifics, but he's accumulated enough educated guesses to be on the mark.

The problem is, the threat of prison isn't the epitome of my concern. Yes, it's up there on the list. Pretty high in fact. But the thought of being arrested and spending my life behind bars comes in second place when I think about Remy and all that's left unsaid between us if we don't face each other again.

I need to talk to him. And not only in the hopes he can get me out of the Hugo situation. It's so much more than that. I just can't bring myself to go in search of him when the thought of him turning his back has me tied in knots.

"Hey, hon." Ivy slides onto the ornate park bench beside me. "Can we talk about some of the people who attended…?" She cocks her head to take a better look at me, her brow furrowing. "What's wrong?"

"Nothing." *Everything.*

"It doesn't seem like nothing." She grabs my hands, clasping them with hers in my lap. "You're shaking."

Am I?

I don't feel it.

The constantly building ache in my chest paired with the increased threat of nausea doesn't leave room to notice much else.

"Why don't we go to the staff break room and get some privacy for a little while?" Ivy pushes to her feet, the long lengths of her black dress swishing around her calves as she drags my hands with her.

"No, I..." I shake my head, unable to move from fear of throwing up. "Maybe later."

She's quiet a moment, the excited chatter of so-called mourners in the wake room filling the void.

"Liv, what's going on?"

I scoff a manic laugh.

Well, both my parents are dead.

I'm going to spend the rest of my life in prison.

And the icing on the cake is that despite all that upheaval, the only thing I can think about is Remy.

Where he is.

What he's doing.

My eyes burn, the increased threat of tears spurring my gut to counteract with a mass production of bile. I wince at the agonizing churn.

"Liv?" Ivy crouches in front of me. "You're worrying me."

Me, too.

I'm not sure how to recover from this. How to survive.

I'm lost. In pain. Yet I'm so goddamn numb.

"When was the last time you ate?" she asks.

I scrunch my nose at the thought.

"Do you want me to get you some sandwiches? I can check with the catering staff and see if there's more food waiting in the kitchen."

I pull my hands from hers to place a soothing palm over my abdomen. I'm definitely going to be sick again. There's no escaping it.

I can already feel my body creeping toward the starting line. There's a slight burn in my throat. A heated tightening takes over my temples.

"I need to use the bathroom." I push to my feet, dizzy with the insurgence of nausea.

"Liv, you can't keep doing this." Ivy stands, running a comforting hand down my back.

The concern in her eyes undoes me, increasing the burn, triggering more bile.

"Please stay here," I beg. "I'll be back in a minute."

She winces but nods.

I hustle for the wake room, accelerating my pace, trying to outrun the inevitable.

"My deepest sympathies, Olivia," a woman says as I enter the building.

"Your dad was such a great man" comes from someone else.

Condolences shadow me across the room, hounding me like wraiths.

"I can't imagine what you're going through."

"You're in my thoughts."

"He'll be missed."

I blink through my blurring vision, stumbling my way across the room only to stop at the edge of the mingling mourners.

Remy's brother stands guard in front of the men's bathroom, making it impossible to discreetly escape into the ladies.

Oh, God.

"Are you alright, dear?" A woman I don't recognize touches my arm. "If it's the bathroom you're after apparently there's a plumbing issue, but I was told if you walk through to the reception area—"

"Excuse me." I turn and flee in the opposite direction.

I don't have time to reach the other bathrooms.

My chest is too tight. My throat too hot.

I burn everywhere. My lungs. My eyes. My nose.

I head for the catering kitchen, shoving past the swinging doors, praying for privacy and an empty sink.

My feet freeze in place at the sight of two women crouched and rummaging through the cupboards beneath the counter.

I suck in an emotional breath. Are they stealing from me? At my father's funeral?

The women abruptly turn to face me, rising to their full height, apprehension written all over their gorgeous faces.

One of them is familiar. The beautiful blonde with blue eyes.

Is she the woman from Smoke & Mirrors? Remy's date from the night I'd been attacked?

The memory is a blur. My panicked unease makes it irretrievable.

I blink and blink, trying to clear my vision. My mind. My heartache.

Is she his lover? His girlfriend?

She has to be famous. I'm sure I've seen her before.

I swallow, willing the nausea back down my throat, but it doesn't quit creeping higher, pushing harder.

"Hey." She levels me with sympathy. "I hope it's okay that we're in here. We wanted to help—you know, the whole *family helps family* thing —and didn't know what else to do apart from washing dishes." She indicates the sink full of suds with a wave of her hand. "It's just taking a while to figure out where everything belongs."

I stare at the bubbles I'm about to destroy in front of an audience. Can I even make it the few steps across the room? Everything is too much—the tightening in my chest, the ache in my nose, the sting of my eyes.

"Family?" I croak.

"Yes, Olivia." She nods, smile pained. "I'm Remy's sister. We're all family."

Sister?

I could laugh with the idiotic relief. I probably would if I didn't find it so hard to breathe. I can't get enough air.

"Are you okay, honey?" The woman inches forward.

No.

I yank at the top buttons of my blouse. My blazer is too tight. It feels like every gasp fills me with pressure but not oxygen. I'm a balloon about to burst.

"*Go,*" the woman demands of her dark-haired companion. "Get Remy."

"No," I beg, the word coming out in a sob.

"Hey, it's okay." Remy's sister runs gentle hands over my arms, hesitant with her touch. "You're going to get through this."

She doesn't understand.

Does she even know what her family have been doing? What *I've* been doing?

Is she aware of my love for her brother? Or that I pushed him away?

Nothing is right without him.

Nothing ever will be.

"Things will get better," she soothes. "You're in the worst of it right now. You're under attack."

That's exactly what it feels like—a battle. A *war.*

Everything is out to get me and I don't know if I should hide or defend myself.

I hunch, sucking in ragged breaths.

My eyes worsen—the blur, the burn. It takes over everything. My face. My throat. My lungs.

"Sweetie, are you having a panic attack?" she asks.

I shake my head.

This isn't panic. It's pain. Misery.

A squeak of hinges carries behind me.

"*Ollie?*"

I swing around at the sound of Remy's voice, finding him standing in the doorway, his stark eyes cutting through the final string of my control.

"Remy," I sob, my knees giving out along with the lifetime's worth of restraint on my sadness.

He lunges forward, arms outstretched to catch my fall. He drags me into him, calling me home against his chest as the tears I've enslaved for years finally fall free.

"It's okay." He holds me tighter. "I've got you."

One by one the heavy cascade heats my cheeks, accompanied by deep, ratcheting cries. I bury my face in his neck, the nausea receding as my sobs increase. I shake with the weight of them. Convulsing. Heaving.

Someone places a handkerchief in my hand.

Softly uttered words are spoken between brother and sister.

I don't understand any of it. I'm too deep in hysteria. Forming a bond. Becoming best friends with grief.

Then I'm being lifted. Carried.

"I'm taking you home," Remy murmurs in my ear.

I don't protest. There's no will to do anything but cling to him as my tears soak the shoulder of his jacket.

He takes me through the external door to the side of the building, the high hedge shadowing us, my uncontrollable weeping echoing off the wall.

I'm carried into the parking lot.

Remy talks to others. Instructs. Makes subtle demands.

I'm too busy sobbing. Devolving.

He continues holding me as we're nestled into the backseat of an unfamiliar sedan—plush creme leather, new car smell.

I'm strapped in against his chest, his arms never losing their grip, his comfort unwavering.

I close my eyes as someone drives us from the funeral home. I let the tears take over. The pain run free.

"I'm right here, Pyro." Remy nuzzles my cheek. "I'm not going to leave you."

God, the way he appeases me. How he soothes.

It's more than just his words. It's his touch. His gaze. His existence.

He nourishes my soul, welcoming me into the destruction instead of forcing me to shut it out.

I let my sorrow surge free, wild and with abandon, as we're driven through sightless streets and paused at innumerable intersections.

"It feels so good to hold you," he whispers.

The tears fall harder. I don't know where they come from. How they keep flowing.

We go somewhere dark. Somewhere echoey.

A multi-level parking lot.

Not *my* home. *His.*

The car stops and I'm carried from the vehicle, Salvatore's surprisingly empathetic stare following me from his position behind the wheel as I cling tight to Remy's neck.

I'm taken into the private elevator.

We ascend to the soundtrack of my hitched breaths.

Then it's just the two of us on Remy's sofa, me nestled on his lap while the tears slow to a trickle.

He coaxes me back to the land of the living, holding me, consoling me, whispering to me.

"You're not alone…"

"I'm here for you…"

"Your grief is safe with me…"

One by one, he picks up my broken pieces, fitting me back together, making me whole. The silence stretches, allowing me to relax into its cocoon, the weight of my problems still right there, just no longer as heavy.

"Can I get you a glass of water?" he finally asks.

I nod through the exhaustion, my head aching, my eyes puffy and sore.

He places me gently on the seat beside him and walks for the kitchen, returning moments later and handing over a chilled glass.

"Thanks." I keep my head low and take a sip, not ready to look at him and face the damage that's been done.

He reclaims a seat at my side, his leg against mine, a gentle hand coming to rest on my thigh. I watch as it slowly glides against the material of my skirt, back and forth, the slight rasp of fabric the only accompaniment to my sniffs.

I don't know how long he lets me sit there, quiet in my grief, but time stretches enough for guilt to creep back in.

I take another sip and place the glass on the coffee table. "I bet I look a treat."

"You're always beautiful."

I keep my head downcast, hiding my wince. "Even when I accused you of killing my father?"

His hand raises from my thigh, lazily dragging along my jaw, gently adding pressure until I lift my chin to meet his eyes. He stares at me with such hardened sadness I'm almost plunged back into tears. "Even then."

I crunch my nose against the burn. "I'm sorry."

He frowns. "Why?"

"Because I accused you of something that never should've been thought, let alone spoken."

He brushes away the stray strands of hair clinging to my cheeks. "Ollie, you were justified in what you said. I gave him the pento. It was ridiculous of me to think he wouldn't use it."

"No. It was ridiculous for you to believe he wouldn't keep his word with something so important. I would've trusted him, too. Even after he'd lied to me over and over again."

His thumb strokes my jaw. "He lied because he loved you."

I meet his eyes. "And you gave him that pento for the same reason. I should've realized you'd never do anything to hurt him… or me."

His lips kick in a bittersweet smile as he continues dragging that thumb over my skin with attentive reassurance.

He's so good to me.

So patient.

So understanding.

"Do you forgive him?" I ask, hoping not to trigger his own grief.

I'd found his letter screwed up in the parking lot, the two written words packing a savage punch. I'd regretted the way I spoke to Remy before then, had endured multiple hours of guilt while at my father's bedside to know I'd reacted horribly. But *forgive me* was my undoing.

"I don't know, Pyro," he admits. "I'm still angry. I've done a lot of bad shit over the years, but this hits different."

I wince, leaning into his touch, wishing I could place a kiss to his palm, but we're not where we once were.

"I think the worst part is what was left unsaid." His brow furrows. "Carlo ended up meaning a lot to me. It was more than a working relationship, and I'm not sure he knew that."

"He knew." I choke on my words, trying to rein in my sympathy.

He shrugs. "Maybe."

"No, not maybe." I slide a hand into the pocket of my blazer and retrieve my father's letter. "I want you to read this."

He eyes the envelope with trepidation. "That's between you and your dad. I don't—"

"Please." I reach it toward him. "I want you to read what he had to say."

She holds out the envelope that matches the one I carelessly discarded at the funeral home.

I don't want to read it.

What I want is to remain composed for her, and I'm not sure I can do that with Carlo's voice in my head.

"Maybe another time." I gently guide her hand back to her lap.

"Remy, please."

My chest tightens. It's so fucking hard to deny her. "Ollie—"

"It's important." She pulls the folded piece of paper from the envelope and places it in my hand. "Trust me."

I drag in a calming breath and take the paper and ink grenade.

I itch to stand up, to pace, to get a fucking drink as I unfold the cardstock and stare at the familiar writing.

Dear fragolina,

I know you're reading this with sorrow in your heart but please believe that this path led to the least painful outcome.

I could never have said goodbye to you.

Not in a million years.

If I was a stronger man, maybe things would've been different. I could've told you the truth, and you could've held my hand as I took my last breath. But I think we both know you would've fought to delay the inevitable, and I would've caved to your sadness.

This way, you didn't have to watch your father slowly die an inhumane death. And your heartbreak won't be the last memory I take from this earth.

In both regards, I'm grateful.

I said my own subtle farewell to you tonight. I made you laugh. I watched you smile. And I can rest easy knowing Remy will be by your side when the news breaks.

Please take care of him for me because through this journey, all he's done is try to take care of you.

He sought the best doctors—for you.

He pushed me to continue the chemo—for you.

He made me vow to tell you my end-of-life plan—for you, my dear fragolina—but my commitment had always been a lie, and for that betrayal, please help him understand I'll forever be sorry.

He deserved better. We all did.

Now that I'm gone, I want you to live your life. Don't cling to family tradition if the funeral home isn't your passion. I'll be proud of you no matter where your future leads.

You were the best thing in my life. And your mother's.

Live for both of us.

Let your hair down. Explore. Create. Get in trouble (just not too much).

And please tell Remy I loved him like a son.

With all my heart, until we meet again,
Dad xoxo

I clench my teeth, trying to keep my shit together.

I loved him like a son.

The words sink under my skin, chipping away at old wounds and new.

I fucking hate this. The discomfort. The ache.

I fold the letter and hand it back, every beat of my pulse pounding heavy behind my eyes.

"You helped him," she whispers. "You gave him the peace I never would've been able to provide."

"I wouldn't have if I'd known."

"I don't believe that." She cocks her head, her somber gaze scrutinizing. "You have a horrible job, Remy, but there's so much good in you. My dad recognized that. I'm sure it's why he trusted you with his plan."

"Until he didn't."

"Until we got too close," she counters. "At the start, he probably thought he could talk his way out of the commitment he made you. But then things changed. *We* changed. And like he said, if I'd known, I would've selfishly talked him out of using the pento."

I drag her back onto my lap, needing her closer. "It's not selfish to have wanted more time with him."

"It is if it's at the expense of his pain and suffering." She turns into me, her shoulder leaning on my chest, her forehead resting against my cheek. "He made the right decision, Remy. I believe that, even though it hurts like hell."

Maybe she's right.

Maybe he had no other choice.

But watching Ollie endure the shock of her father's death, then having her torn from my life is going to take longer to compartmentalize, especially when I dedicated this week to liquor intake instead of forgiveness.

I'm on the journey. I'm sure I'll reach the destination. I'm just not there yet.

What I can appreciate, though, is how fucking phenomenal it feels to have this woman back in my arms.

I know it's not like it was before. Too many things have changed.

Yet for once in my life I have hope.

"Remy…" she whispers.

"Mmm?" I rub my hand over her lower back, trying to memorize everything about her in case it's taken away again.

"Do you remember what you said before you left my father's room?"

I flinch, not wanting to go back there. I'm sure I said a lot of things, all of them panic-fueled. "What did I say?"

"You told me you loved me." Her voice is barely audible, the tone along with her words making me tense. "Do you think you could ever feel that way again?"

Is she kidding?

"Pyro, at this stage, I'm pretty sure you could light me on fire and that feeling wouldn't stop."

She doesn't laugh like I'd hoped she would. Instead, she remains still, the most precious bundle in my arms. "I love you, Remy." I hear her arduous swallow. "I can't stop loving you."

I remain tense as fuck. No words. No thoughts. No speech.

This doesn't seem real.

She pulls back, her eyes glassy as they meet mine. "I've missed you so much this week, but after the way I acted, I couldn't bring myself to reach out to you. Not when it was for my own selfish reasons." She focuses on the ceiling, blinking rapidly. "But I feel entirely alone without you."

I grab her hand and raise it to my lips, placing a kiss to her palm. "You never need to feel that way again. I'll always be here for you."

"Always?" She sniffs. "That's a big commitment."

I'd give her an even bigger one if I thought she'd want to hear it. But there's no point daydreaming about what could be when the mending of our damaged bridges could be temporary.

I drag in a tired breath and place her hand back in her lap. "We need to talk about Hugo."

Her eyes widen. "Oh, God. I forgot about him." Her rapid blinks dissipate her watery sadness, replacing it with shock. "He knows about the retort. Not specifics, but enough to—"

"I know."

Her brow furrows. "Since when?"

"Since a few minutes before I walked into that catering kitchen. We'd been having words in the restroom."

"That's why your brother was guarding the door?"

I nod.

"What did he tell you?" she asks.

Truth is, he'd told me sweet fuck all by the time I jabbed that syringe into his thigh. All I'd had was the vague notion that he'd threatened Ollie and called her a whore. That had been more than enough. "He said something about having information. But he wasn't forthcoming with the details."

"He's been watching the funeral home," she says in a rush. "He said he's seen me coming and going at night. He's even taken note of how many funeral notices have been placed on our website and tallied the amount of times the retort has been used. He knows the numbers don't add up."

He *knew*.

The stupid fuck doesn't know anything about anyone anymore.

I'm just not sure how to break that to Ollie without having her cast me out of her life again.

"What should I do?" Those eyes implore me, the beauty in those hazel depths making me protective as fuck.

I don't want to lose her again. But I'll be damned if I continue keeping things from her.

"He's not going to be a problem, Ollie." I keep my hands where they are—one on the sofa cushion, the other lazily pressed to the low of her back. If she runs, I won't stop her, despite knowing I'll never recover.

She sits taller, her gaze scrutinous. "Ever?"

"Ever."

She drags in a slow breath, her mind working a mile a minute behind those beautiful irises.

I let her digest the implication, my pulse thrumming, my fear of her leaving growing with every silent second.

She'll be my undoing. I'll become a crazed madman haunted with my need for her. I'll never sleep. Never eat. Never function.

Living will be dying.

"Okay," she whispers.

I frown. "Okay?"

She swallows. Nods. "Yeah, okay. He was a horrible person. Maybe not worthy of death, but worth doesn't seem to be a currency this world cares about." She settles back into me, resting her cheek to my shoulder. "I knew the bed I was making when I inserted myself into the agreement you made with my father. I'm a big enough girl to lay in it."

Heat builds beneath my ribs. Fucking pride.

I turn my face toward her and place a kiss to her hair.

She's one of us now.

"Does that make me a bad person?" she whispers.

"It makes you a realist. Nothing is fair in this life, and you don't have to look far to see it. Criminal convictions are determined based on skin color, race, or bank balance. Entire countries starve while others are gluttonous. Wars are started for profit. Sex trafficking is one of the biggest growing industries."

She flinches. "Are you—"

"No." I cut her off. "I'd never play a part in that. But the cartel sure as hell do."

Those sick fucks have streamlined their business model. It's why I give no shits about killing them.

She relaxes again, her retreats from anxiety becoming quicker and easier. I hope one day soon she won't have anxiety about me at all.

"So you're kinda like Batman," she muses. "Living in the shadows. Taking down the bad guys."

I snicker. "You forgot the part where I earn millions from illegal drugs."

She shrugs. "I'm still going to role-play it in my mind for a while. Let me live my fantasy."

That warmth beneath my ribs increases.

Here I sit, surrounded by grief and regret, yet I'm unbelievably happy with this woman. "Out of all the fantasies in the world, you're doubling down on a Batman remix?"

"Well, considering all the fantasies I've had this year involved a man who iced me out whenever things got steamy, I think the Batman stitch is a nice compromise, don't you?"

I don't regret the so-called icing.

There's no doubt in my mind she would've had regrets after fucking me if we'd done it way back when, especially given the circumstances that surrounded our explicit encounters.

But things are different now.

I can't stand the thought of leaving her wanting. I'd do anything to make her happy. To convince her to stay.

I'm all in.

"I need you," she whispers, placing the most delicate kiss to my neck, the featherlight touch electrifying. "Will you deny me again?"

I know I should.

After what she's endured she can't be thinking straight.

"Because, no matter how bad you are at this," she continues, "horrible sex isn't going to come anywhere near the worst memory I'll take from today."

I fight a smirk, fucking frothing over her sass. "I'm not bad at this, Pyro."

She leans back with a raised brow "Are you sure? The constant delays haven't instilled me with confidence."

She's such a fucking temptation—those emotive eyes, those lush lips.

"I would've thought the orgasms I've previously given would've lessened any doubt."

She shrugs. "I've chalked them up to flukes."

"Is that right?" I wrap my arms around her and shove to my feet, increasing my hold when she squeaks. "I guess I need to try harder to convince you."

She wraps her arms around my neck. "Being hard is definitely a good platform for your campaign."

My chest thrums with the need to laugh.

I fucking love this woman.

I steal her mouth for a kiss as I stalk across the room, pulse thumping, cock well and truly hardened. She cups my cheeks, fusing our mouths, moaning into the contact.

"God, I adore you," she murmurs against my lips.

I hold her tighter. Kiss her harder.

I carry her into my bedroom, kicking off my shoes as I approach the bed to sink onto the mattress. "Are you sure you want this?"

"Without a doubt." She nods her forehead against mine.

"Then be a good girl and hitch that skirt so you can straddle me."

She whimpers into my mouth and does as instructed, pulling and tugging the tight material of her pencil skirt to the top of her thighs as she shimmies in my lap.

It's a fucking storm of friction against my cock.

"Like this?" She kicks off her tiny pumps and climbs on top of me, settling the heat of her pussy over my crotch.

"Just like that," I moan. "Such a good girl."

She reclaims my cheeks. My lips.

Her kiss is wild and ravenous, her tongue dancing with mine as she rolls her hips and grinds into me.

I slide my hands up those beautiful thighs to her ass, guiding her into another grind, countering my hips with her movements, simulating sex over and over until she's panting for more.

"I can't wait to be inside you." The rub against my covered cock is already too much. I could come like this.

That's what she does to me. Makes me crazed. Desperate.

"There's no need to wait." She undoes the buttons of my shirt, then pushes my clothes over my shoulders—jacket and shirt combined—the material catching at my wrists.

She leans back, her eyes sparkling. "Looks like you're trapped. What a predicament."

I grin. I'll give her the freedom to explore. To feel comfortable. For now. "Take advantage while you can. The tables will turn soon enough."

She tightens her thighs around me, her nails scratching up my ribs.

She learns my body with her lips and palms, placing kisses along my shoulders and neck, dragging light fingertips over my pecs and stomach.

It's the sweetest oblivion.

A mindless tease.

"You have an incredible body." She drags her tongue up my throat, her breaths panted, the continued rub of her pussy making me groan.

"Just wait until I get my hands on yours."

"I better hurry then." She rushes to undo my pants, discarding the belt and lowering the zipper.

Then she pauses, suddenly timid as she stares at my bulge.

"Take it out." I fist the bed coverings, my fingers throbbing for action.

She does as instructed, lowering the waistband of my boxer briefs over my length.

"Grab my cock, Ollie." It takes all my restraint not to touch her, to keep my fucking arms immobile.

She eyes my dick, her thighs squeezing around me, her want for me making the engorged length throb. Tentatively, those delicate fingers rake over me, light with the first stroke, then harder with a gentle squeeze.

Fuck.

I'm in trouble.

"Protection?" she asks.

"I've got no hands, Pyro. That's your job now."

She bites her bottom lip and looks up at me from under thick lashes. "Do you always use it?"

"Always. Top bedside drawer. Left corner."

"So you're clean?" She makes no move to grab for the condoms. Instead, she shyly licks her lips and stares back down at my cock "And you know I am, right?"

Every. Fucking. Muscle. Tenses.

I incline my head, speechless at her implication.

"Would you mind if I felt what it's like without?" she asks. "Just for a little while?"

Would I mind?

Would. I. Fucking. Mind?

I'd drag my balls through broken glass for the mere opportunity. I'd father her children. I'd make her my wife.

"You can't get me pregnant." Her voice is breathy. "I'm on the pill."

I guess that's a bonus for now, but filling her with my babies is definitely an urge I could explore.

"Do it" is all I can say.

My impatience is excruciating. The way she stares hungrily at my dick is too much of a fucking thrill.

I'm already seeping at the tip.

"Will you talk me through it?" She releases my shaft and rises above me, her expression gaining an apprehensive edge as she discards a pair a black lace panties, then plants her knees on the mattress beside my hips. "I don't know what I'm doing."

"You're going to be so fucking good at this, Ollie. Just take your time and guide my cock to that sweet pussy."

She swallows and reclaims my length, tilting it toward her.

"Now rub me against your slit. Show me how wet you are."

Her breath hitches as my tip presses into her. It's the slightest touch. An excruciating tease. Then she's dragging me back and forth along her slickness, drenching my crown with her need.

"Good girl," I groan. "You're so fucking ready for me."

She nods. Pants. "I've wanted you for so long."

"I'm all yours. Sink down on me."

Her exhale is ragged. Shaky.

She's nervous.

"There's no rush." I fight against temptation, my palms sweating. What I wouldn't give to tear that blouse and expose her tits. To force her mouth to mine as I thrust balls deep. But we can do all that when she's ready.

She won't get another first.

She slowly lowers, the tight grasp of her cunt fitting perfectly around me.

I tense my muscles. Clench my teeth.

She's so perfect, I can't fucking take it.

"Just like that, Pyro." My tone is guttural. "Keep sinking onto my dick. You feel incredible."

"You're bigger than my toys." She latches onto my shoulders, lowering farther.

"Go slower. I don't want to hurt you."

"It doesn't hurt." She meets my eyes, her nails digging into my skin. "I'm enjoying how you stretch me."

Fuck.

My pulse thrums in my gut. My thighs. My groin.

Every nerve tingles with a heightened sense of her as she continues to lower, inch by agonizing inch, until she's fully seated.

I groan at the perfection.

She whimpers, rocking her hips, beginning to gently ride.

Fucking her without protection probably wasn't the best idea if I wanted to play my A game. As if that flawless virgin pussy wasn't enough. Now I have to deal with heightened sensation and the incredibly smooth glide.

"Fuck, Ollie. You take me so well."

The oscillation of her sheath is phenomenal. The roll of her ass in my lap a goddamn dream.

"How does it feel?" I swallow over the desert claiming my mouth.

"Amazing." She guides her lips over mine, the contact frazzling my control.

"Take advantage while you can." I kiss her hard. Fast. I rock into her as she slowly undulates, each glide of her tight cunt a thrill and a curse. "I can't keep my hands off you for much longer."

She whimpers, fucking me like an angel, tempting me like the devil.

Up. Down. Up. Down.

Heaven and hell.

Bliss and torment.

"Touch me," she whispers into my mouth. "I want your hands everywhere."

The green light has me frantic.

I start yanking my arms from their confinement, my right escaping, my left getting stuck on the buttoned shirtsleeve.

Fuck. Fuck. Fuck.

I swing the material around her back, ravaging her mouth as she continues fucking me while I use my free hand to fight the restriction.

I yank. I tug. I pull.

She chuckles into my mouth. "Do you need help?"

"I need you to quit feeling so fucking good because if I don't get my hands on you soon I'm going to die."

She rocks her hips a little harder, the taunting minx dragging a hoarse growl from my throat. But I get that goddamn arm free, and then I'm all over her, my fingers undoing her blouse buttons.

"Keep riding me, Ollie. Don't you dare fucking stop." I drag my tongue over hers, stroking harder, deeper.

She increases her pace.

"You're at home on my dick, aren't you, my pretty little Pyro?" I release the last button and drag my palms up her waist to cup those phenomenal tits. "You were born to ride it. It's fucking yours."

She mewls, the needy, feminine sound driving me wilder. She grinds harder.

I drag a palm over her sternum, my fingers touching metal, the contact making me spiral.

She still wears my ring—after everything she's been through, despite all the suffering and the pain—*she still wears my fucking ring.*

"You can get rid of this," I growl.

She breaks the kiss, pulling back with concern.

"I want to put one on your hand." I glide my finger through the white-gold loop and drag her back to me. "It can be a commitment ring." I kiss her. "An engagement ring." I kiss her harder. "Hell, I'd make it a fucking wedding ring if you'd let me. But I want it somewhere everyone can see."

Her breaths shudder against my lips as she kisses me back, fucking me, shoving me closer to the edge of oblivion.

"Tell me you'll wear it." I release the ring and grasp her chin, unable to get enough.

She nods. Panting. Gasping.

"Tell me," I demand. "I want to hear it, Ollie."

She cups my cheeks, inching back and looking me in the eye, her pussy not pausing in its agonizing assault. "I'll wear it. I'll *always* wear it."

I grab her hips around the bunched skirt and drag her harder against me, the two of us moaning in unison.

"You're mine," I growl.

"And you're mine," she demands.

"So fucking yours, Pyro. Nobody else's." I shove to my feet, taking her with me.

She wraps her legs around me and clings to my shoulders, never stopping the rock of those smooth hips.

I shuck my pants while she uses my dick, testing my restraint, fucking tempting me to blow.

"Are you ready for something different?" I inch us back toward the bed.

She nods. "Please."

I groan. "I fucking love when my good girl begs." I climb onto the mattress, laying her on her back, settling between her thighs.

I hover above her, poised on one elbow as I take charge, pulling out, then thrusting home.

"*Oh, God.*" Her eyes widen.

I smirk. "It's deeper."

Her head rolls back, her chest arching into mine. "So fucking deep."

"Do you want me to fuck you like this?"

She nods. Whimpers. "I never want you to stop." Her nails scratch my shoulders. My back.

It's too intense. The pleasure and the pain.

Each thrust shoves me closer to the edge.

I've waited too long for this moment. Fantasized too much.

"You're so good at this." My voice is guttural. "I can't wait to spill inside you."

She sucks in a ragged breath.

"Do you like the thought of that, Ollie?" I lean down to murmur in her ear. "Does my good girl like picturing my cum seeping from that tight little cunt?"

She shudders, her core clamping around me. "You need to stop, otherwise I'm going to come."

"Stop what?" I palm the base of her throat, my rings gently grazing her skin while I nuzzle her neck. "Stop fucking you?" I thrust harder. Faster. "Or stop telling you how much my dick loves being inside you. How much your sopping wet pussy makes me feel like a fucking king."

She gasps, her back arching. Her grip pulls tight in my hair, my scalp burning.

She's my undoing. I can barely think through the frenzy.

All I know is that I can't come without her.

She has to cross the line with me.

"We're so fucking good together." I pound into her, adding slight pressure to her throat. "I'll never get enough."

"I'm close." She pants. "Oh, God. It's right there."

"That's it, Pyro." I graze my teeth along her jaw, praying, *begging* for her surrender. "Take my dick like a good girl." I close my eyes, focusing on anything but the way her pussy strangles me. "Come all over my cock."

"*Shit.*" She tenses around me, her thighs a vise. "I'm… I'm…"

She cries out her release, the flutter of her core opening the flood gates, the fucking ache of my shaft giving way to pulsing pleasure.

I claim her mouth. Kiss her hard.

We're all tangled tongues and smashed lips. Panted breaths and thrusting hips.

I lose myself inside her, each pulse of my orgasm rocketing through my entire body.

I groan for her, eating up her whimpers, ringing out each thrust with a delicious grind until we're one gasping, heaving mess.

I press my forehead to hers as we come down from the peak. I roll onto my side, taking her with me, our bodies still entwined, our legs entangled.

We stare at each other, panted breaths receding, her gentle hands coming to rest on my chest.

"You okay?" I ask.

She nods. Boneless. Maybe even mindless. "I'm perfect."

She sure is.

In every way imaginable.

Her attention strays from mine, her gaze casually moving over my left shoulder.

Shit.

She stiffens, the sudden tensing threatening to push my softening cock out of her.

"I can explain." I palm her waist, refusing to let her run as her eyes widen on the wall beside my bed, the floor-to-ceiling space filled with hundreds of pictures of her. "It was one of Flynn's pranks. He did it the night he saw you at Smoke & Mirrors. I think the kid got an inkling I was in over my head with you and decided to exploit the situation by downloading all your social media pics."

Her gaze returns to mine. "That's a lot of photos."

"It is." Three hundred and sixty-one. When I can't sleep, I lie here counting them.

"You didn't think to take them down?"

"Are you kidding? Why would I do that? Those images have been the inspiration for a lot of stress relief."

Her smile turns shy, her breathy laugh tightening my ribs in a way I've never felt before. "I'd like to see that so-called stress relief."

"Give me a few minutes and I'll be happy to demonstrate." I kiss her cheek, her nose, her lips. "I'm not ashamed to admit I'm obsessed with you. I don't want those pictures to ever come down."

"I'm obsessed with you, too." She skims her fingers over my pecs. "You make me happy."

The quiet stretches as we stare at each other, the humor gradually fading from her expression as grief worms its way back in.

She grows cold. Distant.

It fucking guts me to watch her suffer.

"Remy..." Her nose scrunches as tears build in her eyes. "I'm really sorry, but I promise what's about to happen has nothing to do with the sex."

45

OLIVIA

Bursting into tears isn't the most opportune way to show appreciation for the mind-blowing orgasm. But there's no restraint to hold back like there previously was. The nausea option is no longer available. There's only painfully blinding tears. And given the trauma surrounding Remy's first sexual experience and his fear about causing issues with mine, it only makes me cry harder.

I apologize over and over.

He holds me tighter, stroking my waist, slowly coaxing me back from the darkness with his words of affirmation until I fall into an exhausted sleep.

When I wake it's to an empty stomach, my need for food so painful I have to figure out if I'm willing to do a midnight walk of shame or raid Remy's kitchen.

Given I don't have my phone, which means no money and no way of calling a ride share, I opt to creep from his bed and help myself to his heavily stocked fridge.

It doesn't take long for him to find me.

A few minutes later he's back between my thighs, spoiling me with more bliss.

I swear I didn't think history would repeat itself with a renewed bout of post-coital blubbering—it's definitely not a routine I want to encourage—but as soon as the orgasmic high is over, I'm back, digging in the trenches of my sorrow. Sobbing. Sniffling.

It can't be healthy for any man's ego to have a woman bawling uncontrollably after sex, but Remy takes it in stride. Always supportive. Forever my savior.

I think my downfall is caused from guilt.

I want so badly to be distracted from my grief that I seek out his affection. Then once the euphoria is gone, the weight of sadness returns ten times heavier than it was before.

But as I blink awake to the morning sun creeping around the edge of the curtains, Remy isn't beside me, and the sheets where he once laid are now cold.

"Don't go snooping down that hall," his whisper-shout carries in the distance from the other side of the closed bedroom door.

The patter of little feet scurrying along the hall makes me stiffen.

"Tilly," he coos.

Tilly? Does he have a dog?

I sit up, carefully holding the covers to my naked chest, the pile of folded clothes on my bedside table catching my eye. There's fresh underwear, a white lace bra, my favorite *Too peopley outside* T-shirt, and my loose grey yoga pants.

He went to my house to get clothes?

I wait for the irk of apprehension to take over. It doesn't come. I don't care if he's been in my home without me. I can't even summon the will to care if his men did.

All I feel is gooey gratitude.

I trust him. More than logic and commonsense should allow.

I pull on the underwear while still beneath the covers.

"Little miss Tilly," Remy warns. "Get your butt back here now."

A tiny girl giggle sounds from the other side of the bedroom door, followed by the quick scurry of retreating feet.

Not a dog. A *child*.

I hustle into the clothes then sit on the side of the bed, taking stock of my senses. My head is heavy, all the tears having left my face a little swollen and sore. And apart from attributing those same sensations to much more intimate parts of my body for much more enjoyable reasons, I feel okay. Not great. Not perfect. But a small step closer to stable.

I freshen up in the bathroom… finger-brush my teeth… re-braid my hair. Then I pad into the hall, nervous over the indecipherable murmurings of adult conversation between Remy and a woman coming from down the hall.

Facing unfamiliar people isn't my preference on a good day, but this morning my introverted nature is heightened at the thought of seeing anyone other than Remy.

My heart is in my throat as I approach the opening to the living room when a little girl's face peeks into the hall, her beautiful blonde hair loose around her shoulders.

Her eyes widen at the sight of me. She squeaks, then dashes back out of view.

I can't help smiling. Okay, so maybe I can handle the contagious exuberance of an angelic child. Adults, on the other hand…

I reach the end of the hall in time to see her jump onto the sofa in her bright pink dress and fall dramatically into Remy's lap.

He grunts with exaggeration, then wraps her in his arms. "I hope you weren't getting into mischief." He narrows his eyes on her with playful scrutiny. "You know I can smell trouble."

She nuzzles into him, completely at home in his arms.

I stand stunned, in awe of the man capable of such viciously violent atrocities who is equally adept at dispensing compassion and protection.

I never imagined this side of him, though. The paternal aspect.

"You, my dear girl—" He tickles her ribs. "—are a gremlin."

"She is not."

I turn my gaze toward the woman's voice carrying from across the room, my heart poised to break at the thought of him fathering someone else's child until I see his sister standing in the kitchen, palming a steaming coffee mug. She's flawless in a stylish pantsuit, her blonde hair cascading down her back.

"She's a *principessina*."

Remy rolls his eyes. "Since when do you know Italian?"

"Since Bishop started whispering things in my ear during adult-time that I don't understand."

Remy gags. "Do you want me to vomit on your kid?"

"Yuck, Unkie Remy." The little girl claps a hand to his chest.

I clear my throat, wanting to make myself known before I intrude any further. I slowly pad into the room, the weight of everyone's attention making my cheeks heat. "Morning."

"Hey." Remy plops the little girl on the sofa cushion beside him, stands and walks toward me, entirely edible in dark jeans and a black T-shirt. "How are you?"

I force a smile, then find it isn't hard to maintain once he sweeps an arm around my neck to place an affectionate kiss to my temple. "I'm doing better."

"Did the gremlin wake you?" he asks against my skin.

I shake my head and snuggle farther into him. "Thanks for the clothes. Did you go out while I was sleeping?"

"No. I'd never leave you without notice."

I pull back. "Then who?"

"Abri and her scary-ass husband."

His sister snorts. "I heard that."

My heart gives an exaggerated thud. "Who's her husband?"

"Bishop. He was at the funeral yesterday. Apparently Lesley took a shining to him. The old girl must be a sucker for ugly bastards with hideous scars."

"I'll tell him you said that." His sister takes a sip from her mug, still standing in the kitchen. "I'm sure he'd love to hear your opinion on his appearance."

"It's not like I wouldn't say it to his face…" Remy speaks into my hair. "If I had a substantial head start at a run to freedom."

I lightly tap his chest in a subtle attempt to regain his attention. "They spoke to Lesley?"

"Mmm." He nods. "Spoke to her *and* got invited inside for iced tea, apparently."

My brows knit. "You're lying."

"I'd never lie to you." He nuzzles his nose against mine and kisses me, sweet and soft, only to pull away with a growl at the sound of a kiddie giggle. "I guess I should introduce you to the gremlin." He entwines his hand with mine. "Tilly, come meet my Ollie."

My Ollie.

The heartbroken organ inside my chest heals itself a little.

The sweet girl runs along the sofa, plops down at the closest end, and peers up at me with shy eyes.

"Say 'hi,' Til." Abri approaches her daughter.

"Hi." The girl shrinks into her tiny shoulders, her long, dark lashes framing beautiful blue eyes.

"Hi, Tilly." I smile. "It's lovely to meet you."

"Don't be fooled by her timid act. Once she gets to know you she'll cling like super glue." Abri places her mug on the sofa side table and continues toward us. "We haven't formally met, but I am this smitten man's older and wiser sister." She scowls at her brother. "Release her so I can get a hug."

Remy sighs with exaggeration. "Fine. I'll make Ollie breakfast." His hand skims my lower back as he walks around me to the kitchen.

A second later I'm engulfed in the beautiful woman's arms.

"I'm so sorry for your loss, Olivia."

The pity pokes at my grief, but the hug is warm and inviting. A genuine embrace full of solace and loving energy.

I hug her back, surprisingly soothed by her presence. "Thank you for yesterday," I whisper.

"You might want to retract that statement after you spend months retrieving Tupperware from the wrong cupboards in your catering kitchen." She releases me and retreats. "But I promise Layla and I tried our best." She turns to reclaim her mug from the side table, then saunters away. "Come sit with me at the dining table."

I glance from her to Remy, who stands at a Keurig machine, a subtle frown marring his brow.

"Don't scare her away, Abri," he warns. "She's been through enough."

"Pfft." His sister waves a dismissive hand as she reaches the glass table with its orchid centerpiece. She pulls out a chair for me before moving to sit on the one beside it. "I think you did enough scaring away for all of us. What could I do that you haven't already mastered?"

I fight a chuckle.

I love these two together. They're light and fun. A far contrast from when Remy and Salvatore are in close proximity.

"So tell me all the gossip." Abri palms her mug and takes a sip of the steaming liquid. "I've heard my brother's side of things for months, but I've been going insane waiting for the second half of this telenovela."

I blink at her in confusion.

"I'll call security, Abri." Remy growls. "Don't think I won't."

"You threatened me with that yesterday, and I still tidied your apartment. I'm starting to regret my efforts."

"You tidied up?" I ask, wanting to double back to the whole second-half-telenovela conversation, but this is a far safer option.

She nods. "You should've seen this place. It was a mess. There were empty liquor bottles and take-out food containers everywhere. Now it's a shrine in comparison."

A pang of guilt twists my gut. What exactly has Remy been going through?

As if called by my thoughts, he walks over and places a coffee down in front of me. "Strong, cream, one sugar."

My confusion increases. "How do you—"

"Berkeley Springs." He strides back toward the kitchen and clatters pans on his stove. "I asked that A-hole chef."

"The same chef you told me you envisaged gutting like a pig?" Abri asks.

"Don't test me, sis," he mutters.

I hide a smile behind my coffee mug and take a sip. "Thank you, Remy."

He shoots me a wink and carries on with his project at the stove.

"So…" Abri drawls. "Can you see yourself having kids?"

I choke, the hot liquid shooting up my nose.

"*Abri,*" Remy shouts.

Tilly giggles from the sofa.

"What?" Abri looks at me in mock surprise. "I'm just making conversation."

I can't help laughing as I wipe my nose, my cheeks, my lips, cleaning up the spluttered coffee.

I'm lighter than I have been in months, the weight of pain and heartache easing. There's something about the playful camaraderie between mother, daughter, and uncle that makes me feel at home.

"All jokes aside," Abri says quietly. "He's been beside himself. I had high hopes after your weekend away. But the past few days have had me worried you two wouldn't pull through."

I ignore the sadness attempting to edge its way back in. "I wasn't sure how things would pan out either. I guess I'm still uncertain," I admit. "This isn't a typical sort of situation. I'm new to all this."

She levels me with a kind smile. "It's not typical, but it doesn't need to be complicated either. He loves you, and I have a feeling you love him—"

"I do." I nod.

"—so just spend time loving each other for a while. The family business might not be something you're accustomed to, but neither is Remy. You can work it out together."

I turn my gaze to him as he remains at the stove, focused on something in the pan in front of him while he lazily holds a spatula.

For a second, I could almost kid myself into believing he could leave 'the life' and become an average Joe with a nine-to-five, a mortgage, and a predictable routine.

Yet despite *the business* being new to him, it's his vibe.

I think it's where he belongs. And given the lines I've recently crossed, I think I could see myself belonging there, too.

"If you choose to give him a chance," Abri continues, "I have a feeling he'll obsessively adore you for as long as you'll let him. He'd move heaven and earth to make sure nothing else came between you."

Warmth builds inside me. Hope, too.

I believe her.

I believe *in him.*

"Exactly what has he told you?" I ask with narrowing eyes. "I didn't picture Remy as the type to kiss and tell."

She pulls an expression of disgust. "Believe me, I wish he wasn't. There are things that shouldn't be shared between siblings. But apparently he didn't get the memo. Or he's just been so caught up in the thought of losing you that he doesn't care. Which means I've heard a whole heap of stuff that I've had to unpack with my therapist."

My cheeks heat. "Like…?"

"Well, obviously I was at the club the night you got attacked, so we've talked a lot about his guilt concerning that. Then he told me what happened the night he got shot." She raises a brow and sips from her mug. "And I'm not talking about your suture skills."

The heat turns to an inferno.

Remy told his sister about the orgasm he gave me in the bathroom?

"And there were the unending phone calls about his hang-ups with your—" She winces "—inexperience. That guy has an unhealthy amount of trauma from childhood, but apparently not enough to dissuade him obsessing over getting in your pants."

I gape and snap my devastation toward Remy. "He told you I was a virgin?"

"*Was?*" Abri grins.

Oh, God.

I cover my eyes with a hand, trying to hide my mortification and the uncontrollable need to laugh.

Scurrying footsteps patter toward us. "Momma, what's a ver-shin?"

I drop my mug to the table, needing both hands to hide the mortified humor mix as Abri cackles.

"What the hell are you two talking about?" Remy's thudded footsteps approach. "Abri, did you upset her?" He pulls out my chair and grabs my wrist, hauling me protectively into his chest. "I can't tell if you're about to laugh or cry." He drags the remaining hand from my face as I struggle to compose myself.

"Unkie Rem, what's a ver-shin?" Tilly asks.

He stiffens.

Abri releases another uprooting cackle.

I lunge forward, hiding my face in Remy's neck as I burst into a fit of laughter.

"Okay, time to leave," he demands, wrapping a tight arm around my waist as I convulse against him. "Out, Abri. And take your little demon spawn with you."

"Aww. Unkie Remy. I wanted to go to the park."

"Blame your mother. She's the ruiner of all things."

"No." I place a hand to his chest, struggling to breathe through the laughter. "Don't be ridiculous."

"It's okay." Abri pushes from her chair, still chuckling. "I told

Bishop we'd only be an hour, and that was two hours ago. We need to get back to D.C."

I wipe away the happy tears streaming down my cheeks and turn to face Remy's sister and niece who both smile at me—Abri with a knowing glint and Tilly with clueless exuberance.

"I'd thank you for the visit," Remy mutters, "but that would require gratitude I currently lack."

"Oh, stop it." I nudge him in the ribs with my elbow, earning an *umph* and a tighter hold around my waist.

"Watch it or you'll unlock a new kink," he growls in my ear. "I think I might like it rough."

My laughter dies as more heat floods my face... parts down south, too.

I may be swollen from his enthusiastic attention last night, but apparently that has no effect on the rabid hunger of my libido.

"Out," he snaps again.

Tilly whimpers and rushes around the table, throwing her arms around Remy's thigh. "Bye, Unkie Remy."

He releases me with a frown and stumbles backward, shaking his leg as if trying to dislodge a humping dog.

"*Remy,*" I say, aghast.

"Don't take any notice of him," Abri murmurs as she comes to stand beside me, rolling her eyes as Tilly giggles against her uncle's thigh, having the ride of her life. "They have a theatrical relationship. They play-fight and mock each other all the time. I'm sure showing affection through sarcasm and ridicule will affect her later in life, but for now, it's a dynamic they both need." She shrugs. "And apart from Bishop, nobody makes her smile like he does."

She turns to me, her expression thoughtful. "I feel slightly ill saying this—" Her voice is almost a whisper. "—But my brother is a great guy. *This brother,*" she clarifies. "Not the middle one. He's got a few screws loose."

I chuckle and Tilly screams as Remy hefts her into his arms, smothering her with an attack of kisses.

"I understand we don't know each other. And this is seriously left field. But if you ever need anything please call me." Abri grabs my hand and gives a squeeze. "I'm not usually a people person, but I really like you. And us women in tricky situations need to stick together. So I'm giving an open-ended invitation if you ever need a shoulder to cry on, or a drinking buddy to celebrate with." She cringes. "I'd prefer not to talk about my brother's sex life if that's at all possible—because, ya know, psychological trauma and all that—but I'm here for you both if you ever need it."

I wiggle my hand from hers and wrap my arms around her, shamelessly becoming a hugger for the first time in my life. "I can't wait to get to know you better."

She hugs me back. "Again, you may regret that, but until then..." She pulls away with a grin. "Look after my brother and make sure he looks after you."

She walks away, wrangling her giggling daughter from Remy's arms before leaving in the elevator.

As soon as they're gone, the penthouse descends into palpable silence, the sound of Tilly's giggles still ringing in my ears.

"They were too much, weren't they?" He meets my gaze from a few feet away, his expression pinched. "I should've told them not to come."

"Not at all." I go to him. "Your sister is incredible." I sink against his chest, loving how easily I find comfort in him.

"Incredibly annoying," he mutters into my hair.

I grin, understanding the insult for what it is—disguised love.

"How are you?" I ask.

He plants a kiss to my temple. "You don't have to worry about me."

"Yes, I do." I lean away to meet his gaze. "That's how this works. At least it's how I want it to work. You're grieving, too, Remy. I want us to be there for each other."

His lips lean in a sad smile. "I'm holding up okay, Pyro. Having you here makes it easier."

"I'm glad." I sink back into him. "I've enjoyed being here."

"Is that because of the sex that makes you sob uncontrollably or the fact you have to scavenge for food?"

"It's definitely the sobbing sex. I don't think anything has branded my award-winning level of unhinged quite like that does."

He snickers into my hair, his palms skimming my hips. "You're not unhinged."

"And you're not responsible for me sobbing after sex. I really hope you understand that."

He plants another delicate kiss to my temple. "I do. I just wish I could take away your pain."

"Nothing can take it away, Remy. But being with you distracts me from it like nothing else does."

"Good. I was hoping to create an unhealthy reliance so you never want to leave."

I chuckle. "Consider me well and truly ill."

"Does that mean you plan on staying a while?"

I should ponder my answer. Should think it over extra hard considering the potential for disaster. But I don't want to.

I love Remy.

I want to be with him.

And while his presence fills the gaping hole in my chest, I want to remain as close to him as possible. "I'll stay until I wear out my welcome."

"Forever it is then." He palms my cheeks, tilting my face up to his. "I'll always want you here." He places more pieces of my broken soul back together as his lips brush mine. "But before I get carried away, I want you to eat breakfast."

He releases me.

"Wait." I grab his hand. "I want to ask you something, but I need you to promise you won't feel obligated to respond in a certain way."

"Ask."

I drag in a deep breath and entwine our fingers. "I have to do something, and I'd really like if you were there with me, but it's not the type of request someone would usually make."

"I'll do it, Ollie. Whatever it is, you don't need to ask."

"For this, I do. Because as much as I want you with me, what would make me happier is if you made the choice that was right for you… but I won't know what that is unless you answer honestly. Can you do that for me?"

His shoulders straighten as he scrutinizes me. "If that's what you want."

"It is."

"Then tell me what it is."

I wince against the resurgence of grief that's impossible to ignore. "I have to finish things with Dad."

His chin hitches. "The cremation?"

I nod. "I want to take care of the formalities as soon as possible. For his sake as well as mine."

His eyes narrow in confusion, the slightest frown marring his brow. "And you want me there?"

"Yes." I wrap my free arm around my middle. "And I know Dad would, too. But like I said, I'd prefer if you told me what's best for you and the way you want to approach your grief."

His gaze softens, his lips kicking slightly in a sad smile. "Ollie, I'd be honored."

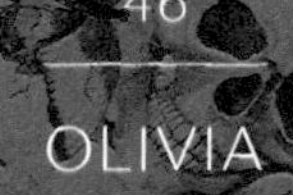

46

OLIVIA

Remy keeps a protective arm wrapped around my waist as we walk toward Stanley, standing at the open delivery room door to the funeral home.

"Good morning." My temporary replacement shakes Remy's hand and squeezes my shoulder in greeting. "Everything is ready as requested."

"As requested?" I ask.

Stanley shoots a questioning glance to Remy.

"I asked for a few things to be arranged while you were doing your hair." Remy kisses my brow.

"What things?" I whisper.

"It's nothing to worry about." He leads me across the delivery room as Stanley murmurs a farewell, the overhead door closing behind him.

After I posed the cremation question earlier, Remy and I shared a quick breakfast, my stomach appreciating the sustenance for the first time all week. Then we showered together, his roughened hands gently washing my hair and massaging my scalp, the luscious feel of it making me moan… which led to those talented hands doing a range of other things that inspired far louder and more uncontrollable sounds.

This time though, the bliss didn't end with an encore of blubbering.

Yes, my eyes had watered, and I'd definitely felt the rush of sadness. But not a single tear was shed.

I'm making progress, although through baby steps. And the relief had been clear in Remy's proud gaze as he'd kissed me back from the brink.

I'm still clinging to that comfort as he leads me through the quiet funeral home, the faint hiss of burning flame carrying from the retort room.

I thought I'd dread this moment. I know I had after Mom died. But there's something about Remy that gives me strength.

"Do you want to take a minute?" He slows his approach. "There's no rush."

His voice soothes me. Everything about him does—his patience, his thoughtfulness.

"No, I'm okay." I take the lead, approaching the open door to the windowless room that's usually bathed in darkness but now glows in hues of orange.

I rush the remaining steps, panicked that Stanley left the retort open and unsupervised while heating. But it's not the open retort that paints the walls in flickering amber. It's the mass of delicate flames illuminated from hundreds of candles spread throughout the room.

My heart stops.

My eyes heat with that familiar burn.

My father's casket rests on the feeder platform before the closed door of the retort while a picnic rug adorned with a mass of floor pillows sits in the middle of the room.

I step inside, gratitude clogging my throat as one of my dad's favorite Phil Collins songs plays quietly from a speaker somewhere in the corner.

"This looks slightly more romantic than I'd anticipated." Remy stops beside me. "I promise that wasn't in the design brief."

I scrunch my nose and turn into him, burying my face in his neck.

I need a second.

Just one.

"I'm sorry." He strokes my braided hair. "It's too much."

"No. It's beautiful."

I'm so glad he's here with me. I don't even want to think about what this would've been like without him.

I pull myself together and turn back to the beauty of a room that has only ever been known for its sterility.

Without a word, Remy helps me load Dad's casket into the retort.

He's cuddled in behind me as I hold my breath and increase the rush of flame. Then he takes my hand, leads me to the rug, and holds me in his arms while the body I ran to for comfort, and strength, and the best goddamn hugs, is burned to nothing but bone and ash.

I cry.

I ache.

I listen to my father's music and fall victim to the memories that awaken.

For more than ninety minutes I endure a gamut of emotions while Remy remains a protective force at my side.

Once it's over, he takes me for a drive to get lunch while the retort cools.

We're both quiet. Comfortably reflective in our own ways.

Then we return to the funeral home, hand in hand again, to sweep what's left of my father from the retort and place him in the cremulator.

"What's your favorite memory with my dad?" I ask from my perched position on the stainless-steel bench.

A grin pulls at Remy's lips. "Without a doubt, it was when Carlo took me on my first walk through of the funeral home. It was two in the morning. Pitch black. And I swear he kept most of the lights off on purpose just to fuck with me." He moves to stand between my legs. "He took me into the cool room—I'm pretty sure as a test to see how tough I was—and pushed one of the trollies out of the way that was carrying an elderly lady. I swear to God, Ollie, that woman groaned loud enough that my soul left my body."

I burst into laughter.

"And that's how I learned that dead bodies can sometimes make noise." He grins at me. "Worst lesson of my life."

I can imagine my father's delight. How he would've chuckled at Remy's fear.

"I love that story." I continue to snicker as a vibration carries from Remy's jeans pocket.

He doesn't acknowledge the sound. Instead, he keeps staring at me as if I've hung the moon.

"Are you going to answer that?" I ask.

"It can wait."

"It's okay." I reach into his pocket to pull out the cell and hand it over. "We're almost done here."

He takes the device and answers the call, his free hand lowering to squeeze my thigh in a silent gesture of appreciation. "Hey, Lorenzo."

"*Figlio*," the voice murmurs in greeting. "Are you with your Olivia?"

I lower my gaze, trying to hide the joy that crosses my face whenever I'm referenced in such an addictively anti-feminist manner.

"Yeah, she's right here. Why?"

"You might want to kindly ask her to reach out to her friends and let them know she's all right. I've received a call from a local police informant that an Ivy Diaz has attempted to file a missing person's report and has made mention of our family being responsible for the disappearance."

"Oh, shit." I push off the bench.

Shit. Shit. Shit.

I left from the wake yesterday without saying goodbye. Ivy and Allison must be in hysterics.

"My phone," I rasp as I run from the room, trying to remember where I left it. I check Allison's desk, then my prep room, finally finding it on the kitchen counter in the staff break room.

Eighteen missed calls.

Twenty-six text messages.

Eight insta DMs.

All from Ivy in less than twenty-four hours.

"Oh, God, I'm the worst." I dial her number, my heart in my throat as the call connects.

"Liv?" she asks in panic.

"Yeah, it's me. I'm so sorry. I couldn't handle the wake yesterday so I left, but I didn't take my cell. I should've called—"

"It's okay." Her voice is fragile. "Where are you?"

"At work. I wanted to take care of—"

"Are you safe?" She cuts me off again.

"Yes. And I'm doing well." The statement shocks me, but it's the truth. Remy has salvaged my worst days and turned them into something I can cherish. "Are you okay?"

She's quiet a moment, the sound of traffic carrying through the speaker. "Yeah. I'm good. I just—"

"That's enough."

I stiffen at the muffled male voice murmuring across the line.

"Ive?" I hedge. "Are you with someone?"

"No one important." Her voice is off, that uncomfortable edge still present despite the assurances I'm okay.

I turn in search of Remy, finding him walking into the break room. I rush for him and his hands immediately claim my hips, his gaze questioning.

"*Something's wrong,*" I mouth, placing the call on speaker. "Ivy?" I ask again. "Tell me who you're with."

"She's with a friend."

My eyes widen at the male voice that comes through louder this time. Perfectly clear.

Salvatore Costa.

Remy grabs my phone, raising it to his mouth. "What the fuck, Salvo?"

Salvatore's snicker sinks into my ears, igniting panic. "There's no need to worry," he drawls. "She's in good hands. We just have a few things to discuss, like her fake name, and why someone with her lineage would be stupid enough to frequent Smoke & Mirrors."

"What fake name?" My voice breaks. "What lineage?"

"Those are questions you can ask once I'm done with her. Until then, you two need to stay out of it. I'm handling the situation with *mi bella reina*, and I won't tolerate being interrupted."

The call disconnects.

My stomach free falls. "What is he talking about? Will he hurt her?"

Remy scowls, his teeth clenched tight.

He doesn't know.

Oh, God, he doesn't know.

"I'll call Lorenzo. He'll shut this down." He pulls out his cell and navigates to his uncle's contact.

"Could you decipher what he called her? It wasn't in English." My fingers tangle nervously in his shirt. "Bella means beautiful but..."

"Queen," he growls. "He called Ivy his beautiful queen. But he didn't say it in Italian. For some reason, that fucker spoke in Spanish."

ACKNOWLEDGMENTS

This is a tough one. Not because it's hard to thank those who helped make Remy what he is, but because the long months spent writing this book were the hardest my career has faced.

At one point I thought I'd reached the end. That crafting words would no longer be a future for me.

If it weren't for the exceptionally special people around me, those fears would've become a reality. So to everyone who held me up while hackers tried to drag me down - thank you.

Remy wouldn't exist without you.

ABOUT THE AUTHOR

Eden Summers is a bestselling author of contemporary romance with a side of sizzle and sarcasm.

She lives in Australia with her own sarcastic, dark-eyed hero and two equally sarcastic teenage boys who are well aware she's circling the drain of insanity.

If you'd like access to exclusive information and giveaways, join Eden Summers' newsletter via the link on her website.

For more information:
www.edensummers.com
eden@edensummers.com

www.ingramcontent.com/pod-product-compliance
Lightning Source LLC
Chambersburg PA
CBHW050956210726
48287CB00004B/1249